To Andy!

The skies are _not_ the limit,

David G. Uppline

11/24/08

The Highest Seat
Does Not
Hold Two

David Williams

PO Box 221974 Anchorage, Alaska 99522-1974

books@publicationconsultants.com—www.publicationconsultants.com

ISBN 978-1-59433-084-1
Library of Congress Catalog Card Number: 2008933636

Manufactured in the United States of America.

Dedication

To those at the beach, for teaching me to ride the waves.

Acknowledgements

First off, I'd like to thank my dad for spending a week teaching me to write and editing the rough draft. Without his help, this book would not have been publishable.

Thanks also to:

Marthy Johnson for editing;

The teachers at Lumen Christi for letting me use the copy machine at the last moment;

William Clarke for being an editor/agent/advisor/best friend;

And of course, to Evan Swensen for agreeing to publish this book and going out of his way to make it happen.

List of Abbreviations

AAA	Antiaircraft Artillery
AA	Antiaircraft (machine gun)
EMP	Electromagnetic Pulse
E-V	Extra-vehicular
FDA	Federal Defense Agency
HE-AT	High-explosive-antitank
HQ	Headquarters
IA	Immediate Action
ICBM	Intercontinental ballistic missile
IDF	International Defense Force
LWCV	light weight cargo vehicle
MAA	Mankind Against Aliens
MPG	Magnetically Propelled Grenade
NCO	Non-commissioned Officer
OP	Observation Point
SFB	Since the Federation Began
SMG	Sub-machine Gun
VDN	Vehicle Designation Number
XO	Executive Officer

Table of Contents

Prologue

Earth. A planet occupied by beings who believed they were alone in this universe.

They were wrong.

In the year 468,197 SFB—or 2552 AD as the humans remembered it—the human race had just celebrated the tenth anniversary of the creation of a unified world government. This had come about after 50 years without war. Since there were no major grievances among the nations or their leaders, some long-forgotten genius suggested there be one government presiding over all nations, while the nations remained independent. In short, a confederation of nations that came together in cases of emergency.

It seemed as if the human race had finally learned to live in harmony with others.

The militaries unified along with the rest of the world, and with the exchange of technology and secrets, they became the most powerful force in their solar system.

Despite their might, they had not fought a war in more than half a century. They trained rigorously to make up for this, until they began to ask what they were training for. The only way a military force would be needed is if a country broke off from the confederation and declared war, but since no military unit was controlled by any one country, whom would they fight?

To justify its existence, the military was assigned the task of colonizing new planets.

Technology for making other worlds inhabitable had recently been developed, and a small settlement was started on the moon. Most cheered this progress. But a few began to worry.

And even fewer were human.

Chapter 1

How It All Began

Lieutenant General Grossen was double-checking his presentation. In a few minutes, he was to speak before the Federal Defense Agency's governing body, the Council of Generals. These forty-seven aliens were the minds behind all military—and most political—policy.

He was a Waas, the most common race, especially in the military. They were humanoid, about two and a half meters tall, similar to humans in appearance, except they came in shades of light to forest green and had no ears or hair. They were more heavy-set than the average human and had V-shaped foot pads to support the weight. With three fingers and one thumb to a hand, and a rather long neck, they managed to present a familiar, yet entirely alien look.

Right now Grossen could care less about what anyone thought of how he looked, especially this new race that had been discovered less than six months ago. *They're going to be added to the Federation anyway, and everyone knows it, so why do I have to go through the trouble of finding a reason to conquer them? I'm sorry—enlighten, not conquer. The pleasures of a bureaucracy.*

"Time to tell beings what they want to hear," he said, looking at the time.

Two unarmed guards escorted him to the chamber. According to regulations, the hallway leading to the chamber was to be free of weapons.

They're not entirely ceremonial, at least in theory. If an enemy did manage to sneak in a force, I doubt unarmed guards would stop them. Not that this facility is secret, but it's just one of thousands of military installations, and we don't tell that this is our HQ to anyone who doesn't need to know.

Glancing up at the open arch entrance the Council, he thought about the war that would ensue after his speech. *From what Intel has said about their current level of technological development, there won't be much space combat, if any at all. Since they only recently began to colonize their surrounding planets, their space fleet can't be too advanced. No, the battle will be fought on the planet's surface. They have a decent military force; they should be able to put up a good fight before they are overwhelmed.*

Before he could think about the predicted casualty count, he arrived at the center platform where he would address the Council. On the platform was a thin pole, in which a small data capsule containing the speaker's notes was inserted from the top. The speaker's notes were then projected in front of him. Surrounding the platform were the Council members, placed on a level above the speaker and arranged in a ring so each member could see the other in the eye. A cool blue light was cast down from the top of the huge dome that formed the council chamber, making the place feel decidedly colder than it was.

Grossen walked to the platform and inserted his capsule. When this was done, General Pathk immediately asked the traditional opening question.

"What have you deemed grave enough to bring before this Council?"

Grossen gave a sigh of relief as he turned his notes to face him. Pathk was going to be leading this session. Pathk was a no-nonsense type of person, so this wasn't going to take more than a few minutes.

"Sir, I have come to present my case for the addition of the planet Earth to the Federation," he replied.

"State your reasons for your opinion."

"As you know, sir, the planet Earth was found only recently. Though its inhabitants do not have anything technological to contribute, during the geological survey a new mineral was found. The inhabitants of this planet call the mineral 'diamond.' It is capable of deflecting any laser weapons we have, if it is shaped properly. And unlike our mirrors, it is quite hard and will not shatter when dropped."

This drew murmuring from the Council members, Grossen noted with pleasure. Obviously, he had surprised them.

He continued, "Based on their history, they will not voluntarily join the Federation, nor will they hand over the formula for synthetically producing this metal, although they do not yet realize its potential. However, if we ask for it, they will quickly find the reason for our asking, and equip their soldiers with armor made from the mineral, making their armies nearly invincible.

"As they have begun to colonize, they will eventually assault the Federation when their own galaxy is not sufficient to hold their numbers. Although they will never have numbers enough to rival the Federation, we do not have a way of penetrating diamond. As a result, they will be able to inflict heavy casualties before they are defeated.

"We must strike NOW if we are to avoid these losses. An immediate surprise assault would catch our enemy off guard. If we hit them without warning, they will be overcome before the potential of the new mineral is developed and used against our forces."

"I thank the Council for hearing my say on this matter." Grossen retrieved his notes, and then snapped to attention, did an about-face, and swiftly marched out of the council chamber.

Smiling inwardly, he listened to the buzz of conversation he had created. Now it was time to lay plans for the assault that would soon be coming.

Chapter 2

An Unexpected Development

Global Military HQ, Earth: General Abacker was hurrying down a hallway as an aide filled him in on the events that had recently taken place.

Abacker, at forty-eight, was the youngest person to make full General in the military, and also the youngest member on the International Defense Force Chiefs of Staff, which consisted of twenty-five generals from all over the world. He was representing the U.S. Army. He was in relatively good shape, but not particularly handsome. His hair was greyer than it should've been at his age, mainly from the stress from being one of the top decision makers in the world.

"Wait a minute, you mean to tell me the moon colony has been destroyed?" Abacker said doubtfully to his aide.

"That's what's believed to have happened. However, we do not know for certain. The last transmission from the Colony said, verbatim, that a large asteroid was on an intercept course and they only had forty minutes to figure out what to do about it."

Abacker smiled. *That would be Clarence. Always adding his two cents' worth, even when he is in danger. It's almost cost him his career a dozen times and he's yet to learn his lesson.*

They came upon the door leading to the War Room, where only generals were allowed access.

As Abacker entered the room, his aide dropped back and went to the Intel room to get any more information he could while Abacker met with the other generals.

Abacker entered the room and was greeted by his old friend, General Malcolm.

"Abacker, come take a seat." He gestured to an empty chair. "I imagine the briefing your aide gave you was pretty incomplete."

"That would be a major understatement." Abacker smiled. "Now what's this business about the moon colony being wiped out by a giant asteroid?"

Malcolm suddenly became serious. "It wasn't an asteroid. You see here," he motioned as a screen unrolled from the wall, "this photo was taken by one of our satellites. At first we thought it was an asteroid, but then this happened."

The screen showed pieces of the asteroid coming off. It zoomed in and showed the asteroid was shaped like a supersized sub. As it continued to zoom in, it became clear the asteroid was smooth. It was then one of the pieces of the asteroid came into view. The suspicion that had been growing in Abacker's mind was realized when the piece of asteroid fired up what was obviously an engine. It was a small, blue circle that was varying in intensity, showing that it was heating and cooling down. The screen then zoomed out, showing the asteroid was a huge spacecraft of some sort.

The colony was then pictured on the screen. The smaller spacecraft were flying all around it, like bees swarming an intruder. Small lights emitted from the craft, and when the lights impacted on the colony, they caused massive damage.

Abacker wasn't as surprised as he'd expected he would be. It was sort an odd moment. What really worried him was these enemies obviously had plenty of information about the colony. Their attacks targeted the key sections of the colony, such as life support and power.

"Well, what do you think?"

"I think this was planned," Abacker replied. He thought about what he said for a second. "Sorry, of course it was planned. What I meant was the attack was deliberate. This is no army just stopping by on an intergalactic tour; this is an attempt to conquer the human race, though I have no idea why they want to.

"Also, they have intel on us. When they hit the colony, they attacked only the vital areas. I don't think there's going to be a 'take me to your leader moment'; more likely, they will show up at the White House and move directly to the Oval Office.

"And I take it the reason we lost communication with the moon was they jammed us."

"We had just arrived at the same conclusion. I—hold on a second, I got a call coming in." He tapped the mike piece imbedded in his lip. He had the receptor in his ear.

He excused himself from the room and returned a few seconds later.

"Our satellites were knocked out about five minutes ago, and my wife told my son he couldn't go to tonight's dance and he's acting like it's the end of the world."

They all laughed, although it wasn't that funny.

"Okay, now we go back to what we were discussing before you walked in," said General Yomaha. "What do we do about it?"

"I think we should inform the world, then fortify the most strategic and vital places, and have a reserve force ready to respond to any assault, plus a secondary reserve force in case they make an attack to draw us off."

General Rason interrupted. "Do you really think we should tell everyone? It could cause a lot of panic."

"Not more panic than if a bunch of aliens land without warning," Abacker replied. "Besides, it will give the militia and police time to form up and make a defensive plan for their communities."

"I agree with Abacker on having two reserve forces. I would also recommend we prepare our ICBMs for launch against their space fleet by adding large booster rockets. Though they could probably dodge or shoot down our nukes, if we set the missiles with time detonators, several missiles would get through and cause widespread damage among their fleet. Now before any of you object, hear my reasons." General William had noticed several mouths opening in objection.

"Any way the people are told, there is going to be some level of panic," he continued. "And let's face it, we have an unmeasured enemy force which is technologically, and most likely numerically, superior. If we win, it's going to be a close battle. When things get too close, some panicking person or government might use the nukes on Earth. If we get rid of them early, we won't have to worry about that. Besides, the nukes are our best antispacecraft weapon, as there is little or no friction in space to slow the explosion, and our atmosphere should be able to deflect most of the radiation.

"And on the subject of anti-aircraft defense, I think we should scatter it around, some of it being placed around strategic positions, but most of the mobile stuff being scattered around the countryside, capable of hitting resupply ships and concentrating quickly against any mass airborne assault. I think heat seekers are going to be the most effective, mostly because we know their ships are propelled by heat, and we don't know if they have stealth technology."

"Using nukes seems like a good idea. However, I don't think our anti-aircraft should be randomly scattered. I think they should be placed in positions where they can be easily moved to cover a different place, which would allow us to cover more area with fewer units," said General Josef.

Malcolm spoke up. "I agree with Josef, on both points. But I was thinking ..."

"That's always a bad sign," Yomaha whispered to Abacker.

"As I was saying, I think they are going to ask us to surrender—then we tell them to go to hell and they'll attack us. No army would pass up a chance for a win without a fight. So when they do, why don't we ask them a bunch of scientific questions, act interested, and get some info on them."

"Although this is an incomplete defense plan, we should adjourn for a few hours and get what we have in motion. If we get things going now, they should be complete by midnight," said General Grudieran.

"Alright, let's get started." Malcolm rose from the table.

The defense of Earth had begun.

Chapter 3

How Malcolm Went to a Peaceful
Conference and Ended Up Declaring War

Malcolm was talking to Abacker by the espresso machine.

"I can't believe they're making me talk to the ambassadors with only two hours sleep," grumbled Malcolm.

And before he has brushed his teeth. Abacker turned away.

"Well, it was your idea." He tried to avoid Malcolm's breath.

"I know, but I wasn't expecting to get the job, so I have no idea what to do," Malcolm replied.

"You can start by brushing your teeth," Abacker said as he left the room.

"And to think I called you a friend," muttered Malcolm. "Hey, Colonel Walker, do you have that list of questions yet?"

Walker hurried to Malcolm.

"Whoa, sir, are you trying to kill them with your breath?" he exclaimed as he neared Malcolm. "Yes, the questions are all right here, as you requested." He handed over a sheet of paper.

"That will be all," Malcolm said curtly. *This is the result of being so lax on discipline.* He looked at his watch. "I'd best get moving," he proclaimed to no one in particular.

He walked toward the exit and the door automatically opened before him. *We truly do live in the future.* An open-top, solar-powered vehicle riding on a cushion of air pulled up on the curb in front of him. The sun beat down upon the building brightly, giving it an almost white color. The sky was a brilliant blue, with no clouds to speak of. It was one of those days which never seemed real, like time was just passing by, only stopping to say hello.

This is a beautiful day. He entered the door that had swung open before him and climbed into the vehicle, still staring at the sky.

As it began to pull away from the curb, he popped a breath mint in his mouth and closed his eyes as he leaned his head back, thoroughly enjoying the day's heat.

Relaxing, he began to think over last night's events. The Global Military HQ had been buzzing with activity all night. *The people have taken the news that an alien race is intent on annihilating us pretty well. Fifteen people died rioting during the night, which is considerably less than expected. After that, things kind of settled down as order was restored. What helped restore order the most was the knowledge that though they can shoot through our atmosphere, the most powerful of their weapons can destroy only five city blocks, making the fear that they are going to blow up the Earth groundless.*

He smiled. *Those Intel boys did a thorough job on these aliens. They spent the night studying the images that had been recorded, and found the power, range, and weak points of almost every weapons system the aliens have in their arsenal. Their fleet of small spacecraft consisted of six-man fighter craft and twenty-man transports. I have no clue how they figured that out. The large spacecraft was about half the size of the moon and they estimated it held 600 million enemy personnel. They just might outnumber us.*

At about midnight, all the comm. equipment at the Global Military HQ received a message that ambassadors for the Federation wished an audience with representatives from Earth. They contacted us by voice only.

The meeting is to take place in Nevada, at a remote location, to which they gave us the latitude and longitude. The aliens had sarcastically suggested Area 51 as a meeting place, which surprised us all because not only did it show they had a sense of humor, they also knew the significance of meeting in Nevada.

Each side is allowed two armed guards, and the details of the meeting do not have to be kept secret, but during the meeting itself, knowledge of what is happening is not to be released.

The Chiefs of Staff picked me to represent Earth, and I've spent the whole darned night trying to figure out what to say. In the end, I've decided just to improvise as I went along, but had to make sure to ask the questions that had been prepared.

His train of thought got derailed as he gradually dozed off, and the next thing he knew he was being awakened by one of the guards.

"Twenty minutes till we arrive, sir."

He spent the next twenty minutes trying to recover from his nap. The vehicle came to a halt, and not feeling quite ready, he got out and entered the mobile home that was the agreed upon meeting place. A blast of cool air hit him as he entered the house and he felt immensely better.

More confident, he strode into the dining room where the alien dignitaries were waiting. One of them was a Waas, and the one sitting to his left was a Rotain, which looked for all the world like ET, except his skin was grey, and his head was shaped like a half-meter-long French bread loaf. Both were wearing what looked like an alien business suit.

Clad in turquoise uniforms that appeared to be almost baggy, with gear and objects dangling and shoes that looked like a series of leather straps which held together fabric in between, the guards somehow managed to cut a sharp appearance. The two guards were Pratins, tall, thin, sinewy creatures, with long necks and snakelike heads. They held their weapons with the long hook-like finger they had on each hand. The most warlike of any creature in the Federation—as all of them served in the military at one point in their lives—they were also keenly intelligent, possessing an IQ above an average human's. Malcolm was mystified as to how they ever learned to hold their weapons with their hook-like fingers.

The Waas said something in a language Malcolm didn't understand. The Rotain on his left then said to him, "Welcome. Please take a seat," as he motioned to a table.

Malcolm and the Waas took their seats facing each other, while their aides stood to the left of their respective bosses.

"I'm General Malcolm." Malcolm offered a hand.

"And I'm Ambassador Qunit." The interpreter was giving the hand a strange look.

Malcolm retracted the hand. "Let's get straight to business. Who are you, what do you want, and how did you learn to speak English?"

"The last question I can answer without consulting the ambassador. My species possess a talent for understanding languages. Some of your transmissions were intercepted and from those I learned how you speak."

After a quick dialogue with the ambassador, the interpreter continued, "We are the Federation of Species, who work together in peace to advance science, technology, medicine, and to generally help each other in our various needs under one unified government."

"Do its members have a choice in whether they join?"

The ambassador looked surprised as the message was translated to him.

"I mean, are some of its members forced into this Federation against their will?" Malcolm explained.

"Some races have to be *enlightened* about the benefits, but in the end they all chose to join us."

"So that's why you blew up the moon colony."

The ambassador and his interpreter debated amongst themselves for a bit. "That was an unfortunate mistake. It was so small we assumed it was a defensive outpost. It was, after all, manned by military personnel."

Malcolm was about to hurl a stream of obscenities, when his aide, seeing what was about to happen, hurriedly whispered to him, "The list, sir."

Malcolm nearly yelled "What list!" when the mission he had designed came back to him. "So, uh, how many species have been enlightened?" He was not entirely successful in keeping the venom out of his voice.

"Sixty-three to date, out of sixty-four discovered. You are the sixty-fourth race. There is one small matter on that account. We like to study and document every new race, so we would need ten live specimens of your species, five male and five female, to, I believe the word is, dissect."

As this was being interpreted to Malcolm, there was a slight explosion in his mind as control vanished from his system.

"I can tell you right now there is no way we are going to give up ten people to be dissected, nor is there anything you can say or do to make us join your Federation."

Qunit kept his poise. "We don't expect you to send us ten randomly selected beings. Beings that have been slated for execution or political prisoners for life, the refuse of society that are going to die anyway, those are the sort of beings normally given."

"These negotiations are over, Ambassador, and we will not sacrifice a single human being." Malcolm stood up and turned around to leave.

"May I remind you there is a battleship hovering over your planet."

Malcolm stopped and faced Ambassador Qunit. "Is that a threat?"

"It does not have to be."

Taking a moment for dramatic effect, Malcolm said gravely, "Then, by the powers invested in me, the Confederation of Nations on Earth declares war on the Federation of Species. You have twenty minutes to leave, Ambassador."

And with that Malcolm stormed out of the door, his aide and the two guards falling in behind him.

Once outside the building, the aide asked, "Sir, what powers *are* invested in you by the Confederation?"

"None. I just said that to make it sound more official."

Marching to the waiting vehicle, the driver saw Malcolm and asked, "Was the mission a success sir?"

"No, it was a horrible failure. The only new thing we learned is there are sixty-three other species in the universe."

As he climbed in the vehicle, Malcolm added, "By the way Sergeant, we're at war."

"Oh, good," said the sergeant, "I was wondering how long it was going to take."

Chapter 4

The Battle for Earth

While the vehicle sped away back toward the Global Military HQ, Malcolm began placing calls to inform everyone of what had transpired. The message he received in return was what he'd expected. In exactly twenty minutes they would launch the nukes.

Malcolm kept glancing at his watch. At twenty minutes he said, "Everyone, I want you to look to the right."

Their heads turned and they saw a missile streaking across the blue sky. In the distance they could see other missiles heading for space.

As they watched the missiles, Malcolm said, "You are witnessing the first blow of the war. Pray to God we survive it."

In the Federation battleship, little alarm was evident as the nukes went into space. All the nukes had missed them, which they attributed to the enemy's primitive aiming systems.

Without warning, the nukes exploded, sending massive shock waves throughout the surrounding space. The battleship crumbled under the force, opening its insides to the vacuum. The air was sucked out of the ship, suffocating the crew. Only a few scout ships that were on patrol survived the holocaust. Within the hour, all Federation forces had vacated the solar system.

When the news of the stunning victory was passed out to the public, they were cautioned not to begin celebrating, as it might be premature. For once, the public listened and waited patiently for further developments.

<hr>

In the Federation, the repercussions were felt immediately. 600 million personnel killed by a technologically inferior race was unheard of. The horrific loss of life caused tremendous anti-Earth sentiment. A huge battle fleet consisting of hundreds of vessels of all shapes and sizes was gathered for the invasion.

When the fleet jumped to Earth, the ships were prepared for nukes to be launched at them, but not for what the Confederation of Nations did instead.

Several nukes had not been fired in the first strike. After the battle, these nukes were sent into orbit around Earth, appearing to be nothing more than circling space junk. When the second Federation fleet arrived, they detonated these nukes in the middle of the FDA fleet.

These bombs caused even greater damage and loss of life than the first, but some of the Federation fleet survived. The surviving ships launched their fleets of shuttles bearing avenging soldiers toward the now defenseless Earth.

Chapter 5
The Enlightenment of Earth

Anti Aircraft fire and Surface to Air Missiles streaked across the night sky at the invading shuttles. Several of the shuttles were hit, but the rest kept on coming. Federal Defense Agency and International Defense Force fighters tangled in the air, the night briefly lighting up when a laser was fired or a missile launched. On the ground, tracers and lasers flew back and forth as soldiers engaged each other. Slowly but steadily, the Federation pushed Earth's soldiers back.

After about two weeks, it became clear the Federation was going to win. All across the Earth the IDF was being pushed back, surrounded, and destroyed. Seeing the military was being defeated, the Chiefs of Staff recommended the civilian population be loaded onto shuttles and sent away from Earth. Speedily, old spaceships were reconditioned. The inhabitants of Earth who had not already been killed began to board these spaceships at designated loading areas. Each of these loading areas had a military platoon guarding it from alien attacks.

Lieutenant Young, United States Marine Corps, was the commander of one of these platoons. Reports had told him 24 FDA soldiers were coming to capture the loading zone. He had deployed his troops away from the loading zone so stray shots would not hit the civilians.

As close as they were to battle, he wasn't feeling fear; rather, it was excitement. "Marines, listen up," he shouted "Soon we will be engaged with the enemy. Our foe is technologically superior to us, but there is something we have that they don't.

"We have marines! We are the best of the best, and have always been throughout history, and will always remain so. Look at the past. We have fought from the halls of Montezuma to the shores of Tripoli. We defeated the German advance in Belleau Wood. We did amphibious assaults at a time when no one believed they were possible. We took the island fortress of Iwo Jima. We fought our way out of the Chosin Reservoir. We fought and won at Hue. All this was only in our first two hundred years. And today we shall add a new victory to this long and glorious list. OORAH!"

"OORAH," his marines shouted back at him.

A plan quickly formulated in Lieutenant Young's mind. "Fix bayonets," he yelled.

The marines pulled out their bayonets and attached them to their M-24 rifles. The M-24 rifle looked like an M1 Garand with a synthetic stock and a grenade launcher slung underneath. Carrying a forty-round clip, the rifle was able to fire single-shot or fully automatic. On top of the rifle was a small transparent box with a red dot in the middle that served as the sight.

Once the marines had fixed bayonets, Lieutenant Young said, "Private Smith, you used to be a sniper, right?"

"I was until they caught me driving drunk and busted me to private," Smith replied.

"Find a good position and start taking long-range shots as soon as you see the enemy. Make them keep their heads down."

Smith disappeared as he went around the top of the hill to a sniper position.

Young turned to his platoon sergeant. "Staff Sergeant Chopin, take a squad and get behind us a little ways. When the enemy gets close enough, we're going to make a bayonet charge as the two machine gun teams provide cover fire. While we're doing that, you and the squad will go around and flank the enemy. We should catch them in a nice little pincer."

Staff Sergeant Chopin hurried to comply with Lieutenant Young's orders. The rest of the platoon quickly took up defense positions. They were on top of a rocky hill, a good place to defend. A hundred meters below the hill was a thick forest, but behind the hill the terrain became too rocky for trees to grow.

Private Smith fired a shot, splitting the silence that had fallen over the area. Several laser shots crashed into the rocks around Smith, but they all missed him. Smith's shots increased in rapidity as he cried out, "Sir, twenty-six enemy soldiers coming up the hill fast. I think I got two of them."

"Up and at 'em, marines," Lieutenant Young shouted.

The marines appeared from their cover and opened fire. They could spot quick glimpses of figures scurrying from rock to rock, moving a little too fast to shoot at—not that it stopped the marines from blazing away.

After missing a couple of FDA soldiers, Lieutenant Young mentally marked the rock behind which a soldier he had been shooting at disappeared. His grenade launcher had a full clip of five grenades, so Young decided to fire a pair at the rock. He pulled the secondary trigger twice and two grenades streaked from his rifle. The first grenade blew away the side of the rock and the second exploded at the now exposed soldier's feet. With his legs and stomach blown out, the alien fell dead.

Other marines caught onto Young's idea and started lobbing grenades all over the place, but the enemy continued to advance. Lieutenant Young let the enemy make it about three-quarters up the hill, then yelled, "Chaaarrge!"

The marines stood up and started running toward the enemy, shouting loudly as they went. Young had counted on the enemy's not knowing how to react to a bayonet charge, and his gamble seemed to be paying off.

Lasers streaked through the air and struck down several marines, but the momentum of the charge was too great for it to be stopped. The marines came among the enemy and engaged the aliens in hand to hand combat.

Lieutenant Young jumped on top of a rock, and leapt down on the alien below, abandoning his rifle. Rolling with the alien, he went for a short distance until the alien shoved him off. The alien—who unbeknownst to Lieutenant Young was a Waas—had dropped his weapon when Young leapt on him, so the two of them went at it hand to hand.

Young threw a couple of punches the Waas dodged and the Waas made a fast left hook at him. Stepping out of the way of the blow, he grabbed the alien's arm and twisted hard, then sent his elbow into the Waas' chest, knocking his opponent's wind out. He took a step back and then delivered a powerful sweeping right leg that caught the Waas in the same place as the elbow. The Waas was knocked off his feet and went flying backward. Landing headfirst, the Waas collided with a rock, instantly breaking his neck.

Firing broke out in front of Lieutenant Young as Staff Sergeant Chopin's group hit the enemy on the flank. Struck by two surprise maneuvers, the FDA force was annihilated.

One of the marines yelled a stream of highly vulgar words at the dead bodies, daring any other aliens to attack them.

The platoon regrouped back at the top of the hill. Doing a quick head count, Lieutenant Young discovered eight of his men had been killed and six wounded. He was about to order the platoon back into defensive positions when he spotted a man in a general's uniform walking towards him. Somewhat mystified, he stared hard at the name on the uniform. It read "Abacker."

"How's your platoon Lieutenant?" Abacker asked him.

"We were just hit by an enemy unit and took some casualties, but we're still ready to rock and roll, sir."

Abacker looked at the dead aliens stretched out on the hill. "Good job. Get your marines and pull out. Board one of the shuttles. We need to get out of here."

"Sir, we're going to stay here until they get us all. As long as one marine is still alive, no alien is going to rule Earth. We will not abandon our post."

Abacker stared at the Lieutenant for a second. "You, me, your marines, and a naval fighter pilot flying one of those shuttles are all that's left of the military. The rest has been wiped out. Right now I'm the only living general. Little platoons guarding loading zones still exist, but those are being taken out by advancing FDA units."

A distant look came into Abacker's eyes. He continued in a lower tone. "And after they've eliminated the guarding platoons, the aliens blow up the shuttles, with the civilians still in them. They must really hate us, but I can't say I blame them. We killed a lot of them." Abacker shook his head and came out of his trance. "When the military men die out the human race will fall. When those who have learned war are no more, we will never be able to take back Earth. Do you still want to stay, Lieutenant?"

Lieutenant Young was quiet for a moment, then surrendered his warrior's pride to his sense of duty. "We will leave, sir," he said. "To preserve the Corps."

"To preserve the Corps," Abacker repeated.

Chapter 6

Abacker's Law

The shuttles blasted off from Earth, fleeing into space above. The naval forces were too busy finishing the humans still on Earth to bother with them. These shuttles formed up with the group that had gathered above the planet. When no more shuttles were forthcoming, this small group bearing the remnants of the human race began to run away from the doomed planet in a futile but defiant gesture.

Once every last human on Earth had been killed, the Federation forces chased down the shuttles. This time, the Federation showed mercy, and made the human race join the Federation. However, in punishment for the massive loss of life the humans had caused, the 'race was prohibited from ever returning to Earth.

Abacker, being the highest-ranking person, naturally assumed command of the human race. He was forced to sign the agreement entering the 'race as part of the Federation, but he never officially declared the war over. It was an unnamed assumption that the war had ended with the fall of Earth.

After he signed the agreement, Abacker decided to make an address to the human race, knowing he could speak in relative security because only a select few aliens could speak any of the human languages.

Abacker walked up to a podium in front of a crowd that had gathered to hear him speak. "My fellow people, today the human race nearly became extinct. To save what remained of the 'race, I was forced to bow to the wishes of the Federation.

"I would like to congratulate you all on becoming the newest members of the Federation of Planets," Abacker said sarcastically. "Aliens will now populate our empty world."

He paused. "I know many of us would have preferred to have fought to the death, but that cannot happen. The human race must never cease to exist. We will do whatever is necessary to survive.

"One of the conditions forced upon us is we can never return to Earth. In a few hours they will load our shuttles into their hangar bays and take us deep into the heart of the Federation. Then they will hide the location of Earth from us as punishment for all we have done to them. They think by taking away our home they have taken away our strength, our identity. They mean to assimilate us into their society so we forget who we are and won't cause any more problems.

"But we shall not lose ourselves. We shall not settle on a new planet and just become another member of the Federation. We shall fight, and we will remember who we are, until the last of us are destroyed. I swear to you, no human shall ever set foot on another planet until we have found Earth."

Thunderous applause broke out at the strong statement. Every man, woman, and child among them knew they would abide by this rule.

Abacker continued, "Several marines and a naval pilot have survived and are among us now. While I will teach the marine platoon leader and the naval pilot the art of strategy, the enlisted men will train you in their ways. In secret we will build an army, until one day we are strong enough to challenge the Federation and take back our planet.

"Now we must look to the present. Survival is paramount. We cannot live as we lived in the past if we are to survive. No longer can we afford to discriminate based on sex, religion, race or color; we can only prejudice against species. Equality is a must, for if we are fighting amongst ourselves, we cannot fight the real enemy. Old grudges have to be dropped in favor of the new one, the one against the Federation.

"No one will be forced into the military, but I doubt finding volunteers will be a problem. However, some old freedoms we have previously enjoyed will have to be sacrificed if the 'race is to live. Anything preventing reproduction must be strictly prohibited. We need to grow to be able to challenge the Federation, and only when we are great enough in number shall we begin fighting back.

"Above all else, one law shall be upheld. No human shall ever take the life another human, not even in justice for a wrong committed. The minute we start fighting against ourselves is the minute the Federation will win.

"Though battered and bruised, we are not beaten. We will resurrect someday, and on that day we will fight the Federation again, and that time we shall prevail!" Abacker finished.

Booming shouts and cheers rang throughout the room. The speech would be replayed over the intercom on every ship, then destroyed so the Federation would never find it. But its destruction would not make it forgotten. The words were engraved into the hearts and minds of all those heard it, to be repeated again and again to future generations.

As he stepped down from the podium and started to walk away, one of Abacker's assistants confronted him. "I think you let some of your personal beliefs influence your law. You can't force your ideas onto others. That is a freedom that should never be taken away. If you do that, you become no better than the Federation, you are nothing more than …"

Abacker turned to face the assistant and interrupted him. "Look around you. Look at the facts. There are only a few of us left, a couple million out of an original seven billion. One Federation battleship carries many times that. And the Federation has several hundred battleships out there. If there is not some sort of power running the universe besides us, then we don't stand a chance."

Shortly after the speech, the human race was packed into the hangars of waiting Federation battleships and sent deep into Federation territory.

Abacker's Law led to a slight difficulty. The 'race had originally intentioned to remain in their shuttles until they found Earth, but they encountered the problem of fuel. Things would have turned ugly had they not ventured near one of the Federation planets. They were searching for some kind of aerial re-fueling system when they discovered a space station that formed a belt around the planet. This solved their problem, as setting foot in a Federation space station was not setting foot on a Federation planet. Soon a flourishing human community was established on the orbiting space station.

Not everything was going perfectly, however. The Federation made demands on the human race, including the turning over of ten people for experimentation. Naturally, the humans refused. The Federation took the ten people by force. With their small, newly trained army, the humans made several raids in retaliation. The Federation returned the favor in kind, but then the humans made several revenge raids against the Federation's retaliatory raids.

The vicious cycle did not stop there, and each side continued striking back, ensuring they would never find peace. Eventually, this simply became the way things were done.

Chapter 7
Three Thousand Years Later

By the year 470, 854 SFB major technological and political changes had occurred.

Shortly after the war, the FDA managed to acquire samples of diamonds. They made extensive studies upon it, and through trial and error discovered a cheap method of producing synthetic diamonds.

These diamonds were mass-produced and turned into a suit of armor impervious to any weapon. It was made airtight and had an oxygen-generating system so the armored suit could be used as spacesuits. To allow for eating, a small hole could be opened around the mouth. Building armor suits became something of an art, and by the year 470, 548 SFB, diamond armor suits were so thin and crystal clear they were invisible. When clothes were worn over the suit it was impossible to tell if someone was wearing one.

The only thing that could defeat diamond armor was the specially developed ice bullet, which used the same principle as a HE-AT round. When the bullet impacted the armor, a jet of water was sent between the molecules of the diamond and then flash-frozen. The frozen water would expand and explode, sending jagged pieces of diamond into the suit's wearer.

An ice bullet was about the size of a pellet. About 250 shots were in a standard assault rifle or sub-machine gun clip. Eventually, weapons were developed that sent projectiles so fast they shattered every bone in the body when they impacted the diamond armor. Nevertheless, the ice bullet was so successful it stuck around.

This new form of super-high-speed propulsion for bullets was known as magnetic acceleration, so named because when two magnets of the same charge are put side by side they repel each other. Two metals that reacted incredibly violently to each other were found, and ice bullets were made out of one of the metals and the chamber of firearms out of the other. When the bullet entered the chamber, the two strongly repelled. The bullet was forced out of the barrel at close to the speed of light while the weapon recoiled into the shooter's shoulder.

To take some of the kick out, the force from the recoil was used to power small repulse-lifters placed all around the weapon. These repulse-lifters pushed air into an enclosed layer surrounding the weapon—making the weapon more or less resistant to motion, a feature extremely useful in long-range or one-handed shooting—using the principle that every action has an equal and opposite reaction.

The discovery of magnetic acceleration ended the use of armored land vehicles. Soldiers armed with a clip of bullets that were heavier than an ice bullet were more than a match for armor. At the speeds the bullets were traveling, they would punch right through any armor other than diamond armor. When fired in fully automatic, the devastation on an armored vehicle was tremendous. Armored vehicles quickly became obsolete, but soldiers continued to carry one clip full of heavy shots for anti-vehicle or demolition operations.

Marines used an assault rifle that looked the same as the one they had used in the Battle for Earth, without the grenade launcher. Also, they had old-fashioned iron peep sights instead of the laser sights, and added a sling. The biggest difference was a rod that projected past the barrel. This rod, when turned on, projected a small field along the length of the rod that would vaporize anything it touched. In effect, it was a really sharp bayonet.

To fit the needs of all its species, the FDA adopted an assault rife that was about as long as an average human's arm and had two hook-like hand holds, one forward and one back. The rear handhold had a firing stud. Like the Marines' rifles, it used a peep sight. Their rifles had a banana clip just forward of the rear grip, and fired single-shot or fully automatic as did the Marine assault rifle. The true rate of fire was unknown as it increased during volleys, but the 250-shot clip would be emptied in a second and a half if the trigger was held down. Since shoulders varied widely from species to species, the rifles had no stock, nor did they have the bayonet-like rod the Marines carried, as hand to hand combat was considered primitive and out of date. Since all FDA soldiers were required to have a weapon on them at all times, most of the noninfantry troops used a much shorter SMG version of the FDA assault rifle.

One thing all rifles had in common was ancient peep sights. The reason behind this was sometime after the conquest of Earth, the FDA had built a series of bio-robots, which combined the best qualities of living things and machines. Then the robots rebelled and started taking over the universe.

Unable to stop these terrible machines, the FDA trained their soldiers to fight without electronics, and deployed Electromagnetic Pulse fields that knocked out all electronics within their range. Having lost their mechanical precision, the bio-robots became easy pickings. The FDA discovered most of their enemies had become technologically dependent, and began to employ

EMP fields in all their battles. The human military adapted to the FDA's new tactic and began to employ their own EMP fields.

Gangs and paramilitary units did not totally adjust, and among them one could find the wild array of lasers, guided bullets, and other electronics that were not anachronisms.

After the Battle for Earth, the FDA had begun to downsize their battleships to prevent so many deaths with the loss of one ship. By 470, 854 SFB, two main classes of battleships existed, the *Dousier* and the *Avendor*. The *Dousier* was shaped like a rectangle with all the sides concave, bending in to meet at the center. All the armament on a side converged at one point, giving a high concentration of fire. *Dousiers* were out of date, however, and had many weak points, so they were primarily used in antispacecraft defense. *Avendor*-class battleships were the latest and greatest, and were far too strong to be challenged by anything other than another *Avendor*-class battleship. Because of this, most navies got rid of their other vessels and kept only battleships and support vessels.

On the political side, the human exiles had split into two groups. The first was the Human Alliance, known simply as the Alliance, and became recognized as the official government of the human race, as no human would serve in the congress of the Federation. The other, Mankind Against Aliens, or MAA, was a terrorist organization. They believed the only way to secure peace was to kill or subdue every alien in the "'verse." The MAA was responsible for the mass murder of alien civilians from time to time. The Alliance always publicly denounced the MAA's actions but privately often supported the MAA on military raids.

A strong Marine Corps and Navy grew from the Alliance in captivity, one that was rivaled by no other except for the FDA. The FDA did not have separate branches of the military, only different units, so they did not quite comprehend why the Alliance had two different military chains of command. This gave Alliance soldiers a slight edge in that their training was more specialized to their branch of service, while the FDA trained their units more roundly to prepare them to take on any job that might be required.

The Federation had stopped expanding its borders about four hundred years after the fall of Earth. All 103 intelligent species that had been discovered joined the Federation, in the end.

Growing rapidly, the human race went from endangered status to being one of the major species in the three millennia since the fall of Earth. One galactic language was spoken, and to better adapt, all humans learned this language and forgot their native tongues. Despite the loss of culture, the ability to go anywhere in the 'verse and be understood could not be undervalued. Decent-sized human communities were established in space stations above almost every planet. All of them, throughout this entire time, had followed Abacker's Law without fail and never set foot on a planet, until now. One human dared to break this law. His name was John.

Chapter 8

John on a Mission

He was arrogantly striding down the hallway, partially blending in the darkness, wearing a black combat suit with his blouse tucked into his trousers, and a thin black belt that was almost invisible against the rest of his uniform. On his right thigh a pistol slightly smaller than an M9 Berretta was strapped into a low-slung holster. His left thigh had a small SMG on it. He had six spare clips on his hip. The cargo pockets were loaded with explosives, except for the one on his upper left, which contained a small holster for his second-most-favored weapon, a small handgun about half the size of his other pistol.

His favored was in his hands, a medium sized SMG. The grip for his forward hand was close to the end of the barrel. His hand was too large for the pistol grip, just the way he liked it. The clip was inserted into the front of his forward grip, so the ammo went straight into the chamber. With the short stock firmly in his shoulder and the weapon pointed forward and seeking targets, he looked exceptionally dangerous, which was actually a bad thing in his business.

He was an assassin, known as John. No one knew his last name. He was a human, and anyone who saw him would have assumed he was an Alliance operative, except he wasn't wearing any facial covering other than his diamond armor, which did not distort his image. In other words, his identity could be easily discovered if you got a good look at him.

Once you got a good look at him, you would know who he was. His face was posted all over the 'verse. Right next to it was a price. The price his life was worth. At only twenty-eight, he was the best assassin in the history of the Federation, which meant he had taken down more government workers than anyone else. Hence, the nine-digit number next to his name and face.

He was currently on a mission. His target was a Federation general, whose crime was he was too successful in cracking down on illegal arms dealing. John was unfamiliar with his contractor.

The general was on board a *Dousier*-class battleship. John had already breached the ship, and everything was in its place. Now it was time to make the first move.

His plan was to make as much noise as possible. Standard procedure for an intruder alert was to lock down all high-priority areas and to start slowly searching; locking down each area they cleared, essentially driving the intruder into a corner. The trick was to get into the place you wanted to be before they locked down, thus trapping the target in the room with you. From experience, John knew he could make it.

He had breached the ship just before the bridge. As he strode across the floor, he swept the area with his eyes. With no one in sight, he quickly dashed around the corner. Not breaking his stride, he dropped the two bridge checkpoint guards with one shot apiece.

The remaining members of the guard contingent burst out of their guard room. John tossed a grenade into the middle of them. Though it wouldn't pierce their armor, the blast knocked them off their feet. Not needing to kill them, John placed another explosive on the door. The small blast didn't hurt him.

John heard a whirling of motors manually closing a door behind him as he entered the second checkpoint. Half the guards were waiting for him. Before they could fire, John killed several of them and entered the guard room positioned midway in the short corridor. He cleared the room of its inhabitants, then spun around and shot guards who had rushed in after him. John ran back into the corridor as the remaining guard hit the alarm. He cut the soldier down, then placed an explosive on the roof. Climbing into the resulting hole, he crawled till he judged he was at the middle of the bridge.

Drawing his second SMG, he placed them both on full-auto. He looked through a ventilation grating at his feet and made a quick survey of the area below. Once he had the layout of the bridge, he kicked out the grating and fell onto the middle of the bridge. Spraying fire in a full circle around him, he forced all the bridge officers to dive for cover, although he didn't hit any of them. Rolling forward, he discarded the empty SMGs and whipped out a pistol as he stood up. He put two bullets in an officer who jumped in front of him and entered the general's quarters before anyone else saw him.

The general looked up from his desk. John shot him between the eyes as the alarm went off.

John slapped a circular device with about the same diameter as his body onto the roof of the office. At the touch of a button, a small, powerful laser cut a hole through the ship's hull. He opened the circular device and crawled through the hole until he was on the surface of the battleship.

Launching a grappler to his ship, he reeled himself in. His ship was in one of the blind spots of the battleship, where he had attached himself like a limpet while the battleship was at a space port. He got aboard the ship quickly and detached from the hull. Before he even registered on the radar, the small ship launched into midspace.

Chapter 9

Beginnings

In his gleaming white uniform, the Alliance admiral strode through the corridors crowded with marines. Catching sight of the admiral's rank, a marine yelled, "Officer on deck!"

There was a mad scurry as marines scrambled to brace themselves against the bulkheads. Two long columns of marines stood stiffly at attention.

"Is Sergeant Heyligher here?" the admiral demanded.

A marine broke ranks and walked within a few paces of the Admiral. He made a sharp salute. "Sir, Sergeant Heyligher reporting as ordered."

The admiral returned the salute. "Are you the sniper who's closing in on the record?"

"Yes sir."

"I've been told you're an expert at infiltration, nigh undetectable. Am I correct?"

"I've yet to be spotted by the enemy on a mission, sir."

"How well can you handle your battle rifle?"

"I'm as proficient with my battle rifle as my sniper rifle, sir."

"Perfect. Accompany me to my shuttle."

"With respect, sir, who are you?"

The admiral laughed at that. "Isn't that the question we all must ask ourselves? My job is Head of Alliance Intelligence. Now let's leave."

A few minutes later, the two of them were alone in the admiral's luxurious private shuttle.

The admiral said, "Your secondary objective for this mission is to take out the head of Intelligence of the Varsis sector. He's landing on Jannet in two weeks, where he'll be attending a conference."

Pulling out a holographic map, the admiral continued, "You'll need to take the shot from here."

"I can't do that, sir. That location is on a planet, which you know as well as I do we're forbidden to go on."

"Once you learn what your primary mission is, you'll understand why we've decided you can set foot on a planet. And while you're on the planet, you're to contact the Assassin."

"*The* Assassin, sir?"

The admiral nodded. "I had to deploy half the department and nearly a third of our budget, but we found him at long last."

"Then I take it my primary mission is to eliminate him."

"I'd better explain the whole thing to you."

Once the admiral finished, Sergeant Heyligher said, "I'll get my things, sir. I should be ready to go in less than half an hour."

"The shuttle will be waiting for you."

— · —

She was a hotshot Alliance pilot. Ready for anything, courageous to a fault, and talented like few others. Yet she lacked an enemy. So far, there hadn't been anything more than short skirmishes with the FDA.

Sighing in boredom, she ran her fighter through the preflight checks. She then rocketed out the airlock and rendezvoused with her wing mate outside the battleship.

After setting her autopilot, she settled in for another long, eventless patrol.

Upon landing, she discovered she was starving. She headed toward her quarters. Despite the presence of many others, the battleship's corridors felt empty. Arriving at her room, she changed out of her flight suit and went down to the pilot's lounge.

The doors slid open, revealing a mass of pilots standing in a dimly lit room. Light from the corridor flooded in, silhouetting her form in the doorway. Most of the pilots immediately recognized that form and backed away, exercising a careful avoidance.

She didn't mind the reception. Her beauty was great—many had told her so—and therefore her pride held no grievance.

One of the bolder pilots approached her. "How was the flight?"

"Oh, it was nice, but kind of boring."

"Yeah, there hasn't been a lot of action lately."

"I hope it's the calm before the storm."

The pilot shook his head, then spoke with a touch of respect. "Well, you're probably good enough to weather it. I might make as well—once I almost got a lock on you in the simulators."

She smiled at the compliment. "Thank you."

"It's not a compliment, just a statement of fact. Hey, are you hungry?"

"Very. Always am after long flights."

"You want to go get something to eat?"

"Not with you."

There was smothered laughter from the crowd. The pilot paused as if considering whether to press his cause, then retreated.

Striding slowly through the other pilots, she sat on a stool and ate without any further advances.

Sitting behind a desk in his quarters, the FDA general wearily put down the datapad he'd been working on.

He would have to give his biannual report to the Council of Generals in a few months. That meant a long trip from the borders of the Federation.

The general hated doing this. He'd much rather take on a fleet of enemy warships than a room of bureaucrats. At least the enemy warships fought fairly.

Chapter 10

Back at Home

John landed back at his mansion. It was in a secluded place, built in a mountain range, right under a ledge. The first thing he did was take a shower.

I have left the rest of my race. I broke all ties with them. I ran from them. I ignored their rules. But most importantly, I live on a planet other than Earth. And I don't care.

He turned the shower off. He put on his dark green and black striped bathrobe, and similarly colored slippers. Like the shower, this was an ancient human custom he enjoyed. Almost everything in his mansion was a replica of old Earth fashions and designs. It was, of course, expensive, which was the point.

He walked to his desk, which was on the top floor of the structure. The room was about the size of a gym, with huge floor-to-roof windows stretching across the length of the room. Both ends were large polished hardwood walls, with an elevator at one end. The floors were also polished hardwood and without decoration.

The only object in the room was a wooden desk and a chair. Wood was rare and expensive. John liked the expensive, glossy look, mostly because it served as a giant mirror, allowing him to monitor the whole room with a glance.

Standing over the desk, John began sipping a small glass of water when he spotted something in the corner of his eye. Looking up, he saw a fully armed Alliance marine. The marine had a ragged look to him. His black and grey shaded Battle Dress Uniform was dirty and wrinkled, the small pack on his back bulging, and his assault rifle was held in a loose grip at a 45-degree angle across his body.

Three things went through John's mind in that instant. *This guy has a boonie hat on, which means he's a sniper. So the Alliance has finally gotten tired of me breaking their rules. What is an Alliance soldier doing on a planet?*

John was so intrigued by the last thought he didn't draw the SMG concealed in his desk. "So, what are you doing on a planet?"

"I'm here to make an offer on behalf of the Alliance."

"As you probably know, I don't do jobs for the Alliance. And my question was, what are you doing on a planet?"

Apparently not hearing him, the marine continued, "As even *you* know, the location of Earth has not been known for thousands of years. The Alliance has decided it is time to find out where it is. You are not alone in wanting to live on a planet. The Alliance and the MAA want you to find out were Earth is. The payment will be substantial, and you will be forgiven for breaking Abacker's Law."

"I thought the Alliance and the MAA never worked together. And you still haven't answered my question as to what you're doing on a planet."

"The answer to both questions is a two-man team has been put together to find Earth, one from each organization. They have been authorized to do whatever is necessary to accomplish the objective, even if we have to break Abacker's Law. If you accept the offer, you would become the third member and the leader of the team. To put it simply, my leaders feel your experience in getting into secure government areas has made you the best person for this mission. In addition, by getting into so many secure areas, it is believed you have some hint as to where Earth is."

I admit I sometimes looked for hints about Earth while I was on missions, but I never found anything. Still, there is something about this guy. He seems ticked off that he was chosen to deliver the message to me. I think he doesn't appreciate that I have broken most of the rules the rest of the race holds sacred. But there is something else he disapproves of about me.

"What's your name?" John asked him.

"Sergeant Heyligher. Sergeant Gregory Heyligher."

"Do they call you Greg for short?"

"No."

"All right Greg, do you know who I am?" John liked acting a lot more comfortable around Greg than he really was because he could see it was getting under the sergeant's skin.

"Who in the 'verse doesn't."

"Then you know I'm an assassin, and what you're asking me to do is to spy, and I don't do spying. I don't like trying to get a piece of information without anyone knowing I was there. I don't sneak around and do things quietly; I prefer to hide in the light."

"Your last sentence was purposely confusing so I would have to ask what you meant by that. Under normal circumstances, I would not respond, but as I have a mission, I am required to find a way to accomplish it, and this is an obstacle which must be cleared. So, what did you mean by your last sentence?"

Interesting. He likes to be in control of the situation. He made it clear he wanted to be the one asking questions, not answering them.

"It's basically the same principle as a fighter flying with the sun to his back, or using a flash-bang. You blind the enemy by making so much noise and confusion they cannot respond."

"Interesting philosophy."

A thought occurred to John. "You said your leaders felt my experience made me the best choice for the job. You do not hold this opinion?"

"I think my squad could do the job just as well."

"How old are you?"

"Twenty-two."

"Well, there are some things only experience can teach you. For instance," John said, looking at a monitor on his desk, "did you know two assassins followed you to my house? They are going to be here in a minute."

They heard a thump on the roof. John put down his glass which he had been holding and picked up his SMG. Greg covered the right while John covered the left.

Suddenly, two aliens rappelling from the roof—one on either side—appeared holding the line in one hand and their weapon in the other. With one shot, just before his target broke through the giant window, John put a round into the assassin's heart, instantly shattering the window as the bullet passed through it.

John spun around, just as the second assassin burst through the other window, firing wildly with one hand. Greg waited half a second and then fired, straight through his target's head, a perfect shot.

John asked him, "Why did you wait so long to fire? He could have got us both."

"One well-aimed shot is worth a million misses." He paused, and then continued, "If you're not going to accept the offer, do you mind if I accomplish my second objective?"

John shook his head and picked up his glass as Greg took off his small pack and quickly assembled his sniper rifle. The sniper rifle was three quarters of his height. It looked like a hunting rifle, except it had a pistol grip and a small five-round magazine that contained ice bullets the size of a .223 shell, casing and all. Inside the scope was an inverted post that served as the sight, much superior to the old-fashioned crosshairs that had a habit of getting lost when sighting in on a target. The scope also had an internal gun-camera to confirm kills. There was a bipod on the front that folded forward and the entire rifle was in the same camouflage pattern as the uniform Greg was wearing.

Greg went to the shattered window on the right and lay in a prone position. Though he could not actually see the target, satellite imagery was feeding data into his scope, allowing him to spot his target 18.342 kilometers away, well over the horizon. His bullet would be traveling fast enough to follow the planet's curve, so he could hit the target, but if he was off even the smallest fraction of a degree, he would literally miss by a kilometer. John was surprised when only a half second later Greg fired. As Greg disassembled his rifle, John commented, "That was fast."

"I take half a second for every shot. It sometimes seems a miracle I survive close-quarter combat."

"So who was that?"

"The head of Intelligence for this sector. He was at an outdoor conference."

John waited for a second, and it occurred to him that in a blink of an eye the same thing could happen to him. No one would know who he was a hundred years from now, except for when someone beat his kill record, and then would he be remembered only as second-best. "I accept the offer. I've got a pod to take us to the space station."

"May I ask why you've made this sudden reversal in opinion?"

"Immortality. If I do this, no human is ever going to forget it. While someone might become a better assassin eventually, you can only find Earth once."

"Alright, where's the pod?"

"This way." John began walking toward the elevator.

Chapter 11

At the Space Station

The pod was a small spacecraft designed to go from planet side to a space station. Most, like John's, were preprogrammed with coordinates to a docking bay on the space station, making piloting unnecessary.

Greg broke the silence on the way up. "I didn't think you would accept the offer. I always figured you would never have anything to do with the race again. I should have guessed you wouldn't pass up the opportunity to make history."

"Hey, I could be better than that. I could be doing this because I feel this is the right thing to do. Or that it is time for me to help with my race's cause," John said almost sarcastically.

"You really have no morals, do you."

They were silent until about two minutes later when the announcer said, "Prepare for docking."

John asked, "Where are we going?"

"To where the leaders of the Alliance and the MAA are waiting for news on whether or not I have succeeded. The meeting spot is in room 14034, sec589, midstation."

With a rapid series of taps on his eyelids, John input the location of the room into his electronic contacts, or eye-sights. Now he would always know its location by a marker pointing to it. He then powered up the two SMGs he had brought with him. A red dot and a blue dot appeared on each of his eye-sights, showing exactly were his SMGs were aiming. Red for right, blue for left. This made shooting with two weapons at once practical. Next his "rear view mirrors" came on. These gave him a 360-degree line of sight.

All of this was exceedingly helpful for nongeneral warfare situations, but useless in combat, as both sides deployed EMP fields that rendered eye-sights ineffective. This forced soldiers to rely on old-fashioned iron-sights, but every soldier wore eye-sights just in case the EMP fields didn't work. However, for an assassin, these made their job a lot easier since no one other than Federation or Alliance forces could afford EMP fields.

Before they left the house, John had put on full combat gear, so he was ready for anything. "Alright, let's go."

They stepped out of the pod into a small room with an airlock behind them. There was only one door out to the interior of the space station. They moved through it quickly as it was a natural place for an ambush.

The sight of two heavily armed men clearing a doorway in a crowded area would have been considered strange anywhere else. Not here. If they had walked through the door casually and unarmed, then they would have attracted attention, in the form of pickpockets and conmen taking advantage of someone who was obviously new to space stations.

There was no law enforcement on space stations and almost no government presence period. The crime bosses were the rulers here, although the Alliance and the MAA were the biggest powers around. The crime bosses and the humans rarely messed with each other, but when they did, it got ugly, with the criminals getting the worst of it. Although humans were not powerful enough to fight the Federation directly, they were more powerful than any other force in the 'verse.

John and Greg moved into the crowd, making their way to the designated room. The corridors were about the size of an average one-way, one-lane street, with vendors lining the walls. The ceiling was about four meters high, with red lights casting a glow on everything. The smell varied from mouth-watering to putrid. Beings of all descriptions—most of them not very complimentary—passed them. They made their way through the crowd for about half an hour, not taking the lifts because going along at a set speed, to a set place, at a set time was an invitation for an assassination.

At the end of the half hour, they entered a lift, which sent them three corridors up and two corridors left, too short a distance for them to be ambushed.

The new corridor had restaurants and bars lining the walls. Restaurants were a counter and some tables with no walls around it. John was constantly scanning the crowd, looking for danger. He eventually found it in the form of three former clients who were sitting at a bar. The three aliens walked in front of him, forcing him to stop.

"Excuse me," John said.

The leader spoke. "For you ... no excuse."

Noticing a fourth alien sneak into position behind him, John figured they intended to have violence.

"I'm sorry if you misunderstood. I mean to pass."

"You should have taken down that snitch."

"You know my rules well. I decide what jobs I take, and that is why requests are sent to me, not orders. You see, if I took every request as an order,

I wouldn't be much more than someone's private assassin. Since I make a lot more working freelance, taking orders would be a losing proposition on all accounts."

"When Isnen Orday sends a request, it is an order."

John was relieved to know who he was dealing with. "Let me put it to you this way. You are nothing more than a petty little crime boss who thinks he's a lot bigger than he really is. I'm assuming the two assassins who hit my house were yours. Like I have said, I have my rules, and trying to kill me breaks several of them. There is a heavy price to pay if those rules are broken."

"Get him." Isnen Orday drew his weapon.

Before Isnen could level his pistol, John had drawn his two SMGs and was firing so fast he had hit all three of them at least five times before they fell to the ground. And he was only using semi-auto. He spun around to find the fourth assassin with a hole in his chest where Greg had bayoneted him.

John said, "Thanks."

As he turned off his bayonet, Greg replied, "You're welcome."

"Alright, let's get moving."

Now that the problem with assassins was over, they got in a lift and made good time to their destination. John reflected on the encounter. *That guy was dead when he inferred the assassins were his. My rules are simple. You try to kill me and I will wipe out the 'verse's memory of you. It's probably a good thing I took up this job, for the sake of the other members of the organization. If I had the time, I would have killed every last being who was part of Isnen's gang. I've had to do that five or six times. I thought the message had been received.*

It's all these beings really understand. Violence. To be honest, I'm sick of it. I need this break to do something where the beings are slightly more civilized.

Before he could do much more thinking, they arrived at their destination. They walked quickly through the door into the large conference room. Sitting there were about ten representatives from both the Alliance and the MAA. Greg walked up to the head of Alliance Intelligence. "Sir, both missions have been accomplished successfully."

All those in the room turned to look at John.

"As soon as you're done basking in my presence, I would like to hear the details of the mission. We can work out payment when I do the job. I do require, however, that you tell me how both you and Orday found my place."

The politicians didn't seem bothered by his comments. Instead, one of them said, "The briefing will be ready in about an hour. In the meantime, you should meet the third member of your team. Sergeant Heyligher will guide you to him."

"Alright, let's go, Greg." The admiral to whom Greg had been talking looked at Greg strangely.

"It's a nickname," Greg mouthed as he rushed out the door opposite of where they had entered.

The new area had white walls and was clean. This was where the Alliance had an outpost. Main human colonies were similar to this, but those were guarded to prevent aliens from entering. Greg led John to the dormitories and entered a room without knocking.

Once inside, Greg said, "Hey, Carol, you in there?"

"Yes I'm in here. Where else would I be?" a voice replied from another part of the room.

John looked around. The dorm was in the shape of an L, with a shower and a sink in the block that made it an L. It was a spartan room, with no decorations, and little furniture. A suave but tough-looking man appeared, saying, "Sergeant Heyligher, you'd think they'd take the time to train you to knock." He noticed John. "And who's the guest?"

"John. And you are?"

"Oh, you're that assassin guy aren't you? Well, come on in."

They followed the man around the corner of the L, into his living room. On the floor—next to a glass coffee table—was a disassembled rifle. The man sat down next to it. "Take a seat, make yourselves comfortable. I'm Carol and I fight with the MAA. I'm on Assault Team Blue. They picked me to be the representative of the MAA on this team."

John was impressed. Assault Team Blue was feared among Federation forces for their aggressive tactics. Although the MAA was responsible for some atrocities against aliens, the Assault Teams never took part in them, as their only mission was to inflict as many casualties on the Federal Defense Agency as possible. Assault Team Blue was responsible for some interesting ways of doing that, such as attacking a division head-on, battling enemy units during parades, and ambushing platoons during live fire exercises.

John took a good look at him. Carol was completely bald, but despite this he seemed young, not yet out of his mid-twenties. His uniform was a variety of shades of grey. John's eyes turned to the weapon he was working on. It looked like a modified Ferndi Rapid-Fire assault rifle. John decided to ask about it.

"Is that a Ferndi Rapid-Fire?" John asked.

"It *was*," Carol replied. "I gave it a longer barrel so I could get more stability. Then I modified the receiver so it could take the new two-thousand-round box magazine. I also gave it a square forward hand grip and locked it into automatic fire mode."

At this point Greg interrupted him. "Why would you want to do that? All that does is put a lot of ice in the air. If you took the time to aim, you could take the target down much faster."

"Yeah, but the objective isn't always to kill the guy. Sometimes all you need to accomplish is to make the other side duck. And lots of bullets heading toward you are going to make anyone duck."

"There are many examples in history of a single sniper pinning down units much larger than he. That makes him a lot more cost-efficient."

"And a lot more examples of automatic weapons doing the same thing," Carol shot back.

"Hey, remember, it isn't each other we're here to kill," John said. "I personally think both of you are right, depending on the circumstance. Otherwise, both weapons wouldn't still be in production. History has a way of getting rid of what it doesn't need."

John turned to Greg. "Greg, have you guys had this argument before?"

Before Greg could answer, Carol spoke up. "I didn't know you were called Greg,"

"I'm not," Greg said tersely.

"He is, but I think he just likes to pretend he isn't," said John.

"No, that's not true; you gave me that name."

"Sensitive about that are we, Greg."

"I am not sensitive about that, Caroline, I'm just annoyed."

"Caroline?" said John inquisitively.

"My parents always wanted a girl." Carol sounded apologetically.

A palpable silence ensued.

They spent the rest of the hour talking about tactics and trying to get along decently.

At the end of the hour, they went back into the conference room. The politicians were waiting for them. One of them motioned for them to take the three empty seats.

After they sat down, the senior Alliance representative spoke up. "It is good to see all three of you doing well. As you all know, you are here to find Earth. The planet's location has been hidden for the last three millennia. It was believed that without a home, our race would drift aimlessly across the 'verse.

"We have been fighting a war against the FDA for three thousand years, but to what purpose? By our own law, we can't just conquer a planet and call it Earth. If we do not know were our planet is, we can never win. We will never be strong enough to defeat the Federation completely, but we can take and hold something small—like our home planet—and convince them to leave us alone.

"Earth's believed to still exist, but it is one of the FDA's greatest secrets. What we have to go on is that the FDA does have an HQ where information regarding Earth's location might be found, but the HQ location is also a well-kept secret.

"However, we do have a break. We know General Hindes has just been transferred from the HQ back to a field assignment. We do not know when this is to happen, but we know it will happen eventually. If you can intercept and interrogate the general, we believe you will be able to discover the HQ's location. From there you should be able to find the right person who knows Earth's location."

"So all you're asking us to do is to find the two best hidden locations in the 'verse, not to mention that the FDA's HQ is probably the most secure location in the 'verse as well," John said.

"I never said it would be easy," the representative replied.

"I'll say it won't be. I've assassinated several congressmen, and although they aren't much more than puppets, security is tight. I had half a battle fleet on my tail the last time. Speaking of which, what do we have for transportation?"

"We have a shuttle for your purposes. All other information you need is on this data capsule." The representative handed him the capsule.

"We'll need three days to plan before we go," Greg interjected.

"Granted." The representative continued, "If that is all, this meeting is adjourned."

John walked beside Greg. "It took them an hour to come up with that? I don't get how you stand it." There was a pause. "By the way, why did you say we needed three days to prepare. You know we could go this second if we had to."

"You'll see in the morning."

And at 0400 the next morning, John saw what it was. Greg was standing in the doorway with a light beam pointing at John's face.

"What in the 'verse are you doing?" John said.

"Be at room 19 in ten minutes."

"Do you know what time it is?" John was not certain Greg actually knew.

"Yes. 0401. Hurry up, you have only nine minutes left."

At 0410 a sleepy-looking John and Carol entered room 19. They were greeted by an energetic Greg and an obstacle course.

"You can't be seriously thinking of making us do that," Carol said.

"We need to learn to work as a team. Pain is bonding."

When a buzzer went off, John and Carol reluctantly followed Greg into the course. Within ten minutes they were working hard to complete the obstacle course as fast as they could. The room was only about the size of an average basketball court, but as soon as they crossed to the other end, an infrared signal was interrupted which changed the room's course—and allowed the team to return across the same ground, but with a different field problem. They kept at it for three days.

From Greg's military experience, he knew that to get through the course they had to learn to work as a team. By the end of the third day, his plan had worked.

As they rested at the end of the third day, John said, "So, did you do any planning while we were exercising?"

"As a matter of fact, I did," Greg replied. "The general's battleship needs to stop at Eveni to pick up the general. We get there before the battleship, attach ourselves to the battleship, and jump the general before he hits planet side."

"Not bad. Only a few thousand holes in it," Carol said sarcastically.

"I know, but I was thinking we could improvise as we go along."

"Sounds like a deal," said John. "Let's try to leave in about two hours.

Chapter 12

The Mission Begins

None of them could believe the sight before them. What was in front of them looked like a piece of junk, shaped like a spacecraft. On closer inspection, it turned out it *was* a spacecraft.

They had been told it would be small enough not to be noticed by the FDA. And small it was, if nothing else. It could barely hold five people without making them rub elbows. The shuttle was rusting, light green, and economically constructed to resemble an old wine cask, constricting into a rounded bulb nose. Slapped onto the nose were metal scraps welded on to cover microfractures. A darkened windshield covered most of the front of the shuttle, with a bar in the middle and four spokes for support.

Aside from the bulbous cockpit, the remainder of the vessel was a large, cylinder-shaped escape pod that could function independently from the rest of the vehicle. Externally strapped to the sides of the cylinder were two large engines that poked out beyond the back. At the rear of the spacecraft was a small rectangular hatch used for entering and exiting the shuttle.

Featured inside was a one-man cockpit and the open-faced escape pod that served as the rear of the craft, with a bench seat for three and a small vacuum-assisted latrine. The casings for the two engines jutted through the sides, with two steel plates welded on top of them for sleeping. The ship itself was slow and ungainly—its only redeeming feature was it could go to midspace and make planetary landings, though the team was convinced it would fall apart if a planetary landing was attempted.

They piled in through the rear hatch, with the distance between them measured in centimeters. Once onboard, they discovered another problem after detaching from the space station. Greg said to John, "So, are you going to fly this thing?"

John replied, "I have no idea how to fly. Everything I travel in has preprogrammed coordinates."

"Hey, Carol, you used to fly a while back, didn't you?" Greg asked as they continued to drift.

"I did some work on the simulators, and did a couple flights under instruction, but after that it was too expensive to continue."

"But you do know how to fly?"

"I have some basic knowledge, but little experience. Still, I guess I could probably manage to control this ship."

"Good," said John. "You're our pilot."

"Okay," Carol slid into the pilot's seat. "Is there an operation's manual?"

"Sure, and a warranty too. How about looking at the diagram on the panel in front of you?" John muttered as he climbed on top of the left bunk.

He ignored the sarcasm. "Give me a little time to see what everything does."

Carol gave the rudder pedal on his right a good hard push. They immediately began a flat counter-clockwise spin, swiftly swinging around 180-degrees. Carol hit the left rudder to stop the spin, which worked, but was followed by the sound of a wire frying. "I suppose we'll avoid any unnecessary rudder inputs in the future," Carol mused. Then he glanced at the diagram and pushed the throttle lever forward. The sudden burst of power sent them skyrocketing through space, right toward an incoming freighter. Carol pushed down on the yoke, narrowly missing it, then suddenly pulled to the right, dodging another craft. "Yep, definitely got the hang of it now," he offered to his white-faced companions.

Although it seemed like they were going fast, they weren't. Their full speed was only the docking speed of some of the other ships. After a period of hectic maneuvering, they managed to reach an empty portion of space, much to the crew's relief.

Carol was the first to speak. "Can we call this the *Mercy*?"

"Not exactly what I planned on dealing out," John replied.

"Oh, sorry, that was her nickname. You see, the shuttle reminds me of a girl I used to know, Mercedes. Short, vicious, and ill-tempered."

When John didn't say anything, Greg said, "In that case, I think it's a perfect fit."

John and Carol began figuring how to work the computer. After it started and stopped several times, they were able to get it to stay on long enough to make the calculations and to slide into midspace.

Centuries earlier, it had been discovered a laser beam using the right gas at the right frequency would cut a hole through the fabric of space and time. A vessel could travel through this hole and enter another dimension, known as midspace.

Using the same laser, another hole could be made to reenter real space. After some experimentation, it was found midspace worked like a wormhole, creating a shortcut through space.

Without midspace, crossing the galaxies of the Federation would take many lifetimes. Instead, using the shortcut of midspace, it took only a decade at most to cross the Federation from end to end.

It was while going through midspace that their computer gave out again. This knowledge was communicated to the rest of the crew by Carol slamming a fist into the computer.

"So what's happened now?" John asked.

"The midspace computer's gone out again," Carol replied with disgust in his voice.

"Okay, let's see what we can do. What does the chrono say? Or has that given out too?"

"Nope, still working. It says 1838."

"Good. I remembered the time we left. It was 1541. We should be able to figure out when we need to slip out of midspace based on the time when we left," John said.

After a series of simple algebra problems and unpleasant memories of grade-school math, they had a good estimate on where they would appear.

"All we can do now is hope we did all our math right and the whole midspace apparatus doesn't give out as we're entering a star." Greg walked over to the bedding pads.

"You sure you're not overdoing the optimism?" John said sarcastically from the escape pod.

"That coming from you is almost funny. And besides, that was barely pessimistic. I could have said a lot of things a lot more depressing."

Intrigued, John asked, "What do you mean, that coming from me is almost funny?"

Greg rolled over on the bunk. "Among human communities, it is automatically assumed you are a pessimist. I guess it is because you avoid the rest of the 'race."

"That doesn't make me automatically a pessimist. Not being with the rest of the 'race has almost nothing to do with whether I'm a pessimist or an optimist. The only way it could be connected was if I had given up on the whole 'race."

"Not exactly. If you had an optimistic outlook on everything, why would you have avoided the rest of us? You would've kept in contact with your friends and might've accepted missions from the Alliance or the MAA. I mean, yeah, you could say it would be bad for business as a lot of aliens hate anyone and anything that has to do with the 'race, but with your reputation, anyone who really needs someone dead would get you. And besides, do you see the glass half empty or half full?"

"I see that I need half more than what I got."

"Then you're a pessimist who doesn't want to admit it." Greg rolled back over in his bunk, leaving John alone with his thoughts.

He's right, John reflected. *I am a pessimist who doesn't want to admit it. I see everything in a sadistic light, after seeing so much moral decay. I've seen how the 'verse really works. Whoever is the most powerful rules through the language every being understands. Violence. Violence in action, violence in threats, violence in word, violence in everything. The message everyone gets is a body count.*

With that, John closed his eyes and instantly fell asleep for the next two hours.

When he awoke, Greg and Carol were conversing in low tones. He heard Carol say, "But even if we do end up killing the guy, we should be able to get the info from his dead body."

Greg replied, "How? Besides, I'm telling you, they keep that information only in their heads. They wouldn't trust anything else. Besides, there is a regulation against copying sensitive info. And even if there was a copy kept, if we come in guns a-blazing, the first thing they are going to do is destroy the copy."

"Not if we move fast enough. And in the middle of what looks like an assassination attempt, the last thing the general's going to be thinking of is destroying that info."

"If it was an assassination, what *is* the general going to do? Pull out his side arm? He probably hasn't used that thing in the last couple of decades, and he knows it. He can't run anywhere when the ship is in lock-down. So all he *can* do is destroy vital documents." Looking up, Greg noticed John had opened his eyes.

As John slowly awakened, Greg motioned him over. He then proceeded to explain what he and Carol had been discussing. "You're finally awake. I need you to explain to Carol why we need to capture the general quietly and not go in shooting everything in sight."

"I don't see what's so bad about going in shooting, as long as you hit what you're shooting at. The FDA has a standardized way of dealing with situations. They are methodical, and it works, but it is slow. That's why for us, speed is the key."

Carol said, "See, that's exactly what I was saying."

Greg replied, "No, you said we should hose the area down with automatic weapons."

"Same principle."

"John, can you give me a hand with this one?"

"Actually, I'm curious to see how this turns out."

"That proves my point, Greg," Carol interjected, "because if he thought I was wrong, he would have tried to talk me out of it."

"I'm sorry," John said apologetically. "Did I give you the impression decisions would be made democratically?"

"Well, no, but I thought we all would have an equal say in what we do." Carol seemed somewhat confused.

"Ah, that's where our understandings diverge. I have a lot more combat experience than you two. Which means I know what it takes to survive and to win. Now, it would be a real tragedy if we all got killed because I was out-voted. Are we green on this?"

In the silence that followed, John asked, "Okay, so what were you guys thinking of doing?"

Carol spoke up. "I was thinking of capturing the general as soon as he gets aboard, and then making a quick getaway."

"Hit them when they least expect it, not bad. Only problem is, the reason they least expect it is because security is the tightest at that point. So Greg, what did you have in mind?"

"How about prior to the general's change of command, he will want a few minutes alone to plan his speech, think about what he wants to do with his new command, and so forth. As soon as he does that, we move in and nail him."

"Alright, it could work, but we are taking a chance that he has not already done so on the ship. Never make the mission dependent on what the target does. That is the quickest way for the mission to spin out of control.

"What we should do is hit him when he's on the shuttle coming up to the planet. It is much easier to hit him then since there is a blind spot in the bat-tleship's defenses. Plus, in the shadow of that much firepower, they become overconfident and have only a small contingent of guards on the shuttle itself. If we can do it in less than four minutes, they won't know what happened.".

"A four-minute window or else we fail. Oh yeah, much safer than either of the plans we proposed," Greg said wryly.

"That's a good point," John replied.

"It's funny, I keep expecting you to say something more. You know, explain your reasons, offer a justification, or something, but I keep getting disappointed."

"I understand completely. Don't worry—eventually you'll learn not to hope for the impossible."

Carol interrupted. "In about ten minutes we should be reentering real space and I'm hoping *that's* not impossible."

John and Greg stopped talking and walked over to the cockpit, and stood staring at the chronometer, not speaking a word. As the estimated time for reentry came closer, they just waited patiently. At the exact second they ar-rived at the estimated time, Carol hit the lever that brought them back into real space.

Then there was a small burst of activity as they took stock of where they had landed.

Carol said, "Where are we?"

"At grid 16, sector 78, at least we're in the right galaxy," Greg replied.

"We are off by 207 grids to the northwest. We need to get to grid 475."

"Everyone, let's get started on the new calculations. We are going to have to do this by hand."

They worked with a sense of urgency they did not need. After doing nothing for so long, it took a good shot of adrenaline to start thinking again. It was a great relief to be given something that engaged their minds. Their next jump brought them to a point almost opposite their current position relative to the galaxy, but slightly closer to the target planet. They kept jumping back and forth, slowly but surely making their way closer. After a while they reached the planet.

"Look, there's our planet." Carol pointed to a small dot that had appeared in front of them.

"Let's not make another jump, we'll just approach in real space," John said.

"I'll try to find an asteroid or comet to hide behind and get us in close and undetected."

"The planet has an orbital space station," John pointed out. "See if you can find a broken-off piece of it and use that to take us in."

Although their ship was relatively slow, it could go at speeds of about three-quarters of light speed. The faster ships went about seven-eights of light speed, and military ships went about nine-tenths the speed of light. Space battles were never fought at that speed, however, as both sides would have passed each other before they could fire a shot. The main purpose of all this speed, for the military at least, was to get past an enemy's defenses before the enemy could respond.

It took them another hour to reach the planet. They waited behind a piece of the orbiting space station that had broken off and was circling the planet. The first thing Greg noticed was something was missing. After thinking about it for a minute, he said, "Hey, where is the battleship?"

Worried, Carol looked out the window for anything that had not shown up on the radar. "They couldn't have already left."

"They haven't," John assured them. "It hasn't arrived yet. They wouldn't just stop by a planet, pick up some general, and then move on. They would take advantage of the stop to effect some repairs or take on supplies. Nothing works perfectly on a ship that big, and they always have to fix something. No, if they had arrived, they would still be here."

"So how long do we wait?" Greg asked.

"Knowing the FDA, about a year."

"A whole year," Carol exclaimed. "We can't wait a year."

"Let me remind you we are searching for something that beings have sought for centuries. Not to mention the FDA is the biggest bureaucracy that has existed in the history of the 'verse. You weren't seriously expecting to find Earth in a couple of weeks," John replied.

"Well, I was kind of hoping."

"You guys need to understand this mission is now our lives. When you accepted it, what you said was that you were going to spend the rest of your existence doing this. Though I would also like for this to end in a few months, the reality is we are probably going to spend anywhere between ten and twenty years on this. We are going to spend a lot of time in a state of boredom, so we had better get used to the idea of waiting."

"What are we going to eat?"

"I've packed enough ration capsules to last us six months."

Fortunately for them, they had to spend only the next three days wasting breath on idle subjects, trying to sleep, and wishing they had brought a deck of cards, or any other form of entertainment, when the battleship appeared.

Greg was the first to see it. He was idly staring out at the stars, wondering if he would ever visit any of them, when the blank patch of space he had been staring at was suddenly filled with the sight of a battleship appearing from midspace. Although he had spent most of his career on Alliance battleships, he was still taken aback by the size of them. The *Avendor*-class battleship was almost four kilometers long, and half a kilometer in height.

It had a long, sloping triangle shape, with a small indentation in the front and a large one in the rear that held the engine. Its gun turrets could cover almost any point on the ship. This was possible because when the turrets rotated inward, they rose up like a screw and went above the guns in front of it, allowing all the guns to be fired at the same target. Weak points were found only directly above or below it, or in the back because the engines blocked the line of sight for the guns.

To defend the ship from enemy fire there were hundreds of thousands of small computer-controlled rifles that shot tiny bullets at incoming shells, big enough to cause an incoming shell to explode but small enough to bounce off any ship's hull, which prevented friendly fire incidents. The bullets fired from these defenses would cause the incoming shells to splinter into pieces because of the incredible energy caused when the opposing shells met. Only an EMP charge could disable the computer controlling the rifles.

The black paint on the ship with a red stripe running around the middle signified it as a Federal ship. Over a thousand small lights shone from inside the battleship, blending in with the stars at a great distance. Time had proven the only thing that could destroy one of these behemoths was another. Even an entire fleet of star-fighters would not have the firepower to penetrate the thick hull, and the battleship's own small fleet of starships would decimate the attacking fighters.

It was such a sight that Greg forgot to inform the others of its appearance. He was broken out of his trance when John said, "Oh look, there's our battleship."

Greg was slightly startled. "Yeah, there it is."

Carol said, "We're orbiting toward it. As soon as we are close, I'll drift off the piece of space junk and right up to the ship."

They waited as they slowly approached the battleship. The huge spacecraft grew as they approached it, until it filled their sight completely. Carol began to pull away from the piece of flotsam and soon they were drifting in the open, right toward the battleship, but at an obtuse angle so as not to cause the collision avoidance matrix to go off. At the last possible second, Carol pulled up and attached the *Mercy* to the hull of the Federation spaceship.

"We're on," said Carol.

Greg let go a breath that he hadn't realized he was holding. John stood by passively, not showing any emotion. "Can we hack into their docking port's computer?"

Carol answered, "It shouldn't be hard, but how do we know which docking port they are going to be in?"

"There is only one docking port on this space station large enough to hold them."

"Oh, in that case, just give me a few minutes to look it up."

"I want a direct feed from the docking port's computer so when the battleship attaches to it we have access to its computer."

John knew the way the FDA guarded against hacking was to prohibit other computer systems from interfacing with it. As soon as another computer system was connected to the battleship a virus was launched into the interfering computer. But this safety mechanism was suspended during docking when the ship's computer had to be slaved to the docking station's. During that brief time, the docking port's computer and the battleship's computer were linked and the bug could be placed in the battleship's computer. The window of opportunity was only seconds long. It took Greg and Carol a slightly fewer number of seconds to realize what John was trying to do.

Carol said, "We're in. Okay, the battleship's about to begin docking right about … now. We've got power."

Greg asked, "What do you mean, we have power?"

"Sorry. It's a thing we say in Assault Force Blue. Knowledge is power, and so whenever we get information we say we have power."

"Does the computer have anything on the location of Earth or the FDA's HQ?" Greg asked.

"Let me see. Ah, no it doesn't. Oh well. Should have figured it wouldn't be that easy."

"It didn't hurt to try."

At this point John spoke up. "They'll pick up the general as soon they are ready to depart. The general will want to stay in his planet side accommodations as long as possible. Are any soldiers going on planet leave?"

Carol quickly searched through the battleships computer. "No, but we got a lot of guys going onto the space station for leave."

"That's fine. So any personnel shuttles that are going planet side will be going to pick up our general. That eliminates a lot of variables. The fewer the better. Are we all in accord that we nail the general on his shuttle?" John asked.

"I'm in agreement."

"Got no problems with it," Carol added.

"Now we just wait," John said.

One month later

"So we're still waiting," Greg said.

"How was I supposed to know they would overhaul the engine at this stop? Besides, even if I had known, there is nothing I could have done about it," John replied.

At that instant, the computer beeped.

Greg was the first to speak. "This is it."

"I don't think so," John replied. "Although it is a personnel shuttle, I don't think it is the one we're waiting for. Look, it says right here it is going planet side to get a couple of expensive parts for the engine. They have a platoon riding in the shuttle to guard it."

"It seems like the sort of cover-up a cautious general would use."

"Don't log me on this, but I have to agree with John. Sure, it could be our target, but why would the general come on board now? Repairs are at least a week or two from being complete. I say we wait."

Greg was silent for a while. "The escape pod can launch and return without damaging the cockpit, right?"

"Yes, and I know where you are going with this. I won't stop you, but I won't help you either," John said.

"I just can't allow the chance that we miss the guy."

"And so it's better to take on a platoon of FDA soldiers?" Carol objected. "You may want to reconsider this."

"Besides, you're going to break our cover," John said.

"I can make it look like an engine failure," Greg replied.

"And when they kill you before then?"

"I'll have a dead-man bomb. It'll look like a suicide bomber attack."

"Which is what it will be. Let's suppose you are right. When you get shot, you ended up blowing the general to kingdom come; we no longer have anything to go on and the whole mission fails. Whatever you do, we lose. So what if we miss the general? We know where he has to go, and we can get there before him and have a second chance," John said.

Greg slid a magazine into his rifle. "You still want to wait?"

"It's not worth the risk," John stepped back from where they had assumed the escape pod ended and the cockpit began.

Carol said, "The shuttle is returning."

"This is a mistake," John said to Greg.

"Too late," Greg pushed the escape pod launch button.

The escape pod sealed off, and much to John's surprise he discovered he was on the wrong side of the seal. As Carol hurriedly tried to stop it from launching, the escape pod rocketed away.

They could see the FDA shuttle looming closer through the viewport. It was a big blunt silver mass, half as wide as it was long. The back had a cargo door that came down as a ramp when opened, and on either side of the door the shuttle engines poked out of the shuttle. Short stubby wings were placed about midway on the ship to improve handling in the atmosphere. Just behind the cockpit was a small door that would permit only one being to walk through it at a time. The shuttle had twelve rooms that held five beings and a small cargo area in the back. However, the personnel shuttle was primarily used during peace time. For assaults, the cargo shuttle was used. The cargo shuttle was simply a personnel shuttle without any of the rooms, allowing it to carry 378 soldiers or a whole lot of gear.

During the short ride, John didn't speak a word until they attached to the shuttle. "When we go in, I'll take the corridor on the right, you take the one on the left. And try not to get killed."

Greg just nodded.

To ensure its inhabitants could be rescued by any vessel, the escape pod could extend its own airlock and breach a hull. Using this feature, John attached them to the shuttle and opened a breach. Once the hole was made, John swiftly crawled down it.

Less than a second later, John was in the FDA shuttle, firing away. Greg crawled out of the ship to the sight of three bodies, and John was marching down the hallway, creating more. They had dropped into the rear cargo hold of the shuttle, right with the valuable engine parts.

FDA personnel shuttles were so large they actually had two corridors, allowing them to fit more rooms inside of it. Greg began to move down the left corridor. Two FDA soldiers appeared running down the hallway. Before they could fire, Greg ran one of them through with his bayonet, and turning quickly knocked the other's SMG aside and slashed him across the chest. Looking up, Greg shot another soldier who was running toward him.

Meanwhile, John was moving down his hallway quickly. Two soldiers appeared in front of him. John fired twice, and they fell dead on the deck. Further down the hallway, three soldiers opened fire on him. As John dashed for cover, he managed to bring down one of them. He crouched down in the doorway that provided him cover for a second until they slowed their fire slightly. He then stuck his head out at knee level, and fired a few quick shots that finished off the remaining soldiers.

Running forward, he gunned down another soldier who was coming at him. A doorway opened right next to him, and an armed alien came rushing at him. John turned and snapped off a couple shots that sent the being reeling into the wall. He then faced the hallway again and with a short burst dropped the soldier who came out from a door slightly in front of him. John put his back to the far side of the door and fired two shots, which took care of the two who had followed him down the corridor. Whipping around the door, he pulled his trigger three times in rapid succession to take down a Pratin who had entered the front of the hallway.

John busted into the cockpit and slew the two pilots before they realized he had entered. Exiting the cockpit, he waited for about ten seconds before Greg reappeared.

"Is the ship secure?"

"It is. I think only about half a platoon was on board. And there is no general," Greg said crisply.

"Have you created the engine failure?"

"That's what took me so long."

"Let's leave."

As they walked down the hallway John had come down on, Greg looked at the pile of bodies with something between shock and amazement.

"You did all this?" Greg asked. "I only met three."

They arrived at their escape pod. Climbing into it, they launched away from the shuttle and back to the rest of their ship. When they had almost reached the blast safety zone, Greg triggered the device that superheated the engine, causing the shuttle to explode. The bodies of the beings they had killed were scattered into space, as their diamond armor prevented them from destruction by the flame. By the time the FDA could attempt to retrieve the bodies, the corpses would be so far away as to make recovery impossible.

Greg used the escape pod's automatic return feature to take them back to the *Mercy*. The escape pod would attach to the shuttle on its own—a plus, because neither John nor Greg had the piloting skill to do it.

When the escape pod reattached to the cockpit of the *Mercy*, Carol was relieved to see both of them had made it out okay.

"Good to see both of you made it back in one piece. I take it no luck on the general?"

Annoyed and angry glares answered his question.

Eight days later

As they sat looking at the ground, an alarm went off in the computer. Rushing over to the console, Carol said with excitement, "This is it. This is the general. We've got him."

As John and Greg peered at the console, Carol continued, "Yeah, this is definitely it. It has a planet side destination, a squad of soldiers, and it even says they are picking up a flag officer."

"Yeah, I think this really is the right one," Greg said.

"For once, you're probably right," John agreed with him.

"They'll be back up with the general in about twenty minutes."

"Okay, get your weapons ready now, detach from the battleship, power down so we look like a piece of space junk, stop near where they will exit the atmosphere, then put on a short burst of power and board them. Greg will lead with his bayonet thing to take care of anyone quietly; I will be behind him, and Carol will cover our rear. When we enter a room, I will take the lead; Greg will follow me, and Carol will be outside the entrance of the room and covering our rear. We want to do this as quietly as possible. Everyone understand?"

They nodded.

"Alright, then let's get started."

In about five minutes they were in full combat gear and were drifting toward the enemy shuttle's exit point. Ten minutes later, they were waiting a short distance from where the shuttle would enter space. During the next five minutes, the tension began to mount. Although they were all confident in their abilities, the entire mission rested on the success of this strike, and they couldn't stand the thought of messing up something they had waited for over a month.

The twenty-minute mark passed. By the time the shuttle was three minutes late, they began to worry. Had they missed the general? Had the enemy become alerted? Was there an ambush waiting for them? When the shuttle arrived eight minutes late, it suddenly burst out of the atmosphere, putting their fears to rest. They had to start their engines earlier than expected since the enemy was going faster than planned, probably in an attempt to make up for the time they had delayed; but it wasn't too difficult an obstacle to overcome, and they fastened to the shuttle in the same manner as they had before—only this time the rest of the shuttle was attached to the escape pod.

As the breaching device cut a hole into the shuttle, Greg slid noiselessly down into the rear cargo hold, but unlike last time, he was alone. After Greg's signal that it was clear, John and Carol joined him, only slightly disturbing the cold, still air. They moved quickly to the V.I.P. room, which wasn't much different from the other rooms except it was designed for one person.

John quickly disabled the locking device on the door with a small explosive charge placed in a vacuum seal to prevent noise. He moved in without a sound, and spotted the general walking to the door. John roughly shoved the general on to his back as Greg entered. John then began to interrogate to him.

"Are you going to a change-of-command ceremony to take control of the Fourth Command sector of this galaxy?" John asked as he put his foot on the general.

"Yes, I was."

"And was your last assignment at FDA HQ?"

"No, the general I was replacing had just been assigned there. I was coming to fill the gap he would be leaving."

Just then, they heard Carol fire a short burst, breaking the silence that had reigned since they had entered the ship.

"We need to get out of here." John started leaving.

Not hesitating, John and Greg were out of the room in an instant and began running down the short corridor to their ship. Carol followed behind them, running backward and blazing away at the soldiers who were chasing them as he went. In about five seconds they were out into the rear cargo area, and in eight seconds they were in the *Mercy*, and detached from the enemy craft.

"Launch for the change-of-command ceremony. Intel has screwed up," John said.

Without hesitation, Carol used one of the preplanned coordinates they had figured out in their spare hours. Within seconds, they were gone to midspace.

Chapter 13

A General's Abduction

Carol, who hadn't heard the exchange with the general, asked, "So, this makes twice that you guys came back without a general. Is this the start of trend?"

Humorless stares greeted this suggestion. Carol wisely shut up.

John replied, "Intel misinterpreted the data intercept. The guy we are going after is going to the HQ, not coming from it. The one we hit was his replacement."

"Do you think word has got out as to our intentions?" Carol asked.

"The moment we boarded the Federation shuttle, word of our intentions was out. Even if we had just shot the general when we realized he was the wrong one, they would have put the person he was intending to replace on alert as it might be a move against that particular command," John answered. He thought for a second. "Carol, what is your opinion on the atmospheric handling of this thing?"

"Can't guarantee it'll hit the ground. That said, I'd say the odds are good we'll survive breaking atmo. The real question is, at what speed and in how many pieces do we land? Trust in the ability of the repulse-lifters to keep us flying planet side will probably be misplaced."

"All I need it to do is to get in and out of the atmosphere. The plan I have in mind is for us to land in the new space port they are constructing, the one about 160 kilometers from the military base. We enter the construction site quickly, steal one of the ground vehicles, and use it to get to the change-of-command ceremony. Then we get the general, put him on it, interrogate him on the way back to the shuttle, and then move to the HQ as fast as possible. Are we all in agreement about this?"

"Sounds good," Greg agreed.

It was a short jump, and only about forty minutes later they reached the planet.

Carol began to dive toward the planet, trying to get the right angle of attack so they wouldn't burn up upon reentry. No one ever paid attention to the space-traffic controllers, so when they cut off the traffic controller, it was seen as routine.

As they entered the atmosphere, a wall of fire began to form around their heat shield, quickly engulfing the entire shuttle. Carol was having serious doubts as to whether or not they would reach the ground. The *Mercy*'s speed began to slow rapidly, until they were no longer engulfed in flame.

Carol put the engines in full reverse, and aimed at the point where they had decided to land. They slowly lost speed, until they reached an altitude of about 15,000 meters, when the shuttle went into sub sonic velocity. Carol then guided their glorified falling rock to a landing point about a kilometer away from the construction site. He turned on the repulse-lifters, but as he had expected, they failed.

With the ground rapidly approaching, Carol pulled up until they were pointed nearly straight up, mushing through the air. Then he turned on just enough engine to slow their descent without sending them back into space. The *Mercy* slowed until it was hovering nose up. Carol gently lowered the shuttle down on its engines. Though they were jolted, everything was basically intact. The biggest problem was they were pointing straight up at the sky, which meant the exit in the escape pod was blocked off.

Greg thought about this for a minute. "Can the windshield on this shuttle open?"

"It might, but it wouldn't open on purpose. I haven't seen any button that would do that," Carol replied.

"In that case, we should search the manual to see if it does."

"No, what I meant was I have memorized the manual and there isn't a button on it that will open the windshield. In other words, to get out of the window we would have to destroy it."

"We have breaching devices. Those things are airtight, and they place a sealed covering over the hole if you detach it. If they weren't sealed, everything loose in the ship would be sent into space, which is bad if you intend on getting anything out of the ship. There shouldn't be a problem if we use one of them to get out of our shuttle," John said.

"Are you certain it wouldn't fall off when we exit the atmosphere?"

"Yes, for two reasons. One, the breach will be on the inside, so there is little chance it will be ripped out by the speed. The second is I have breached ships planet side and hidden in them until they were in deep space. As far as I could tell, everything seemed to work fine."

"Well, it's worth a shot."

John pulled out his breaching device. He broke it out of its rectangular storage position and into its circular breaching position. It was a little wider than the width of a man, and about two centimeters thick. When he placed it up near the windshield, it conformed to fit the curve of the hull. John grasped the lever protruding from the center of the device, and then quickly whipped it in a circle, which moved the cutting laser around the circumference of the device, making the hole.

With the press of a button, the top centimeter lifted a little bit above the rest of the device, still attached to the device by a hinge. John put his fingers in the crack, and then opened the portal until it was resting on the hinge, revealing a back mat that was divided into four sections by a crack that ran in a cross. These sections were airtight, and as John hauled himself through them, the mats conformed to his shape and clung to him to prevent any air from escaping.

John kicked out the metal disk the breaching device had cut out, and shut the portal. Releasing the portal, he fell about a meter to the ground. Carol was out next, followed quickly by Greg.

They set off toward the construction site at an easy jog. The terrain was mostly grassy hills, unbroken by any rocks or foliage. The hills were long and not very high, which made going up and down them easy. A light breeze played across the grass. The sun was hot, but not unbearably so, and the breeze provided a nice cooling effect.

All this was lost on John. He had got a glance at the construction site as they descended in the shuttle, but it was not enough, and everything would have moved by the time he got there. The terrain also bothered him. It was so open any fighter craft could find them without much difficulty, and surveillance satellites would spot them approaching the military base long before they could breach the perimeter.

While John was pondering this, they reached the last hill before the construction site. As soon as they could see over the hill, they hit the deck and then crawled to the top of it. They stuck their weapons over the edge of the hill, using the feed from their eye-sights to survey the site.

The construction crews were working on the foundations of the new space port. Vehicles and equipment were scattered across the site. It was a field of dirt, punctuated by holes into which they were putting foundations and partially completed sections of wall. As they looked, John spotted a vehicle on the far side of the site driving behind a partially constructed wall. About five minutes later, a loudspeaker announced a lunch break. The worker who'd driven the vehicle appeared with about five other workers who were walking to the collapsible dining facility.

John pulled back, and the others followed him. "There's a vehicle on the far side of the site, behind that partially completed wall. We can run around the site, stay behind the hills and get to it without being seen."

"Let's go." Greg started moving.

They slid down to the bottom of the hill, got up, and started to run. The construction site was a level area surrounded by a ring of hills. They ran, keeping the hills between themselves and any observers at the construction site. It took them about five minutes to reach the other side of the site.

John crawled up the hill, and then poked his SMG up. He scurried back down. "We need to go about four hills to the left."

They moved the distance, and John went up again. He swiftly returned. "One to the right."

Moving once again, Carol and Greg waited for John to come down the new hill. "This is the one. Once we crest, we'll need to crawl about halfway down the hill before we can stand up."

Carol stopped John. "Are you absolutely certain this really is the right one?"

"Very funny. Start walking."

They crawled to the top of the hill, and then slowly went over the top. Inching their way down, they kept crawling until they were completely covered by the shadow of the nearest wall of the construction site. They slowly stood up, and then dashed to the vehicle.

The vehicle was next to the wall and held a large vat of welding material. Carol and Greg dumped the vat off the end of the vehicle, then Greg jumped onto the command platform. The vehicle appeared not to have any security features in operation. Carol and John hopped up into the front section, and Greg pulled out in a quick right turn. He put the throttle at full speed, and they were up and over the hill before anyone noticed.

As they sped over the terrain toward the change-of-command ceremony, Greg looked at the vehicle they had stolen. It was a standard construction light weight cargo vehicle, or LWCV. It hovered about a meter above the ground, and was five meters long and two and a half meters wide. The guard rails were at waist height, and took a dip about two-thirds of the way back along with the rest of the LWCV to make room for the command platform. The command platform consisted of a platform with a windshield in the corner fronting a small joystick and throttle. It was designed to be loaded from above, so it had no roof or walls other than the guard rails.

The LWCV rose and fell automatically with the hills, so all Greg had to do was point it in the right direction and put it at full speed. John was busy making calculations. They were 150 kilometers from the military base, and they were going 120 kilometers per hour. He figured it would take them an hour and a half, adding in the extra distance caused by the hills.

When they were only about forty minutes away from the base, they passed through a valley that had a slight dip in the middle. The hills to the left rose gently away from them, but the ones to the right were relatively steep. The hills on the right were about one hundred meters away, and those on the left two hundred fifty meters.

John was noticing this when he spotted movement. Looking closer, he saw what looked like a series of rocks on the crest of both hills. He realized what that meant as his eye-sights went out. They must've entered an EMP field, and only the FDA had EMP fields. A hail of bullets began to rain down on them from both ridge lines. John immediately began to return fire.

Standard ambush response was to force your way through. But, for reasons Carol and Greg would never be able to explain, they slowed down, stopped, then got out of the vehicle, and engaged the superior enemy force. John would always say he knew if they wiped this group out, their leaders would not know what had happened to them for a period of time, long enough for them to get the general.

For whatever reason, John and Greg rolled out on the left side, and Carol went out on the right. The larger enemy force was on the left, so John and Greg began to advance toward them at a fast walk. Carol rushed around the vehicle and followed them, forming an inverted triangle with John and Greg three meters abreast of each other and Carol in the rear, walking backward.

John fired a quick series of single-shots. His intent was to make his opponents duck, not to kill them. John knew even if he was not good enough to hit a target two hundred fifty meters away while moving, he could at least come close. Carol was blazing away with his modified rife with the same intent. The two of them put out a huge volume of fire, forcing the enemy to make only quick snap shots, never having enough time to aim.

John took a glance at Greg. Greg would take a few steps forward, drop into a crouch, wait his customary half second, then fire, killing anyone who was foolish enough to leave his head up for more than a second. Normally, John would have preferred another person like Carol in this situation for the extra suppressive fire, but Greg's ability to hit anyone who took the time to aim made anything the enemy fired at them nothing more than a wild shot, which was the only reason they were still alive.

At the speed they were moving they quickly closed with the enemy. Bullets were cracking all around John's head, but he didn't mind. He was only a hundred meters away. This was his territory.

A soldier poked his head up. John nailed him on the first try. Another appeared, and John hit him with two quick squeezes of the trigger.

As if on cue, three soldiers leaned over the edge to fire. With a series of rapid shots, John swept his fire down the line, killing all of them before they had time to duck or fire a second shot.

That pretty much broke the enemy's back. After John and Greg had knocked off a few more soldiers, they received no more fire from the hill in front of them. After three seconds of this, John rushed up the crest and swept both sides. He yelled, "Clear," and Greg whirled around and hit the deck. John and Greg added their fire to Carol's and in only a couple of bursts the other side was also silent.

As John began to run over to the other ridge, Greg motioned for him to stop. Greg took out his sniper rifle and looked through the satellite feed. He stood up. "It's all clear."

John said, "This was a hastily made ambush. If they'd had more time, they would've done a lot more preparation. This must have been a security detachment sent out when they spotted us. If we move quickly, we can hit them before more reinforcements can be scrambled."

They started out again. Along the way Greg looked through his satellite feed to give them a heads-up on what they would encounter.

At the gates there was a full guard contingent. But the fence was relatively unguarded, with only a few soldiers patrolling it. The plan was simply to ram it at full speed while John and Carol fired at it in full auto. They appeared over the last hill only two minutes from the base wall. They were only one minute away by the time someone fired at them.

John and Carol began to blast off clip after clip, punching holes through the diamond fence. After several clips of firing at the foundations of the fence, it fell over. John and Carol switched their attention to the guards who were firing at them.

As they laid down a base of fire, Greg drove full speed ahead, crashing over the remains of the fence.

They drove across the long, flat metal runway. Greg skillfully danced the hovercraft around the spacecraft revetments that dotted the edge of the airfield. Small yellow circles ran the length of the runway, looking like a distant string of Christmas lights. Though he was not certain, Greg thought these might be landing spots, as everything that landed here was a V/TOL aircraft.

Greg steered them right toward the largest hangar, where the change-of-command ceremony was to take place. Although the ceremony was not due to start for another hour, they figured the general would already be there waiting for the other general they had hit earlier.

As they approached the hangar, John leapt off the LWCV and into the hangar door while Greg pulled a hard right to avoid the door. John held his hand out in front of him, counting on his diamond armor to smash through the hangar door. His gamble paid off, and his hand plowed through the door, along with a small but powerful explosive.

John pulled his hand back as he released the explosive, and then began to run toward the LWCV, which Greg had turned around by now. As John and Greg closed on each other, the bomb went off, sending John soaring. Greg jumped-up from the command platform and caught him, bringing the two of them down in a heap. Both of them were on their feet in an instant, but it was almost too late for Greg to regain control of the vehicle and avoid a large obstacle that resembled the remains of a stage.

John's bomb had wreaked havoc in the hangar. The large door had been blown off, and everything inside was destroyed. Wreckage and ruin were scattered across the floor. Although no enemy personnel were injured because of their diamond armor, nothing could compete with a bombing for pure shock effect.

All the beings in the room had been knocked to the floor, so it was a simple matter to figure out which one was the general and pick him up. Greg turned the LWCV around while John secured the general with a quick-cooling metal he poured on the general's hands. Then they hit the accelerator and drove back out the base.

A few guards had gathered to from a weak resistance, but Greg simply by-passed them. Carol turned around and fired a couple of bursts at the fading soldiers. Then suddenly they were through the hole in the fence and outside the base.

As they sped toward their shuttle, John said, "Greg, I want you to be look-ing for fighters. I'll take over driving."

Greg nodded and they switched positions. Greg began scanning the ho-rizon, searching for any black specks that might appear in the great, blue, cloudless sky above them. John pushed the engine as hard as he could, trying desperately to get away before the FDA figured out what had happened. In the hour and a half it took them to get back to the shuttle, he had seen no presence of the Federation.

Wondering if this was a trap, John reentered the *Mercy* through the breech he had created. Seeing nothing amiss, he gave the all clear. Carol and Greg came in dragging the general between them. "Carol, get us out of here. Greg, you help him. I'll keep an eye on the prisoner."

After taking only one look at the general, John had severe doubts the gen-eral would be trying anything for a long time. He was still dazed from the explosion. Obviously, the shock from the bombing had confused the general to an extent John had not even hoped for. This would make the interrogation so much easier.

Carol turned the engines on, and pushed them to full power. Since the en-gines were beneath the ground, they blasted all the dirt away from them. The grass caught fire and spread out in a blazing ring. The shuttle stayed in place for a second, and then shot out of the ground like a bullet.

The shuttle began to shudder as it entered the upper atmosphere. It was rattling so bad Carol was convinced it would fall apart before they entered space. With much rattling and noise, they burst out of the atmosphere. They sped away from the planet at full speed until they were far enough away from the atmosphere to go to midspace.

Chapter 14

The First Interrogation

John could still not believe their luck. While he had gotten away with these sorts of things many times in his career, the stakes had never been so high. In his experience, the higher the stakes the more things go wrong. Once in the safety of midspace, John began to interrogate the general.

"Is your next assignment to FDA HQ?" John asked.

"Yes, it is," the general replied.

"How were you to get there?"

"I was to go to a designated point, where a shuttle would pick me up. I know nothing more than that."

"Was there a signal you were supposed to give to say it was all clear?"

"None that I know of. But as soon as they hear I've been kidnapped they will leave."

"Knowing the Federation as I do, I doubt they will be told anytime soon."

John forced the general to reveal the coordinates for the rendezvous, then injected a sleep drug into him. He then unwound a little, only enough take to the tension off. John never allowed himself to completely relax. If he had, he would have been dead by now. However, being constantly on alert extracted a huge toll from his body. John had learned to deal with fatigue in a cost-efficient manner by taking advantage of these little moments. Even this only helped so much, and John knew it was a matter of time until his body couldn't take any more stress. But he figured that day was at least half a decade away, so he didn't worry.

Greg closed his eyes and slept until Carol woke him an hour later. Carol was careful to wake Greg by sounding a time alarm in the ship. Had he placed a hand on Greg or spoken into his ear, Greg would have reacted instantly and probably attacked him.

As Greg slowly stood up, Carol said, "We just came out of midspace."

"Great, anything interesting happen while I was asleep?" Greg asked.

"Not unless you consider staring blankly at a console fascinating."

Greg walked over to the cockpit and looked out at the scene before him. It was a space station around a planet he did not recognize. John told him, "The coordinates are to a docking bay off our starboard side."

"I thought the Federation didn't use docking bays in civilian areas." Greg looked at the map of the space station.

"They don't. Which makes it a good bet this is the place we're looking for."

Carol took them to the docking bay nearest the rendezvous point.

"Excuse me," Greg asked, "I don't mean to bother you, but isn't parking our shuttle right next to the Federation hangar a little obvious?"

"It is." John casually rose from his seat at the back of the shuttle and sauntered over to the cockpit.

"But you see," John continued, "the FDA isn't going to arrest us for parking next to their secret hangar. It might give away their location."

Greg noted the undercurrent, *don't give advice,* but he pressed on undeterred. "I was thinking of after we hit the hangar. They will suspect our shuttle because it landed next to their hidden base just before it was wiped out."

"That's assuming we want deniability." Stopping his slow walk to the cockpit, John turned and faced Greg. "All we need is to hit the target and get out. What happens afterward is of no consequence."

"But they might get a description of us," Greg continued to argue.

"We're riding in this undersized prison of a shuttle so we don't have to worry about things like that." Conceding the point, Greg let the subject drop.

Carol gently let the shuttle drift into the docking bay next to the FDA hangar. Shutting down all power, he let the artificial gravity of the space station bring the shuttle to a halt just before the main exit.

Greg used a marine frequency to contact a couple of Alliance operatives to pick up the general and deliver a new computer.

As soon as Greg had contacted the Alliance operatives, they moved out to the Federation docking bay. John was in the lead, with Greg and Carol watching his back. John looked at the markings on the docking bay door. "This is a medium-sized cargo hangar. The guards are those two guys in civilian dress hanging around to the right. We should use the Delta room entry."

Carol and Greg nodded. The Delta room entry technique was the fastest and most violent of the various room entry tactics, but required the assailants to be firing close to each other. Any missed shots would likely result in hitting a friendly.

John withdrew his SMG, and began to walk toward the door. Greg and Carol hung back, waiting for the guards to expose themselves when they attempted to stop John. The two FDA guards fell for the bait, and as John was coolly placing a breaching charge on the door, the guards pulled out their concealed weapons, only to be cut down by a burst from Greg and Carol. Then things exploded into action.

John slapped the breaching charge onto the door's locking mechanism. He stepped back as Greg and Carol hit the wall on either side of the door.

It took three seconds for the charge to drill a hole in the door and fill the hole with water. The water was flash-frozen, shattering the lock.

John kicked the door open and hurled a flash-bang inside.

As the flash-bang went off, John dashed into the room, dropping the first soldier he spotted. John moved at a dead run along the wall to the far left corner, firing with perfect accuracy as he went.

Greg and Carol waited a half second, just long enough for the soldiers' attention to be drawn toward John. Once the soldiers were distracted, Greg and Carol made their entrance, moving into the room and taking positions in the two corners nearest the door.

This arrangement allowed the three of them to cover the entire room. The soldiers in the middle of the docking bay were caught in a perfect crossfire.

After a few seconds, the firing stopped. Eight FDA soldiers and technicians lay dead on the floor, while the remainder had raised their hands in surrender. Carol, being the only one familiar with prisoner snatches, quickly disarmed and secured the seven surviving FDA technicians.

John and Greg separated a pair of pilots from the rest of the group while Carol kept an eye on the prisoners. John looked at the higher-ranking of the two pilots.

"You were to bring a general to the FDA HQ. You will give me the coordinates of the destination you were told to deliver the general to," he said forcefully, counting on the disorientation of the flash-bang to make the pilot temporarily forget his POW training.

The ploy worked, and before the pilot realized what he was doing, he blurted out the coordinates. From the look on his face, John could tell the pilot realized he had made a mistake. The pilot attempted to cover it up. "These are only the coordinates to another shuttle, and I have no idea where that one goes."

Although he was certain the pilot knew were the second shuttle went, John decided to leave it at that. He could always find that out later.

Greg contacted a couple more Alliance operatives to pick up the prisoners. He waited until the operatives were right outside the door, and then made his way to join John and Carol in the *Mercy*.

Chapter 15

To Steal a Computer

As he walked to the shuttle, Greg thought about the events that had just occurred. *It truly is amazing how little responsibility society feels. In plain sight, we blew open a door and killed FDA soldiers, their own troops, the protectors of their way of life, and none of them did anything to stop it. None of them will report this to the authorities, give an anonymous hint to the police, or even discuss this with their friends. All they think is that it is none of their business. This apathy has nothing to do with just trying to make their way through life without any trouble; it is merely citizens not caring what happens to their society.*

When we find Earth, everything will change radically. A full-blown war will break out, the first one for the Federation in a while. Hundreds of millions will die. Possibly billions. Enough for everyone to notice.

It was several days before they reached the coordinates the pilot had given them.

Carol and Greg immediately suspected a trap when they discovered the co-ordinates dumped them into empty space. John just stared at the endless stars stretching out before him, as if he was waiting for something. Carol began to reach for the controls to get them out of there in a hurry, but John stopped him, simply saying, "Wait."

After a moment, John relaxed. "I have a thought. Any experienced military man heading for a rendezvous and arriving at a blank patch of space will au-tomatically think it's a trap and leave. However, the pilot might be told what to expect, and an information satellite could launch if the craft remains there for, let's say about an hour. It sends a data burst to the spacecraft, and then returns. I know something like this has been used for passing information, so why not use it as a secret navigation buoy?"

Carol said, "The idea sounds reasonable, but any data sent to us will be encrypted."

John thought for a minute. "Greg, your armor is space-worthy, right?"

"Yeah, it should be."

"And marines are trained to do extra-vehicular breaches?"

"It's part of basic. You want me to go E-V?"

"That would be nice. In the plan I'm thinking of, you go space-side before the satellite arrives, and when it shows up you quickly detach the comm-box. Get it back to the shuttle, and we should be able to physically hook it up to our computer and rip the info out of it."

"It could work," Carol said thoughtfully. "It's kind of weird how almost no one thinks of doing anything physical anymore. So far as I know, the FDA doesn't have any defense against actually getting next to the computer and retrieving the data."

Greg ran over a check of himself, and seeing his suit was all in order, he gave a thumbs-up to John and Carol, and exited the craft via the breaching device John had placed on the hull. He shut the breach on his way out, and waited until he could be seen through the windshield. As soon as he caught sight of John and Carol, he tapped his head twice and tested his comm. gear. "Can you hear me?"

Carol replied, "Yep."

"Roger that, out."

They went into comm. silence for the next hour. Greg adjusted his position using small one-way air jets that shot small bursts of air to control his movement. He stopped about one hundred meters away from the shuttle.

Without warning, something appeared out of midspace. John, looking expectantly for the satellite, was chagrined to see an FDA shuttle accompanied by two fighters. "Can anything go right?"

Carol lurched for the controls, and began to make a beeline toward Greg, who was directly underneath the shuttle.

To their surprise, Greg launched up toward the FDA shuttle and activated his bayonet, cutting a hole about halfway up into the interior of the shuttle. He reached in and grabbed something. Holding onto the object he had grabbed, Greg kicked himself back to his own shuttle.

As Greg slid back inside, the pair of Federation fighters peeled off and came to a halt off the nose of the *Mercy*. Carol could clearly see the fighters' pair of long, shark-fin-like wings, and their short, pointed cockpits, but it was the two machine guns in the wing roots that caught his attention. As the fighters called for them to surrender, Carol launched them into midspace and safety.

John said to Greg, "That was pretty impressive. I wouldn't have thought of using the bayonet."

"Yeah, well that's why the marines have them. They give you that unexpected edge," Greg replied.

"What was it you took from that shuttle?" Carol asked, turning around in the pilot's seat.

Greg held up a box. "This is the nav computer to that shuttle. They should have input the coordinates for their next jump by the time I got it. I assumed they would be returning to their starting point."

Carol took the computer and looked at it. "Yeah, I can extract the data stored in this. It shouldn't be all that hard."

Carol hooked up the stolen device to the ship's computer, and spent the better part of two hours extracting the data. When he finally finished, there wasn't a moment's respite before John input the data and they were off again.

———◆———

This time, the jump took only about ten minutes, and suddenly they were staring at a deep-space station run by the FDA, complete with a hangar for twelve shuttle-sized craft. The small station was crewed by pilots and mechanics, plus a small support and command crew. In all, it held about seventy-five personnel, not large, but far too many for the three of them.

Realizing they had most likely been spotted, John said to Carol, "Head straight to the hangar's door, and attach the shuttle there. We'll make a breach, then fast-rope down to the floor. You and Greg hold the hangar. I will find the pilot lounge and take one of the pilots prisoner. We've got to do this fast."

Carol attached them to the top of the hangar door, then followed John and Greg out of the shuttle. John breached the door, attached the line and fast-roped down.

As John's feet hit the ground, he did a roll to get out of Greg's way. He began firing as he stood up. With a rapid series of shots he took out the soldiers in the hangar. Greg and Carol took up defensive positions in the two doorways that led to the hangar. John stepped out of the closest door and immediately grabbed a lone mechanic who was walking down the hall.

As John disappeared with the FDA mech, Greg and Carol hastily constructed defensive positions. Greg took a couple of tool boxes and wedged them in the door to prevent it from closing. Then he spied a large, flat spare part for one of the shuttles. He took a replacement nav computer and used it to prop up one end, then grabbed a couple of tool boxes and scattered them randomly in front of his position.

Greg put his black combat helmet on and pulled his darkened goggles down. With his chin strap buckled, his face was almost entirely covered. He then crawled under the flat spare part into his makeshift sniper position. The scattered tool boxes covered most of the front of his body, and the spare part cast a shadow that made him nearly invisible. Since ice rifles were flashless, this would do for the time being. Carol simply wedged his door open and took cover behind a large cargo box.

It wasn't long before someone entered Greg's sights. Trying to take attention away from John, Greg fired, hitting his target. Another soldier came dashing around the corner to see what had happened. Greg dropped him with another shot. Carol let loose with a burst, cutting down a soldier walking toward him. More soldiers came, and it wasn't long until a couple of small units with weapons drawn were advancing toward them.

"Where is the pilot lounge?" John demanded of the mechanic.

"It is down that corridor, third door on the left."

John held the soldier in a head lock, leaning back so the hostage had to support John's weight, and was unable to touch John with his arms. As soon as John had him in this position, he moved out to the indicated door.

Entering the room, John encountered four pilots sitting on couches. John grabbed his hostage near the top of his neck, and spun him around so he was between John and the bullets. As he did this, John dropped his SMG and drew his pistol from his upper left pocket. Running to the end of the room, John used the now dead hostage to soak up the incoming bullets. He had hit three pilots when he reached the end of the couch where the highest-ranking pilot was standing.

John let go of the hostage and reached over and grabbed the pilot's arm, then spun while ducking, resulting in the pilot being thrown over his shoulder. He continued his spin and kicked the senior pilot's side arm away, which the pilot had drawn while lying on his back. John bound the pilot, picked up his SMG, and made his way back to the hangar with the senior pilot.

A small pile of bodies lay in the hangar's doorway. As John entered the hangar and walked to the rope, Greg and Carol abandoned their positions. Ascending the line, John opened the breach door.

Carol and Greg tied the pilot to the rope, and John hauled him up through the breach and into the shuttle. Greg and Carol came up next, and just before Carol entered the shuttle he pressed a detonator, then hurriedly shut the breach and dived into the shuttle. Carol detached them from the station. They were into midspace a minute later.

"Another successful mission." Greg reclined on a bunk. "You know, I wouldn't mind a mission where all the enemies gave up upon arrival."

"Yeah, but we would be out of a job if they made it that easy," John replied.

"I guess you're right," Greg yawned, then climbed onto one of the bunks and tried to get a few hour's sleep.

John said to Carol, "I imagine the button you pushed triggered some explosive that disabled the other spacecraft."

"That's about the size of it."

After a short silence, John asked, "So how was the action on you guys' side."

"Actually, it wasn't all that much. I think we got about a dozen soldiers between us. It didn't take them long to figure out we had much heavier weapons than they did, and as long as we were holding the doorways, we could take them out one by one. Even numbers can't prevail in that situation."

Standing up, John went to the back of the shuttle, where they had secured the pilot. He sat down, cross-legged. John and the prisoner stared at each other.

After about five minutes, John broke the silence, saying, "What was your mission?"

The pilot remained silent, just staring at John.

John tried again, this time saying, "What spacecraft do you pilot?"

More staring.

"Are you even a pilot? Is that uniform you're wearing earned or are you some big shot who thinks the uniform looks good on you?" John was looking for a reaction. Seeing none, he waited for a bit.

"Did you fail POW school? I think you did. They teach you to give half-truths, you know, something that is true from a certain point of view, something you can remember. If you say nothing, I've no choice but to kill you."

John had a feeling he was on the right trail, but the pilot wasn't showing it. John thought about what the prisoner had been doing, and started eliminating possibilities, searching for what motivated the pilot's silence. A disturbing and worrisome motive entered John's mind. "Okay, I'm going to take your clothes, and then I'm going to find whatever it is you are hiding."

He put the prisoner in a drug-induced sleep, and then began to search him. He took off the pilot's armor and flight suit, searching every hole, every pocket, making sure there was nothing dangerous. John turned his back on the prisoner, then walked up to Carol whispering, "Do a search for anything embedded in his body."

Carol switched the radar to electronic search mode so it would scan for electronics. Pulling out the radar, Carol pointed it at the pilot and narrowed the beam. He scanned the prisoner for any embedded devices. Finding a miniature electronic bug in the pilot's ear, Carol removed the device and modified it so he would be able to monitor what it sent and received. Carol replaced the device in the prisoner's ear.

As he put the radar back into place, Carol noticed John pulling something from the pilot's flight suit.

Carol asked, "Did you find something?"

"Yeah, I found a kill pill." Seeing Carol didn't get what he was saying, he explained. "A kill pill is a term used in the spy/assassin community for a suicide device. I got rid of it."

Carol nodded in understanding.

John gave the pilot back his flight suit, but kept the armor. He woke the prisoner. "Well, I found your suicide pill, so you're not getting away that easy. You have no other option than to tell us where your destination was."

The pilot said nothing.

"I'll let you think about your options for a while." John walked toward Carol.

John whispered to Carol, "Got anything?"

"Take a look at this." Carol gestured to the screen in front of him. John looked at it, and saw the text of his latest sentences, and a second list of a conversation next to it. The second conversation told the pilot not to respond to the questions until they got an ID on the voice.

"It seems like higher headquarters has taken an interest in us. That confirms this is the guy we want. I'll give him an hour, and then spend the rest of the day pumping him for information. You keep an eye on the screen, and see if there is anything we can use against him. Oh, and when Greg wakes up, make sure he doesn't talk. We don't want them to know how many of us there are."

John spent the rest of the day asking the prisoner pointless questions, hoping to get a response, even if it was only the pilot telling him to shut up. John had no such luck, and ended up talking to himself by the end of the day. Finally, after about twelve hours, John gave up. He walked over to Greg—who had awoken by this time—and Carol.

As soon as John entered the cockpit area, he could see Greg and Carol shaking in silent mirth. Carol, seeing John's puzzlement, pointed toward the screen with the messages.

John read "We have an ID on the voice. You're dealing with a human assassin, only known as John. He is extremely dangerous and has taken out a number of Federal workers. What we know of him is this: he has been doing assassinations since an early age; he is scared of the rest of the human race for unknown reasons; and generally avoids others of his race. However, he might be using this as a front; there is a strong belief he is an Alliance operative.

"It is believed he doesn't take a job unless it is highly dangerous. We think he is an adrenaline junkie.

"Whatever his reasons, he has killed a lot of your fellow soldiers, and needs to be eliminated. We will attempt to find a way to trap him but until we give you more instructions; do nothing."

John smiled. "Adrenaline junkie, I like that," he whispered.

"It's funny what they assume," Carol whispered back.

"Yeah, they probably are laughing at what we assume about them," Greg said softly.

"You have a point, but we should stop talking about this. We could be heard." John nodded toward the pilot.

They typed on the shuttle's computer to settle on a plan. It was decided John would push for info and hope the pilot or his directors would give away a hint, a clue, or anything regarding the location of the FDA HQ.

John got a few hours of sleep while Greg stood watch over the prisoner. Though it seemed like days to Greg, it wasn't much more than four hours. Having nothing to do, he just stared at the prisoner and the pilot just stared right back at him.

When John finally woke up, Greg took over monitoring the computer screen while Carol got some sleep. John began with the usual battery of questions, getting nowhere. John got a random idea, so he broke off his interrogation and walked over to Greg.

In a relatively loud voice he said to Greg, "How's it been going?"

Looking at John in horrified astonishment, Greg went mute until John gave him a reassuring wink. Still mystified, Greg played along. "Everything's going fine."

"Good. This guy's ready to break. I can feel it. As soon as he does, we need to be in the FDA HQ before anyone notices. Keep the shuttle running, we'll need to leave quickly when they discover I killed one of their generals. Got it?"

"No, not really, but I hope it makes sense later." Greg looked pointedly at John.

John did not go back to the pilot. He waited with Greg for a message to appear on the screen. After a couple of minutes, it arrived and read, "So all they want to do is to break into HQ and assassinate someone. In that case, go ahead and tell them where it is; we'll be waiting."

He started to interrogate the pilot again. In the middle of one of John's sentences, the pilot interrupted. "If you want to know where the HQ is, fine. Just let me get back to my family."

"Okay, where is the FDA HQ?"

"How do I know you won't kill me after I tell you?"

"Didn't you just say you were going to tell me?"

"I want some sort of insurance against becoming expendable. So I ask again, how do I know you won't kill me after I tell you?"

"You don't. You're just going to have to trust me."

"Trust an assassin? That isn't something most sentient beings would do."

"I guess that makes you exceptional. I told you to consider your options, but obviously you did not. Let's say you never give any answers, and it reaches the point that I have run out of time, so I kill you and get a new prisoner. Or I don't kill you, and I keep you in captivity for the rest of your life, and you still never get to see your family."

John paused for effect, then continued, "The other two options are you tell me the information, and I kill or detain you, or you tell me the information and I let you go.

The pilot waited for a minute. "The HQ is based on Gauss 1, Thriem Galaxy. It is one of the old underground bases. I don't know anything beyond that."

"Okay, thanks for all the info." John reached over for a painkiller and injected it into the pilot. He then took out a knife and ripped out the device that was embedded in the pilot and crushed it. Taking a small med kit, John repaired the pilot's damaged ear.

The pilot, who hadn't felt a thing because of the painkiller, stared at John with a blank look, realizing he had been duped.

As the FDA officers on the other end of the listening device heard John crushing the device under his foot, they entered a state of shock. It took them a minute, and then the officers started giving a torrent of orders. They assumed John would give the information to an Alliance battle fleet. While the FDA officers were confident their numbers would prevail, they feared the Alliance would be able to inflict considerable damage. In their hurried defense plans, they completely forgot about John's attempt to infiltrate.

John said to Greg, "As soon we jump to the planet, you take the escape pod and the pilot, and stow him away in some spacecraft going far away from here."

"I really appreciate your not shooting me so my superiors will have a scapegoat to blame for everything that went wrong."

"Greg, get some sealant for this guy's mouth." He turned to the pilot. "The reason I don't kill you is because word has a way of getting around, and sentient beings will learn if you give me the info I want, I'll let you go. It provides a good incentive program."

Greg sealed the pilot's mouth shut, then woke up Carol, and told him what had happened.

Carol walked over to the dashboard and looked at the last message the pilot's superiors had sent him. He read the last bit out loud. "*In that case, go ahead and tell them where it is; we'll be waiting.*"

When he finished reading, Carol added, "I'm getting the impression their security is a whole lot better than we expected. To allow someone to walk right up to your HQ means you've a lot of faith in your security forces."

"Then we'll just have to be better than they," John said. "Hurry up and enter the midspace coordinates."

Chapter 16

John's Surprise

Unfortunately for them, they were several days away from Gauss 1. They would have been bored out of their minds had not Greg pulled something out of his pocket.

"I can't believe my eyes." Carol looked at them in disbelief. "Where did you get those? Well what are you waiting for? Deal them out."

"When we were on the FDA space station I noticed a deck by a dead mechanic. I found out it was a deck of cards. What should we play first?"

Since they now had something to entertain them, time passed quickly and the days became a blur. One incident, however, was seared into their memory. It began when Carol said, "My high beats John's by three, which means this round goes to me, yet again."

"Not so fast," said Greg. "If I play the wild card as a warlord, then all high cards are subtracted by five, and all low cards are added by seven, which puts John in the lead."

Greg put down his hand and John reached for the pile of bullets they used as tokens to bet with. Carol, having bet big this round, lost almost everything he had won.

In disgust Carol threw down his cards. "Now why are you and John ganging up on me? I'm just good and I can't help it I won the last twelve rounds in a row."

"Well, seeing as you couldn't lose, John and I decided to help you out with that," Greg replied.

"The rules clearly state two players cannot combine forces."

"Stop whining. You were beat with only the smallest amount of treachery. Now that we finally beat you and have split your winnings, John and I are enemies again."

"You are never going to get married, you know. No woman could stand such a black-hearted beast as you."

"I don't plan on getting married. I take lives; I don't make 'em."

"Nice one liner."

"I know, I'm very proud of it."

"So I take you're one of those guys who say they're never going to fall in love and forget what they said when a certain girl comes along."

"Yeah, that's about it. You see, I just haven't met that girl yet, so until then I see no problem presenting the tough-sergeant appearance." As Greg was speaking he dealt the cards.

"I'm curious, have you ever even had a girlfriend?"

"Not really. My concern when I was in high school was becoming a marine. I just exercised like a madman. I was considered something of a freak, someone who was going to get killed volunteering for some hopeless mission. I never really thought about girls and they never really thought about me."

"I was into girls before I left middle school. Of course, none of them were into me then. As a matter of fact, they still aren't."

"I wonder what it was they don't see in you."

"Well, I don't see anything all that bad about me."

"No, neither do I. Other than that you have joined an organization even some humans consider to be a terrorist group, which implies you are a violent, brainless killer. While I know better, most people don't."

"I understand what you're saying, but that shouldn't matter. Even Hitler had a wife."

"You know, it's funny that we are talking about a subject neither of us knows anything about." Looking over at John, Greg realized that John had remained strangely reclusive in this argument. Still looking at John, Greg dimly heard Carol say something to the effect that he knew all about girls.

Greg replied, "If you know so much about girls, then why do they cross the 'verse to avoid you?" Continuing to look at John, Greg said, "Hey, have you ever had a girlfriend?"

An image of a young, pretty face of about 15 with long, black curling hair flashed through John's mind, accompanied by a white flash of sheer pain that coursed through his body, a pain so unbearable that mere words could not describe it.

Greg was surprised to find John's pistol pointed at him.

"Don't ever ask again," John said.

And he never did.

Chapter 17

Planets and Plans

When they arrived out of midspace and in position above the planet, Greg got in the escape pod and took the prisoner to the planet's space station. They waited about half an hour before Greg returned.

Greg reattached to the rest of the shuttle, and as the doors opened, he stepped through them, saying, "Everything went off without a hitch. I took a little extra time to ask around and I discovered the location of the local military base. Since there's only one old underground base on the planet, it's got to be the HQ."

"Great, so where is it?" John asked.

Greg pulled out a map. "I marked the perimeter with a red line. The area around it is mostly pine forest and tundra. Small bushes scattered all over the place, so cover is good all around. No civilian buildings within ten kilometers in accordance with the military perimeter law, but all the base's entrances and exits have roads leading to the cities. The last fifty meters before the perimeter have no plant life, so there's no cover that can take us all the way in."

John looked at the map and nodded. "Okay, we land in the city as close as we can get to the ten-kilometer zone. We do a recon on the place, then make our move."

Carol dove down to the planet. He wove a careful pattern around the spacecraft coming out of the atmosphere. Gauss 1 was one of the most populated planets in the 'verse. The Federation's capital was in the next solar system, only a twenty-minute ride in midspace.

It made sense to John that the FDA HQ was on Gauss 1. In the ancient times, when the Federation was just beginning, it had consisted of three races that possessed the technology of space travel and eventually found each other. They formed a single government, realizing they would continually be at war if they did not.

After a century, a fourth race had found them, and a great war was fought, with the fledgling Federation barely surviving. At that point, the Federation understood there were other races throughout the 'verse, and each one would have to be conquered or the Federation would fall. That was when the military gained power.

The Federation expanded, and through a series of military victories, their power increased. They sent scouts to every corner of their galaxies, and kept moving, slowly discovering the vast size of the universe.

As they conquered, they acquired new and faster ways to travel. No one knew when, but at some point they reached a race wiser and more powerful than any of the others. Thousands of legends sprang up about this race, but all agreed they were the ones who taught the Federation about midspace, before the Federation wiped them out. Because of this, that race was not in official records.

The Federation found it more convenient to open membership to all, saving them the trouble of conquering some planets. Those who did not join voluntarily became members of the Federation anyway.

Fewer and fewer new sentient species were found, and it was discovered most of the 'verse consisted of many variations of the same races. The exception, of course, was the human race. Humans were found on only one planet, which was why John thought the 'race had such an obsession with Earth.

John gazed down at the planet below him. The city lights were shining like a nova, lighting the entire sector they were heading toward. The entry into the atmosphere was as harrowing as ever in the *Mercy*, but John didn't notice. He was absorbed in thought, looking at the city in darkness.

John broke out of his thinking and started looking for a good place to land.

He pointed out a spot on the ground to Carol. "Land there."

Carol brought them down onto the spot John had pointed out. It was on a street in one of the back alleys which no one traveled. Carol parked the *Mercy* in one of the allotted parking spaces behind a large apartment building. "While I don't have much to say for this heap of junk, it is small enough to be a regulation-size hovercraft. We should be allowed to park just about anywhere."

"Okay guys, we have two options," said John. "We can move fast and plan as we go, or, knowing the FDA is already alerted to our presence, we can take the time to thoroughly recon and plan this operation."

"Well, because they already know we're coming, taking some time to plan might do us good," Greg said.

"If we hit them now, we might catch them by surprise," Carol said.

"It looks like the finial decision is mine. We've been in almost nonstop action for who knows how long. We need the rest before we throw ourselves onto a task this big. So, I say we take the time and plan while resting."

Carol concurred. "Then let's get started."

"First move, we rent a room. I will be the one renting, as my face is recognized and everyone knows enough about me to not ask questions."

John climbed out of the shuttle through the hatch in the rear of the escape pod. He stood up and stretched. The night air was cold and refreshing. No matter what you said about the Federation, one thing they did right was trash disposal. No whiffs of rotting garbage, no backed-up sewers, none of the scents that destroyed the feeling of fresh air. John enjoyed the moment and then walked around the building.

When he got to the front, he encountered a dead street. No hovercrafts rushing by, no lights, nothing moving—period. Seeing this, John knew he had picked the right landing spot. This was a poor sector of the city, which meant police would pay it no attention.

He walked up to the door. The door opened with a groan, showing its age. As the door slowly retracted into the roof, John entered the building. He was in the lobby and there was a ragged-looking Rotain behind a desk tucked away in a corner.

The alien did nothing, so after a minute of just standing there, John said, "Excuse me, I would like to rent an apartment."

The Rotain finally looked up. "We have three apartments available."

"Do you have any that give me a view of the forest?"

"Yes, we have two rooms, one on level six, the other on level four."

"I'll take the one on level six." This was a stroke of luck John had not expected. Now they would be able to recon the HQ from their apartment.

"That will be six hundred for your first week and a thousand for every two weeks after that."

He walked up to the Rotain and gave him the amount requested, and the alien gave him his card-key.

Using the lift, John went to level six. Arriving at his room, he used the card to electronically unlock his door and stepped inside.

He looked around the apartment. It was clean, but run down. The bed was in decent repair, wrinkly, but it didn't have any holes. All the appliances appeared to work. The apartment consisted of a main room—which held the bed and the couch—a latrine, and a small kitchen.

John activated the mike in his diamond armor suit. "I'm in the fourth room from the left, facing the HQ, and at the sixth level."

Greg replied, "We hear you. I think we can see the room from the shuttle, but I'm not sure."

John walked over to the window facing the HQ. The window was a transparent force field. John found the service panel and deactivated the field, then stuck his head out and spotted the shuttle below him.

Greg called him on the mike. "Okay, we can see you. It should take us about a minute to get up there."

John retracted his head. Greg and Carol launched cables up to the top of the apartment building along a path that had no windows. The cables were thin strands of a flexible metal, contained in a cylinder smaller than a hand.

It could launch the cable to its maximum length of fifty stories. They made sure the cables were secure and hooked them to their armor. The cables began slowly reeling them up until they were adjacent to John's window. They swung through the window and into the apartment.

Chapter 18

A Night at the Apartment

John waited until they had gotten their cables loose and recoiled them. "I'm sorry to say there isn't any food here, so we'll have to continue living off the rations we brought onto the shuttle. There's a bed and a couch. I'll take middle watch."

Taking the middle watch was something everyone dreaded because once you finally got to sleep, someone woke you up, and after your shift was done, you spent the rest of the night trying to get back to sleep. First and last watches were coveted positions.

The night passed uneventfully, and in the morning they all woke up feeling better than they had felt in a couple of months.

John ate the cold but not quite stale rations. "I have a plan in mind. We get on a hovercraft, and blast our way inside, just like we did with the general."

Greg hesitantly spoke up. "I don't think that's going to work. Last night, during my shift, I used my spotting scope to check out the HQ. I marked all the guards and security measures I could see on the map."

Greg pulled out his electronic map that was marked by a pattern of dots, each representing a security measure.

"The blue dots are security devices. The green lines are the routes of patrols. I marked the time and number of guards at the end of each line. The green dots are the stationary guards and black dashes are the entrances."

John looked at the map with concern spreading across his face.

"Most of this stuff is fresh, not more than a couple days old," Greg said. "You can tell by the color of the dirt. When you let them hear our plan on the bug, they started preparing for us. From the way their defenses are positioned, I think we can safely assume they're expecting us to make a direct assault."

"How did you get that detail during the night?" Carol asked.

"My spotting scope's infrared, at least when there's no EMP field" Greg answered.

"I expected there would be additional security, but not this much," John stepped closer to the map. "We're going to have to find a new plan, and quickly. Right now I don't see a way to get inside, so the only thing we can do is observe and hope we find a weakness.

"We'll each go to a piece of high ground, and observe the area. We do this for about eight hours. Rendezvous back here at the end of the eight hours, compare notes, and then do the exact same thing tomorrow, and the day after that. That should give us a reliable estimate on where all the guards are."

"I'll take that high rise over there." Carol pointed at a skyscraper in the distance.

"The highest building on this side is not far from here. I can make it there without any difficulty," Greg said.

"I'll go to the far end of the city, and on the subject of transportation, Carol, I assume you will be taking the *Mercy* and Greg will be moving along the rooftops. Make sure no one sees you are human. Unless anyone else has something to add, I suggest we get started."

They began to move out to accomplish their objectives. John removed all his weapons except for a pistol, but Greg and Carol kept their weapons with them.

Greg went out of the window first. He stuck his head out, launched his cable to the top of the roof, stepped out the window, and attached the cable to his armor. Jerking to a stop, he activated the cable's reel and ascended to the building's top.

John and Carol attached their cables and jumped out the window. They came to a slow halt on the ground.

Greg was looking at them from the top of the building. He gave them a two-fingered salute and walked off to his position. Carol got into the shuttle and John began walking. As John was strolling down the street, Carol took off and soared over him.

John walked far enough to be in an entirely new neighborhood. Once there, he began looking for a public transport.

Public transports were large hovercraft that held up to fifty beings. They were long and thin, with curved walls coming together at the top, creating a semicircle with the repulse-lifters on the flat bottom. The pilots took direct money—also know as cash—so it was an untraceable method of travel.

Finding one, he took the public transport about halfway to his destination, walked for another half hour, and took a second public transport the rest of the way.

John traveled the last fifteen minutes on foot. He stood next to the building he intended to use as his observation post. The building was the tallest in the area, but it was not quite a skyscraper. It was in the classic square shape, with force shields for windows. There was only one entrance, a large double door employees could pass through three abreast.

Although it had taken John over an hour and a half to arrive, it was still a few minutes before the workday started. Large groups of beings entered the building, providing perfect cover. Moving among them, John quickly managed to fade into the crowd, and made his way to a lift service area. He knew lifts had a safety margin of half a meter between them and any wall. It would be a tight squeeze, but he could make it.

He waited until he heard the lift go below him, then opened the maintenance shaft and hopped down. John fell only one story before he landed on the stopped lift.

Before he was ready, the lift shot up. John forced himself into a ball on the roof of the lift, expecting to go all the way to the top. When the lift stopped after traveling only a few stories, John realized his mistake. Only high-level executives would use the upper floors.

His plan failed, John waited for the lift to go about halfway up the building. When the lift ceased moving, he jumped to the door above him, bracing himself in the doorway, and jammed down the emergency-open button.

John stepped through the door, and to his surprise, there was no one in sight. Knowing the seclusion would not last, he looked for a piece of furniture to hide behind. The small lobby had a three-seat couch and two small, uncomfortable chairs, plus a small coffee table with a plant on it. Hearing footsteps, John dove underneath the couch.

A pair of employees entered the room on their way to the lift, neither noticing John. They selected a level and a tracking signal was sent to the lift. The lift came to their position and took them to their desired floor. As he watched the employees go through this process, an idea occurred to John.

As the employees stepped onto the lift, John dashed from his cover and stuck his fingers—which were protected by a diamond-armored glove—in the outer door to prevent its closing. The lift went down without waiting for the outer door to close.

He wedged his body in the crack and used a free hand to order the lift to the top floor. Seeing the lift come rushing toward him, he hurled himself down the shaft. The lift met him halfway, bringing his descent to a sudden halt.

Stopping briefly at the level John had come from, the lift traveled to the highest floor. As soon as the lift reached the top, John reached up and placed a breaching device onto the roof. Cutting a hole, John opened the breach and fired his cable through the hole. The cable went out to its full length, and as it started to fall to the ground, the lift went down again, leaving John behind.

John began to fall, so he buckled the cable onto his armor. Since he had fired it at an angle, he could only hope it would catch the edge of the building. When it caught an edge John came to a jerky stop. Slowly, the cable began to reel him up.

After climbing through the breach, John arrived at the roof. He detached his cable and took a look around at his surroundings. The top of the building was slightly angled to allow rain to slip off, but it was by no means smooth.

Rough gouges and bumps caused by centuries of cooling and heating covered the roof. One of the gouges had caught his cable's attachment device.

John went into the prone and crawled around to the reverse side of the slope. Since this was the highest building in the area, he was counting on not being seen from behind. He stuck the tip of his pistol above the incline, using his eye-sights to survey the base. Zooming in, he had a great view of the HQ.

He began recording on the map in his palm every patrol and defensive measure he could spot. The first hour of the watch was the most interesting, but there the level of interest began to decline as it became more repetitive. In his first hour, John noted a number of soldiers returning to work after a night in the city. Several patrols swept the area first thing in the morning and returned later to conduct more patrols at random times.

So many patrols and security forces were coming and going John barely had time to note their location. He spotted one patrol arguing over which route to take. They decided on a direction, and a few minutes later one of the soldiers blew up without warning. The patrol picked up the body and carefully retraced their steps.

Minefield, thought John. This was new and deadly information. Minefields were hardly ever used for base security, especially when the base was surrounded by a city. The risk of an accidental death was high and even in wartime they were only rarely used.

At that point, John ruled out any attempt to sneak in by the pine forest. With all the security measures, it would be impossible to get inside without detection. Instead, he focused his attention on the entrances. The two hundred meters before the entrances were barren, without even a grass cover.

The entrances themselves were holes that seemed to swallow up the road. The holes were reinforced by strong metal frames that continued down the tunnel. No gates blocked the holes and only a five-man guard stood by the entrance. This relaxed scene was deceptive, however. On closer inspection, John spotted a series of doors in the tunnel that could close and catch an intruder between them.

Although the last two hundred meters to the entrances were dirt, the area on top of the entrances had been allowed to grow into a pine forest. In this forest, John spotted at least half a dozen snipers and concealed machine gun emplacements. It was enough firepower to stop an infantry company.

Discovering these positions took up most of the day. John spent his time staring at only one entrance, using his peripheral vision to watch the rest of his area. Eventually, a small movement, a tiny shift in body position would give the location of the enemy away. The snipers' weak points were hunger and thirst. Sooner or later they had to eat or drink, and make enough movement to be spotted.

Since he had had breakfast and dinner, John did not need to eat or drink, so he fasted to avoid being noticed.

After studying the entrances, he turned his attention to the incoming and outgoing shuttles. The FDA shuttles flew low and disappeared into large holes in the middle of the base area. Hours later the spacecrafts left through the same holes.

When the eight hours were nearly up, John slowly brought his pistol back under the reverse slope. He began backing down the building until he was at the edge. Worried that one of the snipers might notice him crawling over the reverse slope to the hole, John decided to take the chance of being reported by a civilian. He hooked his cable onto a gouge and rolled off the edge. He went down straight, his head aimed at the ground. At the last minute, he snapped upright and landed safely on his feet. Getting some slack on the cable, he gave it a whip, and the loop created traveled up the length of it, popping the cable out of the gouge. The cable slid off the building and back into his launcher.

Several beings walked up to John to see if he was alright, but when they caught sight of his face they turned around and pretended they hadn't seen him. Most assumed John had killed someone, but for once they were wrong.

John moved away from the area as fast as he could. He pushed through crowds politely but forcefully, entered a public transport. After a series of turns and twist in his route, he managed to make it back to the apartment by the rendezvous time. Seeing no one on the back side of the building, he sent his cable up to the roof and made a quick ascent to their apartment.

<hr />

Greg and Carol were waiting for him. Greg was reclining on the couch with a hot drink in his hand and Carol was poring over a map on the table. Spotting John, Greg waved his unoccupied hand at him.

"You finally decided to show up. While you were away, I discovered a heating unit. It's been a long time since I've had a hot meal, even if it's only heated ship's rations."

"Did you find anything interesting today?" John asked.

"Other than the heating unit? As a matter of fact, I did. I looked at the gates in my area, and discovered how far the guards let vehicles approach before they stopped them. They halt hovercraft about twenty meters out, right in the middle of one of the biggest crossfires I've ever seen. Security is tight here. Tighter than anywhere I've ever seen."

"Fortunately for us," Greg continued, "their snipers are lacking in some vital areas. They never bothered to cover up the seams on their hideouts, and you could see the dirt was padded down or spread lightly. I think these guys are just hauled from basic, given a scope and a rifle, and called a sniper. I mean, how else would the FDA be able to spare so many snipers?"

John realized how little he knew about snipers, so he kept his mouth shut while Greg was speaking.

"I didn't find even half of what Greg found. Take a look at this; he even marked where he spotted footprints." Carol pointed at Greg's map.

John walked over to the map. On it was an array of colors, showing every bit of detail Greg had documented. It made his and Carol's efforts seem pitiful in comparison.

Carol interrupted his thoughts. "The one thing I did discover was a group of five civilians that went into the base during the morning. I had to leave before the end of the workday, so I didn't get to see if the civilians left the base."

"Shouldn't it take only a couple seconds by shuttle to get here?" Greg asked.

"It does, but I had to fly around to several different points around the city to throw off any pursuit."

"Oh, I didn't think about that."

Carol continued, "I caught only a glimpse of them as they went into the base, but I'll leave earlier tomorrow morning to get a better view."

John said, "I think you've found the opening we need. It won't be too hard to infiltrate if civilians are allowed on the base. I don't know if any civilians came through my sector in the morning. Certainly none of them left. But I encountered delays on the way to my OP. I didn't arrive until all the morning traffic had disappeared, so I really have no idea what happened in the morning."

"It seems we're all in agreement with getting up earlier. I think one hour should be good."

Carol and John nodded.

John asked, "So where is this heating unit you were talking about?"

"In the kitchen, above the oven."

"Don't you mean the heating unit above the heating unit? Isn't an oven a heating unit?" Carol's question went unanswered.

John walked under the open arch that separated the kitchen from the rest of the apartment and went to the oven. The oven was a small, black square at knee level, built into the wall. It had a little handle for opening and closing, with temperature controls arranged on a panel. John looked up and saw the heating unit right above it. The heating unit looked almost exactly like the oven, the difference being that it had Heating Unit written on the top.

John took out his rations and placed them in the unit, set the timer, and waited for a couple of seconds. He took his meal out as the timer went off. His rations were nothing more than powder in a capsule about the size of his hand. When the capsule was opened, the powder mixed with air and became a sort of soup that looked less than appealing, but it was filling.

Pouring the powder into a cup, John took a seat on the table with Carol. Greg came over to join them and the three of them began to compare notes. Taking what they each had observed, they compiled a complete map of the HQ.

Chapter 19

A Plan to Die For

Greg said, "We've pretty much ruled out any possibility of sneaking in by the forest. Our best bet is to disguise ourselves somehow and use the civilians to get in."

"You've said that at least twice," John said, "and have yet to give us an idea as to how."

"How do you expect us to disguise ourselves? Buy an alien costume? At those party stores they sell costumes of famous beings? We could try bluffing with one of those on." Greg was being sarcastic, knowing as they all did, that costumes looked ridiculously fake.

Carol and John were quiet for a moment. Greg thought about what he had said. "You know, that might not be such a bad idea. It would hide our basic human form and allow us to get close enough to make a dash for it. Besides, the guards would be curious enough to ask what we are doing. They would wait for us to get to the twenty-meter mark, then stop us. It shouldn't be hard to rig some sort of booster to get us past them."

"We could strap a shuttle's engine to a hovercraft, and be past them before they could open fire," Carol added.

"It has the highest possibility of working," said John. "Tomorrow, I will make a foray into town to get the costumes and the booster engine. Until then, I suggest we get some sleep. Who's got first watch?"

After sleeping through most of the night, Carol woke John up for his shift on watch duty. Carol went back to the bunk to try to get whatever sleep he could. John dressed and went over to the window. Greg had thoughtfully placed his spotting scope on the windowsill.

John sat at the window, staring out at the enemy base. He spent his entire shift of two hours and forty minutes doing this. At the end of that time, he set the alarm on the chronometer next to the bed to start blaring in one minute.

A loud beeping began, and from the depths of the bed, a hand appeared to shut the alarm off.

A voice from under the bed said, "Who dares disturb me at this ungodly hour?"

John replied, "Greg, I seem to recall someone getting me up at 0400 to do an obstacle course."

Greg's head appeared from under the blanket. "Well, I'm certain whoever did that will be punished. Is breakfast ready?"

"No, it's not." Carol slowly rose from the couch. "Consider it your punishment."

"And a cruel one at that." Greg yawned.

They began to move about accomplishing the duties of the day. When they were finished, they left the apartment as they had the day before.

To vary his route, John took the nearest public transport. He rode a series of transports to the new position he had picked out the night before. It was near his former position, but a good two blocks away, so no one would recognize him from the day before. About six buildings were in a small area, grouped close together. John walked between them until he was out of sight from the street. Seeing no one around, he launched his cable up to the top of a building and let the cable reel him up.

Seeing this building had a standard, rain-deflecting sloped roof, John hid on the reverse slope. Once again, he put the tip of his pistol over the edge and began to detail information on the FDA HQ.

The sun was just coming up over the horizon, sending its first red waves down upon the planet. Dawn slowly crept toward John until he was bathed in light. The city began to come to life. Beings started to get up and prepare for the coming day. Soldiers began to return from a night out, and small groups showed up at the HQ. One by one they came to the entrances and passed the checkpoints, disappearing into the base.

John kept a careful eye out, but he didn't spot any civilians. He wondered where the soldiers' families lived. Not all of the FDA troops could be single, and most would not accept a station that required them to be away from their families for most of a year. John felt if he could find the answer, he could use it to find a way in.

The day went by in much the same manner as the first, except it became old and boring faster. Time went by agonizingly slowly; the sun was beating down with a murderous heat, and John was forced to endure it without moving.

A piece of new intelligence was the guards for the entrances changed at 0600.

It took all his endurance to stay attentive to the details taking place below him. He feared repetitive occurrences would lure his mind into a false sense of security—that's when mistakes were made.

At last the day ended and John rappelled down the building. Detaching his cable, he began to make his way back to the apartment by a route different from the one he had taken that morning.

Meanwhile, since he was close to the apartment, Greg returned through the window before John or Carol arrived. He had set his weapons down, and was about to make a meal for himself when the door opened. A Waas with cleaning devices started to walk into the room.

Aghast, Greg walked over to the alien and blocked him from entering the room. "What are you doing here?"

The Waas looked at him. "I am part of the regular cleaning service offered by management."

"Get out of here. If I want cleaning service, I'll ask for it. Now move." Greg hustled the alien out of the room.

"Okay, okay, I'm leaving." The Waas hurriedly backed out of the room and into the hallway.

A few minutes later Greg looked into the hallway to make sure the Waas was gone and saw two armed gangsters walking toward him. Before he could decide how to deal with the gangsters, they turned to a door. Breaking the door in, they strode into a room, and began making demands on its inhabitants.

"Do you have the money this time, Remaro?" one of them demanded.

"No, but next time I will have it. I promise," said a voice from inside the room.

"That is what you said last time and Grenci has lost his patience. If you don't have the money, he will make it easier for you by removing those who depend on you for a living," said the second gangster.

The voice began to plead, "Please, do not harm my family. I needed to pay for the rent; it's my fault, not theirs."

The second gangster interrupted him, "You're right, it is your fault, not theirs, but they can't pay your debt. So we'll start with your youngest, and every week we will kill another member of your family until the debt is paid."

At this point, Greg grabbed his battle rifle and ran down the hallway to the room were the drama was playing itself out. A Waas and his family were huddled in a corner, with the two enforcers standing over them, their weapons pointed at the family. The Waas man was trying to shield his family in a futile attempt to protect them.

Greg shouted, "Drop your weapons, NOW!"

The gangsters slowly dropped their side arms, and turned around to face him.

Greg had his rifle leveled at them. He nodded toward the Waas. "That man, how much did he owe you?"

"Five thousand," one spat out.

"Okay, here is the money," Greg pulled out a chit worth the required amount and tossed it to them. "Leave, and don't return. Your weapons can stay here."

The gangsters left without a word.

Greg picked up their weapons. He turned to the Waas man. "I suggest you find a line of work that doesn't require you to go through their territory."

He walked out of the door and back to his apartment. John was waiting for him. As Greg walked into the room and turned around to close the door, John said, "What kind of a crazy stunt was that? You jeopardized the whole mission. Do you understand that?"

"Yes, I understand what I did. I saw someone in need and I helped him."

"You nearly wrecked everything we've done so far. Do you seriously think those gangsters are going to take being shown up on a hit? They and their boss are going to want revenge. You're wearing the uniform of an Alliance marine and you were on a planet. Don't you think the authorities might be interested in this? Is there any reason to think the scum won't report you?"

"Look, they've got their money. There's no reason to take revenge, and the last thing they want is Federal attention. All that aside, they were threatening that family's lives."

"You made an enemy. There is no telling how this will play out, but I wouldn't be surprised if it ends in our capture."

"If you become so caught up in the big picture you don't take the time for individual beings, then you've lost sight of what really matters. What would you have me do, let the family be slaughtered one at a time?"

"I would."

Greg returned John's cold stare. "You're a cold-blooded killer. That's all you are, and that's all you will be."

"I know."

In the short pause that followed, Carol entered the room. John then said, "As I was given command of this mission by your superiors, in the future you will not do anything to jeopardize the mission, nor will you go off gallivanting to rescue every passerby in need."

Carol exclaimed, "Whoa, did I miss something?"

"You did. A family was about to be murdered and I prevented it. John has a problem with that."

Carol looked at Greg with a surprised expression. "You exposed yourself? You might have blown everything we've done so far."

"Do either of you even care a family was about to be murdered? When beings are in a mess like that, you've got to help them."

"No, you don't," John said. "Beings don't want your help. It's called pride."

Greg was about to argue the point, but seeing it was useless, he left it at that.

Carol broke the silence, saying, "Well, I do have some good news. I think I found the entrance where civilians on the FDA payroll are allowed access."

Immediately, the argument stopped and all interest turned toward this new piece of information.

"What happened exactly?" John questioned.

Carol displayed his map on the table. "As soon as I got to my position, I saw a civilian vehicle enter the HQ. I thought I had missed it again, but then another vehicle showed up, and then another, so I took down all the details I could. What they had in common was they all wore business suits and they drove in decent-looking hovercrafts."

"I'll go into town and get the equipment. I should be back in two hours." John walked out the window.

John walked down the street and didn't have to go three blocks before he encountered a used hovercraft dealership. He sometimes wondered how all the dealers managed to stay in business.

The dealership was a tall, open-faced building that spiraled upward, with hovercrafts crammed into every corner. John walked through the door at the bottom of the building.

Inside was an empty waiting room. It was furnished in the usual way—chairs and couches, small round tables with ancient magazines scattered across them, and some sort of machine that produced a coffee-like substance.

At the front desk, John spotted an eager-looking clerk—a blue humanoid alien John did not recognize—about to unleash a barrage of sale pitches.

John hoped to forestall this. "Just give me the best hovercraft you've got and I'll take it."

The alien, seeing he had already made a sale, searched for the most expensive hovercraft on his computer. "I've found the one you want. It costs only seventy thousand, quite a bargain for a hovercraft like this."

John wondered what kind of being knowingly ripped off the most notorious assassin in the 'verse, but he paid the outrageous price, not wanting to waste time bargaining.

The clerk said, "One of our sales assistants will show you the vehicle."

A sales assistant with feathers covering his body appeared through a door opposite the front entrance. "This way, sir."

John followed him through the door. They went up three levels, and then the sales assistant went up to the car on the edge of the building's exterior spiral ramp. John walked up to the hovercraft and inspected it.

It was about half his height, with short walls along the sides. It was open-topped like almost all other hovercrafts, with a deployable force field to provide cover during rain. The hovercraft had a rectangular shape with rounded edges to increase aerodynamics. For seats, it had four shallow depressions with gravity generators that kept the occupant firmly in the seat.

Control panels were in front of every seat. These could unfold into a steering mechanism. The sides had a sleek blue finish, and the interior was jet black, showing it was clearly an upper-middle-class vehicle but still nowhere near worth the 70,000 John had paid for it.

As John looked at it, the sales assistant handed him a card that served as the ignition key. John took it, his eyes never leaving the hovercraft. Then he hopped in the vehicle and put the ignition card in a slot in the middle of the hovercraft. The vehicle roared to life, springing off the ground and floating on a cushion of air produced by the repulse-lifters.

The sales assistant said, "Good luck on your next assassination. Unless, of course, it's someone I know, or …"

John didn't listen to the rest of the feathered alien's sentence. He deployed the control panel in front of him and sent the hovercraft sideways over the edge of the building. At first he fell relatively fast, but as he approached the ground, the air cushion slowed him down, stopping him before he hit. He pushed the throttle all the way forward, and went zooming down the street.

Most hovercrafts skimmed between one and ten meters above the ground, so John picked the middle ground and went at five. He made his way past swarms of traffic, weaving deftly. There were no set rules governing hovercraft traffic, at least none that were followed. Police forces were spread so thin they could not be spared to govern the roadways. The result was traveling by hovercraft was extremely fast and dangerous, with midair collisions common.

Rushing down the streets at speeds in excess of 800 kilometers per hour, it didn't take John long to reach a costume store. The store was at the bottom of a large skyscraper, tucked away in the corner. John parked his hovercraft in the street, as all the sidewalk positions were already taken.

It's a good thing they make hovercraft so low to the ground. He turned his hovercraft off.

He ran at a low crouch to the sidewalk, dodging incoming vehicles. In the short but harrowing journey, he managed to safely cross the street. Catching his breath, he noted the store didn't seem much bigger than twice the size of his apartment.

However, the outward appearance was deceptive, and he found the store loaded with costumes of every shape and size. The small crowd of costumers squeezing through the overloaded aisles caused John a slight bit of worry. An assassin could easily be hiding in here.

John's eyes swept around the building; scanning for quick exits should he need them. The checkout counter was at the front of the store. The positioning of it was such John could not leave through the front door without being noticed. A red sign in the back caught his attention. On closer inspection, it became apparent this was the emergency exit.

Satisfied he had a second escape route, John turned to the business of shopping. The store had grown silent since John walked in. It didn't take him long to figure out why. At the front of the store, prominently displayed high upon the wall, was a costume of himself, complete with a fake SMG strapped to his side.

Studying it, John decided the costume looked lifelike, but the thought of buying it did not even cross his mind. Moving on, he selected three costumes of leading politicians. He purchased them in complete silence. No one in the building spoke, or even moved for that matter. John walked out and went back to his hovercraft at a leisurely pace.

He wasn't bothered at all that he was recognized wherever he went. Though it gave his presence away, the 'versal recognition and fear helped him in acquiring just about anything he wanted. On top of that, the average citizen never reported sighting him. And finally, John didn't care because a human walking on a planet was going to stand out, anyway.

John got back into his vehicle and waited for a break in traffic. As soon as there was a gap, he powered up the hovercraft and poured on speed as he entered mainstream traffic. Making his way through the city quickly, he went to the nearest shuttle parts dealer.

The shop was a square one-story building with a scrap yard in the back. This time, John had plenty of parking room and was one of four costumers at the parts dealer.

He walked up to a worker and asked for a spare shuttle engine. The worker showed him around back and John found an engine to his liking. After a quick exchange of money, the engine was his.

A cart fitted with repulse-lifters was used to load the engine on the hovercraft. Small blocks that fit into the curve of the spare seats were attached to the engine. When dropped into the seats, the gravity generators secured the engine to John's vehicle.

In another minute, John was off again, returning to the apartment. For an errand run, it had been done quickly, mostly because of John's huge pocketbook. He did not have to spend a long time looking for the best prices.

All this spending did little damage to John's financial situation. Killing was a profitable business as long as beings were around; someone always wanted someone else dead.

Chapter 20

Some Assembly Required

Taking a roundabout route back, John arrived at the rear of the apartment and parked the hovercraft in the far corner of the lot. When he entered through the window, Carol asked. "Did you get it all?"

"Yeah, it's all in the back." John jabbed a thumb at the window he had come through.

Carol walked to the edge of the window and dropped to his knees. Since he could not risk being seen, he poked the tip of his rifle out and used his eye-sight to survey the goods. He withdrew the rifle a minute later and asked, "Can I keep the hovercraft when we're done?"

"No, you cannot. When we finish, it needs to be wiped and destroyed," John said.

"Excuse me for asking, but what does "wiped" mean?" Greg asked.

"It's an assassin's term that means you remove all traces of your ever touching it."

"I thought we didn't need deniability."

"We didn't, right until the point where messed with those gangsters. Should they tip the FDA, this apartment will be searched. We wouldn't want them to have confirmation of a human presence."

After a short pause, Carol said, "Can I get to work on the engine?"

"I don't think you should; we want beings to think I'm the only one here. I'll go out and disassemble the sections you need and bring them to the apartment."

"That'll work."

Seeing Carol about to ask a question, John preempted him. "Now I understand a human walking around will attract suspicion, but I'll be wearing a welding mask."

"Well, that answers my question. If we get started now we can finish in a couple of hours."

John went down to the *Mercy* to retrieve the tool kit. The welding suit was an old-fashioned, thick, brown padded suit with a hood and mask. Quickly donning the suit, John stepped outside the shuttle.

The parking lot was a barren wasteland, with nothing moving in it save the wind. The wind did its best to make up for the lack of noise and howled at the top of its lungs across the empty space.

While John was preparing, Carol used a cable and pole to create a make-shift pulley.

John removed the first piece of the engine and tied it to the cable. Taking a quick look around to make sure no one was watching, he gave a thumbs-up to Carol. Carol hauled the piece into the room and untied the cable. He threw the line back down as soon as he finished. By this time, John had removed the second piece and was waiting to attach it.

Things proceeded like this for about a quarter of an hour, quick for disassembling an engine, but long enough that John began to feel exposed. It was with relief that he hauled the last piece up.

John ran around the building and came up through the front entrance. Upon entering the room, he found parts scattered about in a haphazard manner.

Carol was busy modifying the engine in a way that would have shocked the manufactures. Even to an untrained eye, it was obvious his improvements would cause a massive amount of damage.

John commented, "What happened to the engine I bought?"

"I should have told you earlier, but this will be a one-way trip, at least for the engine."

"What exactly is going to happen?" John asked.

"The plan is to use a burst of speed to get past the guards," Carol explained. "Only problem is, we'll be going too fast to slow or turn and will smash right into any roadblock inside the tunnel. To prevent that from happening, I've installed a system that will cause the engine to go into reverse immediately after the initial burst of speed."

"The sudden reversal will shred the gears, making my engine useless. Unfortunately, you're right. I think your plan will work."

"It had better," Greg interjected.

"Have I ever given you reason to think I would fail?" Carol asked indignantly.

"Yes."

It took Carol an hour and a half to finish the job. John spent another half hour reassembling it in the manner Carol had painstakingly described, but at that point he had stopped worrying. The mission was a go.

—◦—

John took off the welding suit and replaced it along with the toolkit in the shuttle. Making certain no one was around, he returned to the apartment. Carol was sleeping on the couch. Greg was waiting for John to begin a shift as sentry.

The instant John enter the door, Greg made a beeline for the bed. After lying down for a second, he got out of the bed just as quickly as he'd got in, remembering he had forgotten to set the caffeinated-drink maker to start when he awoke.

As he set the heating unit, Greg asked John, "Do you think we missed anything? I mean, for making a complex engine modification, we did it kind of fast."

"Greg, if I thought we had missed something, I wouldn't have stopped working,"

"Yeah, I know. I just don't think I could stand it to get this far and be blown up because of some stupid mistake."

"I know what you mean, but you don't have to worry. If it doesn't work, you won't have any regrets because you'll be a smear on a wall."

"That's comforting to know." Without another word, Greg fell face forward onto the bed, drifting off into a deep slumber.

The night passed by peacefully. Greg had the middle shift. He spent his time contemplating the events he was privileged to take part in.

This was to be the last night in the apartment. They had agreed to forego the final day of observing and start the intrusion in the morning. Not only were they impatient, but John worried Greg's intervention on behalf of the Waas family would have negative consequences, and the sooner they left, the less the odds were the gangsters would take revenge.

Greg enjoyed his shift to the fullest. He knew he would not have another chance for peaceful thought for quite some time.

The importance of what he would do in the morning filled him with anticipation. Something many had attempted and failed to accomplish lay at his feet, waiting to see if he could pick up the mantle the others could not. No one else had gotten so far, at least that Greg knew. The problem with being this close was a message couldn't be sent without alerting the FDA.

Morning came swiftly. Greg did not remember waking Carol for his shift, but he knew he must have, seeing as Carol was the one who woke him up. Greg rolled off the couch and began to make preparations for the coming day.

A quick meal and then he went work, securing all his gear on his body, making sure it would all fit beneath the costume. The sense of gravity had not deserted him from the night before, making all the unimportant details seem to have greater meaning.

John, on the other hand, did not care they were breaking into the FDA HQ today. He gathered all their belongings and piled the gear next to the window, then had Carol and Greg sit on the pile. Starting in the far corner, John worked his way methodically backward, wiping the apartment free of fingerprints and DNA traces.

When he hit the small enclave by the window where Greg and Carol were waiting, John said, "Okay, let's get our costumes on now. Make sure your diamond armor is on as well."

They slid the costumes over the web belts that held their weapons. Underneath the web belts were their clothes, and beneath all that was their diamond armor. There were enough layers that extended wearing would cause discomfort, but they did not intend to wear the costumes for long.

The plan was to arrive early and say it was "Wear a Costume to Work" day. It was an explanation so ridiculous the guards would assume it was the truth, since no one would be crazy enough to make up a lie like that. When the guards asked for their ID cards, they would have an excuse to reach in their pockets for their weapons.

Carol and Greg gathered all the gear in their arms, attached their cables, and jumped out of the window. John finished scouring the room and followed them down.

Dawn was still a few hours away. They gathered by the *Mercy*, loading the equipment they wouldn't need inside.

John said, "Okay, we need to put our weapons in the shuttle. Anything that can't be concealed has to be left behind in the shuttle."

Greg put his sniper rifle and battle rifle inside. He slipped his pistol into the costume along with a couple of spare clips. "I've got a grand total of a hundred and fifty shots. That should be enough."

Carol said, "I don't have anything concealable. I only took my Ferndi; I didn't think I would need any other weapons."

John said, "That's fine. I have a small SMG; it shouldn't be hard to hide in that costume of yours."

Carol took the SMG and said, "Thanks."

"You can have all the ammo I have for the SMG. It takes the standard assault rifle clip. I would take about five, so if Greg and I run out of ammo, we can break open one of the clips and reload our clips from it. I'll be taking along both of my pistols, along with as many grenades and explosives I can carry."

"I'll go ahead and move the shuttle. Let's go, Greg."

Before they left, John welded the booster engine to the bottom of the hovercraft, where it could not be seen by the guards. That work took only a moment to finish. The hard part came when he needed to wire the engine controls into the hovercraft's system. Carol helped him with that, and between the two of them, the modified hovercraft was made operational.

Greg and Carol entered the *Mercy*. They activated a beacon that John's eyesights would home in on, allowing them to rendezvous where Carol decided to park the shuttle. Though more complex than simply giving directions over a radio, the homing beacon was advantageous because they didn't have to risk someone's monitoring their conversation.

The shuttle lifted off the ground and rocketed overhead. Once the *Mercy* was out of sight, John got in the hovercraft.

Since the hovercraft was facing the apartment building, John turned it around quickly, then shot out of the parking lot. Shoving the throttle all the way forward, he accelerated to speeds just short of the sound barrier. Other hovercrafts swerved out of his way, nearly causing accidents, but that was okay with him.

At the speed he was going, it took him twenty minutes to reach the place where Greg and Carol had hidden the shuttle. They stepped out of an alleyway when they caught sight of the hovercraft barreling down the street.

John nodded in approval of their method. From his eye-sights, John knew the shuttle was a distance away. By emerging away from the shuttle, Greg and Carol lessened the chance of discovering it.

Slamming on the brakes, John slowed at an extreme rate. Greg and Carol leapt on board before it stopped moving. Greg took the remaining front seat and Carol sat in the back, where he could activate the booster engine.

John put them in a hard spin, ending with them pointing in the direction of the FDA HQ. Speeding forward, he weaved an aggressive pattern around the traffic.

It took John only two minutes to reach the road to the HQ. He put that tidbit of information in the back of his mind. It might come in handy later.

Chapter 21

A Break-in and Entrance

As they approached the ten-kilometer perimeter around the HQ, John slowed down to the mandatory two hundred kilometers per hour, and dropped to the required height of one meter above the ground. Unlike in the city, these rules were enforced strictly. Any deviation would result in being shot down.

The road to the FDA HQ had no obstacles restricting access other than a sign that warned the base was ten kilometers away. The ten-kilometer zone surrounding the area was not Federation territory, so legally you could not be turned around until you reached the gate.

This did not mean you could walk freely around this area. By law, anything the FDA perceived as threatening could be met with violence. That was why anyone sneaking around in the pine forest was risking his life.

John entered the road cautiously. It presented a drastic change from the city. After the pavement ended it turned into a dirt road flanked by a pine forest.

To go from the city to the woodland military base in a few meters was of special significance to Greg. It meant they had reached the point of no return, because it would be too suspicious to start down the road, then turn back.

The three-minute ride was filled with suspense. The constant worry of a shot ringing out made the air so tense it could be cut with a knife. A strange quiet had descended upon them. Everything became unreal. Reality did not return until they rounded a corner and the guards outside the HQ came into sight.

John slowed down for this last two-hundred-meter stretch. He came to a stop where the guards were standing, about fifteen meters from the entrance. The guards lazily walked up to them, surrounding them slowly.

One of the guards asked, "What in the Federation are you doing dressed up like that?"

"It's 'go to work in a costume' day, at least for our department. Didn't anyone tell you?" John replied.

"No, actually they didn't. Oh well, no one ever tells us anything. Show us your ID and we'll let you through."

"Sure, it's right here." John as he reached into his costume.

This was the signal for Carol to turn the booster engine on. There was a tremendous bang as the engine fired up. A flare of exhaust, a cloud of dust, and the hovercraft was past the guards. An instant later Carol's programming kicked in and the engine reversed itself, firing backward in a desperate attempt to slow down.

They flew into the tunnel. The road descended steeply for a short distance. At the end of the descent was a sharp right turn. In that instant, Greg knew they were going to hit the wall.

Greg held onto his pistol, hoping the engine would slow the impact down enough for his armor to be able to survive the blow. He knew his odds for survival weren't the greatest. Bracing for the impact, Greg saw the wall rush up to meet him. A giant lump formed in his throat. He had not expected to end his life as a mess on a wall. His eyes desired to close, but a morbid fascination kept them open.

Suddenly, a massive impact threw him out of the hovercraft. As the nose of the vehicle bent inward, Greg felt himself become airborne. Out of the corner of his eye he saw the same thing happening to Carol.

John had managed to get in a crouching position, and as they hit the wall, he sprang off the hovercraft, sailing through the air and landing in a roll to absorb the impact at each point of contact his body had with ground, evenly dispersing the shock.

Getting up as fast as he could, Greg was pleased to discover he was fine, with nothing broken or bruised. All three of them had their costumes torn to shreds, revealing their uniforms.

So pleased was Greg to be alive he forgot what he was doing for a moment. He was snapped back into reality as John pulled out both of his pistols and began firing.

Bringing out his pistol into a two-handed grip, Greg faced the direction of the road. Not far from where he stood was a barricade with five guards.

John blazed away with his pistols as he maneuvered toward the guards at a right oblique, killing two. Greg dropped down to one knee and took his customary half-second to aim. He fired a couple of times and one of the soldiers collapsed.

Meanwhile, John had managed to maneuver around the right side of the barricade. In the rapid exchange of fire, the pistol in John's left hand exploded for no apparent reason. Ignoring the problem for the moment, John continued shooting with one hand. In the short shootout that ensued, John came out the winner.

By this time Carol had gotten up and brought his SMG to bear, but no more fire was coming from the barricade.

Greg and Carol dashed over to where John was standing. John switched his pistol to a two-handed grip. "Everything's all right, my smaller pistol survived."

"What happened?" inquired Greg.

"The pistol that exploded was in a holster on my leg. It must have absorbed more of the impact of landing than my diamond armor. When I started firing, the recoil finished the job and destroyed the pistol," John explained.

With that, John placed one of his explosive charges on the floor. When the charge went off, a gaping hole appeared in the road. At the bottom was a room filled with officers working on computer screens.

Leading the way, John went down first. Shooting at everyone in sight, he dashed for the door. Greg dropped into the room and tripped on some of the debris. Recovering his balance, Greg found an FDA officer standing in front of him.

Greg momentarily hesitated. The alien before him worked in an office and that made the alien a noncombatant, didn't it? As the alien reached for something on his leg, Greg remembered all FDA personnel were required to carry a weapon. If they all had a weapon, didn't that make them all enemy combatants?

The question became academic when the FDA officer began pulling out an SMG. Greg swung his pistol toward the officer, watching the red dot in his eye-sights move correspondingly. The dot settled on the alien's chest and Greg pulled the trigger, knocking the officer off his feet.

Carol dropped in behind him. Together, they followed John to the door. Carol fired a few scattered shots to keep the officers under cover but otherwise they met no more resistance.

Once in the hallway, John gunned down the pair of soldiers who were walking towards him. As the soldiers fell to the floor, Greg and Carol fanned out to provide security.

John halted and placed another explosive on the wall to his left. The wall was blasted open, with pieces flying through the room. Through the smoke and confusion, John strode into the room, Greg and Carol flanking him. Cubicles and panicking FDA employees were entangled in a jumbled heap. When John reached the opposite wall, he blew it down as well.

Stepping into the next room, John held his fire. The flying pieces of wall had done his work for him. He ran for the door on the far side and kicked it down. A surprised Waas stood in the entrance way. John smashed the Waas's head into a wall, knocking him out.

They burst into another hallway. A lift was at the end of this corridor. Looking around, Greg noticed the walls were made of a smooth black metal. The air felt a little cooler than it had outside, but was still warm enough to be comfortable. Nothing seemed to have been recently cleaned, which Greg took as a good sign. If there wasn't regular maintenance, then there wouldn't be janitors walking all over the place.

John took up a position next to the lift. Greg and Carol leveled their weapons at the lift's door.

Though the others couldn't see it, Greg was nervous. He had no idea what would come through those doors. It could be an entire security squad, or a civilian. Either way, he was expected to shoot, and Greg wasn't sure if he would.

The door slid open to reveal a couple of senior officers. Before Greg could decide whether or not to open fire, Carol shot them both. When the shooting stopped, John went into the lift, making sure it was clear. Greg and Carol followed him in. They went one level to the side and down three, a trip too short for an ambush to be prepared.

During the ride, Greg mentally berated himself. His indecision had put his comrades at risk. Debating the moral correctness of killing FDA personnel without a combat military occupation specialty had caused him to freeze up.

If I have to murder to complete the mission, is the mission worth completing? Greg shoved the thought away. Now was not the time for questions.

As the lift came to a halt, fear gripped Greg. If there was an ambush, he would die. A voice inside him screamed for him to turn around and take the waiting lift back to the entrance and escape, or to surrender to the nearest FDA soldier. With effort, he fought the fear.

The door opened, and John went out first. Greg came out next, while Carol provided suppressive fire.

Several aliens were in the hallway. Some fled, while others reached for their weapons. Greg concentrated his fire on the aliens reaching for their weapons. He figured he hit a couple of them before the hallway was clear.

An information station was built into the hallway's side. Once the FDA troops were gone, John accessed the station and looked up all the janitors' rooms. Knowing reinforcement would arrive at any moment, he spent only enough time to memorize the rooms' locations.

John kicked in the door of the nearest room. They entered another office area. A worker stood to challenge them. Greg swung his pistol toward the alien but did not shoot. Instead, he fetched the FDA employee a hard kick. The alien collapsed on the ground, rolling in pain.

Hearing the commotion, the rest of the office workers dived for cover, leaving the team unhindered. John rushed them through the area. Upon coming out of the offices, they discovered they had entered a long corridor.

John placed an explosive on the ground and detonated it before he got out of the blast zone. His armor absorbed the shock wave and deflected the shrapnel. The section of floor he was standing on collapsed, falling away in large chunks. Keeping his balance, John rode one of the pieces to the floor below him.

From above, Greg saw a soldier draw his side arm. Taking aim, he dropped the soldier with one smooth pull of the trigger. He and Carol then jumped into the room.

By then, John had flattened the door in front of him with a hard-running shoulder. Carrying his momentum across the hallway, John plowed through the next door in a like manner.

—◆—

A large room with dozens of small construction vehicles was on the opposite side of the second door John had flattened. He selected the fastest vehicle he could find. Greg and Carol got on board while John hot-wired the vehicle. John leapt on as the engine fired up and drove through the exit.

They came flying out onto a roadway. Lining the roadway was a city underground, with buildings built like large rooms, vendors lining the sides, and just about anything else needed for life. Yet it managed to have almost no splendor or majesty, nothing interesting about it at all, for that matter. The city was simple, with the same dull grey color on every building.

A lot of aliens were walking around. Because all FDA personnel were required to carry a weapon, every one of the walkers might be an enemy. Greg felt fear rising in him again. If the crowd turned against them, they would not live.

"Start shooting," yelled John.

Greg and Carol looked at each other. Both knew this crowd contained many sentient beings who had nothing to do with this. Innocents would be killed. But enemies were in the crowd, along with those who wished to be neutral, and those enemies might rally the masses against the team. Carol and Greg knew the only way for them to survive was to create panic.

With a heavy heart, Greg swung his pistol toward the mass of sentient beings. Dropping the red dot in his eye-sights over one of the aliens, he began to apply trigger pressure. Behind, he heard Carol open fire. As he pulled the last pounds of pressure, Greg thought, *What I'm doing is wrong. This is murder.* The pistol barked in his hand, and an alien fell, bleeding heavily. *But it can't be helped.*

The roar of the screaming crowd reached his ears. Many began to flee in all directions. Some stood their ground and shot back. Using his eye-sights, Greg was able to accurately target these soldiers. Most of the time, he hit only those using weapons. But there were misses.

They broke through the city, leaving a trail of bodies. It was mostly empty streets after that, with few enough sentient beings that Greg and Carol did not needed to kill any more.

John drove them until they had descended four levels. Stopping at one of the few enclosed hallways, John got out of the vehicle and placed an explosive on the wall. The resulting explosion disintegrated most of the wall.

FDA employees cowered behind their desks. John strode aggressively through the room and kicked open a door on the opposite side, stepping into a hallway.

As he followed John into the hallway, Greg realized they had reentered the footpaths. He breathed a sigh of relief. Now he wouldn't have to worry about crowds.

Instead, Greg worried about the security squad that came out of a nearby lift.

Not having time for a fight, John led Greg and Carol down the hallway in the opposite direction, heading toward the nearest lift. Unfortunately, the other lift was at the far end of the corridor, a good kilometer away.

The security squad came in hot pursuit. Knowing they could not run a kilometer with a squad on their tail, John turned and started shooting, forcing the security team to take cover.

Carol went a little ways beyond John and dropped into the prone. He yelled for John to pull back as he laid down suppressive fire.

Catching onto the plan, Greg stopped running a short distance from Carol. As he got into the prone, he felt a little ridiculous. Against a fully armed security squad, all he had was a pistol.

Greg watched intently as John came running back, racing past him and Carol. Carol held back the enemy for a few seconds more, then retreated as well, leaving Greg to face the security squad alone.

Now it was his turn. Greg danced his eye-sights over the opposing squad members, squeezing the trigger of his puny pistol every time his red dot was covered by the body of an alien. He couldn't see if his bullets were having any effect. It certainly didn't feel like it.

FDA bullets whistled past his ears and pinged off the floor. The noise blended into a sort of music, like a symphony out-of-tune. It took all his willpower not to flinch in the face of this storm.

Greg's pistol clicked empty. It was time for him to pull back. Standing up, he turned and dashed down the hallway. John was in position and providing cover fire. Ice bullets zinged overhead.

He felt naked with an empty clip in his pistol. Slapping in his last clip on the run, Greg made certain to place the used magazine in a pocket where it wouldn't fall out. Later, there might be a chance to reload the clip.

As soon as Greg was past him, John hurled one of his grenades at the security squad. The grenade exploded and scattered the squad across the corridor. John coolly shot the soldiers lying exposed on the ground. However, most of the squad survived, more cautious, but still willing to pursue.

John signaled for Greg and Carol to continue running. The three of them hurried down the hallway. With its many twist and turns, the corridor allowed for an abundance of ambush points. If the FDA got a second squad in front of them, they wouldn't stand a chance.

Having suffered casualties, the security personnel moved with care. Some provided cover while the others made short dashes forward. Despite the safety of this tactic, the squad leader soon realized their quarry was getting too far ahead. He decided to abandon the slow, safe way in favor of simply running after them as fast as possible.

Noticing the FDA was catching up, John chose to end the problem. Picking a straight section of the hallway, John hid himself and Greg behind the corner. Carol saw what they were doing and entered a door about three-quarters of the way down the section. A couple of shots were heard from inside the room, then silence.

Waiting for the security guards, Greg felt his fear rising again. Shoving his doubts away, he tried to concentrate on what he needed to do. Their corner would not provide enough cover for both of them. When the time came, one of them would have to go into the open corridor.

Greg knew he should be the one to go out. John was more valuable to the mission, whereas he, a simple marine sniper, was expendable. But he did not want to go.

A heavy clump of boots came down the hallway. John gave him a nod. Now was the time to spring the trap.

Greg rolled out into the open. Though the action was dangerous by itself, Greg wasn't planning on its becoming suicidal, so he lay in the prone to minimize his target profile. Bringing his pistol to bear, he engaged the enemy.

John had already dropped at least one soldier. The others spread out, caught in the middle of the straight section. Knowing their chance of survival lay in blowing through the ambush, they turned their weapons to full auto and charged.

For Greg, it was like a solid wall of ice bullets coming his way. When one round plinked off the ground close beside him, it occurred to him these bullets could kill him. Death would mean the end of all his hopes and dreams, the end of any chance of having a family—something he privately hoped for but publicly denied—the end of all of life's pleasures and sorrows he suddenly found himself attached to.

I do not want to die. Every one of those incoming bullets was a bearer of destruction. The matter of his life or death hinged upon the accuracy of his enemy. If but one of the soldiers adjusts his aim by a centimeter, he would cease to exist. He could survive only by surrendering.

Greg momentarily stopped firing and looked at his pistol in indecision. All he had to do was release the weapon and raise his hands. It would be so easy.

He pulled the trigger twice. An FDA soldier collapsed on the ground. Pity for the soldier momentarily flared in Greg's heart, and then he swung the pistol onto a new target. A few more shots and this soldier fell as well.

Though the security squad suffered heavy casualties, they would have succeeded had not Carol stepped out of a room as the FDA soldiers passed him. Carol's SMG spouted a torrent of lethal ice bullets on the soldiers, catching them by surprise and making short work of them.

After the last soldier had fallen, they began running again. Because of their work on the obstacle course, they were in excellent shape and able to run the distance without flagging.

As they neared the final corner, John found himself a good ten meters ahead of Greg and Carol. That didn't worry him too much; he assumed having to watch the rear was slowing them. They were so close to the lift there shouldn't be any trouble.

Almost the instant that last thought entered John's mind, he turned the corner and saw the lift door open. A small security team of four was inside. John's pistol was pointing and shooting as the guards reached for their safeties.

Fortunately for John, the security team was bunched up in the lift and half of them could not fire. In the mad scramble to get out of the lift, they were able to get off only a few wild shots. Trapped like fish in a barrel, the security team was dead by the time Greg and Carol arrived.

Coming to a halt beside John, Greg was surprised at the pile of bodies inside the lift. Had not the guards been carrying weapons, he would've said it was an execution. The jumble of limbs blocked the lift door from closing. Greg thought the constant opening and closing of the door was kind of morbid.

"Sorry we were late," Carol said. "We stopped for a second to see if anyone was following us."

"Don't worry about it."

John reached inside the lift and attached a shaped charge to the roof. Kicking the alien soldier's arms and legs back inside, he stepped back and let the door close. The explosion blew away the top half of the lift.

John dashed into what remained of the lift, with Greg hard on his heels. They found themselves falling down the lift shaft, for when the top half of the lift had been blown away, all the electronics failed, along with the repulse-lifters that kept it floating.

Chapter 22

The Descent

Whereas Greg and Carol were caught completely off guard, falling down the shaft had been John's plan all along. He had destroyed the top half of the lift so he could use the bottom as a wind breaker.

Staying only a meter behind the lift, they fell down level after level. The guards' limbs were caught by the air, causing the bodies to be pushed above the lift and among the three of them. Greg thought it a little eerie to be falling with the dead. To avoid looking at the corpses, he tried to peep over the edge of the lift. Below him, he could see the lift shaft stretching for almost eternity. He decided there were other things he could look at.

Because lifts went sideways as well as up and down, tunnels lined the side of the shaft. At the end of these tunnels vertical shafts could be seen, and beyond the shafts, more tunnels appeared, and so on. Seeing this extensive underground system, Greg thought the HQ had expanded past the borders of the above-ground perimeter.

Looking at the shaft itself, Greg discovered to his surprise it was lit. The whole area was engulfed in a dim blue light. Nothing came to his mind as to why the energy was wasted on lighting these areas.

John broke the silence that had reigned during their descent. "Once we go down ten more levels, we shoot our cables through the horizontal lift shaft on the right."

In the time it took them to get their cables out, they had traveled the required distance, and only half ready, they fired their cables into the horizontal shaft. Snapping their lines to their armor, they waited for them to attach to the shaft. When the cables did hit the shaft, they stopped descending with a sudden jerk. Slowly, the cables reeled them up.

Rolling out onto the horizontal shaft, they removed their cables from the floor and began to walk down the tunnel. The shaft was a little taller than head height and about as wide as it was tall. The three of them walked abreast toward the other side. A ditch ran along the middle, and before Greg could wonder what it was for, a lift came hurling through the shaft.

As the lift came roaring at them, John led the way in a mad scramble to the side of the tunnel. They pressed themselves against the wall and the lift missed them by centimeters. Looking to the side, Greg noticed the lift was above the ditch. Doing some quick mental math, Greg figured they could lie down in the ditch and avoid being run over by an incoming lift.

The lift stopped in front of one of the doors that lined the shaft. A metal rod extended from the lift and depressed a button on the shaft door. They heard the door slide open, then the lift went zooming off in the opposite direction.

As they pushed themselves away from the wall, Greg said "I think if we walk along the ditch in the middle, we can lie down when a lift passes us."

Carol walked to the ditch and lay down in it. John could not see any of Carol above the floor. "Okay, it looks like it will work. Let's get moving."

They went at a fast jog along the ditch. At the edge of the tunnel was another vertical shaft, with horizontal shafts coming out of it at even intervals. John looked down at the massive collection of tunnels, counting downward to the shaft he wanted.

Greg, however, was not interested in the tunnels. Instead, his attention was directed toward the side of the vertical shaft. "Take a look at this."

John and Carol turned their heads in the direction Greg had indicated.

Greg said, "I was wondering why they took the expense of lighting the tunnels, so I was looking for some sort of walkway or something. It turns out they have a whole ladder system built into the walls. The reason I hadn't picked it up before was because we were going down too fast to see it."

"The FDA must keep a record of this somewhere," said John. "They'll assume we also have access to this information, which means they're going to search this area sooner than I expected."

John found the tunnel he was looking for and fired his cable down into it, then leapt off the edge. Greg and Carol followed him, and together they fell past the tunnel, allowing the cables to slow them. Coming to a slower, gentler stop this time, they let their cables' reels do all the work and waited to be hauled to the tunnel's entrance.

John said, "We need to go sideways for the next forty-three shafts and down for a hundred twenty levels, which will put us in about the middle of the southern section of the HQ. I input the coordinates of a janitor's room in my eye-sights so when we are below it I can cut a hole through the floor. We'll sit tight for a few days until security goes back down to normal levels."

Carol added, "Just in case something happens, remember all the shafts curve slightly so everything in the HQ eventually leads to the center. From what I could tell, that's where the Council of Generals meets. If everything blows up in our faces, then maybe the survivor could make an assault on the generals or something."

They began the long, arduous journey. To get across from horizontal shaft to horizontal shaft, they fired their cables across and jumped out as far as they could into the vertical shaft. The cables caught and reeled them up

Lifts kept coming by, forcing them to dive for cover in the ditches. They would wait for the lift to go into another tunnel before moving, as the lift might suddenly launch toward them after taking on a new load of passengers.

The biggest danger however, was presented not by the lifts that traversed the tunnels, but the lifts that came hurling down the vertical shafts. Every time they crossed to another tunnel, they risked being suddenly caught in midjump by a lift that might appear without warning. There were several close calls, but they always made it through in one piece.

It took them nearly half the day, but at long last they reached the point where all they had to do was descend. Attaching their cables, they went down fifty levels, the max length of their cables. They repeated the process once more, then after a pause went down the last fifteen levels.

They walked to about midway in the tunnel, where John stuck a breaching device on the roof. Quickly cutting a hole, John pulled himself up. Taking a look around, John gave the "okay" signal for Greg and Carol to come up.

—◦—

Coming behind Carol, Greg scanned the room as he brought his legs through the hole and closed the breach behind him. John had been exactly on target in selecting the point on which to come through the floor. They were inside a janitor's room, more aptly called a janitor's closet. There was enough room for one of them to lie down and for the others to stand, or for all of them to be standing or sitting, but that was it. There were old cleaning utensils scattered about the place and the smell was less than pleasant. From the dust on everything, Greg figured this room had not been used for some time.

Racing through the security concerns, Greg felt confident they would not be discovered. Patrols would be sent out along the lift shafts, but only the vertical ones, since one could look through the horizontal shafts from the outside. At the speeds they would be going, they would be able to see a man in the tunnels, but the breaching device was too small to be seen from the outside.

A thorough search would be mounted in the western section where they had made their entrance, but in all the other sectors only a hasty search would be made. Soldiers would run through the entire area, locking the doors behind them in an attempt to herd the intruders into a corner, but they would not check out every single place, just running through each room, not searching the room. Since the standard procedure was to lock a janitor's room when it was not being used, the soldiers would just pass it by, seeing that it had not been unlocked.

After about ten minutes, an alarm went off. It rang out ten times, the signal for an intruder alert.

Carol asked, "Why did it take them this long to sound the alert?"

"Remember, this is the headquarters of the largest bureaucracy in the 'verse," John replied. "Verification is needed to prevent false alarms, but the first level of command lacks the authority to make a basewide alert. The next command level will require the first's proof proven before they too decide to pass the info to a higher level. The process is repeated until it reaches the top of the chain of command, where the alert is finally given."

"Then why was a security team chasing us?"

"I was talking about basewide alarms. Local alerts can be issued without higher clearance."

Carol nodded in understanding.

John said, "It would be best if we were silent from now until the FDA finishes searching."

Carol took a seat on the ground and leaned his head against the wall. Greg followed his lead, looking forward to the rest.

Greg was feeling good about making it this far safely when two thoughts hit him at once. The first was, *We're trapped inside this tiny room and cannot escape.* The second, *I murdered those sentient beings in the crowd.*

John continued to stand, listening to the sound of the search taking place. Soldiers were running around the area, scrambling to their intruder positions. He thought it was kind of humorous. Most of the "soldiers" were office workers who carried arms and wore diamond armor only because FDA regulations required it.

Still, fools with powerful weapons could do a lot of harm, especially at ranges where aiming didn't matter. John stood perfectly still, not wanting to make noise and have some passerby discover their hiding place.

Soldiers kept running around for about an hour, at which point they finally got into position. They were poorly trained in this respect, for it should have taken no more than fifteen minutes.

These "soldiers," the first part of any FDA search team, had set up a series of checkpoints and roadblocks. The second part of the team really worried John. Real soldiers and security guards would rush through the area, locking the doors behind them and driving the intruder into the checkpoints, where the intruder would hopefully be slowed long enough to be caught.

By the time the second part of the search team reached their area, four hours had passed. The security guards ran right by them, apparently not even noticing the janitor's room.

Once the soldiers had gone, they were in the clear. The soldiers would not be back to check a place they had already secured. However, John felt it prudent to wait a couple of days for security to calm down and unlock the doors.

After a short, whispered conversation, a sleep rotation was decided on. Greg and Carol stood first watch while John lay down on the floor and slept.

I'm a murderer, no better than John. Those people didn't need to die. Greg tried to shove the thought away, but failed. *Imagine how many of them felt the same fear you felt in the hallway today, wondering whether they were never going to have a family or complete their dreams. Imagine how for many of them, that fear became a reality. And it was all your fault.*

No, Greg mentally screamed. *It's all a lie. I'm a good person; I couldn't have done something like that.*

But you did.

The faces of those he killed during the day flashed through his mind. He tried to count them, but couldn't. He knew it wasn't a bad dream. The sound of their screams still rang in his ears. It had not only been murder, it had been a massacre.

I DID NOT MURDER. I only aimed at those who were trying to kill me. Anyone else I hit was an accident.

But you knew there would be misses. You knew innocents would die, yet you opened fire anyway. You started shooting because fear for your own life was greater than your respect for theirs.

Greg couldn't deny it. Deep in his heart, he knew that was the truth. His act was not one of violence; it was one of cowardice.

And with admission came resolution. *Never again,* he swore. Though he would forever be unable to atone for what he'd done, no matter the cost, no matter the pain, never would he kill needlessly.

They kept a continuous rotation every couple of hours, giving all of them a chance for sleep.

The only change came at 0600 hours, when a general came on the public address system. "Soldiers of the FDA, I congratulate you on your exemplary performance by standing guard all last night without complaint. For that, I feel you deserve to know what's happened. Intelligence believes the intruders escaped during the night, leaving the base by an exit in the lift shafts we had not known about until last night. The purpose of the raid seems to have been a statement they could infiltrate and exit our base at will. If they try this again, they will find this is not so now that we know their secret exit."

There was a pause, then the general continued, "Until they try again, however, I believe you are deserving of rest. All personnel have the next twenty-four hours off. Enjoy your day soldiers—you earned it."

Wild cheering erupted from down the hallways as soldiers made their way to their quarters to first get some sleep and to spend the rest of the day doing whatever.

"I wonder if he was telling the truth about their intelligence experts thinking we escaped through a previously unknown exit," Carol whispered.

John replied, "I wouldn't doubt it. This place is so old there are probably dozens of unknown exits."

"If that's the truth, then why did he say it over the announcement system? Even if they do think we're gone, it's common sense to take precautions in case we're still here." Though it had been Greg's turn to lie down, he hadn't really been sleeping. His dreams were disturbing, being filled with images of him slaughtering civilians.

"It's a trap. By giving the soldiers leave for today, he's trying to trick us into thinking the base is clear. Undoubtedly there are special units waiting for us to appear on a security camera."

They were silent for a long period. Time passed slowly, with nothing really changing. Most of the HQ was empty, with soldiers sleeping in their dormitories. The day eventually ended. The second day was mostly a repeat of the first, except for one small incident.

John was leaning back against the door, when he heard voices speaking outside. Listening closely, he discovered he could hear conversations that were going on outside by putting his ear against the crack between the door and the wall. After about ten minutes, he heard a pair of soldiers conversing as they walked along the hallway.

One soldier said, "Yeah, it's about time they got around to it. I haven't seen my wife in two months."

The second soldier replied, "That's the way it always is, isn't it. They never get around to bringing family along the first time. It's almost like an afterthought, you know."

"I can just see them going 'Hmm, you know what, I bet those soldiers would like to see their families. Let's see if there is anything leaving for that base we can put the civvies on. Nope, nothing available for the next month. Too bad, but I know our soldiers can take it.'"

The soldiers laughed, and then the first soldier said, "So, do they send all of them at once, or do they send them over here one by one?"

"That would be just like them." The second soldier chuckled. "No, they all should arrive tomorrow. By the way, have you seen that ..."

The voices faded. His question answered as to what the FDA did about the soldier's families, he knew he could exploit that information. Security would be tighter, of course, but it still wouldn't be able to entirely compensate for the advantage of confusion.

Later in the night, when John and Carol were standing guard, they woke up Greg and held a council of war.

John said, "Tomorrow, the families of the soldiers are arriving. There will be a lot of confusion, with beings getting lost all over the place. The security system will be overtaxed with a mass of calls about civilians in places they shouldn't be. We should be able to slip through unnoticed."

"Wait, you mean to tell me real civilians live here?" Greg asked.

"They probably live in cities like the one we drove through."

Greg turned a couple of shades paler and was silent.

"What about security? With this many people living in the HQ, you'd think its location would've been leaked by now," Carol said.

"All the secret and important places are in the lowest levels, while most of the sentient beings live near the top. I bet most of the soldiers don't even know they're in the HQ."

"So how are we going to find Earth in here? I mean, we can't exactly ask someone for directions."

"Well, for one thing, the Federation has an obsession with documenting everything. That'd be a good place to start."

"Doesn't the FDA have a big library or something that is supposed to have everything ever documented in it?"

"As a matter of fact it does. It is supposed to be in the FDA HQ. If we can get to an information station and download everything onto a map, we should be able to find directions."

"Won't they detect us downloading the schematics of their base?" Greg asked.

"With all the lost family members they will probably overlook it," John replied.

"It's a plan," said Greg.

"Let's do it," Carol agreed.

The next morning they got up and waited until about noon, when the new arrivals would be pouring in thick and fast. They had a brief discussion on how to best carry out their plan.

Greg said, "So, are we going to do this like the first day? Are we going to use the lift shafts and breaching devices to appear from underneath our objectives?"

"No, not this time. You see, the problem is I only have one breaching device and three explosive charges left. I do have five grenades, but those are only antipersonnel weapons, they can't blow through a wall. We are going to have to rely on conventional sneaking around," John explained. "Speaking of armament, let's reload our clips."

"By the way, something I learned accidentally is if you shove the muzzle of your weapon into your enemy and fire, most of the sound will be silenced. The guy's armor contains most of the noise of the bullet's breaking the sound barrier," he continued.

Greg briefly wondered who that "accident" had been. *Probably a civilian like the ones you killed.* He winced at the thought. Learning those sentient being were not only non-combatants but were genuine innocents had only made things worse.

Oblivious to Greg's mental agony, Carol and John continued talking.

"I had thought that was something that only worked in theory. I never heard of anyone actually trying it," Carol said.

"Like I said, I learned this purely by chance. I've only used it twice since then, but it should come in handy for today's work," John replied.

"Since we aren't going to be using the lifts, how are we going to get out of this closet?" Greg asked.

"Simple. We break it down."

Chapter 23

A Casual Day Turned Upside-Down

A soldier was casually walking to his duty station. He had taken his lunch break early and was bringing back the leftovers for his co-worker, who was too busy to take off for lunch.

As he walked down the hallway, a door about midway blew out, falling down with the hinges broken and the lock snapped in two. A black-clad man walked out, and spotting the soldier he began to run at him, reaching for the weapon at his side.

The soldier foolishly stood still and tried to draw his own weapon. The black-clad man reached him and grabbed the soldier's side arm, twisted it, and jammed it into the soldier's armor. The man pulled the trigger of the side arm, the muffled sound of a shot came out, and the soldier slid down to the floor, slain by his own weapon.

Although this was done in full view of a security camera, there were only a certain number of screens that could possibly be monitored at one time, so the FDA actively watched only high-priority areas, and looked at the others only when an emergency occurred.

John quickly dragged the soldier into the janitor's room and shut the door. After Carol jammed the door shut to give the appearance it was still locked, they ran as fast as they could to a corner where they could hide.

Not finding an available corner, they took the next best thing, a restroom. After Greg and Carol got into toilet stalls, John went to the doorway and opened the door using the emergency opening mechanism.

All FDA doors could open with a push in case an EMP field was employed and the electronic opening and closing failed. Moving the door open less than a crack, John stuck the tip of his pistol out, using it to survey the area. Seeing it was all clear, he quietly whispered for Greg and Carol to come out.

Not too far down the hallway was an information station. Greg went to the info station and attached a blank electronic map to it via a small cable. Greg hit several buttons on the map and everything on the station began to download onto the map. The progress could be traced by the 3-D objects that slowly transformed into the HQ.

It took four long minutes for it all to download, but as soon as it was done, Greg yanked it out and they were back in the restroom, crowded into one stall and poring over the map.

As they were staring at the three-dimensional map, Carol said, "It just occurred to me, if they decide to see who just downloaded a map, we're in the area they are going to search."

"Good point," Greg concurred. "Maybe we …"

Greg's words trailed off as someone walked into the restroom. They were perfectly silent until they heard a flush and the alien cleaning his hands. The door hissed open, then closed with a thud.

A silence came upon them. Greg and Carol were standing on the toilet seat while John stood on the floor to give the impression there was only one person in there.

At last John spoke. "Even if they did search for who downloaded the map, they aren't going to look inside the latrine."

With that they went on staring at the map until they had worked out a decent plan.

They exited the restroom and made their way slowly and cautiously through the base. They walked as fast as possible, always waiting until the next piece of cover was unoccupied, and then moving to it with all possible speed. Although the base had an overabundance of personnel, it was so big that beings were in hallways only every two minutes on average. Their other advantage was most beings were at their work stations. Even on the first day most of the beings they met were in offices.

It took them a harrowing thirty minutes to reach their destination. Behind a series of boxes, they peered out at the scene before them. It was a large parking lot filled with all sorts of trash removal vehicles. A couple of soldiers were loitering around, obviously waiting for their shift to begin. After about a quarter of an hour, the soldiers got on a pair of trash removal vehicles and left the garage.

As soon as the soldiers were out of sight, they were out of hiding and looking among the trash disposal vehicles for a particular Vehicle Designation Number, or VDN. In the FDA, two letters preceded this number, the first giving the vehicle's function, the second its operating area.

Finding the VDN with a library designation, they climbed into the rear garbage hold, which was about halfway full from the morning's haul of trash.

Carol covered the others with garbage, then made a large pile for himself. Making a dive into the pile, he vanished under a sea of trash. The three of them had completely disappeared inside the junk.

It was an hour later when Carol remembered the garbage workers should be taking their lunch break right about now. Mentally cursing his timing, he waited for the workers to return and pick up the next round of trash.

Though the stench was blotted out by their diamond armor helmets, the disgusting sight of the filth was enough to put any thoughts of eating away indefinitely. It took two hours of waiting before someone came along and turned the vehicle on.

With a lurch the hovercraft started forward. The carefully made pile of trash Carol had made shifted, leaving him open for any passerby to see. Looking over, he saw the same thing had happened to Greg and John.

Fighting a losing battle, the three of them constantly tried to reapply the covering garbage. Despite their best efforts, they were only partially successful, for the hovercraft kept slowing down and speeding up.

After a long journey and a lot of jostling, the vehicle stopped and did nothing for five minutes. John slowly peaked his pistol out of the garbage container. Seeing no one around, he climbed out cautiously, and made certain they were alone. He hid behind the vehicle and whispered the all clear to Greg and Carol. The two of them swiftly joined him behind the vehicle.

The area they had arrived at was a barren lot behind a building surrounded on all sides by large walls reaching the roof. Pieces of fallen scrap littered the ground. There were two entrances, the large one at the rear the trash disposal vehicle had come through, and a small door at the front that allowed only a man-sized object to pass.

Looking for a piece of cover, they spotted a series of discarded electronic bookcases. Hiding behind these, they waited for another half hour before the FDA soldiers were finished removing the trash.

When the soldiers finished at long last and the hovercraft had left, they broke from their cover and took up position on the sides of the smaller door. Opening the door a crack, John surveyed the area with his eye-sights before entering. Spotting two soldiers still waiting around after the job was done, he waited for them to leave.

When the soldiers left, John waited for another minute, and opened the door all the way and stepped inside. He got behind a trash can a few meters from the doorway. Greg and Carol came in behind him and the three of them crowded behind the relatively small piece of cover while John scanned for the next place to hide.

They had done it. They had managed to make it into the Library of the Federal Defense Agency. Nothing could stop them now. Soldiers in sufficient force could not be rushed here in time to stop them from accessing the electronic book that held Earth's location. But to ensure they survived finding where Earth was, they had to stay quiet, avoiding all contact.

Too close to risk losing it all now, they moved slowly and cautiously, not making any mistakes, doing nothing chancy or stupid that would ruin their effort.

After safely making it to the main library area—where all the books were held—they took a moment to survey the area around them. The book stalls were towering giants that scraped the roof. All the dividers had blue illumination lights, and between these lights were rows of thin black cards, the books.

Row after row of books, all lined with military precision. There were stairways leading up and down to other levels, giving an indication of how much information was stored in this area.

At the end of each stall was an electronic card catalog. Grabbing the nearest one, John quickly found what he was looking for, a record book called *The History and Conquest of the Planet Earth*.

Fortunately for them, the book was but five rows away. It took them only a moment to find the row and begin searching for the book.

Carol gestured wildly for John and Greg to come over. He pulled out a book and showed its title to them.

This was it. The book they spent so much time and effort looking for was held before them in Carol's hands. Even in this great moment immediate tactical concerns were not forgotten, so John turned around and provided security while Greg and Carol turned the book on.

Putting the voice at the lowest volume, Carol asked the book for the info on the history of the conquest of Earth. The book began to give an account of the battle for the planet.

To cut time, Greg asked, "Book, where is the location of Earth?"

The book replied, "That information was stored separately. For security reasons, it has been moved to General Grossen's office."

"Where is General Grossen's office?" Greg asked the book.

The book gave him the office number of the general.

Taking the office number, Greg looked for it on the map. He looked at the position of the office. "This guy used an office near the bottom of the HQ, close to the Council of Generals. He must have been a regular customer or something; maybe he gave the Council a morning briefing. Security's got to be tight."

"You're assuming this guy is still alive," John said. "Book, when was the last update on the contents?"

"In 468,200 SFB, on the ninth hour of fourth day of the third month," the book replied.

"That was just after Earth was conquered," said Carol. "This guy is long dead."

"Chances are Earth's location is still at that office, seeing as there was no good reason for the FDA to move it again."

"Okay, what's the plan?" Greg asked.

"First, let's get out of here," John answered.

They went out the way they had come in, this time with a little more speed and less caution. Their good luck continued and they were not spotted— nothing short of a miracle.

After they emerged from the library and into the barren lot Carol said, "We can't do any more sneaking around. Sooner or later someone is going to catch us. We've got to find a method to move faster and still remain hidden, like we did with the trash disposal vehicle."

They continued walking until they were in a corner so they could observe both entrances at a glance. Then John said, "I agree. The thing is, no one goes down to the generals' territory."

"The lift shafts would work. Although we can't bust out anywhere we want, we can still appear at the right level," Greg offered.

"Tell me what you have in mind." John walked over to Greg.

Greg pulled out his map and held it in front of him. "If we get into the lift shaft that's inside the library, we can use it to get down to the level we want."

"That part I knew already," Carol said. "How do you propose we get out of the lift shafts?"

"When the lifts opened, I saw them extend a rod to depress a button on the shaft door. I think if we can push the button, we can open the door," Greg explained.

"How many security rooms do they have?" John asked, referring to the rooms security personal gathered in to watch the video feed from the various cameras in their area.

"Three. The one on the far right keeps an eye on the office we want," Greg replied.

John stared at the map. "There is a lift that brings us to the same hallway as the security room. It's the third door down from the lift, so we should be in there before they even know we've arrived."

"I like the plan. Let's do it," Carol agreed.

Without any further discussion, they entered the library for the second time. The journey was short and silent, and no sentient beings crossed their path. They ordered the lift to a level above them and waited for the lift to begin to close its doors.

Carol jammed his legs into the closing outer door. John and Greg jumped over his leg and down the shaft. As soon as he saw they were clear, Carol rolled over the edge in pursuit.

Flying down the shaft at tremendous speeds, they didn't take long to go down to the proper level. Firing their cables down a horizontal shaft, they were jerked sideways and pulled into the shaft. They went across for a few more shafts.

As they walked along the ditch of one of the shafts, Greg stopped and nodded at one of the doors. Greg and Carol climbed up to the left of the door, and John took the right. Since they could not use a breaching device, Greg shoved all his weight into the button that opened the shaft door.

The door opened the instant it felt the right amount of pressure. John came out of the door so fast it was like he entered the hallway before the door opened. Greg and Carol came out as if in pursuit of John, all three of them pumping their legs up and down like pistons. They had to get inside the security room before someone reported them, making stealth secondary and speed primary.

Seemingly without breaking stride, John kicked open the door to the security room. He removed one of his grenades from his pocket and hurled it inside the room. As he stepped back, there was what sounded like a mild explosion.

In the second he waited for the grenade to go off, Greg and Carol had caught up with him. The three of them charged into the security room, each heading for a separate corner.

The handful of security guards inside the room had been knocked off their seats and were spread dazed on the floor, but somehow they maintained the presence of mind to draw their weapons.

Upon entering the room, John shot the two most alert-looking guards. The remaining three, though still on their backs, put up a smattering of return fire.

This would be a good time for you to exercise that newfound mercy. Taking the situation in a glance, he saw John and Carol methodically eliminating the soldiers. However, the soldiers were holding and using their weapons, making them dangerous. He also didn't know what to do if they captured the guards.

Greg held his fire, knowing he could not end this without violence, yet not certain he should shoot. It was not until one of the guards took careful aim at John that he pulled the trigger. The type of alien was unfamiliar to Greg, but he distinctly remembered the grey-green blood that poured out of the hole in the alien's armor.

Greg asked, "Do you think anyone heard us?"

John replied, "I don't think so. These walls are mostly sound proof. That's why the grenade sounded so quiet."

Greg looked around and noticed the grenade had been much more powerful than it sounded. The security consoles were trashed and the seats were shredded by shrapnel. Most of the paint from the walls had peeled off because of the heat. Fabric blown off the chairs littered the floor, some of it on fire.

John stamped out the fires. "Let's go."

Chapter 24

In The Office

Leaving the destroyed security room, they walked causally to the lift. By throwing the grenade inside the room, John not only knocked down the soldiers, he also ensured the security cameras would transmit to broken monitors, leaving no way for the FDA to retrieve the footage.

Taking the lift to the general's office area, they exited quietly and went behind a curve in the wall for cover. Scanning the area around the corner, John spotted no one. They went the entire way to the general's office without seeing a single being.

Greg would've suspected a trap but for one thing. The place to have sprung an ambush was as they exited the lift. There had to be a perfectly normal explanation for this.

They approached the doorway leading to the general's office. As the door blew open from his kick, John marched inside in a businesslike way. Seeing the area empty, he signaled for Greg and Carol to come in. Carol fixed the door so it wouldn't swing open and would retract electronically when used the normal way.

Greg took a glance around. There were many doors leading to offices along this short hallway, but only one office door at the end of the hallway. The last office had to be where the highest-ranking officer worked. Pulling out his map, Greg confirmed his suspicion.

John glanced over at Greg's map and then made a swift march to the door. He walked right up to it and nothing happened. This was surprising only in that most office doors opened automatically. A pad appeared next to the door. "Fingerprint authorization please."

John had half a mind to blow the pad to pieces, but he figured it would be a clear sign they had been here. Instead, John looked up and surveyed the ceiling. Seeing nothing that could help them get into the general's office, he brought his eyes back down. Then he realized the whole thing was a hoax, since wearing diamond armor made all fingerprints identical, which the general should be wearing per FDA regulations. John put his hand on the pad and the door opened.

As they walked in, Greg asked John, "How did you figure it out?"

"All fingerprints are the same when you have armor on. If you didn't know that and touched the screen with your bare hand, you would give security your fingerprint," John explained.

Carol said, "Let's start searching in the far left corner."

They went to the corner and began to methodically spread outward, going over every little detail of the room.

The room was centered around an elaborate wooden desk with a couple of meters of space between it and the surrounding walls. All the walls, except the one with the door, had wooden cabinets of varying sizes, the largest being open-faced to accommodate a small personal library, the other two serving as file cabinets.

From all the expensive wood, it was obvious this was at least a lieutenant general's room, and the occupant was probably up for promotion to the highest rank, full general. John stored this information away for future use.

Going through every single drawer and looking into every little nook and cranny took them almost half an hour. When they finished, Carol announced their discovery with a statement. "It isn't here."

"I don't think we could have missed it." Greg took a precautionary glance around.

"Well, we really have no idea what we are looking for. It could a book, a message, a recording, or who knows what else. But we went over the place pretty thoroughly, so if it was possible for us to find it, we would've. I say we wait for the general to show up," John concluded.

"We have no other lead. This is our best shot."

"I'm of the same mind as Carol. Let's do that. Until then, we should keep looking anyway."

They went back to searching for the location of Earth. An additional ten minutes had passed before they heard footsteps in the hallway. Hearing the noise, they immediately abandoned their current activities and lined up on the sides of the doors, out of sight to any in the hallway if the door opened.

Most of the motion on the other side of the door had abated when a lone set of footsteps approached the door. Gripping his pistol tightly, John watched the door rise up. A Waas came into the office. Seeing three armed men waiting on the other side of the door, he started to back out.

John grabbed the Waas and yanked him inside. The door shut behind him, and the general gave up struggling, knowing whatever happened in this room would not be heard by those outside. John threw the general to the other side of the room and leveled his pistol at him.

Seeming subdued, the general asked, "Are you going to kill me?"

"Not unless something unforeseen happens, such as, oh maybe a security team busting in the door."

"No one knows you're here."

"I would like it to stay that way. Now, my first question is, why was this area vacant so long a period of time?"

"There was an office party for the new families that have just arrived, sort of a meet-and-greet. It had nothing to do with your arrival."

"The location of Earth was supposed to be here. Why isn't it?"

"General Grossen got promoted to the Council of Generals. He took the info with him and stored it under his seat. There is a key needed to open the seat and I have no idea where that is."

"I'll deal with the key later. Where was General Grossen's seat on the Council?"

"How am I supposed to know? I don't have time to memorize pointless facts."

"But you have books and you can look it up. Which book would tell me what seat he was in?"

"I don't know. I have a record book for all major decisions made by the Council. It might be in there, but I've never looked for the seating arrangement."

Greg walked over to the personal library and pulled out the record book. After asking the book a few questions, a diagram of the Council appeared, with one seat highlighted. He downloaded the data from the book onto his map. "I've got it."

John's eyes had not left the general. "Thank you for your help."

He proceeded to go around the room and hit hard on what seemed to be random places on the wall.

John turned and faced the general. "All the security recordings in this room have been destroyed. The monitors upstairs have also been trashed, so there is no record of this ever happening, except for a video I took."

"I see no camera in your hand."

"I put my eye-sights on video mode. And since it doesn't record sound and didn't see me pointing a pistol at you, it looks like you were making a deal with me. You know security will take every scrap of information off my body, so the video will be found if I die."

Nodding in understanding, the general went to his desk and began to work as if nothing had happened.

John opened the door a crack and looked out into the hallway. All the other generals were in their offices, so it was clear of traffic.

John went out of the room first, with Greg behind him and Carol taking up the rear. As they marched down the hallway, a reptilian-like secretary appeared out of nowhere and almost ran into them. John shoved his pistol into him and pulled the trigger. The shot was muffled and not heard by anyone else. John handed the body to Greg.

Great, another noncombatant dead. He hoisted the body over his shoulder.

They walked to the main entrance without any further trouble. This changed when they opened the door. There were two guards facing outward—a Pratin and a Waas.

John ran out of the door and rammed his pistol into the guard on the left and pulled the trigger. He spun and grabbed hold of the other guard's weapon. He yanked the Pratin's SMG to the side as he jammed his pistol into the second guard and fired. The two guards fell dead on the floor.

Carol and John picked up the fallen guards and the three of them made their way down the hallways to the lift as fast as they could. It was short but arduous, and if Greg's obstacle course had not had long sections in which they had to carry each other, they would not have been able to do it.

Carol called the lift several levels above them and did the usual routine of jamming the doors open. Greg threw the bodies down the shaft, where they would probably be found when a search was made. It didn't matter as long as it delayed the discovery of the dead for some time.

Greg looked to John. "Shall we go down?"

"No, it's only a couple of levels down to the Council, and all the lift entrances will be heavily guarded. That general's office is only a fifteen-minute walk from the Council. The best way to do this one is the traditional way."

"Let's get a semblance of a plan together before we do this," Carol said.

They went into a restroom like they had before and tried to work out a plan. Greg peered at the map "The best plan I can see is to just shoot our way in—which won't work—but it's all that comes to mind."

"I have a slight improvement to your plan. I've three charges and a breaching device left. We can kick down a couple of doors and place a charge on top of the Captain of the Guards' office. We could blow it down and mess with security until they were all distracted by a whole series of alerts. Then we sneak in during the confusion."

Carol looked intently at the map. "That would work, but they probably keep an eye on the surrounding area, so it would alert them anyway. If we take out the first checkpoint quietly, we can place a charge on the roof and blow a hole in it. The roof of the Council is an old fashioned one designed to stop armor-piercing rounds, so it has a thick outer band to take most of the energy out of the shot, and a thicker inner band to soak up the rest of the energy. The space between is enough for us to crawl through, and the edges are weaker, so it shouldn't be too much for your explosive to blow through. We could then crawl to the middle and use a breaching device to get down. And if we wait twenty-five more minutes, the workday will have ended, and hopefully the Council will have adjourned and vacated the area."

"That's the best plan I've heard so far, and I don't think there is going to be a better one. Only one modification I'll add. Remember, we have to take out the Captain of the Guards first, and then go into the roof. I think my explosives are modern enough to break through the bit of extra thickness of that ancient wall."

"Why do we have to take out the Captain of the Guards?" Greg asked.

"Simple. There is a key needed to open Grossen's old seat and no one knows where it is. The solution is to take the Captain's master key."

"Makes sense. By the way, how did you know the general was going to be cooperative?"

"He was a lieutenant general up for full general. If it was found out his office was broken into, it would trash his career as he would be under suspicion of dealing with us. The only way for his career to survive is for us to get what we want."

"He betrayed the Federation for his career?"

"By saying he didn't know where the key was, he puts the responsibility on someone else, at least in his mind."

"Only twenty-four minutes left," said Carol.

Chapter 25

To the Council of Generals

At long last, the FDA version of taps was played to signal the lowering of the flag and the end of the duty day. After waiting a little while for everyone to clear out, they left the latrine.

The area had a quiet about it, unlike the hustle and bustle that filled the upper levels. Greg supposed this had to do with the end of the day and everyone's vacating the place.

During their short trip down the hallway, they encountered no one until they reached the first checkpoint.

Stopping at the corner just before the checkpoint, John edged his pistol around to survey the soldiers. After a quick glance, he pulled back and whispered the situation to Greg and Carol. There were six guards ten meters from the corner, all standing around a lever that could close a blast door across the hallway, effectively blocking the way.

It took them about two minutes to work out a plan.

John threw an unarmed grenade over the guards' heads. The guards' eyes followed it for the briefest of seconds.

In that instant, Greg and John crossed the distance and were among the guards. Sticking his pistol into the side of one of the guards, Greg silently eliminated the soldier. To Greg, John seemed to be a blur of motion, taking out multiple guards smoothly and instantly.

The remaining guards turned around to face their attackers. Seeing a Waas' SMG leveled at him, Greg dropped his pistol and grabbed hold of his enemy's weapon. Twisting hard, Greg turned the SMG around and shoved it in the alien's gut. Looking up into the Waas' eyes, he saw the alien's terrified expression as the realization of impending death came.

A pity for him, Greg thought as he slipped a hand along the SMG and pulled the trigger. The Waas' eyes clouded with pain, then went dull and expressionless as the body fell to the floor.

So fixated was Greg on the carcass, he didn't notice Carol had saved his life.

"Come on, let's go," Carol said to him.

Looking up, Greg saw Carol standing over the corpse of a guard who had taken aim at him.

"Thanks for the save," Greg replied.

None of the guards had had time to close the door. Strolling down the hallway, John casually picked up the grenade he had thrown and cast a glance around the corner. He then hurriedly armed the grenade and hurled it down the corridor.

Hearing the explosion, Greg and Carol hurried to John's position. On the other side of the corner was a second checkpoint identical to the first. John had already shot most of the guards, so it was the work of a moment to finish off what remained.

"This checkpoint isn't on the map," Greg said.

"Makes sense for them not to give away all their defenses," John replied. "I'm assuming there are guards around every corner. How many more turns do we have to make?"

"Two."

The third checkpoint was a repeat of the second, with John's throwing a grenade and then moving in and finishing the guards off. However, these guards had heard the earlier explosion and had shut their door. John slapped on an explosive and blew the door down.

Walking down almost to the corner on which the fourth checkpoint was situated, John put an explosive on the wall; but instead of detonating it, he stepped back and threw a grenade around the corner. Turning quickly, he detonated the explosive at the same time the grenade went off, with the grenade's detonation covering the sound of a hole being blown in the wall.

John led them into the hole and entered an empty office area. They took the nearest exit leading to the hallway. As he ran down the hallway, Greg pulled his map out and gave directions.

They reached a room with two guards standing outside. Carol fired two short bursts that slew the guards as John walked up and kicked down the door.

Striding into the room, John raised his weapon and shot the sole occupant, the Captain of the Guards. John bent down and searched the soldier while Greg and Carol stood guard. Digging through his pockets, John pulled out a card. "This is what we're looking for."

As he slipped the card into his own pocket, John rose and pulled out his last explosive. Placing the explosive on the roof, he shaped it to explode in a small concentrated area. John armed the explosive and then cupped his hands around it, directing the explosion upward. The blast blew him to the ground, but it did not harm his diamond armor. Looking up, John could see a jagged hole several meters deep.

Greg offered John a hand. Taking the hand, John got up and jumped into the hole, spreading his arms and legs out to support himself. Bringing his legs up and pushing on opposite sides, John "walked" up until he reached the top of the hole. Pulling himself up, John went into a crouch and waited for Greg and Carol, who came up a couple of seconds later.

Taking a second to glance around, Greg was impressed by what he saw. They were in a curving dome, with huge paralleling walls above and below him. It must've been an engineering marvel to create a structure like this underground.

They crawled until they were in the middle of the dome, the highest point. John placed the breaching device at his feet. Slowly, John began to turn the handle around. Everything was so quiet the click of the handle hitting its starting point sounded like a thunderclap.

John lifted the hatch on the breaching device almost reverently. When he stopped, the three of them stared down at the Council of Generals thirty meters below them. All they could see was the pole on which a speaker addressing the Council would place his notes, but even that managed to give off a sense of majesty and glory.

The Council room was bathed in a dark blue, giving it a cold feeling. John attached his cable to the top of the roof and slowly began to lower himself. Before John's head was out of the breach, Greg attached his cable and began to lower himself almost on top of John, with Carol close behind. The unsophisticated, gangly sight of the three men on cables sharply contrasted with the feeling of ancient power the Council seemed to radiate.

Greg could barely believe he was actually in the Council of Generals. As he looked around, he could see the forty-seven seats arranged in a circle and the large open arch that was the entrance to the Council. The acoustics of the room were such that anything said on one side could be heard on the other, even the smallest whisper. It made their lowering cables seem incredibly loud. He was afraid they would be heard by the guards.

John slowed down his descent until Greg and Carol were level with him. Coming down ever so slowly, all six of their feet hit the ground at once, sending a boom throughout the Council. They had just become the first humans ever to set foot in the Council of Generals.

John did not take a second to feel the moment. "Come on, we need to hurry."

Looking up, Greg saw there were curving stairways on the left and on the right that led to the Council seats, but of course those were not fast enough for John. He ran at full speed and leapt, grabbed hold of the edge, and pulled himself up and over the ledge. Greg and Carol came right behind him.

Greg turned around and looked at the floor from the viewpoint of one of the generals. It was hard not to feel a sense of superiority. Besides sitting a level above the speaker, there was a ledge that came to about knee level when sitting, inside which were computer panels so the generals could do their own research on the speaker's topic. The seats were soft, with a hard metal backing that forced the occupant to sit upright.

A small distance separated the seats from the ledge, creating a walkway around the Council room. Using this walkway, they reached General Grossen's old seat.

John and Carol shared a look as Greg stared in wonder at the Council room. John held out the master key to Greg. "The honor is yours."

"You sure?" Greg asked.

John and Carol nodded.

Greg took the card and held it up to the seat in front of him. He heard a faint click and the seat popped open a crack. Greg stuck his fingers in the crack and lifted the seat all the way up. Peeking inside, they saw an electronic book. Greg reached in and pulled the book out.

Activated at Greg's touch, the book began with the opening, "This is the personal account of General Grossen and the conquest of the planet Earth, renamed Nargartha."

They did not listen any longer. They all knew where the planet Nargartha was, but just to make sure they didn't forget Earth was Nargartha, they downloaded Nargartha as the next waypoint in their eye-sights.

A moment of silence was taken as the book droned on. At last John said, "Nargartha was one of the planets I never set foot on. Kind of ironic."

—◆—

"We need to get a move on," John said.

With that they snapped back to reality. They realized if they did not get out of there alive, everything they had just learned would go to waste.

"Detach your cables," John told them. "By now the guards must've discovered our trail. We've got to leave through the main door."

They hurriedly detached their cables and headed out of the Council room.

Under the arch and out into a long corridor they ran. There were several waiting rooms for beings to prepare their presentations before they gave them to the Council of Generals. The hallway to the Council of Generals was unguarded, as according to regulation no one with arms was permitted inside, but that was not true for the three corridors leading to the hallway.

They reached the end of the three corridors leading out of the Council, each of them having a door and a heavy guard unit to prevent unauthorized personnel from coming inside.

Stopping, John asked, "So, which one should we take?"

"The nearest lift is down the far right corridor," Carol said.

"The faster we get out of here the better," Greg agreed.

"Then we're all in accord."

Walking up to the door, Carol kicked it open and leapt to the side as John hurled a grenade into the guard contingent. They waited until the explosion came, which knocked most of the guards off their feet.

The guards were behind a series of boxes that served as cover, but they were facing out, waiting for an intruder to try to come in, not trying to leave.

Spreading out to the sides, the three of them caught the guards in a crossfire and methodically wiped out the opposition. Hit from behind and at close range, the guards didn't have a chance. Most didn't even last long enough to turn around.

John reloaded once the guards were down. They ran down the corridor, hurrying to escape the flood of security that had to be coming any minute. Rounding the last corner, they were chagrined to discover a guard force of ten waiting in ambush at the lift.

A flurry of bullets zipped past them as they turned around and ran back behind the bend.

"I don't have any grenades left," John said. "We can't take them."

All our hard work for nothing! Greg thought as he caught his breath. *There's no way we can get past those guys and we can't go back the way we came. All we can do is wait for the FDA to surround and kill us.*

Though he'd felt fear of death, never had Greg known for certain he only had a few minutes to live. It was terrifying.

Looking around, he saw Carol and John had also realized there was no escape. The mission had failed.

Chapter 26

Back to Civilization

"I didn't think it would end like this," Carol said.

"I didn't think it would end, period," Greg replied.

Carol slowly swallowed. "At least we found Earth before we died."

"Not that it'll do anyone any good." Greg was staring intently at the ground.

"Even if we had succeeded, the knowledge of Earth wouldn't have helped the Alliance."

Greg turned to face John, surprised he had spoken.

John elaborated. "The Alliance and MAA would've launched an attack the instant they learned that information. The universe would've become engulfed in all-out warfare, taking many lives that need not have been lost."

"I didn't think you cared about that sort of stuff."

"I don't." He looking intently at Greg, "But you do."

John continued, "I'm sorry you guys got involved in this. I should've been here alone."

"What do you mean?" Carol asked.

"The Alliance and MAA needed me to find Earth. They sent you two along so their representatives could take credit in the discovery."

"Oh," Greg said. "I thought I had been selected because I was close to beating the all-time kill record for snipers."

"Don't get me wrong; you were chosen because you were the best, but the main idea was to get me on this mission. Sorry about dragging you guys on this one."

There was silence for a moment. At length Greg spoke. "You know, despite what I said earlier, I was really looking forward to retiring and starting a family."

"A real meal is what I wanted after this mission," Carol said. "A big, juicy meat slab with some sort of fried vegetable on the side."

Another pause ensued.

John peeked around the corner. "I'm not interested in waiting for the FDA to catch us. Since we're going to die anyway, why don't we at least try to shoot our way to the lift?"

"One heroic last charge?"

"At least we could take a few of them with us," Carol added.

Greg wondered about the moral correctness of killing others because you knew you were going to die. Then the sniper in him took over, and a cold, emotionless wave washed over him. There was no anger, there was no fear, no feeling at all.

John gave the last battle orders. "I'll roll out of the corner while Carol provides suppressive fire. Greg, I want you right behind me. I'll take the left side, you take right. We'll try to push into the middle, where Carol can mow them down. Remember, the lack of cover works both ways."

Wordlessly they got into position. John nodded, then rolled out as Carol began opening up in full auto. Greg came out running, sticking to the right side of the hallway.

Pointing his pistol at the mass of guards, Greg pulled the trigger as rapidly as he could. Shocked at the unexpected attack on both flanks, the guards began to bunch up in them middle. Greg kept running and shooting, confused as to all else but those simple motions.

Carol cut a great swath through the soldiers with one, long burst. Reeling in panic, the soldiers fired rapidly and wildly.

Suddenly, all the shooting stopped. Lowering his pistol, Greg looked around in amazement. All the soldiers were dead. Carol and John were still alive.

Blinking his eyes, Greg made sure he wasn't dreaming. *We're going to make it.*

Having eliminated the guards, they did not waste a second. Now that they had a chance, there was no way they would let anything get in their path.

They opened the lift door and fired their cables up the shafts. Twenty levels up they had gone when they heard a lift coming down with a vengeance. Swiftly, they swung into one of the horizontal shafts and disconnected their cables.

While they made it into the shaft well ahead of the lift, their cables were not fast enough and were caught by the lift. They would be dragged along when the lift started going back up.

This was an unexpected boon. They would be able to ascend at a rate far faster than if they were reeled up by their cables.

As swiftly as it had come down, the lift came back up. John figured the lift was going to get reinforcements, having already delivered the first wave. Either way, it didn't matter anymore; the point was they had been discovered.

With a lurch they were pulled off their feet and hauled upward. The lift went up to fifty levels below the ground, so they swung out to level fifty-one and detached their cables.

They ran sideways for a considerable distance and had to constantly dodge lifts that were pouring into the Council of Generals. John knew time was running out and soon patrols would be sent down the vertical shafts.

Eventually they reached a point just below the entrance nearest to where they had originally breached the base perimeter. Naturally they would not use the same entrance twice as the guards would be watching to prevent such a thing from happening again.

Ascending the distance with all possible haste, they appeared at the lift-shaft door they had chosen for their exit. John looked at Greg and Carol, and they gave him a nod. Acknowledging their nod, John hit a button which opened the shaft door. He then dropped into a crouch so low his knees were next to his chest. He moved slowly through the door and into the next room.

The room was actually more of a parking garage. In it were scores of hovercraft owned by military personnel. John had entered at the back. The section he had chosen was empty of sentient beings, while the front of the lot was crowed with soldiers trying to get off base for the night.

Keeping low to the ground, John signaled for Greg and Carol to move forward. Using the hovercrafts to remain in defilade to the nearby soldiers, they gathered around the back side of the nearest hovercraft.

Carol ducked underneath and took out the bottom of the vehicle. Working swiftly, he tried to hotwire the hovercraft. Although it was designed to sound an alarm if someone attempted to steal it, it was not equipped to defend against removal of the bottom section and hotwiring from there. The damage was too obvious, and it would be spotted by the police in a heartbeat. However, being spotted by police was not one of their concerns, so Carol was as sloppy as could be and left the bottom of the front half of the hovercraft on the floor. The hovercraft suddenly rose as Carol managed to hotwire the engine.

Emerging from underneath the hovercraft, Carol whispered, "This one is the same model as the other hovercraft you had, only it's a couple years newer and has the new silver paint scheme. Otherwise it should handle just about the same."

With that, they hopped into the hovercraft in the same arrangement as before, with John at the helm. John sent them flying down the parking garage as fast as he could without attracting attention, which meant he had to slow down several times to stop other hovercraft from running into him; but even at the slow speed of ninety kilometers per hour they were going too fast for anyone to get a good look at them.

At the end of the parking garage, John joined the general flow of traffic going to the city. He had to negotiate the constant turns of the corners that formed the checkpoints on the way in, but he was always able to put himself between two other hovercrafts so he was not seen by the guards.

In a few minutes they were at the entrance and almost on the dirt road that would take them to the safety of their shuttle. Now they would find out if their plan paid off.

They were counting on the presence of many new civilians. These would all be trying to get inside the base or out to the city at the end of the workday. Because there was only one entrance where civilians were allowed access, they figured the snipers would be concentrating on the civilian entrance to help the overwhelmed guards.

The moment came and passed, and before they knew it they were past the guards. Although incoming traffic was checked rigorously, outgoing traffic seemed to be allowed to pass unmolested.

They kept low and wove a path through the traffic to avoid being next to any particular hovercraft for more than a few seconds. The pine trees seemed almost sinister, with their long, dark green branches concealing who knows what dangers. The three minutes stretched out to an eternity. There was a temptation to floor it and get out of there, but they restrained themselves, not wanting to take risks now that the end was in sight.

A sign marking the end of the base perimeter came into view. The instant they passed the sign, John rose to five meters in a heartbeat and pushed the throttle to full. This was what most soldiers were doing, so the action blended in well. Moving as fast as the hovercraft could go, John took the first turn that got them out of sight of the HQ. Going through a maze of buildings, John kept driving into the heart of the city until there was no possibility of being seen by snipers from the HQ.

Having gone into the city far enough, John turned into the main highway and cut across town toward where they had hidden their shuttle.

Greg suddenly felt his hair prickle on his neck. He had a sneaking suspicion they were being followed.

He had to be hallucinating. Glancing around, he could see nothing behind, above or below them. Then he caught sight of the others' faces. Carol's eyes plainly showed he felt it as well. Even John's normally neutral expression had signs of worry.

They all looked at each other. Greg began to say, "John …"

"Yeah, I know," John interrupted.

"I don't see anyone," said Carol.

"Doesn't matter. We're getting out of here." As those words left his mouth, John began to weave through traffic in a manner extremely dangerous for all concerned. Subtlety abandoned, John made a beeline for the shuttle. Cutting through traffic, he took the most direct route while Greg called out directions from his map.

Just outside the lot behind the deserted building, John stopped the hovercraft and they got out on foot. The only way to reach the shuttle was through an alleyway that was only a little too small for a hovercraft to fit in.

Feet pounding the ground, they dashed down the alleyway so hard it felt like their lungs were going to burst, but they pretended the pain did not exist, and forced their bodies to go faster.

They burst out of the alley and into the lot. The *Mercy* was waiting for them. Carol never thought he would be happy to see the shuttle.

Running inside from the back, Carol took the helm. Since he did not know most of the preflight checks, he thought he was ready to go in a couple of seconds. As Carol ran through what checks he knew, Greg asked John, "Drop-Com?"

"Drop-Com," John agreed.

Greg went next to Carol and began to remove the communications gear. Before he could finish, he thought he heard the distant wail of police sirens.

Carol turned the engines on and with a roar they came to life. Pointing the nose slowly upward, Carol put the engines at maximum thrust as soon as there was nothing but the fading sun in their eyes. With a lurch they went forward, singeing the tops of nearby buildings.

Greg breathed a sigh of relief. Working faster, he gave a hard pull and the comm. gear came out.

Greg took his recording device he had been issued for the mission. The device had a false log of what they had been doing, and described them as an independent group of humans, allowing for the Alliance and the MAA to deny they had anything to do with the expedition. Turning it on, Greg quickly recorded the location of Earth and rigged the device to the portable radio so the info stored on the recorder would be broadcasted.

Having made these arrangements, Greg walked out the back of the shuttle with John, who opened the rear door a crack. Greg then hit the play button and tossed the recording device out the shuttle. It took a few seconds for the radio to start broadcasting, at which point the shuttle was already a good distance away. The information telling Earth's location was out, and a few seconds later the device hit the ground and was smashed into little pieces.

The FDA of course was monitoring all Alliance frequencies, but they could do nothing to stop the transmission once it was made. However, the one thing they could do was to triangulate the location of the transmission, which they did with astonishing speed, only to discover what they found was a piece of comm. gear falling to the ground. This left them with nothing to identify which spacecraft had made the transmission.

Having but one course of action left, they called the orbiting fleet of battle-ships and ordered them to set up a blockade to stop anything from leaving the atmosphere. It was a futile gesture since by the time the battleships could stop the constant stream of traffic coming and going from the planet, the intruder's shuttle would've made the jump to midspace.

Like always, escaping the atmosphere in the *Mercy* was an adventure all by itself. The shuttle buckled and groaned as it strained to break free of the planet's atmosphere. It was as if the shuttle wanted to fall apart but was forced to stay in one piece against its will. The shuttle seemed to give a sigh and accepted it would have to be in space again when they broke free of the atmosphere.

Coasting in space, Carol could see the battleships' engines begin to warm up. He imagined the FDA was broadcasting a message telling all ships to stop, but since they didn't have comm. gear anymore, he couldn't hear it.

Almost casually, Carol opened a hole to midspace and went inside, going beyond the reach of the FDA.

Still on his way to report to the Council of Generals, the FDA general received an interesting set of orders. He was to halt until further notice, for the HQ had been deemed not secure. Also, all units were to be at maximum alert and prepared for war.

He pondered what this meant. For the HQ to be designated as an unsafe place, raiders must have attacked it. What did the raiders do or take to cause such an increase in alert levels?

"They must have found Earth," he mused aloud when the answer came to him.

Once in midspace, the entire shuttle seemed to relax. Carol turned around and they all looked at each other. Greg said, "We did it."

"Yeah, we did," John agreed.

"Everyone say hello to immortality. As long as the human race survives, we will always be remembered," Carol proclaimed.

"Assuming of course, the 'race doesn't get wiped out in the war that's about to come."

"Always assuming that, of course."

There was a moment of silence, then John asked, "Have either of you ever seen a full-scale war?"

Carol replied, "No, everything we did was small unit actions."

"Never an all-out war," Greg answered, "but I have been in a few battleship battles, and those things are impressive. You can hear the big boom of the guns all round the ship. The massive impact of enemy shells hitting your ship can be felt through the passageways."

"Once I was on one of the gun crews," Greg continued, "a small anti-aircraft artillery gun. I was the rammer, the guy who shoves the shells in the breach. I will never forget that. You have no idea what is going on in the big picture, only what is happening in your little area. The only one of us who was paying any attention to the battle was our targeter. The rest of us just concentrated on whatever our job was; only thinking of what needed to be done to get the ammo to the gun and shoot it.

"Then of course there were the boarding parties, where marines do most of their fighting. That's what most combat operations are for us. So I guess you could say I've been in a war, but never in a land battle."

"All I've ever seen was gang wars, and those are in no way, shape, or form a land war. Well, more precisely, all I've been in is gang wars. I've seen the FDA prosecute a full-blown land war against some militia factions, but I never had anything to do with those. What I saw wasn't pretty. About half a city was leveled in urban combat."

"John, do you think the FDA has the advantage of previous land wars against us?" Greg asked.

"No one has fought a war on this scale in a while. Both sides will be new to it."

"Then it's just a matter of who can adjust to it first, same as any other battle," Carol said.

"You've probably discovered the greatest truth of war."

Greg broke out the deck of cards, and they all played with their minds distracted, thinking about the upcoming war, with the exception of John, whose mind was always on the present. As a result, he won every game until Greg and Carol were forced to snap out of their thoughts and pay attention to the game. Eventually they put the cards away and slept for a good six hours, the longest they had slept without interruption in months.

Carol slept in the escape pod. When he awoke, he walked into the cockpit and looked at the instruments. "We have about an hour to the rendezvous point."

John and Greg rolled out of their bunks and began to get all their gear together. It took them most of the hour to check everything they had.

Greg picked up his sniper rifle. "It's ironic I never got to use this."

"The mission didn't turn out the way any of us expected," Carol agreed.

They had no idea what to expect at the rendezvous. They were told it was a fixed point in deep space where the leaders of the Alliance and the MAA were waiting for their return and were told nothing more in case they were captured.

All their questions were answered when they came out of midspace to the sight of an Alliance battle fleet. Battleships filled the area. The sight of two hundred of the behemoths floating in space took Greg's breath away.

At the center of the fleet was a large drifter dock, which was basically a space station that did not orbit and had the ability to move from place to place. This drifter dock was the biggest John had ever seen.

One of the battleships flashed out "dock here" with a strobe light, but no one on the shuttle could read strobe light. Fortunately, they just assumed they were supposed to land there.

A fighter squadron and a bomber squadron launched to escort them in. They could see the long, sleek noses of the fighters aimed right at them. The fighters had short, heavily slanted wings which projected downward from the bottom of the fighters. The cockpit was near the back of the fighter, with the headrest being formed by the tail that came up behind it. Just below the cockpit, swiveling machine guns were mounted in sockets on both sides. Two engines, one on top of the other, provided the propulsion. In the crack that ran between the two engines were tailfins, which ran downward sharply and extended beyond the engines. These fighters were creatures of grace.

By comparison, the bombers were ungainly hogs, but they packed a punch rivaled by none. They looked like a sideways "I" with a round bump in the middle when viewed from above, but when you saw it from the front, you could see the wings were thicker at their roots, and tapered down to a thin rounded-off point. On the wingtips a set of swiveling machine guns was mounted, and about midway along the wings was another set of machine guns. Sitting on top of the rounded bump in the middle of the "I" was the cockpit. Directly underneath the cockpit was a heavy-caliber gun that could dish out a load of EMP shells on a capital ship, taking out its computer-controlled defense rifles. Two huge rectangular engines poked out of the back, and on the top and bottom of each of these engines, rudders came out, jutting away from the spacecraft.

None of these spacecraft carried missiles—for that matter, the Alliance Assault Shuttle was the only spacecraft to carry missiles. The reason was simple. Computer-controlled defense guns, more properly called "defense pistols," for they weren't much more than a tube two centimeters long, could easily shoot down an incoming missile. The only way to defeat these defenses was to fire enough objects to overwhelm the computerized gun.

Rather than send a swarm of guided missiles at the target, it was much cheaper to make the firing system guided. Fighters used machine guns that could swivel 30-degrees from centerline and fire 30 millimeter bullets.

To fire, all the pilot had to do was to maneuver the targeting reticule in the radar screen over the box the computer projected around enemy targets, and then pull the trigger.

———

The Alliance fighter pilot was in the ready room when she heard the call go out. Though her squadron wasn't the one chosen to serve as honor flight, she still felt the excitement.

Now that Earth had been found, she was certain combat would be in her future.

———

As the fighters flew into position around them, Carol could see the pilots pointing at them and obviously commenting on his piloting skills, or more specifically, absence thereof. Carol ignored the insinuating gestures.

Greg said, "Okay, when you look at the battleship, there is a line running along the top and bottom where the two sides meet. When you get closer, you will be able to see the lines are a flat strip running along the centerline. A hangar door will open in bottom, and that's where we enter."

Carol angled them so they were below the battleship. Coming closer, he saw a ramp lower from near the back of the ship. Aiming for the crack in the ramp that would allow him to enter, Carol made big bulky turns since he could not use the rudder pedals. As the closed the distance, they could distinguish the dark blue of the Alliance battleships from the black of FDA ships of war.

They began to pass underneath the battleship. Slowing down as they neared the ramp, the first squadron of fighters preceded them into the hangar.

The entrance had an airlock that forced Carol to stop the shuttle once inside. Once the second squadron came in, the ramp closed behind them. Then the airlock opened, revealing the massive hangar.

Looking about the hangar, they could see a full wing of spacecraft packed into it. Greg knew there was also another full wing above them in the upper levels.

At the end of the hangar a large crowd of mechanics, pilots, and marines had gathered. They were not waiting in any sort of formation, but in a kind of disorganized mob. In front of the crowd "Land Here" had been painted across a landing pad.

Carol was able to set them down in the space, back end facing the crowd. Greg walked up to the door and waited for Carol to get out of the pilot's seat and join him. When Carol was ready, Greg opened the door. As it swung out, a thunderous applause broke out from the Alliance soldiers. Greg came out of the door first and raised his fist, the signal for a successful mission. The applause went from thunderous to deafening. Carol stepped out of the door and the applause rose to ear-shattering. Carol walked up to Greg's left. Then John exited the door.

There was almost a pause in the audience. Some recognized him right away; others didn't and were told who he was by those around them. But they put their doubts about him in storage, for if he was on this mission, he must have done something right.

Carol and Greg parted for John to come between them. John walked up and stood right in the center of them. The three of them stood there and did nothing, simply taking it all in. Though they did not know what they were supposed to do next, they knew if they began to move through the crowd, someone would intercept them and give them directions.

Just as they expected, as they moved through the cheering masses a captain in a pilot's uniform came up to them. "Hello, I'm Captain Udesky. If you'll follow me, I'll lead you to where the politicians and generals are waiting to debrief you."

They made their way through the crowd to the lifts. In a short time they reached their destination.

Chapter 27

The Splitting of the Team

Captain Udesky said, "Here's where you get off. I need to get back to my squadron. Congratulations on finding Earth."

With that they stepped out of the lift. They had come into a conference room colored by the black metal that made up the hull of the ship. The room had a long, smooth oval table in the center. Arranged around the table were the leading politicians and generals of the MAA and the Alliance. There were three empty seats at the nearest end of the table.

Without waiting for an invitation, John sat in one of the seats. Greg and Carol followed his lead, hoping this would make John's move seem a little less impulsive.

Once they were all seated, a couple of politicians and generals gave overly long introductions, thanking everyone for taking the time to be here, and praising the success of the mission. After the three had endured that, a long debriefing commenced in which every little detail of the mission was examined and reexamined by each individual politician and general, although they were all in the same room. After a couple of not-so-subtle hints from John, he was given his payment—which, as he had predicted, was bigger than what had originally been agreed, and the debriefing ended before a fourth hour had passed.

At the end, when the others had left, the head of Alliance Intelligence spoke. "Before you leave, John, I have the answer to your question. I couldn't say this while the room was full, but one of our agents monitoring assassin contractors noticed that Isnen Orday had set up a new organization under a different name. We intercepted their signals and learned they'd hired you to kill a general under the pretext that he was cutting down on illegal arms dealing. While you were eliminating the general, they placed a tracking device on your ship. We traced the device to your mansion and got there faster."

"Greg, did you know about this?" John asked.

"No, I didn't."

"We hadn't received any comm. traffic indicating they were sending assassins so soon. We're truly sorry about that."

"Don't worry, I'll never work for the Alliance again."

"Now, for your own security, neither your names nor pictures will be released to the public, with the exception of John's. Since John's features are widely recognized in the FDA, we see no harm in using his participation in the mission for propaganda. We assume none of the sailors and marines present recognized any of you other than John. Understand, however, this does not guarantee your security, for in all probability your faces have been caught on a security recording at one of the locations you hit. As a last word of caution, do not mention to anyone you participated in this mission."

When the head of Alliance Intelligence finished speaking, an aide escorted them to their quarters. Almost by natural impulse, they all went to John's room and held their own debriefing, one that was more a reminiscing than an evaluation. They had compared notes and opinions on what happened for a while, when a call came through for Carol.

He held up his hand for quiet. "Roger that, I'll be there in couple of minutes."

Carol looked at them. "That was the MAA. They said they need me back with my team to get ready for the assault. There is a shuttle waiting for me in the hangar."

"See you sometime later," Greg said as Carol got up and left the room.

"That was somewhat sudden." Greg turned to John. "You know, I should probably head back to my squad. Rodrigo's been handling my duties while I've been gone. I don't want him to get too used to having my job."

After a second of quiet, Greg asked, "What are you going to do now?"

"I don't know."

"You could come hang out with my squad. You're the best at close-quarters combat I've ever seen, and we snipers really need help in that area. If there is a need for us to be boarding a ship, we're really going to want you with us."

"Sure, why not. I don't lose anything."

They got up and left for the hangar. Greg gave the ranking general notice they were leaving for his squad. When they came to the hangar, there was a shuttle waiting to take them to Greg's battleship. Once on board the shuttle it was a short journey to the ship.

As they landed inside the ship's hangar, Greg faced John. "Welcome to the battleship *Adamant*."

They came out of the shuttle, this time without the cheering crowd. Greg led John over to the lift. Mechanics were busy tuning spacecraft, armorers were stockpiling weaponry, and everyone was generally hurrying around to prepare for the invasion.

Greg came to an information station next to the lift. He asked, "Third battalion, Fourth Marines."

A cross-section of the ship appeared, with a section highlighted in red.

"Second Squad, scout/sniper platoon."

The cross-section zoomed in and highlighted the four rooms that made up the quarters for the squad.

Greg and John entered the lift and went up to the indicated area. The lift stopped and opened to reveal a hallway filled with marines engaged in normal deployment activities—that is, being bored out of their minds and trying to find some way of amusing themselves.

They made their way through the bored marines to the scout/sniper area. A group of snipers were practicing hand to hand combat in the hallway. One of the snipers had the other in a headlock. The second sniper stuck his hand in the headlock to prevent it from closing in on his neck and wrapped his leg around his opponent's leg and pulled hard. As the two of them came tumbling to the ground, the second sniper pushed his hand against the headlock and slid out from underneath. He twisted as he came down and placed his hand against his opponent's neck, which would have resulted in a kill had this been a real fight.

The two combatants stood up. The winner slapped the loser on the back and whispered something that made them both laugh.

"Still haven't lost yet, Lorenzo?" Greg said to the victorious marine.

"No, Sergeant," Lorenzo replied. "Hey Sergeant, I heard you did some interesting things on that last mission. No one gave any details to us, but scuttlebutt is something big is happening."

"Where's Rodrigo?"

"He's in Lieutenant Derek's quarters. He told me to send you his way as soon as you got back. There is some sort of briefing going on there, so I wouldn't miss it."

"Thanks, man."

"No problem, Sergeant." Lorenzo made no mention of John. Lorenzo assumed if he was with Greg, there must be a good reason for it.

Greg went through the somewhat crowded hallway and reached the room at the back. On the top of the doorway was a heading that read "Lieutenant Derek."

"Lieutenant Derek is our officer," Greg told John. "He isn't like the others and had his quarters placed right next to ours. His opinion is that an officer is needed near his troops, and if the other officers want to talk to him, they can give him a call."

In a joking tone, Greg continued, "Though he will never admit this, I personally think he hangs out in the enlisted quarters because military protocol won't let an officer share a room with an enlisted man, so he gets an entire room to himself."

Placing himself at the center of the door, Greg knocked once. A voice said, "Enter." Greg walked in sharp and professionally, a distinct contrast to his dirty and wrinkled uniform. Snapping to attention two paces away from Lieutenant Derek, Greg saluted. "Sergeant Heyligher reporting, sir."

The lieutenant returned the salute. "At ease."

Although "at ease" was a drill position, Greg knew Lieutenant Derek was telling him to relax. Also in the room were Platoon Sergeant Ramon and the two other sergeants in the platoon, plus Corporal Rodrigo, who had been standing in for Greg.

Greg said, "So I heard there was some sort of briefing going on."

Lieutenant Derek replied, "You won't believe this, but we found Earth. We're going to take it back as soon as possible."

"Oh, I heard about that on the way here."

"How was the mission, Heyligher?" Staff Sergeant Ramon asked.

"WBB." Noticing the strange look John was giving him, Greg explained. "It stands for Weird Beyond Belief."

Greg continued, "Lieutenant, do you mind if John joins us? This guy has close-quarter combat down like no one else."

The lieutenant looked at John, studying him. Finally, he asked, "You're the assassin guy who lived on other planets, right?"

"That's me," John replied.

Lieutenant Derek thought about it for a second longer. "It's probably against some regulation, but I've done worse in my career. Welcome to the team."

Then Ramon spoke up, "Okay, that's all for today. Heyligher, the only thing on schedule for your squad is for you to get action ready. All units are to be on thirty-minute alert."

The leaders of the squads stood up and left to prepare as ordered. Greg and Rodrigo walked out discussing how the squad had performed in his absence. John followed at a distance.

They walked to the three rooms that had been set aside for the squad, plus the fourth room that served as quarters for the sergeants in the platoon. Each room held four marines, or at least was supposed to.

Walking to the first room, Rodrigo opened the door and yelled inside, "Squad meeting in ten seconds, out in the hallway. Hey, where the heck is Sandusky?"

"He and Walters went down to the range," said a marine from the room.

"Figures. Well, go see if you can drag the two of them down here," replied Rodrigo.

At the next room, Rodrigo opened this door as before. "Schmidt, where is your fire team?"

"Walters went down to the range with Sandusky. Lorenzo's giving hand-to-hand-combat lessons, and White just went down to infantry country to try to beat Sergeant Hanson at chess, again," Corporal Schmidt replied lazily.

"Find them. Get them in the hallway. We're having a squad meeting right now."

Upon reaching the last room, Rodrigo entered it and came back out apologetically, saying, "My entire fire team is gone, Sergeant."

"Hey Corporal, Brauner said to tell you he was going to beat the pull-up record. Yangkin and Lynch decided to come along and see him do it," a sniper in the hallway informed Rodrigo.

"Thank you, Lance Corporal McAlister." He turned to Greg. "Sergeant, do you mind if we wait a few minutes to start this thing? I don't want to give Brauner an excuse for not being able to beat the record."

"You mean to tell me Brauner is trying to beat that thing again?" Greg was dumbfounded. "I thought I'd talked him out of it."

"You did, but a couple of weeks after you left he decided to try it again. I figured when he tore a muscle he would give up, but he hasn't done that yet," Rodrigo replied.

In the next couple of minutes the squad assembled in the hallway in front of their rooms. The last to come was Brauner, right after Yangkin and Lynch came in and announced once again Brauner had failed.

Once they were all there, Greg began his briefing. "Okay guys, the first thing is, I'm back, and the mission was a success. Can't say what it was about, though.

"Second, I'm certain most of you have heard it already, but in case you haven't, Earth has been found, and we're going to take it back.

"Last thing, I would like for you guys to meet John. This guy was our team leader on the mission and you will never see anyone better than him on the battlefield. He isn't a sniper, but he will be on the quick-relief crew in case one of you gets into trouble. Also, he will be with us when we do boardings, and when we board a ship, you do whatever he tells you. As far you're concerned, he is the top of the chain of command. Okay, do I need to go over anything again?"

Greg looked around. "No? Good, then let's get started."

The squad broke up to accomplish the various tasks. Sandusky and Walters went to the armory to get the squad's weapons. When on thirty-minute alert, all weapons were moved from the armory to the gun lockers in each fire team's room. McAllister and Lynch went to work cleaning out the gun lockers, since the lockers had been used to store miscellaneous items. White, Lorenzo, and Brauner went to draw supplies, going to the supply room to get everything the squad would need to live a week on the battlefield. The remainder of the squad was busy finding and arranging the various pieces of gear so they could be grabbed quickly if the call to arms was sounded.

While this was going on, John took Greg aside. "So who exactly am I going to be working with?"

"Ah, forgot about that. Each fire team provides one assaulter, whose job is to be as good with their battle rifle as their sniper rifle. They're basically there in case we get into trouble, at which point they'll heroically sacrifice themselves to let the rest of us get away."

John pondered that. "Okay, but that still doesn't answer my question. Who are my coworkers?"

"Well, you got Sandusky and Walters, who are pretty good. You see, they used to be the worst shots in the squad, so I told them if they ever outshoot me they'd get three days leave. Since then it's been impossible to get them away from the range."

"Who's the third guy?"

"That'd be Yangkin. He's mostly normal."

"What'll the sleeping arrangements be?"

"Each of the fire teams has its own room, arranged so fire team one is the first and fire team three is the closest to the back. There is a room the four sergeants in this platoon share. If you ever need me, there's a good thirty percent chance that's where I'll be. As for yourself, check with Lieutenant Derek; see if he comes up with a room. If you'll excuse me, I've got to go over to the NCO room and get it to thirty minute alert."

Greg walked down to the NCO room and went to work.

Standing around for a second, John decided to do as Greg suggested and went down to see Lieutenant Derek.

Chapter 28

In the Routine

John almost considered knocking on the door, but it just wasn't his style, so he walked right on in.

Lieutenant Derek was standing over the small desk he had in the back of the room, looking at some bit of meaningless paper work he was required to do.

Hearing someone enter, Lieutenant Derek spun around and was momentarily surprised until he remembered John had joined their platoon. "Whoa, you caught me off guard."

"I was told you could find me a room."

"Uh, yeah, as matter of fact, I can. Just drop your stuff right here. I've had a room to myself for way too long, so I guess its time to share," Lieutenant Derek analyzed John as he spoke. He wasn't bothered that John had entered the room without knocking, since he also preferred to ignore common civilities whenever possible, but he was beginning to wonder what kind of person John was.

"Thanks." John began to take off his weapons and gear.

He had not let his medium-sized SMG out of his arms since he did not have a place to put it, but now he laid it down on the gun locker, and took out his small SMG and his remaining pistol. Looking at them carefully, he saw they were still in decent condition, but he took them apart and cleaned them anyway. He removed the small flecks of dirt that had managed to make their way inside and oiled all the moving parts. Having done this, he placed his weapons inside the gun locker, but kept his pistol in his upper left pocket.

Once his weapons were secured, John looked and saw the lieutenant had removed the second bunk bed from the room, and had only kept the first bunk bed to make more room. John walked over to the top bunk and set what was left of his gear upon it.

John was not happy with what was left. He had no grenades, no explosives, and no breaching devices, but he did have six breaching charges he had not brought along during the raid on the FDA HQ.

He asked Lieutenant Derek, "Is there a place I can get breaching devices and explosives?"

"Try the armory; maybe they will let you have them. Actually, I should probably come with you because I seriously doubt they will give away stuff like that to anyone other than a marine officer."

The two of them stepped out of the room together and walked at an almost lazy pace. Derek tried to talk with John to get an understanding of him. He had often wondered if John really was the emotionless killer people said he was. Professionally, he considered it worth his while to figure out John's emotional status to discover the mental side effects of killing a large number of beings in cold blood, something a sniper also did.

Derek began to ask some probing questions. "So, what was the mission like?"

"I take it you mean the one I was just on?"

"Uh, yeah, that one."

"Like they say, hours of boredom punctuated by moments of sheer adrenaline rush."

"I always thought it was hours of boredom punctuated by moments of sheer terror."

"It might be, but we really weren't all that scared. Mostly it was just trying to accomplish the next task."

"So basically, it was a normal combat mission, except a little harder and with higher stakes."

"That's about the sum of it."

Derek deduced John was not interested in talking. He decided it would be best to shut up and avoid becoming pushy.

They picked up the explosives and breaching devices at the armory without saying so much as a word, but for some reason the silence wasn't uncomfortable. John had that effect on people, making them feel more comfortable by not talking.

A bit of time was spent getting to thirty-minute alert, but once all sections had reported ready, the predeployment activities began. For infantry units, that meant hitting the assault course and rifle range. In supporting units, that meant stocking and restocking every piece of equipment, making sure everything worked. The sniper units spent most of their time on the range.

When Greg's squad was on the range, he invited John to shoot with them. The range was a fifty-meter-long open area with a yellow stripe no soldier was to go past. This yellow stripe marked the firing line. Soldiers stood behind it on red X's and fired their weapons.

The targets were electronic circles at shoulder level, which flashed red when hit. Because the range was only fifty meters long, the size of the targets varied from a human head to something so small only a sniper scope could pick it up. This simulated longer ranges, the theory being if you can hit a one-centimeter target at fifty meters you can hit a humanoid at five hundred meters.

Actual bullets were not fired. Although the hull of the ship could stop the bullet, the bullet would ricochet around inside the range, so target lasers were affixed to the muzzle of the rifle.

The sniper platoon was on the range, each squad having its own area. Someone was supposed to be a designated range safety officer, but none of the snipers listened to that regulation. Instead, they got down to the serious business of shooting.

Looking at the squad, John could see most of them were using the twelve-kilometer target, and Sandusky, Walters, and Greg were having some sort of competition at twenty kilometers, the longest one available. Each of them fired five times. Greg's target flashed red all five times, Sandusky's and Walters' four times each.

Leaving Sandusky and Walters to work on their shooting, Greg walked over to John. "They are getting close. I'll have to change the rules so only direct bull's eyes count."

John asked, "How do you guys manage to hit at twenty kilometers?"

"It really isn't all that hard. The scope allows us to zoom in so the target looks like it's only five hundred meters away. Then we make the repulse-lifters on the rifle heavy enough so it won't move without a good amount of force. The bipod on the front of the rifle allows for even more stability. The rest is just good form, proper trigger pull, and the little details, plus a lot of time spent on the range," Greg explained.

"I'm curious; since you weren't allowed on other planets, what did you snipers do?"

"Well, an average space station is about 200 kilometers above a planet's surface. So what we do is we get on top of a space station and fire a heat-protected bullet at a target on the planet below. A satellite that is linked to our scope sends electronic guidance to the bullet to keep it on target, while gravity keeps our bullets fast. By the time the bullet is far enough down to be caught in an EMP field, it's on track and will cross the distance so quickly nothing new can disrupt it."

He continued, "Since you need to have the right angle to get through the atmosphere, there are only a few places on a space station you can shoot from. Sniper battles spring up around those places as each side tries to deny the other access. I'll tell you, if anyone says the top of a space station is smooth they're lying. Tons of dents, divots, and debris make the outside of space stations excellent hiding places."

"I never saw any of this going on."

"Something would be wrong if you did. We're good at what we do."

"Is there a place here where I can work on shooting on the move?"

"Yeah, there's a couple of empty positions at the end of the range you can use."

John fitted his SMG with a laser and turned his eye-sights off. He began to run sideways back and forth along the open area. He shot at the head-sized targets fifty meters away, at first slowly, and then faster and faster as he got into his groove. Every time a laser left his SMG, the target flashed red.

Heads began to turn toward him until the entire platoon was watching him.

Lieutenant Derek was the first to speak. "How long did it take you to learn to shoot like that?"

"Years."

"How are you at long ranges?" Sandusky asked John.

"I can shoot to about five hundred meters."

"So you do most of your fighting at close ranges."

"Most of the time."

"When we board a ship, you need to hang around the assaulters."

Everyone returned to the range and began shooting again.

John had proven he was worthy of their respect. In the following three days, he began to blend in with the normal squad activities, always taking a part in what the squad had to do, even the pointless tasks they were assigned.

———

Staff Sergeant Ethan Ramon was looking forward to a good night's sleep. The last few days had been incredibly hectic, with little time for rest.

It's what—one or two weeks till the wedding, he thought with pleasure. As his eyes closed and he drifted off to sleep, his mind went back to the day he asked the question.

Rosanna was sitting at the table with a huge smile on her face. Despite his best attempts, his nervousness had shown through the entire night. Though she didn't say anything, he suspected she knew.

Taking one last drink to stiffen his resolve, he pulled the ring and dropped to his knees.

"NO!" she screamed.

Ethan was confused. Rosanna hadn't said no; she had leapt from her seat and kissed him.

Then she screamed again.

Snapping his eyes open, Ramon awoke with a start. He heard a shout come from the bunk above him.

Climbing up, he saw Sergeant Heyligher thrashing and turning. Heyligher was yelling incoherently.

"They're not dead, they couldn't be," Heyligher shouted. "I'm not that person. It's all a dream, it's all a dream, it can't be true. What in the 'verse is chasing us?"

Ethan put a hand on Heyligher to wake him. Heyligher reacted instantly, grabbing the hand and twisting, then rolled out of bed, bringing Ramon down with him.

Raising his hand, Heyligher was about to deliver a killing blow when Ethan said, "Gregory, you know me. We've been on a first-name basis for years. Snap out of it."

Panting heavily, Greg lowered his hand and leaned back. At length he spoke, "I'm sorry about that. It was just a nightmare."

The other two sergeants had been awakened by now. Ramon told them, "It was a bad dream."

Nodding in understanding, the sergeants went back to bed. Every marine suffered the same dreams where they relived their close calls.

Ethan was concerned. "You want to talk about this?"

Greg shook his head. "I can't."

"Can you still lead your squad?"

"I can, but please don't tell the lieutenant about this. It would just be unnecessary stress, for him."

Slightly disturbed at what he'd seen, Ethan helped Gregory back into bed. Lying on his own bunk, Ramon wondered what could possibly have happened to make Gregory act this way.

——

After three days, while John and Greg were at the firing range, a call came in from Carol. "John, Greg, can the two of you read me?"

"We hear you man," Greg answered.

"Great, now listen guys. The MAA is about to launch an assault on Earth. They are sick of the debating on a plan and are going to take it now. Can't say I blame them, but you guys know the MAA is not strong enough to take Earth alone. Try to get the Alliance to move. The MAA is en route as I speak, so there is nothing I can do to stop them. Got to go. See you guys soon."

"The race is doomed," said Greg.

"Always was," replied John. "Come on, we need to tell Derek."

They told Lieutenant Derek the news.

"Well, if it comes from me they won't believe it. I would recommend John gives the politicians a call. They'll believe him the most."

"I was hoping you would be the one to talk with the politicians," John said.

"Sorry to disappoint."

"Somehow I doubt that." John called a leading politician. He got them an on the line. "This is John. The MAA has just …"

John hung up. "The politician told me they had just received a message from the MAA telling them this already. He was telling me to hang up when I cut him off."

"John, you are the only person who can turn being told to hang up against someone," Derek replied.

"It really is impressive, isn't it."

In about ten minutes, the ship sounded general quarters. The marines at thirty-minute alert were ready in fifteen and all sections reported ready in twenty minutes. The snipers had assembled near one of the engines, the area they were to defend in case of boarding parties.

Once all departments had signaled ready to go, an announcement came over the loudspeaker about what the MAA had done. All units were to prepare for immediate launch.

Naturally, being told to be ready for immediate launch was entirely different from the actual command to launch. After the first couple of hours, the marines began to stand down, allowing themselves to lie on the floor and rest. At least one soldier stayed awake and alert, but the others were dozing off. Once hour number five had passed, John lost his patience.

"I'm going to find out what the delay is."

"Good luck with that," Derek said.

John took the nearest lift to the bridge. Unlike the FDA, the Alliance did not have checkpoints to enter the bridge, since they had not had as many ship's captains assassinated.

Coming out onto the bridge, John looked around. He was at the back of the bridge. In front of him was a large transparent-steel window. The floor slanted so those in the back could see over the heads in front of them. Three rows of fifteen seats each lined the bridge from end to end. In front of each seat was a control panel. On a level below these, there was one big seat in the middle. This was the captain's chair, and in the oversized armrest were the controls to everything in the ship.

Seeing that only about half the positions on the bridge were occupied, John asked, "Is the captain on the auxiliary bridge?"

The primary bridge was located in the center of the tiny concave indentation at the front of the ship. Any spacecraft that tried to get to the bridge would have to go through a concentrated crossfire.

The auxiliary bridge differed from the primary bridge only in location. It was located on the forward third of the flat strip that ran along the topside of the battleship, allowing the captain to better observe the battle.

"The captain left the ship for the command center on the drifter dock some hours ago," a bridge officer said, recognizing who John was.

"Get me a shuttle to take me there."

The bridge officer quickly scrolled along his console. "The Assault Shuttle *Easy Rider* will take you to the command center."

John nodded and took the nearest lift to the hangar.

Once in the hangar, he turned to an information station and looked up the shuttle *Easy Rider*.

John briefly glanced at the shuttle. Like all Alliance spacecraft, it was colored dark blue. It was long enough to hold sixty-three troops, but so thin it had two rows of twenty-one seats each on either side, forcing the remaining twenty-one soldiers to sit on the floor. The Assault Shuttle's main hull was a round tube with the cockpit at one end and a door at the other. The hull was tapered slightly so the three engines on each side overlapped each other. Able to separately rotate in 360-degrees, the engines provide steering as well as thrust.

To increase the aerodynamics for more efficient atmospheric traveling, a set of short wings was mounted on the top of the shuttle and a set of canards just behind the cockpit, plus a small tail with its top cut off near the back. On that cut-off top was a small turret with an antispacecraft machine gun.

Assuming a shuttle was weakly armed would be a fatal mistake. Along with the tail gun, either side of the shuttle had twin automatic-tracking, antispacecraft machine guns. Racks along the wings carried up to four missiles per wing to clear a landing area.

John went around to the back of the shuttle. Held up by four skids, the shuttle was a meter off the ground, requiring John to make a short hop into it. A loadmaster came behind him pushing a crate on a repulse-lifter cart. The cart elevated the crate so it slid into the shuttle with ease. The loadmaster hopped aboard the shuttle and hollered to the pilots, "Okay, we're ready to go."

The two pilots turned on the engines and the shuttle rose into the air. Pushing a few buttons on the cart, the loadmaster secured the crate in place. "I hope you don't mind I brought along the crate, sir. We're supposed to have two full squadrons of twelve shuttles apiece, but like everyone else we only have ten spacecraft per squadron, still enough to land a battalion in one wave, but it makes us hard pressed to accomplish other tasks."

"It's not a problem."

It was a short flight. In a couple of minutes John was out of the shuttle and inside the command center.

The command center was a large room with a great many maps and figures on the wall, each showing a different part of the 'verse. Marine generals, naval admirals, and ship's captains crowded around the politicians in the middle of the room. The politicians were standing next to a large map in center.

Forcing his way through the crowd, John walked up to where the leading politicians and admirals were speaking. He almost had to yell to be heard. "There has been a five-hour delay. What is the holdup?"

The crowd began to quiet. One of the politicians said, "About an hour after the message was received, the MAA began its assault on Earth. Word got out quickly, and it seems the FDA has advance contingency plans. They sent in a fleet of battleships to deal with the MAA and have five other squadrons waiting a half-hour's jump from Earth. If we try to engage the Earth fleet, the others will hit us from behind. If we try to take out one of the other squadrons, the rest will jump us. Right now we do not have enough battleships available to fight all six forces at once. By the time we gather the necessary force, the MAA will be annihilated."

"You've made your own paradox," John said. "You're not considering what the MAA will do. Knowing the MAA, the first thing they've done is infiltrate the civilian alien populace. The FDA can't bombard them into submission; there would be civilian casualties."

"What makes you think that would stop them," someone shouted.

"The FDA are not monsters. They see themselves as the defenders of their way of life. Killing civilians is not something they do," John replied. "The FDA response will be to evacuate the noncombatants. Once only military targets are left, the FDA will prosecute total war. The FDA knows the MAA will allow them to remove the civilians because the MAA would have to get rid of the civilians anyway, so both sides benefit."

A politician interrupted John. "Which means the annihilation of the MAA will be put off for a few more days—still not enough time to get the necessary reinforcements."

"The solution is simple. Where are the nearest FDA supply depots?"

An admiral spoke up, "I see what you're getting at, but it doesn't have any effect on the modern battlefield. Battleships carry enough supplies to last their ground forces some time."

"Admiral, if you had ever seen a land war, you would understand how many stores a single day takes up. One day of fighting takes up what is normally a week's worth of ammunition. In five days you'll be out of ammo."

A second admiral interrupted John, "I found where the supply dumps are. The three nearest are the planets Hegin, Marselo, and Taam, all in the same solar system. They're about seven hours from Earth. The closest after those are weeks away."

"All three are in the same solar system? This makes everything easier. Now you turn the paradox back on them. Jump what ships you have to the supply dumps. They will be forced to decide which they are going to lose. If they come at the fleet taking the supplies, you jump away and take out the Earth fleet. If they just sit on Earth, you take out their supplies. If they split their forces, you defeat them in detail. Although the MAA made a mistake, they have unknowingly provided you the opportunity to take Earth."

There was a quiet over the whole room. One of the admirals finally broke the silence, "It could work. Gerald, where are the nearest reinforcements for the FDA?"

Hitting a couple of buttons on the map next to him, Admiral Gerald said, "There are three fleets coming in, here, here, and here." He pointed out positions on the map. "With all those reinforcements coming, they are going to split their force because they have doubled their original size and that will allow them to hold both objectives."

A general added, "There're a couple of FDA divisions on Hqurat. Their First Fleet will stop there to pick up those. Our Third Fleet could intercept them there."

"It looks like the other two FDA fleets are going to rendezvous at Garth. The Sixth Fleet doesn't have enough power to stop their combined forces, but we can delay them for some time," added another admiral.

A ship's captain said, "As soon as they hear we have taken up position over their supply bases, they are going to redirect their Second and Third Fleets toward us, and their First Fleet toward Earth. The FDA around Earth will send half of their force toward us at the supply base, and leave the other to defend Earth, expecting the other fleets to meet up with them at their destinations and create a two-pronged assault. If we stop the reinforcing FDA fleets, we can take out what is thrown at us."

The ranking admiral finished the discussion. "It looks like we have a plan. Captains, tell your ships to launch on my command to the supply depot. You're all dismissed."

The captains left in a rush to get to their ships. John was a little faster than the captains and managed to get back aboard the *Adamant* before the captain arrived, which was fortunate because as soon the captain was aboard, the order was give to launch.

Coming back to the sniper platoon, John said, "I got them moving. We're going to war."

Cheering broke out from the snipers. Then an announcement came over the loudspeaker and told the whole ship the news. More wild cheering erupted throughout the ship. It was what they were waiting for, this war.

The ship launched into midspace along with the rest of the fleet, bearing their innocent occupants to a hell none of them could have comprehended.

Chapter 29

Earth

Carol was cold, but not wet since his diamond armor prevented that. Rain poured down on him. Though he could not see them, he knew the rest of Assault Team Blue was nearby.

He was walking down an abandoned alley in one of the cities on Earth. The FDA had evacuated the city to a point about five hundred meters away. Huge, empty buildings just below the size of skyscrapers made the city feel even more desolate. Carol hugged the side of the alley, trying to stay in the shadows. Night vision wasn't working; the FDA had already emplaced their EMP fields.

Making his footsteps almost noiseless, Carol continued to creep closer to the FDA lines. While evacuating the civilians, the FDA had set up a perimeter around the areas that had not been evacuated, and slowly closed that perimeter as more and more civilians left Earth. The MAA constantly put pressure on the perimeter to encourage them to speed up the evacuation and to keep themselves so close to the FDA a naval bombardment could not be used for fear of hitting their own soldiers. Carol was on one of these raids right now.

He was almost there. Carol dropped into the prone and crawled the rest of the way to the corner. Moving forward until his head and rifle poked out around the corner, Carol could make out the shapes of FDA soldiers on the perimeter, only thirty meters away.

Small metal blocks—the equivalent of sandbags—were built into bunkers about fifteen meters apart. They stretched across the park in front of which the FDA had made their perimeter. On the tops of the buildings surrounding the park, several bunkers provided support to soldiers on the ground.

Unable to see his sights in the dark, he looked at the head of one of the soldiers in front of him and trusted in his ability to shoot instinctively. In the sky above him, Carol spotted a small light over the FDA position, so high the EMP field had no effect on it. *There's the signal*, he thought. The small light suddenly burst out into a flare, held up by repulse-lifters so it wouldn't come down.

As the light exploded over the area, Carol took aim with his now visible sights and opened fire on the soldier he had spotted before. Seeing the head jerk back, Carol switched his aim to one of the bunkers on top of the buildings. The fire from the rest of Assault Team Blue joined his and a brisk skirmish had begun.

Scattered around the area, Assault Team Blue seemed greater in numbers than they really were. They fired from a variety of positions, mostly uncoordinated, but it had the effect of confusing the enemy as to their actual location.

Carol let loose a long burst at a rooftop bunker. He knew at this point in the battle both sides would have taken cover and neither side would be able to hit anything.

A couple of flares shot out from the FDA lines, illuminating the area in front of them. Carol froze and was still so the FDA soldiers would not spot him. Then he heard one of the bunkers in front of him open fire on an exposed team member.

Swinging his rifle onto the target, Carol fired a couple of bursts, causing the soldiers in the bunker to duck. Getting to his feet, Carol continued to fire short bursts at the bunker. He ran sideways as fast as he could to the exposed team member, paralleling the FDA lines. Several soldiers tried to shoot at him, but they were quickly suppressed by other team members.

Once he reached the Assault Team member, the two of them began to fall back in turns, one retreating as the other provided cover, and then switching. As soon as they reached the nearest door, they went into it and out of the street.

Taking refuge in the store they had entered, they waited for the controller to turn off their flare. Looking into the sky, Carol saw their flare fade away and return to the controller. That was the signal to shoot down the FDA flares. A couple of well-placed shots and the flares winked out of existence.

In the sudden darkness, everyone was temporally blinded, and Assault Team Blue used those couple of seconds to make its escape.

Arriving breathless at the forward base, the team member Carol had saved said, "Thanks."

"No problem." Carol caught his breath.

When his breath had returned to him, Carol walked inside the forward base, which was set up in the bottom of an old apartment building. The lowest level was filled with command and control equipment, the other levels served as quarters for several of the Assault Teams.

Waved over to a group of senior Team members, one of them asked Carol, "How did you think the raid went?"

"It didn't go badly, but not great either. I think we got a couple of soldiers in the beginning, but then nobody hit anyone else."

"It kind of looked like that from my vantage point. At least we didn't lose anyone," Carol's senior team member agreed. "Before I forget, High Command has said we need to break up into cells. The FDA has withdrawn enough they can begin bombardment on us in a couple of days. We need to make sure our casualties are minimal should they locate and hit one of our safe houses."

"I'll go inform the men."

Carol walked around the apartment building and gathered up all the Assault Team Blue members. Three Assault Teams—Blue, Green and Maroon—had been placed in the same area to have enough strength to repel a strong enemy attack, but it quickly became apparent that was not their biggest problem. In the hours they had been on Earth, the only real threat they had was from the orbiting battleships.

Once all twenty-six members of Assault Team Blue were gathered, Carol gave them a heads-up on the situation, and the team members broke up into their predictated cells. Each of the cells went out looking for a safe house while Carol waited at the forward base for them to return. Assault Teams had only a senior team member for leadership, but often Carol served as the unofficial second in command.

Taking a seat on one of the couches in the lobby, Carol wondered what John and Greg were doing.

—◆—

At that same moment, John and Greg were also wondering what they were doing. It had the distinct feeling of nothing, but it had to be something as they had been ordered to do it.

John was sitting with Greg in the hallway along with most of the other marines. They were bored out of their minds, exactly as they had been before the orders to set sail had been given. The last exciting thing had happened an hour ago when they had been called to general quarters as they emerged from midspace. They stood down when it became clear the enemy wasn't going to appear anytime soon.

Some of the battleships were allowed to commence bombardment of the supply depots, but theirs had not been one of them.

John had a bored look. "I never expected war to be this bad."

"You have to admit, when they say you can have your head turned into mush in war, you assume they are talking literally," Greg replied.

"What do you guys do while waiting for something to happen?"

"This. We sit around doing nothing. We can't do any training or go to the range because we might need to get to our stations in a hurry. Anything remotely entertaining cannot be done for fear we have to deploy rapidly. We can't play cards because—wait a minute—we can play cards. Why hadn't I thought of that before?"

"Probably because you haven't had to think for the past few hours."

"It sounds like a reasonable explanation." Greg dashed to his bunk to retrieve his deck.

A couple of marines joined them and soon they had a game going. Naturally, ten minutes after they started the game an announcement came over the loudspeakers.

"Attention all hands. An enemy transport convoy has arrived. Picket fighters have disabled their midspace drives. Currently the enemy is attempting to flee in real space. We have been given the task of capturing these ships for our own use. All hands general quarters."

"Finally, something exciting," Greg said.

"Don't get your hopes up. In all probability we are just going to guard the engine," John replied as he stood up.

The two of them began a lazy jog to their station. When they arrived, the sniper platoon was waiting for them. Taking a seat, Greg and John pulled out their cards again and began to play.

Lieutenant Derek asked, "What do the two of you think you're doing?"

"A game of chance in which skill is needed to deduct your opponent's hand and what he is going to do with that hand," John answered. "Seriously, what do you think we should be doing? We are not near a window, we do not have a critical job, and if we are called to action the cards can be picked up in an instant."

"Good point. Deal me in," Derek took seat next to them.

Ramon joined them and the chase was swiftly forgotten.

While to the marines the whole chase was boring, for those on the bridge it was somewhat exciting. The battleship was faster than the convoy, but the convoy had a good head start. Fighters had been deployed and had overtaken the convoy. The convoy did not heed their command to heave to. The Alliance captain realized they were trying to fix their midspace drive, so he ordered the ship's engineers to put them in the red.

Traveling faster than they should, they still took an hour to catch up with the convoy. When the battleship commanded the convoy to heave to, this time the convoy listened. Small boarding parties went aboard to assume control of the ships, and the convoy leader and the captain began to work out terms of surrender.

In the middle of their talks, an excited ensign came up to the captain. "Sir, do you have a moment?"

The captain came over and the ensign whispered, "Sir, the enemy has just attacked our fleet."

"Tell the XO to do nothing. By the time we reach the battle it will be over, and the distance is too short for a midspace jump."

The ensign looked wistfully out the window, wishing he could be in the battle. Then he turned aside and carried out his orders.

—◦—

Those inside the battle were not feeling quite as romantic as the young ensign. Several convoys had appeared before the battle, requiring battleships to chase them down. The Alliance was down to 189 battleships when the FDA appeared. There were 203 FDA ships, causing a slight disadvantage in numbers for the Alliance.

The Alliance line of battle was facing outward, pointing toward Earth, where they expected the FDA to appear. The FDA also expected to appear there, but they overshot and came out of midspace on the other side of the planet.

The two lines of battle pulled straight up until they were vertical. Once vertical, the ships began to twist down and backward. Both sides leveled out, bows aimed at each other.

A brief moment of peace was observed, then it was shattered by the thunderous roar of the battleships discharging all their weapons at once. The luminescent tails given off by the shells streaked across the space above the planet Hegin. Gunners adjusted their aim from where the luminescent tails had ended, then fired again. Fighters and bombers began to streak out from the holds of battleships. The battle had begun.

The flagship of the Alliance fleet, the *Star King*, was lined up across from the FDA flagship, the *Rylock*, both in the center of their respective battle lines. They began to maneuver toward each other, pouring out torrents of fire as they went, making the space between them almost a wall of luminescent tails.

Alliance captains usually came up through the fighter ranks, whereas FDA captains usually served on battleships their entire career, making the FDA superior tacticians. But the Alliance knew how to employ their fighter wings better.

The *Rylock* began to descend below the *Star King* with it bow still pointed up at it. Thinking his enemy had made a mistake, the *Star King* maintained its position, aiming its bow at the *Rylock*, but keeping its bow pointed slightly above the *Rylock's* because there were more vital areas on top. The two of them continued their rotation around their horizontal axes, the *Rylock* moving a little downward and the *Star King* a little upward.

Suddenly, the *Rylock* locked a tractor beam onto the *Star King*, using it as a pivot to rapidly sweep its aft up. The *Star King* tried to follow the *Rylock*, but could not because of the tractor beam. The *Rylock* continued to sweep its aft upward until it was upside down and on the *Star King's* rear. Rolling to the left and pulling back hard, the *Star King* attempted to shake the *Rylock*, but the *Rylock* rolled with them, leveling out as they followed the turn.

The *Rylock* was on the battleship's sweet spot. The rear of the battleship had few guns because the engines were there, making it practically defenseless. Despite its desperate maneuvers, the *Star King* could not rid itself of the *Rylock*, and the *Rylock* pounded away on the *Star King's* engines, causing heavy damage.

The *Star King* would have been destroyed had not its one-man fighters and bombers come sweeping down in an attack on the *Rylock's* bridge. The FDA general concentrated most of the antispacecraft fire in defense of the bridge to keep himself alive. While this was happening, two gunships came swooping down along the side of the FDA battleship.

Gunships were massively overarmed small spacecraft used to man picket lines. They were designed to survive the first couple of minutes in an encounter with a battleship, long enough to warn the fleet of the incoming enemy. The Alliance version had a triangular cockpit with the nose blunted, and a long, thick body with low-drooping wings. Arrayed around the gunship were three twin 40 millimeter cannons, four triple-barreled 40 millimeter cannons, eight twin machine guns, and a massive twin 70 millimeter cannon. To propel it, four large engines set in pods of two were placed at the back. It was manned by two pilots, two mechanics, and sixteen marines who served as gunners and could be used as a boarding party if needed.

Running down the left side of the battleship, the pair of gunships let loose their terrible barrage, lathering their fire along the side of the battleship. Because most of the FDA's defenses were employed protecting the bridge, the gunships were unhindered.

There was an explosion amidships on the FDA battleship. Unsecured junk was sucked out of the hole the gunships had created. Emergency doors closed and sealed off the breach, but the damage was done. The *Rylock* could no longer turn right as the engine that faced sideways had been destroyed.

Taking immediate advantage of this, the *Star King* turned hard and came around to the *Rylock's* tail. Already crippled on one side, the *Rylock* did not last long against the *Star King's* furious revenge. Blue light played across the *Rylock's* engines as more and more shells got past the defense rifles and released their EMP charges. Soon all the defense rifles had been knocked out by the EMPs and shells went deep into the engines, knocking out the electronics needed to keep the ship running. The *Rylock* drifted out of the battle, disabled and not much more than a gutted hulk.

Unfortunately for the Alliance, the *Star King* had also suffered massive amounts of damage and had to withdraw from the battle shortly after knocking out the *Rylock*.

At the other end of the battle, two clever Alliance battleship captains did a scissor maneuver together. One got an FDA battleship on its rear and the other came screaming out of the sun and behind the FDA battleship. The Alliance captains had taken out two battleships using this method, when both of them got an FDA battleship on their back.

The captains turned their battleships toward each other, allowing them to fire upon the battleship on the other's tail. The FDA battleships were forced shift their fire to the greater threat. It turned into a slugging match as the battleships faced each other and unleashed full frontal barrages.

Shells sailed by each other, slamming into opposing battleships. Numerous explosions appeared in front of the battleships as defense rifles stopped them, but others got through the screen and played blue light over the surface they had impacted.

Huge chunks of battleship drifted off as the main batteries chewed up the metal hulls. The bodies of crewmen sucked out by the vacuum flashed when the light of the sun hit their diamond armor. Occasionally, a fighter crashed into a cloud of debris, detonating in a brilliant flash.

Neither side could take that amount of punishment for long. The battle might have gone either way, except the Alliance captains kept their backs to each other. Additional fire from the rear guns was added to the other's fusillade. The small increase of firepower was enough to win the fight. Lights on the FDA ships flashed on and off three times, the signal for quarter.

After winning that conflict, the Alliance captains sent marine boarding parties to take control of the FDA ships, then retired, for they had taken too much damage to continue to fight.

This excellent teamwork did much to turn the battle in the Alliance's favor, defeating four Federation battleships at the cost of two of their own ships being forced out of the battle. But by no means was the action decisive, for the FDA still had the advantage in numbers, and was giving as good as they took.

Chapter 30

Sneaky

The opposing lines of battle above Hegin had meshed into one. Caught in a whirlpool of dueling ships, Alliance and FDA fighters and bombers clashed in swirling battles.

The hotshot Alliance fighter pilot had two FDA fighters on her tail. She flipped her fighter around so she was still flying forward but her fighter's nose was pointed at the fighters following her. Just before the fighters opened fire on her, she threw her fighter into a sideways spin, constantly varying the throttle. The targeting computers on the FDA fighters predicted where she would be next based on her current heading and speed, but since her speed was changing randomly, all of their shots went wild. The Alliance fighter pilot locked onto the far fighter and held down the trigger as she continued the spin, taking out both FDA fighters in the same burst.

Looking for a new target, the Alliance fighter pilot spotted an FDA bomber making a solo run on a battleship. The FDA bomber was simply a FDA fighter with half of the engine cut out and an automatic EMP cannon put in its place. Although it was twice as slow as the fighter version, the bomber packed a considerable punch. The Alliance fighter pilot lined up behind the bomber, but before she could pull the trigger the bomber juked hard left and began to execute small side slips, making it difficult for the Alliance pilot to put her targeting reticule over it.

Unable to get a lock, the Alliance pilot suddenly went straight down. The bomber pilot, momentarily losing sight of her, stopped side-slipping for a second to bank down and reacquire her. That was all she needed. Flipping her targeting reticule over the bomber, the Alliance pilot held down the trigger and obliterated the bomber.

Taking a glance behind her, the Alliance pilot caught a quick glimpse of the shark-fin wings of an FDA fighter settling behind her. Instantly she threw her fighter into a series of side slips, just barely missing a burst of fire that raked her previous position. A short burst was fired at her again but her defense rifle caught these shots.

The Alliance fighter pilot slowly began to decrease her speed, allowing the FDA fighter to close on her tail. She waited until the FDA fighter was almost directly on her and was about to hit full reverse and zip behind him, when a pair of Alliance bombers came in guns a-blazing and destroyed the enemy fighter.

On her comm. the Alliance fighter pilot heard from the bombers, "Alliance fighter, this is *Red Eye*. We're making a run on the battleship up ahead. Would you mind covering us?"

Hitting her comm. switch, she replied, "Roger that, moving into position now."

Rolling on her starboard wing, she maneuvered directly above and behind the bombers. The bombers dived down upon the battleship below them. Large blue bursts began to pop around them as anti-aircraft artillery guns fired at them.

Slightly annoyed, the Alliance fighter pilot began evasive maneuvers. Luminescent tails streaked around her in groups of five, indicating anti-aircraft machine guns had locked onto her. She dived right through this, trying to stay in a position to cover the bombers.

The bombers made their run on one of the battleship's main batteries. They opened up with their large-caliber EMP shells, spraying the surface of the battleship. Defense rifles caught most of shells, but a few got through and managed to disable one of the guns. The bombers were pulling out of their run when the attack came.

A pair of FDA fighters came diving on the bombers. This was what the Alliance fighter pilot was waiting for. Dropping in behind the shark-finned fighters, she placed her targeting reticule over the first and opened fire. The fighter's defense rifle stopped the first burst, but her machine guns continued to track, sawing the fighter in half.

Seeing his wingman destroyed, the second FDA fighter pulled a sudden flip maneuver, ending with his aiming at the Alliance fighter pilot while flying backward.

As the FDA fighter opened up, the Alliance pilot rolled up and left while keeping her nose pointed at the enemy fighter. The FDA fighter's machine guns followed her, but the Alliance fighter pilot dodged the bullets while at the same time driving the FDA fighter toward its own battleship.

At the last minute, the FDA fighter pulled up. Having a clear shot, the Alliance fighter pilot let loose with a burst that cut off one of the shark-fin wings. The FDA fighter spun out of control and slammed into the battleship.

Smiling slightly, the Alliance fighter pilot slid back into position to cover the bombers for another run.

Armed with powerful EMP cannons, the Alliance bombers overwhelmed and disabled the FDA defense rifles. Once the defenses were down, the bombers dived on the FDA guns, destroying the artillery with short burst from their EMP cannons.

Other fighter-bomber teams caught onto this and swiftly overwhelmed the battleships. Without defenses and without guns, the FDA battleships were easy prey. In minutes the FDA lost so many ships the Alliance now had greater numbers.

By now some of the Alliance battleships were returning from chasing down supply ships. Seeing fresh battleships joining the Alliance fleet, the FDA decided to cut its losses and leave. By this time the midspace gear had been repaired on all the battleships, so once their fighters returned to their hangars, the FDA disappeared into midspace.

In forty-five minutes of battle, the FDA lost 61 battleships, 23 of them destroyed or captured, 29 forced to withdraw and be sent back to space ports for repairs, and 9 that had to leave the battle but were able to effect their own repairs. Alliance casualties numbered 43 battleships, 19 destroyed or captured, and 24 forced to withdraw, of which 14 were able to repair themselves without having to go to a space port.

John and Greg's battleship did not attempt to join the fight. Instead, their captain had wisely decided to spend the time negotiating for the addition of seven transport ships for the Alliance.

For the Alliance forces, it was kind of strange to be left alone with the destroyed ships floating around them. Since their flagship had been forced to leave, it took a bit of time to find out who was now in command, but once that was done things settled back to normal. Shuttles were launched to pick up survivors who had been blown out of their battleships but had not been killed by flying debris. Enemy soldiers found still alive were taken prisoner.

A quick conference was held, and it was decided instead of destroying the supply depot they would take it for themselves. A marine force was sent down and they quickly overwhelmed the small garrison guarding the depot. Needing more transports, the marines then commandeered the cargo vessels waiting to be filled with supplies. Combined with transports taken by the battleships just before the battle, they were able to haul away most of the supplies. They then destroyed what they could not take.

All this only took a few hours and in that time reports of victory were coming in from all the fleets that had been engaged that day. From Herat, Alliance Forces had been able to defeat the FDA and inflict 50-percent casualties while doing it, all the while only losing 39-percent of its force.

At Garth, it was clear the two FDA fleets would be able to defeat the one Alliance fleet with ease, but fortunately the Alliance escaped to midspace before both fleets could be marshaled against them. Due to the short duration of the battle, the FDA had lost 5 battleships destroyed, 9 that had to retire to a dock for repairs, and numerous others sustained light structural damage. The Alliance had suffered 6 battleships destroyed and 1 forced to a dock.

A common thread that appeared in all these battles was the FDA always suffered more damaged battleships forced to leave the battle and spend a couple months at a dock to be fixed. This was mostly because of the Alliance bombers destroying their guns, for which there were not many spare parts. It was something the FDA generals took note of.

———————

Lying in a patch of bushes, Carol was once again being rained on. It had rained almost nonstop since the first night they had come to Earth. He was starting to wonder what was so great about this planet.

However, there was one aspect about the rain he did appreciate, and that was rain hid your movements and your footsteps. This was an especially good quality right now, since he was on a recon mission.

About two and a half kilometers away, he could see the last of the civilians loading onto transports. A sizeable military force was guarding them, deployed in both obvious and hidden bunkers, a line so small and concentrated the MAA was reluctant to test it.

Four other members of the recon team where also spying on FDA forces, but Carol could not see them. Right now they were at the edge of a heavy oak forest, right in the shrubs at the beginning of it.

Carol could see through the holes in the shrubs, but he was pretty certain the FDA could not see him. He waited until the last civilian was aboard the transport and then pulled out his image-recording device. It was nothing more than a simple square with a cap on it. When the cap was taken off, the light that came into it was imprinted onto a light-sensitive paper, and if the reel was spun, the images would filter continuously, like a movie. Although primitive, it was the only thing that worked on a battlefield when an EMP device was employed. Aiming it at the transport, Carol turned the reel round and round as he recorded the transport taking off and leaving the planet.

As soon as the transport left atmosphere, Carol pushed on the side of his helmet and his speaking rod came out. The speaking rod was the two-cups-and-a-string idea carried to an extreme. A tiny rod inside the helmet was connected to a microscopic wire, allowing the voice to be carried along the string to a comm. station. The operator at the comm. station could then route the call to the correct destination.

Carol spoke into the rod, "Comm. station four, this is Blue recon, over."

"Blue recon, this is comm. station four, receiving you, over," comm. station 4 replied.

"Roger that. I need a connection to Blue HQ, over."

"We are connecting you to Blue HQ right now, out."

Then Carol heard on the line, "This is Blue HQ, over."

"Blue HQ, this is Blue recon. All civilians have left the planet, over."

"Roger, all civilians have left the planet. Blue recon, RTB, out."

RTB stood for Return to Base, so Carol disconnected his wire. Soldiers never carried their wires back because they always got tangled.

Having buried and hidden the end of the wire, Carol whispered for his team to form up. They went into a five-man column, with a point man in the lead, a weapons expert behind him, Carol in the middle where he could best control the team, the ambush expert following behind him, and a tail gunner in the rear. Each of them was specialized in his position, and knew exactly what his job was in any situation.

The point man led them through the forest as quietly as he could, usually taking game trails. They could move almost without noise since the ground was wet and the leaves did not crunch underneath their feet.

At the pace they were going, the tail gunner was able to disguise their tracks and keep up. Although the rain wiped away most of the sign, there were still some traces that had to be eliminated. This was essential because the woods were sort of a no man's land, in which the FDA constantly sent patrols to make sure MAA forces were not doing what they were doing right now. If the FDA spotted their tracks, it would not be long before a counter-recon force could be sent out to overtake and destroy them.

<hr />

"Don't worry Greg, there will be other battles. Sure, we might miss them again, but there is a good chance we'll end up in one. Then we can be afraid for our lives as we play cards and wait at our station to repel boarders, who in all probability will never come. And if the current strategy works, all we will have to do is sit here while the MAA takes Earth," John said.

"John, you really know how to cheer someone up."

"It's better to be sitting around wishing you were being shot at than to be shot at and wishing you were sitting here."

"Yeah, but you can only say that if you have been in a war."

"And you have never been shot at in your life, have you Greg?"

"Not in a full-scale war. All the other stuff I've done was nothing more than skirmishes."

It had been three days since the battle they had missed and since then a whole lot of nothing had happened. In two hours the fleet was to set sail for Earth.

The Alliance plan of battle was for most of their forces to be sent in during the beginning of the battle to draw the FDA fleet away from Earth, until there was enough room for the rest of their fleet to jump into the battle just behind the FDA, allowing them a straight shot at the FDA's weak point. John and Greg were to be part of the force drawing the FDA out of position.

The battle was going to be huge, for all the FDA ships that had survived the earlier space battles had retreated to Earth. The relatively unscathed First and Second Fleets were the main component of the FDA task force. Each side totaled nearly a thousand ships apiece, with a slight advantage in numbers for the Alliance. Two thousand ships of war engaged in battle was so mind-boggling not a single being could imagine what it would be like. Both sides were going to suffer massive casualties, and if the Alliance came out the loser, it would spell almost certain defeat for the 'race.

⊷•⊶

Without warning, the point man stopped, and the rest of the team followed his example. After a second of silence, a rustle of movement was heard up ahead and the point man fired one shot. An FDA counter-recon force of about thirty was on patrol and had run into them.

As soon as the point man had fired, they could spot a couple of dim figures making their way toward them. The enemy began to shoot at them, but even as the bullets were fired, the team had begun its immediate action drill.

The entire team switched its weapons over to fully automatic while the odd-numbered men jumped right and the even-numbered men went one step to the left. Pulling his trigger rapidly, the point man emptied his clip and then ran down the middle of the gauntlet they had made.

At the instant the point man stopped firing, the weapons expert did the same thing as the point man, emptying his clip in a few quick bursts and then peeling off and running down the middle of their column. Then it was Carol's turn.

Carol couldn't really see the enemy, but he could spot shapes moving toward him. Blasting off his clip in a couple of seconds, Carol turned and ran between the ambush expert and the tail gunner. The ambush expert had emplaced a mine and was shooting off his clip as Carol ran past him.

Spotting the weapons expert in front of him, Carol ran hard and caught up with him. Leading the weapons expert was the point man. Having fired off their clips, the ambush expert and the tail gunner came running right behind them.

Throughout the whole drill they had been nothing more than a blur of fire and movement. No force could stand against the IA drill, but only for thirty seconds. After that, the advantage shifted decidedly to superior numbers. The team had been able to pull the drill off in a little over twenty seconds, so they were good to go. As they ran, they heard an explosion as the enemy tripped the mine the ambush expert had placed.

Running as fast as he could, the point man led them in a circular path that would take them around the counter-recon team, and back in the direction they had been originally traveling.

They could hear the enemy closing in on them. The point man slowed down and they walked slowly away from the trail they had been taking. They sneaked back alongside their path until they found a dense section of trail, thick with oak trees on either side.

Tossing a couple of small mines behind the pieces of coverage nearest the trail, the ambush expert kept the team on one side of the trail. He arranged them so they formed a slight semicircle, with all their lanes of fire converging into a deadly crossfire.

In a couple of seconds the counter-recon team came running down the trail. When they were in the middle of the crossfire, the ambush expert opened up and the rest of the team joined in. Though they were firing in semiautomatic (with the exception of Carol, who was using his light machine gun), they were highly effective. Several of the enemies were struck down instantly.

Some of the newer soldiers dived for cover, only to be blown up when they hit the mines. The experienced soldiers switched their weapons to full-auto and unleashed a thunderous barrage as they charged the recon team.

The recon team pulled back. The experienced soldiers would have pursued them, but the veterans were alone and the rest of the counter-recon patrol was hanging back. These soldiers returned to their unit to galvanize them into action.

The actions of the combat veterans in the counter-recon patrol were too late, and in the minute or so spent getting their patrol to move, the recon team had gained an unrecoverable lead.

Carol had the team leave a semi-obvious path, strewn with land mines and booby traps. He broke off from that path sharply and went back into untraceable mode. Though he didn't expect the traps to get any of the patrol, he hoped they would make them pursue cautiously.

Chapter 31

The Second Battle for Earth

John and the marines had returned to their quarters to wait for the order to launch.

The two hours they had to wait seemed considerably longer than that. It turned out they actually waited two and a half hours because of a delay.

When everything was finally ready the captain came on the loudspeaker. "All hands general quarters. Before we launch, I want you to know what our target is. Our target is Earth."

Obviously they didn't inform the captain we were told this in our briefing, thought John.

The captain continued, "Today is the decisive day. When we engage in battle with the enemy, whoever wins will gain Earth. I know everyone of you has courage, but it is not courage that will win the contest today. It is purpose. In the past we have fought simply to stay alive. Now there is an end. With Earth, the human race does not only have a home, it has a future. Gentlemen, that's why this day of battle is ours. We have a purpose and there is nothing that will stop us from attaining our purpose. *Prepare to launch!*"

John, along with the sniper platoon, had been in a lift on the way to their battle station. When they arrived just outside the engine room, instead of taking a seat and breaking out the cards, they stood upright and ready for battle. Although they hadn't found the captain's speech particularly motivating, it reminded them of what exactly they were to be doing that day.

"Here we go," Greg said to John.

"I can't wait."

"This is the decisive battle in the 'race's history," Greg said. "You've got to be feeling something."

John said nothing.

There was a slight hum in the engines, then a sudden acceleration as the ship went away into midspace.

Nothing exciting happened during the rest of the exfiltration, always a plus on recon missions. It was but a short four-kilometer jog back to base once they had left the forest. Tired but alive, the recon team reentered the Assault Team Blue area. Assault Team Blue had set up tents in an orchard and made the place their staging area.

The recon team walked over to the command tent and gave a report on what they had seen to their senior team member. After the debriefing had been given, the senior team member said to Carol, "I need you to stay here for a minute. You and I have to come up with a plan."

The senior team member waited until the rest of the team left. "I was told some important news while you were gone. The Alliance has won several major space battles and will soon strike at the fleet stationed above Earth. Our leaders have decided to launch an offensive at the same time and catch the FDA in a two-pronged assault. Since their battleships will be engaged, we don't have to worry about orbital bombardment. My question to you is where can we hit the FDA and cause the most damage?"

Looking down at the map, Carol studied the enemy positions. This was not an electronic map; it was just a piece of paper with objects and lines drawn on it. *Ironic. Several millennia later and still the best we can come up with is paper with lines drawn on it. No matter what great technological advances have been made, war is still as primitive as it was five thousand years ago. Only difference is, now we fight to destroy the enemy, not to take his land.*

As that thought ran by him, Carol suddenly found the answer. "You're looking at this all the wrong way. We don't want to cause the most damage to the FDA; we want to force them to leave Earth. One way to do that is to kill all their soldiers on the planet. Another is to make them surrender."

"Explain."

"Every army needs tons of supplies. From what I could see they have their supply depots right next to where they land their shuttles. We take these depots and set up AA machine gun batteries around all of the clearings big enough to support mass shuttle landings. When the Alliance defeats their orbiting space fleet, they will be left without any hope of being resupplied and have no choice but to surrender."

The senior team member considered it for a bit. "I like it. It could work. I'll pass the idea onto higher headquarters and see what they think of it. In the meantime, I want you to make up a plan for taking out the supply depot in our area of operations."

"I'll get started right away." Carol left the tent.

As John and Greg rode into battle, Greg looked at his chronometer. "Two minutes."

John nodded in response.

A rapid deceleration was felt when they came out of midspace, followed shortly by the boom of the guns. The guns reloaded, and fired again, making another loud boom heard by the below decks. Precise, controlled broadsides gave way to random, hurried shots, creating a continuous sound of rolling thunder.

To the marines, the booms were all the battle was. They could not see what was going on outside.

And that was probably a good thing. The Alliance had come out of midspace in a line almost as deep as it was wide, and was facing an FDA force in the same arrangement, except its back was to Earth.

Fighters and bombers came streaking out of the docking bays in the battleships and met in the middle of the distance between the two fleets. They began their own deadly game as they tried to maneuver onto each other's rear.

While the FDA remained stationary—not leaving the protection of Earth—the Alliance battleships charged at full speed ahead. Shots were fired back and forth across the space between them as the Alliance closed on the FDA. A couple of battleships on both sides were taken out in this furious opening barrage.

Command and control quickly broke down as the Alliance battleships plowed through the FDA lines, penetrating as deep as they could before engaging, bypassing a great many FDA battleships.

Though the bypassed FDA battleships might have simply turned around and taken the Alliance battleships from behind, they could not do so. Had they done that, they would have exposed their backs to Alliance battleships that had not yet penetrated past them.

The intensely close-quarters prevented the battleships from maneuvering and negated the superior tactical skills of the FDA captains. However, the FDA still had a few surprises up its sleeve. Their forces had caught onto the Alliance's bomber tactic of taking out the guns on a battleship and had adjusted their defenses to counter this threat. But the biggest surprise came when the battleships had stopped maneuvering and settled down into their own little individual battles.

Suddenly, the FDA hangars opened to deploy their shuttles. The shuttles crossed the short distance between battleships before they could be stopped. They attached to the hulls of Alliance ships and used breaching devices to cut holes. Through these holes came the shuttles' deadly cargo. Boarding parties.

———◆———

Finally, thought Carol. *I'm on Earth and it's not raining. Not even a cloud in the sky. It is still sunny outside, but dusk is not far away. This might turn out to be a good day. The entire Assault Team Blue even managed to get inside the enemy's front line without getting spotted. We might actually be able to pull this off.*

At that instant Carol was with the rest of his team lying on their bellies in the woods just outside the supply depots. The supply depot consisted of large piles of boxes scattered around the airport, making them impossible to destroy with one strike.

It was a typical VTOL airport, with a lot of open spaces, hangars, and landing pads. Lightly defended, there were only about twenty real guards, with some sixty soldiers stationed there to stock and organize the supplies. The guards would provide the most difficulty, but the supply soldiers would also be a force to reckon with. Tactics and accuracy would be lacking, but they'd be able to overwhelm the Assault Team through sheer weight of numbers. That, combined with twenty guards, was what made this attack so unlikely to succeed.

The plan Carol had come up was simply a frontal assault by the unit. This unexpected maneuver would upset the enemy's contingency plans and force it to reposition. These new positions would be weaker than the prepared ones, making it easy for the team to push past them. Once among the enemy, the team would split up. The FDA would now have to suffer attacks from multiple angles or divide its forces and be defeated in detail. Nothing the FDA could do would be able to stop Assault Team Blue after it got inside the supply depot.

In selecting the place to attack, Carol carefully considered every position around the supply depot. He had considered the front gate, but it was too well defended. Security was lighter on the perimeter, but still difficult to break.

Most of the airport was about 150 meters from the woods, but there was a long, clear open space for about 300 meters to the supply depot. When observing the area, Carol noticed the enemy had only a three-man bunker to defend it. It was an easy decision to choose this as the point of attack.

Carol heard two snaps, the signal for them to get moving. He did not come bursting out of the woods firing. On the contrary, he slowly began crawling forward. Like the rest of Assault Team Blue, he was covered in strands of grass, blending him with the knee-high grass that grew around the supply depot. Inching their way forward, they moved less than half of a meter at a time. It was tedious work, but it paid off since there was a slight hill in front of them they had not seen when standing up. This hill allowed them to get within a hundred meters of the defensive position.

Right around the hundred-meter mark, the single soldier who was manning the position noticed a lump of suspicious-looking grass. Staring at the lump of grass, he saw it move a little. Knowing it had to be an enemy sneaking up on him, he lifted his rifle and took careful aim.

Unfortunately for the soldier, several rifles had been trained on him for quite some time, waiting for him to try something like this. Multiple shots range out, and the soldier slumped over the defensive position.

The little lumps of grass dotting the hill rose and began to run toward the position. A Waas who was checking to see what the shooting was about saw these lumps of grass rushing toward him. Flipping his weapon onto fully automatic, he emptied his clip in the general direction of the enemy.

None of his wild shots hit anything, but it did cause a good deal of return fire to be sent in his direction. As the shots smacked the ground all around him, the soldier snapped back to his senses and ran toward the defensive position. Ducking down into safety, he slapped in a new clip, put his weapon back on semiauto, popped over the top and fired a few inaccurate shots.

By now four other soldiers had joined him. Though the bunker was designed for only three, somehow they managed to squeeze in. Their presence gave him the strength to calm down and get a grip on himself.

Catching his breath, the soldier stuck his head over the top and took careful aim at one of the enemy soldiers rushing toward him. Pulling the trigger, he felt the recoil and saw the bullet impact high and right over his target. He fired again, then a third time in rapid succession. The third shot connected, and the MAA Assault Team member fell. His confidence began to rise as he saw two other enemy soldiers had fallen to their fire. Then a fourth enemy soldier carrying a strange weapon dropped to the ground.

This one had not been hit and began to lay down automatic weapons fire. The rate of fire was considerably slower than normal, but it was enough to make the FDA soldiers duck.

After five seconds of firing with no sign of the LMG running out of ammunition, the FDA soldiers once again stuck their heads above the defensive position. It was hard to aim with all the bullets buzzing around their heads. Two of the soldiers were struck down.

Suddenly, someone began to shoot at them from their left flank. Wondering how the enemy had managed to get past them, the FDA soldier turned to face this new threat. He got off a couple of ineffective shots before the man charging him unleashed a hail of bullets. Death was nearly painless. The impact of the bullet was felt, but before the nerves could send the message of pain, he was already dead.

Seeing they had taken the enemy position, Carol jumped to his feet and made a dash over the enemy's perimeter. A couple of FDA soldiers came running to investigate, but these were mowed down before Carol could fire at them. Reaching the main body of Assault Team Blue, Carol said, "Everyone break into your teams. Let's do this job quickly."

There was a mad scramble as the team members formed up their teams and moved out to accomplish their objectives. Carol ran over to the three who were waiting for him.

"Ready to go?" one of them asked.

"Never been better," Carol replied.

The four of them jogged off in the direction of their objective. Their mission was to take out the guard barracks. Most likely there wouldn't be anyone there, but it still needed to be investigated.

Using the large piles of supplies as cover, they moved cautiously, since they did not know whether there would be two or ten enemy soldiers around the corner. Shots could be heard constantly throughout the supply depot.

Three FDA soldiers ran into them as they rounded the corner. Spotting the soldiers, Carol's unit let loose a couple of bursts that took down two of them. The other one dived back around the corner for cover. While Carol provided suppressive fire, the other three team members advanced on the corner.

The FDA soldier spun around the corner and snapped off a couple of quick shots before he was forced back into cover by a burst from Carol. Then the soldier did the same thing in the same place again. Carol, who had marked the spot mentally, cut the soldier down with a short burst.

These guys must have been supply troops. No experienced soldier would have tried the same thing twice. If we're moving toward the guard barracks and only encountering supply soldiers, then the guard barracks must be empty.

No longer worried about enemy encounters, Carol picked up the pace, and as he had predicted, the guard barracks was empty. The barracks was a long one-story building that had a door on both the front and back and about ten windows on each wall. Before moving on, they rifled through the barracks looking for any useful information, but they found none.

Having accomplished their primary objective, they moved on to their secondary job of blowing up supplies. Standing security while the others rigged the nearby piles for demolition, Carol kept a careful eye out but saw no one. In about a minute they finished rigging the explosives and moved to the next three piles. All they had to do was place a shaped charge inside the pile and then arm the detonator. A simple push of a button would knock everything down.

The four of them managed to rig a total of twenty explosives. Once they had finished, Carol said, "I know we were supposed to wait until the area was secure before detonating the explosives, but I think we should go ahead and blow them now. Obviously, there are no friendlies or enemies nearby, so we don't have to worry about fragging anyone. The FDA should come running to investigate the explosions, then we can ambush them from the guard barracks."

The others agreed to his plan. Carol had them go inside the guard barracks. They took up positions in the windows, crouching down so only their heads and weapons showed. Seeing them in position, Carol hit the button that detonated the explosives. With a tremendous noise the supplies went up in flames. The shock wave was strong enough to both knock Carol off his feet and shatter the windows of the guard barracks.

Getting back on his feet, Carol scrambled to the barracks and made it a couple of seconds before the first FDA soldiers arrived.

John and Greg heard the call go out on the intercom just before they came under attack.

"*Prepare to repel boarders*" rang throughout the ship. The command was punctuated by the sound of shuttles attaching to the hull.

Since they were deep in the ship, they had heard nothing of the battle taking place on the levels above.

Lieutenant Derek was in communication with the other platoon leaders. "Everybody listen up. They need help containing the boarders. I didn't get a complete image of the situation before the ship's defense EMP grid turned on, but from what I could tell, they were being overrun. First Squad, you need to go along the port side and patrol the ship from that point backward. Second and Third Squads, you will go topside and starboard-side respectively, and also patrol backward. Ramon and I will stay here in case something goes wrong."

"Second Squad, let's go." Greg started running to topside. There were access tunnels for climbing to the top of the ship in case of lift failure. Greg decided to use one of these to give him the advantage of surprise.

He reached the access tunnel. "John, take point. Everyone else, standard file deployment." The squad adjusted to Greg's commands as John began to climb up the access tunnel.

Moving with a sense of emergency, they took only a couple of minutes to reach the top. John came out the access tunnel without any caution. He stood upright, looked around, and gave the all clear. The rest of the squad hurried after him.

Bursts of gunfire were heard echoing down the hallway behind them. Greg nodded in that direction, and the squad split up, six on either side of the corridor. The second man in each formation edged to the middle, giving the squad four shooters. Greg went to the middle of the left file and ordered the squad to start moving.

John walked about five meters in front of them, scouting ahead. Unlike the marines, he walked near the center of the hallway. He was relying on his quick trigger finger to get him out of any trouble he might get into.

The marines moved a little faster than normal since they knew John would be the first to be fired on, but they still made sure they always had each other covered when rounding a corner.

The sound of firing came closer. John made a short dash forward, shooting five times as he rounded the corner. The marines hurried to his position.

"It's all clear," John said.

Three FDA soldiers lay dead about ten meters from John. Further down the hallway, they could see Alliance and FDA dead lying near each other.

John made a quick count. "Eight bodies total. The guys I killed must have been the rear guard. The main force is ahead of us somewhere. Is there anything vital in this area?"

"If they keep following this hallway they will reach a turnoff that leads to damage control for this section. We can beat them there if we go down the next access tunnel," Greg replied.

No more time was wasted on words. They ran as quickly as they could to the access tunnel.

John came out the other end of the tunnel. He could see the damage control room. Levers and gear were all around the room, each one controlling some sort of measure to prevent any damage to the ship from becoming worse than it already was. To his relief, they had reached it before the boarding party.

As the rest of the marine squad came out behind him, John said to the five-man damage-control crew, "We have a boarding party heading this way. Do you have weapons, and is there anything we can use for cover?"

The ensign in charge of the station walked over to the wall and inserted a key into a small hole. A panel popped open to reveal two pistols and a pair of clips for each of them. He tossed one pistol and two of the clips to his petty officer and kept the remaining pistol and ammunition for himself.

Sliding a clip into his pistol, the ensign replied, "We have five boxes of fire control and welding gear. Most of it has been distributed to damage control teams, but the boxes should still be able to stop an ice bullet. Petty officer Roberts will show you where they are."

"Schmidt, take your fire team and bring those boxes here," Greg commanded.

John took out his small SMG and his pistol. He gave them to the sailors who had not received weapons. Seeing what John was doing, Lynch gave his backup pistol to the last sailor who was unarmed.

Schmidt and his fire team came running back with the boxes. They set up the boxes farther down the hallway so stray shots would not harm the damage control system. The boxes were arranged with the first two boxes on either side of the hallway, and the second pair about six meters behind them, and the final box in the middle.

The marines and sailor hurried forward to the boxes and took cover behind them. Those who could not get behind the boxes went into the prone or crouched down low. Some stood behind the last set of boxes. They all settled down and made sure their lanes of fire were clear, then waited.

A constant booming came from the guns above. The battleship shuddered with the impact of enemy shells getting through the defense rifles. No noise or movement came from the marines and sailors as they waited for the enemy to appear. Thudding footsteps sounded as the boarding party came closer. The Alliance soldiers' grips tightened around their weapons.

The first FDA fire team came dashing around the corner. Marines and sailors opened a furious barrage and the FDA fire team fell after one volley. The FDA fire teams that had been following the first team grouped together and charged around the corner en masse.

There were sixteen FDA soldiers. Because of the tight quarters, they knew their only chance was to hit the Alliance position and overwhelm the marines before they got wiped out themselves.

Seeing sixteen enemies packed close together, the marines unleashed everything they had. A vicious return fire came from the FDA soldiers, but the boxes managed to soak up most of it. The FDA soldiers tried to set up some sort of system where some were firing and the others were maneuvering.

Greg found himself near the back of the position. Because of the friendlies in front of him, he had to wait for a clear lane of fire. He could hear the whistle of pellets past his ear, but he did not flinch. Shooting at the enemy was more important than his safety.

Unfortunately, he hadn't shot enough to stop their advance. The FDA soldiers were coming closer to their position and nothing seemed to slow them. In a few seconds, it would be hand-to-hand fighting.

A couple of sailors stayed too long above their coverage and were struck down by FDA bullets. Although diamond armor could protect from just about anything, once a bullet penetrated, it was over for the wearer of the armor. The bullet would bounce around inside the armor and turn its occupant's insides into mush. Blood began to pour through the holes in the sailors' armor, spreading across the deck.

John and the ensign—who were fighting side by side—looked over at the bodies, and shared a look. The FDA assault was getting too close to their position. In that look, John and the ensign knew what they had to do.

Breaking forth from their cover, the two of them launched an attack against the advancing soldiers. They stuck close to the left side of the hallway to allow for the rest of the marines and sailors to continue firing on the enemy.

They had managed to take out the advanced element of the FDA force when the ensign was hit by enemy fire. Seeing the ensign fall, John sped up his rate of fire. The marines were able to take the time to aim because most of the enemy's fire was directed at John. Their accurate fire rapidly brought down the remaining FDA soldiers.

Making a quick sweep of the area, John pronounced it clear.

The ground was most certainly not clear, however. Bodies lay all about the hallway. Blood covered the floor at least an centimeter thick. It was not only red blood, but blue and green blood, spilled by the various alien races of the FDA.

Greg took charge of the situation. "Okay, we move down the hallway. There is an intersection that will allow us to intercept all traffic going along this side of the battleship. *Let's move!*"

His words galvanized the marines into moving. They got up and jogged through the bodies of their enemies on the way to their new position.

John stayed behind for a second. He walked over to where the ensign had fallen, and picked up his pistol. He tossed it to the sailor who had his smaller SMG. "I need my weapon back."

The sailor caught the pistol and handed over the SMG. Placing the

SMG back in its holster, John walked over to one of the slain sailors, the one he had given his pistol to. Removing the pistol from the sailor's hands, John inspected it. There was some blood on it, but otherwise it was fine. Dropping the pistol back in his pocket, John walked down the hallway after the marines.

Carol madly scrambled to his feet. *If I have to do this again, I think I'll detonate the explosives after I'm inside the barracks.*

Dashing inside the guard barracks, he occupied a window not far from the door. Right after he had set himself up in the window, five soldiers appeared in the middle of the area where the explosives had gone off. These were clearly supply soldiers, since they had walked into an open area without securing it first. Carol's unit opened fire, taking them out on the first volley.

Seven more soldiers appeared, but this time they stayed at the edge of the explosion radius, where cover was provided by the debris that had been sent flying by the explosion. Two of the soldiers were guards—a Waas and a Pratin—and these two seemed to be leading the others.

First they tried a flanking maneuver, but the fire from the barracks was too heavy for that. Seeing the only way to get to the barracks was a frontal assault, the two guards had the supply soldiers lay down a base of suppressive fire while they moved forward a few meters, then hit the deck.

The guards then provided cover as the supply soldiers ran past them several more meters. Once the supply soldiers had hit the dirt and were firing again, the guards moved, and so on.

Slowly but surely they made their way forward. Little pieces of wreckage were scattered around the area, which the soldiers used as cover. Making short dashes from cover to cover they could make their way across in relative safety.

As the enemy laid down suppressive fire, Carol refused to duck. He knew if he ducked he would have to reappear again and would only be able to get off a few wild shots before having to duck once more.

Instead, he moved to a corner of a window and showed only his gun barrel and the right half of his head. Keeping up a constant fire on the enemy, Carol was kept alive by his ability to make the enemy hide behind their little piece of coverage instead of shooting at him.

The supply soldiers stood up to make a short run forward again. Carol's bullets hit the ground behind one of the soldiers, and as he adjusted his fire, a trail of bullets chased down the soldier from behind, dropping him forward when they connected. Seeing their fellow soldier fall, the other supply soldiers almost faltered, but continued to press on.

One of the guards began to shoot at Carol, who let loose a burst that forced the guard into cover. The guard waited until Carol had shifted his fire, then blazed away at him again. He almost had the range when a burst of fire from one of the other MAA Team members made the guard go back into cover.

When the supply soldiers made another sortie forward, the team members opened fire and managed to bring down two more of them. Seeing they were losing soldiers rapidly, the guards charged the barracks with the remaining supply troops. They fired on the run, not very accurately, but enough to worry those in the windows.

As soon as they gained their feet, one of the supply soldiers was hit by one of the MAA team members. Carol managed to bring down the last one, but he could see the two guards were going to reach the building.

———◆———

Across the space above Earth, the Alliance was pushing back the boarding parties that had come onto their ships. In some ships the boarders had succeeded, but most of the time the marines' superior training showed and the boarding parties were wiped out.

The Alliance captains knew they only had to wait a few more minutes before they could begin to pull back, but they also knew the FDA must have expended most of their soldiers in the boarding parties, leaving their own ships relatively undefended. It was a gamble, but about half the Alliance captains decided to send their marines to board the FDA battleships

———◆———

Assigned to escort a shuttle carrying a boarding party, the particularly skilled Alliance fighter pilot was flying with her flight of four. Knowing the only way to defend the shuttle was to attack the enemy, she had two of her pilots guarding the shuttle while she and her wingman cleared the path in front of them.

A four-man flight came at her head-on. She and her wingman ascended rapidly as they threw hard spins, while the enemy did the same thing in the other directions. Both sides opened fire.

She managed to dodge her enemies' bullets and take out one of the fighters in front of her. Her wingman was not so lucky. Although he had been able to destroy his target, his target's wingman had managed to hit him with a snapshot. His defense rifles had stopped most of the shots, but a couple had got by and hit his wing.

Seeing he was okay but had difficulty maneuvering, she ordered him to fly by the shuttle so the two fighters guarding it could have a shot at his pursuer. Then she concentrated on the fighter in front of her. She was directly on his six o'clock and could see he wanted to flip upside down and engage her while flying backward, but could not because the instant he leveled out she would destroy him.

Unable to shake her, the FDA pilot went into a dizzying array of twists and turns as he pulled up and backward. If he completed the maneuver, he would be able to engage her while flying backwards. Her targeting computer could not get a lock, so she switched to manual aim and fired where she thought he would be next. Seeing the luminescent trail made by her bullets, she walked her line of fire over the enemy fighter, cutting it in half.

It really is sad, she thought, *how many fighter pilots forget about manual aim.*

The two fighters guarding the shuttle had been able to drive away the fighter on her wingman's tail. Seeing the shuttle had attached to the FDA battleship, she escorted her wingman back to the hangar while the other pair of fighters stood guard over the shuttle.

A couple of FDA fighters had tried to make a strafing run on the shuttle as it unloaded its marines, but the Alliance fighters guarding it destroyed one of them and forced the other to retreat. The shuttle detached from the hull and began to head back to the Alliance battleship. As they were leaving, three FDA fighters set upon the pair of fighters guarding the shuttle.

Coming back from escorting her wingman to the hangar, the flight commander saw the three fighters attacking her flight members. Pushing her throttle all the way open, she ordered one of her pilots to pull up hard. As the pilot complied, the FDA fighter on his tail followed him, giving her a perfect shot. She squeezed the trigger and obliterated the enemy fighter. The odds having turned against them, the remaining FDA fighters retreated.

As John, Greg, and his squad of snipers sat waiting in ambush position, they heard on the loudspeakers, "All marines, prepare to board the enemy."

Greg immediately stood up and started running. The rest of the squad followed him, with John in the rear. Needing to save time, they all piled into a lift. Taking the lift down to the hangar, they arrived at a scene of marines and mechanics scrambling all over to get ready for the assault. Spotting the shuttle he was assigned to, Greg led his squad over to the line forming behind the shuttle.

"Before we get in line, let's get into position. Assaulters, front and rear, everyone else, standard positions," Greg said.

The squad formed up with Yangkin in front, and Sandusky and Walters in the rear. This was done so when they left the shuttle, Sandusky and Walters would be in front, and Yangkin would be at the rear of the left file. The reason why Yangkin had to be specifically at the rear of the left file was a twelve-man squad plus a squad leader made an odd number. Since the left file was longer, its tail gunner was the person farthest back in the squad.

Greg said to John, "John, I want you to be the last person on the shuttle. When the infantry makes the breach, you need be right there with them, clearing the way. Once the breach is secure, wait for us and we'll find you."

"I'll see you there."

Counting off sixty-two people, John said to the sixty-third, "Do you mind if you wait until the second wave?"

"Sir, I'm in the second wave."

It was then John realized the high casualties caused by the FDA's assault.

The loadmaster shouted, "Everyone aboard, fill the entire shuttle. If the rest of your unit is not on the shuttle, wait at the breach for them to arrive. Everybody move, let's hurry."

Marines piled into the shuttle. Being the last one in, John was forced to sit in the center row. It was incredibly crowded. They were so close the marines were bumping into each other. The loadmaster pulled the lever that closed the doors.

Five minutes of silence passed and then they heard the pilots turn on the engines. There was a thump as the landing gear retracted and a slight bounce as the repulse-lifters caught the shuttle. The shuttle began to slowly rise and accelerate toward the open hangar door.

As they exited the hangar, the shuttle went to full throttle. The marines inside could not see what was going on since windows were considered unneeded luxuries. It was almost total darkness except for a couple of small red lights. Marines checked each other's gear, making sure everything was in order.

The flight was short and in a couple of minutes the pilots began landing maneuvers. They threw the shuttle into a hard fishtail until they were pointing opposite to the direction they were traveling. Slowly backing the shuttle into the battleship's hull, they heard a loud click.

As the pilots used the breaching device that was part of the ship's rear, the loadmaster said, "Stand up!"

The center row stood up, then the row on the right stood, folding their chairs into the hull behind them. The row on the left did the same thing, then the loadmaster said, "Breach made!" He hit the lever that opened the doors and started yelling, "Go! Go! Go!"

The top half of the door began to swing upward as the bottom half swung down, and through that hole in the middle John came diving out of the shuttle. Hitting the ground in a sideways roll, John came up on one knee firing. Six FDA soldiers had gathered to plug the breach, and John had already dropped two of them before they had recovered from his unexpected maneuver. When they started to return fire at John, he strafed right to evade them. As he did so, the rest of the marines came pouring out of the shuttle. Sweeping aside the rest of the FDA soldiers, the marines turned and began to pour out to the left.

A squad of FDA soldiers appeared around the corner down the left hallway. Half of the marines stopped and laid down a base of fire while the others charged the FDA soldiers. The FDA squad managed to take down several marines, but the marines closed with them and defeated them with their bayonets.

Five FDA soldiers came running down the hallway on the right. Seeing these, John turned and engaged them. In the short exchange of fire, three FDA soldiers died and the remainder retreated. John pursued them back down the hallway.

When the center column had left the shuttle, the column on the right came running out on the heels of the last man, making it seem as if it was still one long line. The column on the right turned to the right and began to run down that hallway so they would not be tripping over the center column going to the left. The left column was to exit and turn to the least defended side.

Greg, who was in the left column, saw John go down the right hallway, and since both sides had little resistance, he decided to follow John. Moving with his squad down the hallway, Greg could see a trail of bodies scattered along the way, most of which he assumed were caused by John.

John was waiting for him at an intersection. "Greg, I found a straight shot at one of the main engines. This access tunnel leads directly to it."

"How did you find this out?" Greg asked.

John pointed to a dead body next to the access tunnel. "I shot this guy as he came out that tunnel. Look at his unit patch, he's an engineer."

"Let's go. John, you're on point."

Opening the access tunnel, John hurried down the ladder with the squad close behind him. At the bottom, there didn't seem to be anyone in the hallways.

The squad formed into their two files, one on either side of the hallway. Hallways in FDA battleships were considerably larger than those on their Alliance counterparts. Their size permitted hovercrafts to traverse the hallways, but it meant fewer soldiers could be carried, something perfectly fine for the FDA, since they had troop transports for that.

John looked at the signs on the hallway. "There are two main engines that can be reached from here. I'll take the near one, you take the far one."

With that John took off and started running down the hallway.

Watching him, Lance Corporal McAlister said, "Sergeant, do you really think one man can do the job of a whole squad?"

"I don't see why not."

The squad followed where John had gone. They passed an intersection that led to the first engine and kept moving until they reached another intersection leading to the second engine. Most of the soldiers on the FDA ship had died on the *Adamant*, and Greg's squad did not encounter a single soldier until they reached the checkpoint that guarded the engine room.

Reaching the left turn before the checkpoint, the squad halted. Sandusky—who was leading the left file—dropped into a low crouch, just out of sight. Walters, since he was on the outside file, slowly crept sideways with short little side steps. As he moved sideways, the area around the corner revealed itself.

When the first soldier at the checkpoint appeared in his sights, Walters fired, taking the soldier down. He moved sideways a little more, and the rest of the enemy entered his line of sight.

Walters yelled, "Maneuver!" as he began to lay down suppressive fire. Sandusky rolled around the corner and fired at the enemy as he advanced toward them along the wall. The rest of the file followed his maneuver, pivoting around the corner and following the wall while firing.

Making a few quick hand signals, Walters ordered a fire team forward and had the remaining marine, Pierre, lay down suppressive fire with him. Pierre crouched down slightly forward of Walters, exposing only as much of his body as he had to.

The double column moving alongside the walls quickly overwhelmed the FDA defenders.

Moving past the checkpoint, they went up to a door "This is the one," Greg said. "L-shaped breach."

Sandusky placed a breaching charge on the door as the columns took up positions alongside. Seeing the columns were ready, Sandusky twisted the handle on the charge and stepped back. The door blew open and the flash-bang went off as the columns burst into the room. One column spread out to the back of the room while the other moved sideways along the wall, preventing a friendly-fire incident.

Taking down the sailors who were in the area, the marines paused and held their positions. They were at the back of a large chamber that housed the rear half of the engines. The engine ran through the middle like a column turned on its side, forming a sort of hallway on either side. Each hallway seemed to stretch for at least two hundred meters.

Greg surveyed the area. "Rodrigo, Schmidt, your teams handle security. Smith, blow this engine apart."

With that Greg dropped into the prone and opened fire on the sailors. Taking careful aim, Greg lined up his sights with a sailor's head and pulled the trigger. The sailor fell dead on the ground.

Several sailors were laying down a base of fire, but Greg did not flinch. Coolly he picked them off one by one.

This is the sort of war I like. It's so much easier now that I have a rifle.

A group of three sailors were behind a crate. Releasing their weapons, they stood while raising their hands.

Greg dropped the first with ease. As he swung his sights onto the second, he suddenly realized the survivors had dropped their weapons and had their hands in the air. *They're surrendering.*

Once his sights were on the second sailor, Greg began applying trigger pressure. This was going to be an easy shot.

Just before he pushed the last pound of pressure, Greg's finger fell away from the trigger, shaking as he did so. *What have I become?*

Waving, he signaled for the aliens to come forward. As the sailors crossed, they were cut down by the crossfire. Looking at their bodies, Greg didn't feel any remorse. And that worried him.

As the other teams were busy covering him, Smith's fire team set the explosives on the engine. While none of them were demo experts, they did understand the principle if you pack enough explosives into something, it blows up.

Most of the engine was uncovered, making it easier for maintenance. It also made it easy to drop explosives down the middle. The fire team hurriedly set the timers on the bombs and chucked them down into the engine. Once they had run out of explosives, Smith said, "Sergeant, we need to get out of here in five minutes."

"Got it. Schmidt, Rodrigo, we leave now," Greg said.

Not even bothering to attempt to provide cover fire, the teams complied with Greg's order. The enemy, seeing their attackers running away so suddenly, realized what had been done and also began to flee. Though their diamond armor would survive the explosion, the shock wave would smash every bone in their bodies.

The squad left the engine room and continued to run until they were a little ways past the checkpoint.

Greg caught his breath. "How long till it blows?"

A small explosion was followed by a huge secondary explosion as the engine began to explode. The whole battleship shook with the force of the explosion.

"Has that John guy done his part yet?" Sandusky asked.

"Most likely. We should head down to the intersection and wait for him."

"That's funny, I didn't feel anything go off," Rodrigo said.

"Unlike us, John *is* an explosives expert. He probably set off one surgically placed explosive that took out the entire engine."

Marching back quickly, the squad made it to the intersection without any trouble. Following their training, the marines set up a defensive perimeter and waited for further orders.

"Sergeant, do you think we should go to the intersection that leads to the first engine? He might be waiting for us," said Rodrigo.

"John wouldn't sit around waiting. He'll be looking for us."

The sound of gunfire echoed down the hallway. It moved rapidly toward them.

Eight FDA soldiers facing an unseen threat nearly backed into Smith's fire team. Both sides were surprised by the other's presence, but the marines acted first and charged the enemy with their bayonets. The other fire teams rushed to their assistance, but they would arrive too late.

Sandusky saw the situation at a glance. His team would be wiped out if something wasn't done swiftly.

Turning his bayonet on, Sandusky batted aside the rifle pointed at him and swung his bayonet across his enemy's chest, killing the Waas.

Moving to the next enemy, Sandusky grabbed the opposing soldier's weapon in his armpit and held it there tightly. He spun around to the left so his back faced the FDA soldier. As he did this he put his foot between his opponent's legs and kicked up hard, tripping his enemy. The soldier fell onto Sandusky's waiting bayonet.

Hearing something behind him, Sandusky dropped low as a bullet went over his head, spotted the shooter, and hurled his rifle like a spear into the soldier's heart.

Whipping out his pistol, Sandusky turned on the remaining soldiers with a fury. He felled two more enemy soldiers who were engaged in hand-to-hand combat with the rest of his fire team. The other aliens were cut down by the slashing bayonets of his team.

At this point John came running down the hallway, clearly in pursuit of the eight FDA soldiers.

John saw the dead soldiers. "I finished my job. I take it the big explosion was you guys. We should head back to the shuttle now."

"Sounds like a plan," Greg said.

Moving speedily but cautiously, the squad managed to get to the shuttle without further incident.

Arriving at the perimeter around the breach, they saw several blood-soaked marines holding the area. A small pile of enemy bodies lay around them. A couple of marines were stretched out on the floor, lying side by side with the FDA soldiers. Other squads were also coming back into the perimeter, some of them dragging the bodies of their comrades. The marine ethic was clear. The shuttle would not leave until all the marines, dead or alive, were inside.

The boarding parties had been sent on board with the objective of destroying one target and returning to the shuttle to get back on board their own battleship. Although standard practice was to keep the ship, FDA boarding parties had caused too many casualties for them to man the captured vessel.

Three shells rocked the battleship in rapid succession. This was the signal for all teams to return to their shuttles. Marines began to rush back. All of them were present in about ten minutes.

Someone pushed a button on the breach that lit a signal light informing the Assault Shuttle they were ready to depart. They had to wait about two minutes for the shuttle to arrive.

Piling aboard, the marines in the first wave lifted off. John looked around, and noticed most squads had lost a man or two. The dead bodies were put in a corner to save room. None of the marines wept or showed any emotion at all. Tears would come later.

Gliding into the hangar bay, the shuttle came to a halt and the marines unloaded.

In the larger scheme of things, the Alliance was ready to make its big move. The boarding parties had been successful in most cases, and though a good many FDA ships had been destroyed, the FDA still held the upper hand. Battered heavily, the Alliance began to retreat. The FDA eagerly pursued them, intent on finishing the enemy while it had the advantage.

Chasing down the battered Alliance fleet, the FDA left the protected position of Earth at its back. Once the distance between the FDA fleet and Earth was large enough, the rest of the Alliance fleet was given the signal to go. The empty space between the battleships and Earth was filled by the remainder of the Alliance fleet, which came out of midspace blasting away at the rear of the FDA formation.

Alliance gunfire chewed up the unprotected rear of the enemy battleships. Great hunks of metal fell off the FDA ships of war as heavy shells smashed through bulkheads. The entire rear row of the FDA's battle formation was destroyed in a couple of minutes, and the next row was also taking tremendous losses. Unable to get off more than a smattering of return fire, the FDA was taking a considerable pounding. Nearly a hundred ships were destroyed in those short minutes and a like number were forced to leave.

Having lost almost a fifth of their total force so swiftly, the FDA knew they could not win this battle. The ships stayed only as long as was needed to get their midspace gear working again and then left Earth to the Alliance.

———◆———

"Ricky, cover the doorway," Carol yelled.

There was a loud BANG as the breaching charge went off, accompanied by a couple of shots. Carol knew they had got Ricky.

He burst out of the room he was in. Down the hallway he could see the two guards advancing toward him along the sides of the walls. Before they could get a shot, Carol opened up, blasting away the one on the left.

Carol and the survivor exchanged a series of short bursts, with Carol emerging the victor.

Checking the doorway, Carol saw Ricky lying face up on the floor, with a big red blotch on his chest were the bullets had hit him. The exploded flash-bang had hit the wall behind him and rolled next to his head.

Outside, the sound of firing had died down. A red flare streaked across the sky, the signal for victory. Stepping out the door, Carol could see red flares hovering all around Earth. Distant thunder could be heard as other units destroyed supply depots.

They had won. Carol took a deep breath of air. Earth was theirs. All they had to do now was to wait for the FDA forces to surrender. Taking one last look at the dimming sky, Carol turned around and went back to prepare Ricky's body for burial.

Chapter 32

The Cheat

Inside the hallways of the battleship, the cheering could not be stopped. The word had just come; the FDA had surrendered to the MAA. All the Alliance was rejoicing, none more so than the marines and sailors who had brought about this victory.

In the sniper platoon, there was extreme thankfulness. All of them had seen war, all had been in it, and none had died. They had been partying for three hours and showed no signs of flagging. Even John was caught up in the moment.

Only Greg was out of it. He stood in the corner, silently observing.

"Something's wrong with Heyligher," Rodrigo whispered to Ethan Ramon.

"I know," Ethan replied. "Usually, he would be the life of the party. Did anything happen while you were on the battleship?"

"Nothing out of the normal. Maybe he's just reflecting on the war."

"Not likely. Everybody's celebrating; even John has a smile on his face."

"Really?" Rodrigo strained to get a better look at John. "I don't see anything."

"It's more of a slight lift of the corners of his mouth."

"Oh, I see it."

Rodrigo seemed to be in deep though. "Should we talk to Heyligher?"

"Why not? What's the worst we could do?"

Greg looked up to see Ethan and Rodrigo approaching him.

"We made it through our first war," Rodrigo said to him.

"That we did."

"Are you disappointed it ended so quickly?" Ethan said.

Greg seemed startled by this question. "What do you mean?"

"You were close to beating the all-time kill record. Now you'll never hit it."

"Oh, that." Greg relaxed. "Actually, I'm sort of glad I didn't. All this killing is getting old. Now that we've taken back Earth, I think I'll get out of the Corps."

Rodrigo and Ethan looked at each other. This was not the Heyligher they knew.

"Okay, what happened?" Ethan demanded.

Greg slowly considered what to say. "When we were on the battleship, three sailors leapt from behind a box. I shot one of them before I realized they were surrendering. Once I knew they were giving up, I nearly killed them anyway."

Neither Ethan or Rodrigo spoke for a while.

"Do you remember what I told you back when I was your squad leader?" Ethan said.

Greg nodded.

"Have you broken that rule?"

"No."

"Then you haven't gone so far you can't recover. But once you cross *that* line, there's no coming back."

Rodrigo said, "Heyligher, you're a sniper, and a good one. If you think you have to leave, then you do. But I think you'll get over this."

"You don't understand; that's not all there is to it. The rest of the story I can't talk about."

"Yes you can. It's just a mental barrier you have to break," Ethan said.

"No, I mean I'm not allowed to talk about it."

Suddenly, it all made sense to Ethan. The nightmare, his screams, Greg's retreat inward. *Something happened on that mission.* "You need to see someone about this."

"Who? A shrink wouldn't understand. No one else has a high enough security clearance."

Ethan pointed his arm at John. "Talk to him about it."

"John's an assassin. Though he's a friend, he wouldn't comprehend."

"Then maybe it is best you leave the military. You could try to start over and forget this."

Greg nodded dumbly. After a moment, he became alert. "By the way, when are you and Rosanna getting married?"

"Since we just got Earth, we decided to have the wedding on the planet. It should be in a week or two at most. We'll send out invitations as soon as we've picked out a date."

"Bet you're looking forward to it."

"Oh, I am, I am. In the meantime, let's join the celebration. Consider it a going-away party."

Forcing a smile, Greg stepped out of the corner. In the center, he saw John and Derek laughing together. *It's good to see John showing emotion. I think he's going to rejoin the 'race.*

To his side, Sandusky and Walters were making some wisecrack. Schmidt and Smith were having an arm-wrestling contest. The rest of his squad was horsing around and having a good time.

At that instant, Greg chose to live. As much as he enjoyed being in the Marine Corps, it was time to leave.

Chapter 33

War's Master

"We're deeply in your debt for coming, sir," an FDA captain said to the general walking beside him.

"Oh, not at all. I was on my way for my biannual report to the Council of Generals. This wasn't much of a detour—and besides—fighting a war is a higher priority than reporting," the general replied pleasantly.

The general was young for someone of his rank. At only forty-two he held the rank of lieutenant general. He was a Viand, a race colored almost pure white due to the lack of sunlight on their home planets. Their hands and feet were almost the same as a human's, as were their nose and ears. They had a chin that jutted out a little more than a human's, plus eyes that were wider than normal.

As a result of the lack of sunlight, their planets were mostly barren, and their bodies were much skinnier than a human's. The biggest difference between them and humans is on the inside, with their vital organs in different places.

This particular Viand's skin was more tanned than normal for his race because of years spent doing field exercises. His dark grey hair was kept cut close to his head in accordance with military regulations.

His uniform was plain, with a name tag that read "Hadrukc"—meaning *rock* in his native language—centered along the seam of his shirt. On the top of his shoulders three little starships signified his rank and job as a fleet commander.

The uniform itself was black, with a long-sleeved shirt neatly tucked into his trousers. One decoration was on the uniform, a red stripe which ran along the sleeves. It mimicked the colors of the Federation—black with a red stripe—but set him drastically apart from the turquoise uniform other FDA personnel wore.

The reason for the uniform, and for his high rank, was he had earned the Ribargo ribbon. To get the Ribargo ribbon, you had to pass a test that consisted of mostly simulated battles designed by Ribargo and all those who had passed the test.

General Ribargo was a military genius who had saved the Federation from defeat, but had been almost drummed out of the military by petty jealously. To prevent this from happening in the future, when General Ribargo was made head of the Council of Generals, he created the test and the ribbon. Anyone who earned it was allowed to assume command of any military unit engaged in battle and could not be kicked out of the military. Those who could pass the test were rare and usually there was only one every two or three centuries. Only once in the entire history of the Federation had two beings worn the ribbon at the same time. The war games between those two had become the basis for all modern strategy.

General Hadrukc had earned the Ribargo ribbon when he was a captain, faster than normal but not the fastest. He quickly rose through the ranks, but like all the others who had earned the Ribargo ribbon he was sent to the outer rim of the Federation, where he would not be able to assume control of any of the other generals' commands. To minimize the time he was in the core of the Federation, they only had him report once every four years.

He had been on his way to report when a message had reached him, asking for his advice on the Earth situation. Hadrukc—who was not particularly eager to meet the Council of Generals—accepted the offer and detoured to the flagship of the fleet that was to reconquer Earth.

As Hadrukc strode into the conference room, all the other generals stood as a sign of courtesy. Acknowledging their gesture with a nod, Hadrukc took his seat at the far end of the table.

When everyone had been seated again, a large three-dimensional map appeared in the middle of the table. The general sitting at the head of the table announced, "General Hadrukc, thank you for coming. Have you been apprised of the situation?"

"As a matter of fact, I have." Hadrukc continued, "Four hundred of our battleships destroyed or captured, two hundred stuck in dry docks for the next six months, and the remaining four hundred in various states of disrepair. On the ground, we were forced to accept terms of surrender because the enemy took out our space fleet and destroyed our supply depots. All in all, a brilliant plan by the enemy."

On the ride to the flagship, Hadrukc had formed his plan, so he was going to ignore all the preliminaries and explain it now while he had the floor.

"Display projected enemy forces on the map. Thank you. Now, as you can see, the enemy is spread out all along Earth. They have not yet consolidated their forces. If we can strike at one side of the planet with a strong force, we should be able to resist the piecemeal counterattacks long enough for the enemy to realize those aren't going to work. He will retreat to one side of the planet and we will wait on ours."

"A stalemate," one of the generals summarized.

"Correct. We will inflict so much damage on him initially he will have to wait for reinforcements to arrive before launching another attack. In the mean-time we will send in our own reinforcements. Since we have the advantage in numbers, as long as we wait on our side of the planet the enemy will see we will outnumber him in the long run. He will lose the game of building up forces, and seeing he cannot overcome us, will have no choice but to retreat."

Hadrukc briefly paused, then continued, "While this is going on, our bat-tleships and troop transports will land infantry on the battlefield. Our plan of battle there will be to force the enemy to use up supplies. We need to force the marines into costly frontal assaults that will cause them to expend tremen-dous amounts of ammunition. The enemy will run out of munitions some-time before we do. Without ammunition, the Alliance will have to withdraw their troops along with their ships. Does this plan make sense to you?"

One of the generals at the table—a Rotain—said, "What I understand is your plan for the space battle is to force everyone to take a side of the planet, then have an arms race to see who can get the most battleships on their side of the planet. Since we have more battleships, we will win the race. The enemy will realize he cannot win, and will have to retreat or risk losing over twenty percent of his total fleet. We win without firing a shot."

"Precisely."

"But then the Alliance gets away."

"The objective of war never is, and never has been, the destruction of your enemy. The objective of war is to benefit your nation at the smallest cost to yourself. The benefit we are looking for is to reclaim Earth. My plan will get us the objective with the least cost in beings and materiel."

"We have the enemy in one place. Why not destroy him now?"

Hadrukc sighed. "Since Earth has been discovered, the Alliance will try again and again to reclaim it. Knowing this, we can set up an elaborate ambush and get them all on *our* terms. The current battle is being fought on the enemy's terms, so this is the best we can hope for. More importantly, if we destroy their fleet and their army now, the survivors will hide on the planet and fight an endless guerrilla wars. Do you comprehend what I'm saying?"

"Perfectly."

"Good; very good. Now, unless there are objections, I would like to lead the attack personally."

There were no objections.

General Hadrukc rose from his seat. "I will now plan my attack."

⸺•⸺

The massive FDA fleet of one thousand battleships appeared into real space on the night side of Earth. It was similar to the first space battle above Earth, as the Alliance once again had a little more than a thousand battleships, slightly outnumbering the FDA.

On the surface, the difference between the battles was this time the FDA was trying to take Earth. However, the biggest difference was standing on the battle bridge of the Federation flagship *Essrock*.

Hadrukc stood staring out at the enemy fleet before him. He had arranged his fleet into a pyramid with the point aimed at the enemy, allowing every single ship in the formation to fire at the same target. The last row was flying in reverse to prevent anyone from coming upon their rear. His bomber wings were divided into four groups, each of them designed to swarm one battleship and disable it quickly. His fighters were divided into five groups, one flying cover above each of the bomber groups, and the final one staying back as a reserve to defend the battleships. To defend against enemy bomber attacks, he had a couple squadrons of *Dousier*-class battleships positioned near the front of the formation where they could sortie out and defeat incoming bombers with their awesome AA and AAA batteries.

Hadrukc gazed down on the enemy. "On my command, have all the battleships fire on the," Hadrukc glanced down at his handheld tactical display, "*Red River*. Ready, fire."

All the guns in the FDA battle fleet opened fire at once, concentrating on a single ship. The Alliance battleship was utterly blown to pieces in less than one volley. The FDA fleet shifted its guns onto the next battleship, which was also smashed into space junk in one volley. Each of the bomber groups descended upon an Alliance battleship. The massive amount of firepower produced by the bombers were able to knock out the guns of the Alliance battleships in a couple of passes.

The Alliance forces were scattered across the planet in a defensive perimeter. They came at the FDA fleet piecemeal, not having any coordination. Every time Hadrukc saw the enemy attempt to organize, he shifted the fleet's fire to the apparent leader, throwing the Alliance back into chaos.

Eventually, the Alliance managed to gather enough battleships to make a real attack. Their commander realized the only way to defeat the formation was to fly underneath it and come upon its rear to destroy the formation from behind. As they flew underneath the pyramid, the rear half of the FDA formation stopped, leaving the first half of the formation to continue forward. The rear half of the formation turned downward to face the Alliance battleships and then commenced destroying them one at a time.

General Hadrukc's attention was not on the battleships, however. Instead, he was staring at the star fighters engaged in battle above the bombers. The Alliance fighter squadrons had intercepted the covering fighters and were engaged in a vicious whirling battle. This, however, was but a diversionary attack, and kept the FDA fighters occupied while the Alliance bombers dived in among the battleships.

The FDA fighter squadrons held in reserve attacked these bombers. Despite being badly outnumbered, the Alliance fighter squadron escorting the bombers actually did a decent job.

With fascination, Hadrukc watched the battle raging around him, having perfect confidence in the ability of his soldiers to protect him. He took particular interest in a certain Alliance fighter pilot.

He called the captain over. "Captain, come take a look at this."

The captain dutifully complied.

Hadrukc pointed out the transparent steel. "You see that Alliance fighter, the one above the battleship *Lulkreen*? Yes, that's the one. Now, observe that it has two of our fighters on it, one in front of it and the other behind it. Notice how the Alliance pilot skillfully keeps making small jukes so our pilots cannot get a lock."

He continued, "I wonder if—yes, just as I expected. The Alliance pilot waited until he—or she, I have heard the Alliance also recruits female pilots—had nearly collided with the fighter in front of him or her, then pulled up hard. To avoid colliding, our two pilots both pulled up after the Alliance pilot, but the Alliance pilot had already turned around at that point and destroyed the two of them in one sweeping burst. Quite a brilliant maneuver, in my opinion."

"Would you like me to destroy the fighter pilot, sir?" the captain asked in an almost tired voice.

"Yes, that would be very nice actually. I would like you to try to destroy the fighter pilot. It will be interesting to see how good this pilot really is. Have a *Dousier* concentrate its fire on that Alliance fighter."

Not being too proud to learn from his enemies was one of the things that made Hadrukc better than all the others. He could tell the captain did not understand this and thought his interest in the Alliance fighter pilot trivial.

A nearby *Dousier*-class battleship opened fire upon the fighter pilot. The Alliance fighter pilot went into a dazzling array of evasive maneuvers instead of trying to get out of the battleship's line of fire. Hadrukc figured out the pilot's plan just before it came into being. As the fighter pilot drew the battleship's fire, a bomber squadron attacked the battleship's guns without fear of anti-aircraft defense.

Seeing the battleship was going to lose its guns to the bombers, Hadrukc said, "Captain, inform the *Dousier's* commander they may resume normal firing."

The captain complied with the order, then walked up next to Hadrukc. "Your curiosity satisfied, sir?"

His mind otherwise occupied, Hadrukc ignored the displeasure in the captain's voice. "Almost. Captain, zoom in one of the targeting cameras on the fighter so I can see the pilot."

Irritated to no end but trying not to show it, the captain gave a few quick commands.

Looking down at the small handheld tactical display he was holding, Hadrukc saw the screen turn from a map with the positions of the fleet on it to a video screen. He looked at the screen. "A female pilot. Interesting."

Turning the display back to the map, Hadrukc said to the captain, "Thank you, Captain, that's all I need for now. You may attend to your duties."

As the captain frostily turned away, Hadrukc stopped him. "By the way, from that excursion we've learned something important. Humans do not consider the consequences their actions will have on themselves. Their sole interest is in the immediate victory. That means they will fall into my trap."

An officer working one of the tactical situation maps called out to Hadrukc, "Sir, the enemy appears to be organizing. Without the rear half of our fleet, the battle computer predicts a 70 percent chance we'll be destroyed."

"Communications, contact the rest of the fleet. Find out where the majority of the enemy is concentrating its fire," Hadrukc commanded.

Only a few seconds later the comm. officer replied, "Sir, there is no pattern. Most ships report the enemy's fire is scattered and not concentrated."

"Notify me if there is any change. The enemy is not preparing an attack. If he were, he'd be concentrating his fire on our midspace drives to prevent our escape."

The ranking tactical officer informed Hadrukc in an even voice, "Sir, while the enemy attack groups are still widely dispersed, they have maneuvered so they are either above or below us. Half the guns in the fleet cannot be brought to bear."

So they have finally started thinking and stopped reacting, thought Hadrukc.

"Very well, instruct the fleet to maintain formation, but they are now permitted to engage individual enemies as long as they remain in pairs. Make sure all ships understand they are no longer to wait for the fleet to designate a target before firing."

Though he could not feel it, Hadrukc noted the battleship was rotating upward by the way the stars changed position. Although the direction the ship was facing had changed, it continued along its previous axis of advance, keeping it in line with the rest of the fleet.

Looking to his right, Hadrukc noticed the battleship next to his had rotated in the same direction. Gazing directly ahead, he spotted in the distance a blue pyramid about half the size of his forefinger. Hadrukc knew the pyramid to be an Alliance *Avendor* class battleship and correctly guessed his battleship would be attacking it.

Long luminescent tails streaked toward the Alliance battleship. Seconds later, more luminescent tails appeared in the empty space between the battleships, but this time they were heading for Hadrukc's flagship.

Hadrukc watched dispassionately as the incoming luminescent tails detonated in a bright blue ball as the defense rifles picked them off. Hadrukc returned his attention to the handheld tactical display. He trusted the captain was competent enough to defeat the Alliance battleship.

His tactical display showed a few small groups of his fleet had broken off and were in danger of being flanked. He ordered them to full reverse and detailed other sections of the fleet to cover their retreat, but several battleships were slow to comply with his orders and were consequently destroyed.

Hadrukc sighed. *You can have the most brilliant orders, and do everything possible to ensure your fleet's survival, but someone always has to question what you say and get killed.*

The comm. officer interrupted his thoughts with an update. "Sir, the rear half of the fleet reports the enemy group that engaged them has been destroyed."

"Good. Instruct them to reform with the rest of the fleet. The enemy should begin a retreat shortly."

As he predicted, within the next few minutes the comm. officer again reported, "Sir, we have picked up an increase in enemy comm. traffic. Also, the majority of our fleet has reported a pattern has developed in the incoming fire they are receiving. The enemy is generally targeting the fleet's weapons systems."

"They are preparing to retreat," Hadrukc said triumphantly. "They don't want us to be able to hit them as they fall back. Tell the fleet to maintain pressure on the enemy, but allow the Alliance to retreat. Insure all commanders understand at this point avoiding becoming disabled is the highest priority."

The comm. officer did as ordered. "Sir, several captains are requesting permission to pursue the enemy and finish them off."

"Permission denied. If the captains will look at their tactical displays, they will notice the portion of the Alliance fleet that was not engaged has moved to the far side of the planet where our sensors are blind. Undoubtedly they have prepared an ambush. Instruct the captains to remain with the rest of the fleet."

Turing to the captain, Hadrukc inquired, "Did you destroy that Alliance battleship?"

The Captain replied, "Yes sir. The *Essrock* will be adding another victory to its long history."

Seeing his fleet was being to cut to pieces, the Alliance commander ordered his ships to the other side of Earth to regroup, exactly as Hadrukc had said they would. It would take about thirty minutes for the Alliance fleet to reorganize and for a plan to be worked out.

Taking advantage of this time, Hadrukc had the troop transports that were waiting at the edge of the solar system make the short jump to Earth. To the horror of the Alliance commanders, shuttles began to stream forth from the FDA fleet, bearing an invasion army. Before they could do anything about it, several divisions had already landed. Any attempt to counter-attack the FDA fleet was forgotten, for if they did not act quickly, the MAA would soon be overwhelmed.

Chapter 34
John's Decision

In the way that is the norm with a bureaucracy, the actual attempt to retake Earth from the FDA ground forces was delayed for two days. Supplies were backed up, invasion plans had to be made three different times to satisfy all the politicians and military commanders, and all the other self-destructive activities had to be accomplished before the assault. During that time, the FDA had poured reinforcements into every corner of the Earth. All nations with a strategic value had at least a corps in it and every continent had at least three corps. The FDA fortified its positions until it had strong defensive lines around every point of importance on the planet.

At long last the plans had been set and the Alliance was prepared to make its counterattack. The marines were to make a planet-head. This attack was extremely tough since only a few places on the planet had enough room for large-scale landings close enough to something worth taking. The enemy heavily fortified these places and the marines had no choice but to charge in.

Greg's unit was slated to go in one hour as part of the third wave. Every-one was busy rushing around the hangar as they prepared for the upcoming battle. Mechanics were making last-minute tune-ups on their shuttles, ord-nance personnel were dragging out munitions, loadmasters were arranging supplies for easy loading, yellow construction hovercraft went up and down the hangar ferrying heavy equipment, and marines constantly checked and rechecked their gear.

Inspecting his marines, Greg was impressed. Wearing their light forest Ghillie Suits with their hoods pulled over their boonie hats, sniper rifles as-sembled and ready to fire, they looked dangerous. On their backs were huge, bulging rucksacks, loaded with everything they would need to survive for almost a week on the battlefield. Extra ammo was stuffed in all the outside pockets of the rucksack. Attached to the sides of the rucksack were the halves of a disassembled battle rifle.

Greg said, "When we go down to the planet, be ready to rock and roll. If you need anything, make sure you have it now. We will be in normal spotter/sniper teams, with the senior man spotter. Any questions?"

Brauner asked, "Sergeant, who goes with John?"

"Good question." Greg glanced around and failed to find John. "Where did he go?"

"I saw him leave the line about fifteen minutes ago. Didn't see where he went," Lynch said.

"I'll go take a look around for him. Rodrigo, you're in charge."

Not really having any idea where he was going, Greg began to wander around the hangar, looking for any sign of John. Finding no trace of him, he decided to try the squad area.

As he was walking toward the lift, he spotted John slouched next to the wall. "You could've left a message where you were going."

He slowly gazed up at Greg. "Take a look around you. All this noise and confusion, all these preparations for an invasion. A straight-on, full-throttle offensive for the great and noble cause of taking Earth back from the hands of the Federation."

"Yes, both of us have fought very hard to get this far."

John shook his head. "This isn't what I do. I'm an assassin. I kill from behind; I kill for money. Fighting for a good cause is not one of the things I do. It was nice for a little while, but I can't continue. There are a lot of clients waiting and I need to get back in the business."

"We're on the eve of an invasion. Whatever you want to do will have to wait till later. Right now we need to concentrate on the job at hand. Besides, you're not just an assassin. I know you; you're better than that. Now's not the time to pull out, the squad's counting on you; I'm counting on you, and in all probability the whole 'race is counting on you. You can't leave right now anyway; all the transports are tied up for the invasion."

The last sentence had come out almost as a plea, a desperate attempt to keep John with the squad.

"I already called the flagship. They are sending the *Mercy* over and have installed an autopilot that will get me out of the hangar. It will be here in about five minutes. I was planning on telling you in a few minutes, once I had figured out what to say."

Almost in a state of shock, Greg said, "John, we go into battle in one hour. You can't leave now. We need you, man. You're cutting out on us, you're …"

Greg never got to finish the sentence. A call came in for John.

Listening to the call, John said, "Okay, I'll be over in few seconds."

Standing up, John looked at Greg. "They arrived sooner than I expected. Got to go."

Somewhere between a state of disbelief, betrayal, and anger, Greg watched as John turned his back on him and walked to the *Mercy*. John opened the rear door and the Alliance pilot who had flown it hopped out. Climbing into the shuttle, John disappeared. The engines on the shuttle came to life and slowly the shuttle rose and flew out the open hangar door.

Greg's eyes followed the shuttle out the hangar, not believing what they were seeing. His gaze lingered on the spot where the shuttle had exited.

Turning away, Greg walked back to his squad in a fury. *To decide this is something you don't want to do was one thing, but to quit on the eve of battle is utterly against any sort of warrior's honor. I had thought he was a friend; now I have no idea what to think. I'm not sure John's even human.*

Reaching the squad, Sandusky asked, "Where's John?"

"He isn't coming. Everyone make sure you got all you need."

The squad had already done as he had ordered, so they sat in silence as Greg took his place in line. They could see the anger shining through Greg's eyes. After about five minutes, there was a change in Greg's expression as he calmed down. But behind his self-control, a cold, hard interior lay, waiting to unleash its wrath on some poor target.

Speaking in low voices, the squad waited for the invasion. In twenty minutes, the first wave took off from the hangar deck. As the shuttles hovered in the hangar on their repulse-lifters, all the marines and sailors came to their feet and started cheering. One by one the shuttles left. Every time a shuttle flew out loud applause broke out from those standing on the deck. Once the last shuttle had left, the marines sat down again and the sailors went back to their duties.

Fifteen minutes later, the shuttles returned. Several shuttles were missing and most of those returning had scars on their hulls. One was shot up so badly it cracked upon landing.

Sailors hurried to rearm the shuttles, replenishing their spent ammunition. The marines who boarded this time were not nearly as confident as the first wave. There was no cheering, no wild applause.

Marines looked anxiously at their chronometers, counting off the time until fifteen minutes had passed. When the expected time had come and gone, they began to worry. Finally, the shuttles showed up a couple of minutes late, putting all the marines' fears to rest.

As their shuttle landed, Greg told them, "Everybody stand up. I want you aboard that shuttle the instant the door opens. No delays, we need to do this quickly."

The shuttle door opened, and before the squad could get on board the loadmaster hauled the bodies of three marines out of the shuttle and dumped them over the edge.

"They got hit by AA fire that came through the floor before we hit the ground. Someone will come along to deal with the bodies," the loadmaster said.

"Get on board, marines," Greg shouted.

Obeying the order, Greg's squad hustled to the back of the shuttle. Being useless in a close-range firefight, they would exit the shuttle last.

As he entered the shuttle, Greg took one last look around. Because of the loss of shuttles, some of the second wave was only now getting on board. The invasion was going to be off schedule.

Greg walked down to the end of the shuttle where his squad was. He sat down where he would be the first into battle. The shuttle was quickly filled with marines. There was a loud noise as the repulse-lifter came on and slowly raised the shuttle from the hangar deck.

Greg felt the shuttle begin to accelerate out of the hangar. *Here I go, off into the abyss of a land war. Down I soar, to meet the great killing machine, the evil that has cursed civilization for centuries. Big frickin' deal.*

Chapter 35

The Third Battle for Earth

Approximately ten seconds after the shuttles had entered Earth's atmosphere, the FDA began to send AAA up. The EMP charges detonated in the air all around them. Fortunately, none of the shuttles were hit.

Coming through the cloud layer, antiaircraft machine gun batteries began to send their torrent bullets up into the sky. Dodging back and forth, the Assault Shuttles continued their headlong dive to the ground.

Breaking out of the clouds, the shuttles could now see some of the FDA batteries. Opening fire with their own guns, they managed to destroy a few of the enemy's defenses.

The ride was rough and bumpy, but Greg did not mind. Every time an EMP charge exploded he could feel the shock wave go through the air. There was a hollow THUNK as a bullet hit one of the wings, but Greg was still unfazed.

Soaring down through the sky, the shuttles began to split up and head toward their different landing points. One was cut in half by a stream of AA shells as it peeled off from the formation. Settling in for the final approach, Greg's shuttle fired a pair of missiles at an AA battery.

The missiles were basically high-explosive battleship shells strapped onto a hypervelocity propellant. An outer casing of ice bullets was packed around the shells for anti-infantry purposes.

As the two missiles arched away from the shuttle, they left long white tails. Two massive explosions announced the missiles had found their target. The AA gun was smashed into rubble along with most of its crew.

Greg's Assault Shuttle formed up with the three shuttles in its flight. The flight dived down toward their landing point. Spotting the mountain overlooking the landing site, the shuttles fired their remaining missiles into it, hoping to suppress some of the fire the marines on the ground were receiving.

"Two minutes till landing," the loadmaster shouted.

The marines stood up. Tensing themselves to spring out of the shuttle the instant they hit the ground, they eagerly awaited the door's opening. Almost unexpectedly the Assault Shuttle leveled out and descended the last few meters on its repulse-lifters.

Before it had touched ground the loadmaster opened the door. Marines jumped out of the shuttle and hit the ground running. By the time the shuttle touched the ground only Greg's squad was still in the shuttle.

"Let's go, marines," Greg shouted as he ran down the shuttle. His squad followed, jumping out the shuttle with him.

Once on the ground, they were confronted with a scene beyond their wildest imaginations. Dead marines lay scattered across the big open plain that served as the landing zone. Several destroyed FDA positions ringed the open plain.

An FDA position on the mountain overlooking the landing zone had not been silenced and was firing into the marines as they exited the shuttles. The first few marines exiting Greg's shuttle were instantly cut down.

Most terrible of all were the mortars and artillery. Though the shells lacked the killing power and range of a rifle, they would wound anyone within thirty meters.

Hundreds of these deadly shells flew over the battlefield. The Alliance had not counted on how well the FDA had prepared its support weapons. Once again, artillery had taken over its rightful place as king of the battlefield, and the Alliance had no answer.

Hearing the shells come whistling overhead, a marine yelled at the snipers, "Get down!"

The squad hit the deck, except for Greg, who only dropped into a low crouch. Several shells detonated around them, but none of the snipers were hit. He stood up. "Don't hit the deck again; you only expose yourself to the air-bursting shells. The best you can do is to get in a low crouch. And spread out; don't get so bunched together."

Greg's marines hurried to comply with his orders, spurred on by the sight of at least one marine dropping every second to one of these exploding shells.

As far as Greg could tell, there wasn't a safe place on the battlefield. He looked at the major concentrations of enemy fire and made a quick analysis. As the shells burst around him, he realized what was happening.

"They've preregistered their artillery," Greg shouted to his marines. "Avoid anywhere that has a lot of shell holes and don't get within five hundred meters of any troop concentrations."

The squad moved as far and as fast as it could from where the shuttle had landed, not heading in any particular direction.

By now the shuttles had left the area. The landing zone itself was mass confusion incarnate. Although the infantry had clear objectives, the support troops milled around, having no idea what to do.

Greg looked around and spotted a major who appeared to be organizing some sort of attack. After ordering his squad to halt, Greg made his way to the major.

The major was standing in plain sight as he yelled out orders. Seeing Greg, he said, "You, you're a sniper aren't you? Go set up a sniper hill over there." He pointed to a hill about two kilometers from the landing zone.

The major took off the speaking wire attached to his helmet. "Here, take my wire. Now move!"

Attaching the wire to his speaking rod, Greg ran back to his squad, which had taken cover behind a slight bluff. Halfway there, a string of mortar shells landed nearby, walking their way toward Greg.

Greg threw himself behind a small cluster of rocks that lay at his feet. The rocks weren't much bigger than two fists, but Greg flattened himself so much he felt he was considerably thinner than the rocks. He didn't go into a crouch as all these shells were ground-bursts.

As he listened to the rounds creeping closer, Greg did not close his eyes. He didn't cringe as shrapnel whistled past his ear. The moment came and passed, and the mortar rounds skipped over him and started impacting the ground behind him.

Greg realized he was now exposed to the shells behind him. He swiftly scrambled around to the other side of the rocks and waited out the barrage.

The instant it stopped he was back on his feet and running toward his squad. A couple of stray artillery rounds landed near him, but these he ignored. He had almost made it to his squad when a shell landed right in front of him.

There was a bright flash and the next thing he knew Greg was on his back. There was a terrible pain in his left foot. He lifted that leg to inspect the damage, and then he noticed Lynch, Sandusky, and Brauner standing next to him. The three marines picked him up and started dragging him back to the bluff where the squad had taken cover.

When they brought him back to the temporary shelter, Greg called out, "How bad is it?"

Corporal Smith delicately removed the piece of diamond armor covering Greg's leg. He took off Greg's boot and inspected the wound. "It's not bad, Sergeant; all you have is a couple diamond shards in your foot."

"Great. Slap a bandage on it."

Smith had to use a spare shirt as a bandage because no one had expected anyone to become wounded and live to tell about it. He swiftly wrapped it around Greg's foot, taking pains to make sure it was tight enough to stop the bleeding but loose enough not to interfere with circulation.

The instant Smith was done, Greg forced his foot into his boot and slapped on his leg armor. He slowly stood up and hobbled forward a few paces.

"We have a job. Set up a sniper hill up over yonder." He indicated the hill with his head.

"Let's move, Second Squad," Rodrigo shouted. The men got to their feet.

They set off at a jog across the landing field. They hadn't gone far when Sandusky yelled, "Poppers!"

Greg suddenly heard the distinctive popping sound made by the air-bursting mortar shells, and dropped into the smallest crouch he could manage. He did not hit the dirt, for he knew the instant he did that shrapnel from above would rain down on his exposed back.

The barrage exploded above him. After about a half dozen shells detonated, the bombardment lifted. Someone cried, "Sergeant, I'm hit!"

Greg and Smith rushed over to the downed marine. The marine was lying on the ground, stubbornly ignoring the pain as he worked to unfasten his hip armor.

When Greg was close enough to tell who the marine was, he said, "How bad is it?"

"Not bad, Sergeant," White replied. "It hurts like heck, but I can still do my job. All I need to do is stop the bleeding."

Greg knelt beside White and pulled out an undershirt from White's overstuffed rucksack. White grabbed the shirt and stuffed it between his diamond armor and the wound, using the pressure to staunch the bleeding.

White climbed to his feet, winced in pain, then snapped to attention. "Ready to go, Sergeant."

Greg maintained his cold expression. "Let's move out."

The squad started forward again. As they marched, Rodrigo called out to Sandusky, "How long did it take you to make up the nickname 'poppers'?"

"About five minutes, Corporal."

"What are you going to call the ground-bursting shells?"

Sandusky thought about that for a minute. "I think I'll call them 'whistlers'."

"You encounter an entirely new weapon and five minutes later you already have a nickname for it," Rodrigo laughed.

Greg silently continued jogging.

They had nearly crossed the landing zone when they heard a loud explosion and then something that sounded like a freight car being hurled through the air. Someone yelled "*Battleship shells,*" and every marine in the landing zone dropped to the ground.

Massive explosions shook the ground as an FDA battleship bombarded the landing zone. The annoying thing about battleship bombardments was the shell traveled so fast it exploded before the sound could be heard, giving no warning of the impending doom to the marines below.

The huge shells tore great holes in ground. Massive detonation sent shock waves that flattened marines. Ice bullets whistled through the air. Greg could have sworn he saw a marine get hurled across the landing zone by one of those shells.

Though it seemed to last a lifetime, the shelling did not last much longer than one or two minutes. Having weathered that bombardment, the squad stood up and started moving across the battlefield again.

Moving at a brisk pace, the squad managed to reach the hill in about twenty minutes. The snipers slowly crept to the top of the hill. Being too far away from the landing zone to be of any tactical use, this hill was unoccupied.

Not more than 28 meters high, the hill was just high enough to provide an overview of the battlefield. The top of the hill was mostly barren of any vegetation, but craggy rocks jutted out all over the place, providing decent cover for the snipers. Greg wasn't quite certain what the terrain of the landing zone had been, since most of it had been turned to dirt by the incoming shells, but the land in front of him consisted of mainly knee-high shrubs with small groves of trees.

Once near the top, the squad deployed in sniper hill formation. Once in sniper hill, the squad completely ringed the hill, allowing it to provide fire support in any direction without having to get on the exposed crest.

In addition to having a sniper placed at every point around the hill, two snipers—in this case Sandusky and Lynch—served as countersnipers, their job being to take out the enemy before the squad could be attacked.

Greg took a moment to rest. The pain from his wound made the climbing excruciating and it was with the last vestiges of his strength he finally made it into position.

As soon as he was ready, Greg reported to the comm. station there were snipers on station. The word was forwarded to infantry commanders and calls for fire support came in almost faster than Greg could delegate them.

When he received a call, he shouted the coordinates to the appropriate sniper. Greg didn't worry about someone hearing him. Most of the fighting was at least ten kilometers away.

The report of sniper rifles became a constant sound on the hill. It was not long until a fire request was sent in for Greg's sector.

Looking into his scope, Greg zoomed in as far he could go. His target was a good eighteen kilometers away, but he was able to find it without too much trouble.

A marine platoon was attacking up a hill. There was a pillbox holding them up. Spotting the soldier in the pillbox, Greg quickly made calculations for the wind and heat factor, took a breath and let half of it out, then gently pulled the trigger back. An invisible hand knocked the soldier in the pillbox down. A perfect shot.

Unzooming the scope, in the bottom of his vision Greg spotted a group of six FDA soldiers making a dash from their bunkers. Taking aim at them, Greg confirmed they were enemy, then let loose all the anger he was feeling.

Pulling the trigger, Greg shot down the last soldier in line. *I can't believe John just left us.* Moving onto the next soldier in line, Greg fired again. The soldier's limbs went into a crazy flopping before he fell, indicating a head shot. *I thought he was a friend, but then he abandoned me on the eve of battle.*

Seeing they were getting shot down, the soldiers split into different directions. Greg tracked the fastest of them, put his aimer just in front of a soldier and squeezed the trigger. Taking the soldier in the side, the bullet caused the soldier do a spin before he collapsed on the ground. *What kind of a person leaves his buddies to their fate just before combat.*

The fourth was running perpendicular to Greg, the most difficult of all shots. Estimating the alien's speed, Greg took the proper amount of lead and fired. The soldier's chest exploded with the impact of Greg's projectile. *I thought John was better than that.*

One—a Waas—had continued trying to make it to where the group had originally been going. Having run out of ammo, Greg quickly slapped in a new clip. Correcting for the soldier's moving away from him, Greg settled his sight on the Waas' head. His rifle barked, and the soldier did a cartwheel forward as the bullet took him square in the back. *I thought he was human, and not a bad one at that.*

Attempting to get back to where he had come from, the final soldier provided the easiest shot of all. Dropping his sight to the soldier's gut, Greg pulled the trigger, and hit him in the torso, knocking him onto his back like he had been hit by a speeding hovercraft. *I thought John decided to fight for a good cause, but then he went back to killing for money.*

The soldiers dead, Greg took his eyes from the scope. It felt good, killing them.

Never kill in anger. Once you do that, you are forever lost. Ethan Ramon's words flashed through Greg's mind.

Greg let go of his rifle. The bipod prevented the rifle from falling, leaving it standing.

He was barely cognizant when the next call for fire support came in. He relayed it to the closest sniper. For him, there would be no more killing.

At nightfall, the squad was ordered off the mountain and told to report to the forward HQ for assignments. They began to slowly climb down the hill.

It was a seven-kilometer walk to the forward HQ, so it took the snipers about two and half hours to reach it. By then night had completely fallen. Sporadic mortar fire continued throughout the night, but none of it was directed toward the squad.

The forward HQ was not what they had expected. It consisted of a series of fighting holes connected by trenches, all of it with some sort of covering on the top of it. For having been on Earth one day, this was quite impressive. The extra motivation had probably been the constant artillery fire.

Reaching the perimeter, a guard sent a challenge to Greg. Greg gave the proper reply and was admitted into the HQ. The squad climbed into one of the trenches and looked for someone to give them a new mission. As they wandered around, they ran into Lieutenant Derek.

Seeing them all alive, he said, "Sergeant Heyligher, how's it been going?"

"We took two casualties, but neither was fatal. Though we're still able to function, the wounds need treatment before too long."

"There isn't anything for you right now. Under the cover of darkness they are going to try to land navy doctors. They have experience dealing with wounds from battleship shells. They should be able to treat all the wounded we've got."

There was a pause as they stood for an awkward second.

"How did you guys do today?" Lieutenant Derek asked.

"Most got two or three kills; Sandusky and Lynch got a sniper team apiece."

"Yeah, they've a lot of snipers here. Me and Ramon spent the day taking out a sniper that had become particularly troublesome. He wasn't a bad sniper, but he didn't have a spotter, typical mistake of arrogance. It took all day, but we got him. Speaking of which, how did you do yourself?"

"Seven."

"Seven? I'll believe it when I see the tape."

"Where is Staff Sergeant Ramon? It's pretty important I see him."

"I haven't seen him in a while. In the meantime. I have some assignments to hand out to you. I'll let you make the actual decision on who does what, but right now I need you to come down to my foxhole with your squad for a debriefing."

Greg mentally sighed. The war called, which meant he would have to kill again.

Chapter 36

Return to the House

John stood outside his abandoned mansion surveying the damage. The windows that had been destroyed in the fight with the assassins still lay shattered. Shards littered the grounds. Otherwise it seemed to be in pretty good shape.

No vandals had hit the mansion; the location was far too remote for them. It was in the middle of a mountain range overlooking a valley with a river running down the middle of it. The mansion was about midway up a mountain, just behind a false ridge that prevented those directly underneath the mountain from seeing it. A huge ledge jutted out of the mountain above the mansion, overshadowing it and hiding it from view from above.

Turning around, John walked over to the *Mercy*, which he had parked just outside the house. He went inside the shuttle, grabbed the little bits of gear he had not taken with him, and locked the shuttle down.

John wasn't worried about someone tracking the shuttle to his location. If someone did track him here, there was only one angle from which they could approach and he had a concealed AA gun to cover that angle. He hadn't been able to reach the gun when the two assassins came because they had come over the top of the mountain and rappelled down the overhang.

John exited the shuttle and strode to the entrance of his mansion. The left half had windows stationed at normal intervals, with a large double door at the lower left hand corner. The right half of the mansion was divided into two sections, upper and lower. The top half held the long room with huge windows; the lower half had no windows at all.

With the huge windows destroyed, the mansion took on a different feel. The office room looked almost like a large porch with walls on either end. John considered leaving it like that, but decided to go back to the old look.

When he reached the large, wooden, five-meter-high double doors, he dropped the load he was carrying and unlocked the door. Gathering the objects he had dropped, John shoved the door open with his shoulder.

The entrance room wasn't big, with only enough room for one small red couch with a wood frame. A couple of ancient artifacts were on display in the room, plus a painting on the wall. Paintings were rare in these times, each one costing a small fortune. John had three.

Proceeding down the narrow hallway, John went to his armory. Inside the armory, racks of weapons lined the walls. He kept several sets of his preferred four ice weapons, along with multiple other weapons he had used throughout the years.

Cabinets lined the wall beneath the weapons racks. In those he stored all the gear that was not used to kill.

After replacing his weapons and gear, John went upstairs to his office. Stepping off the lift, John looked at how bad the damage was from the inside. Shards of the window were scattered across the room. The wild bullets fired by the assassin had cut and scarred the wood floor. He was going to need to get someone to repair this.

A construction company that works for the big gangsters, like Ali-Bettlas, would do. They know the rules, and I could hire them through a couple of blinds. I'll schedule the job for when I'm on a mission. That should be enough to keep my residence a secret.

Slowly making his way around the pieces of glass that had fallen on the floor, John took a seat behind his desk. Hitting a button on the desk, John waited while a hot beverage came out of the far left hand corner of his desk. Picking the beverage up, John leaned back as he turned on his recording device and began looking for a well-paying mission.

———⋆◆⋆———

White had received treatment for his wounds first. While waiting for him to recover, Rodrigo got hit by a shell and had to be rushed into the medical ward. As the squad leader, Greg was seen by a doctor last.

In a few days, White was back on his feet and running missions with the rest of the squad. Greg and Rodrigo were released from the field hospital a little while later.

Greg and Rodrigo were sitting alone at the HQ, waiting for orders. The rest of the squad was deployed on missions. It was about midday and the two of them were eating lunch within easy reach of Greg's fighting hole.

Ethan Ramon crawled up to them. Once next to them, he slowly rose until he was sitting.

"This is really starting to be a problem," Ethan said. "I can't even travel freely around our own field HQ. Someone should do something about those mortars."

"You're telling me." Rodrigo pointed to his bandage.

Ethan laughed. "Heyligher, I heard you were looking for me."

Greg nodded his head. "I broke the rule."

The atmosphere suddenly seemed to become darker. Rodrigo involuntarily moved away from Greg.

Hoping he had heard wrong, Ethan asked, "Which rule?"

"I killed in anger." Greg continued in almost a whisper, "And I enjoyed it."

Ethan spat an expletive.

No one said anything for a while.

"I've known you since sniper school. I think you still stand a chance of changing," Rodrigo said.

"No," Ethan said. "In peace, maybe. But there is a war going on. Gregory, I need you on the front lines and I need you killing. As destructive as it is to your soul, you're perfect for the war effort."

Greg did not reply. *Ethan's given up on me. But I can fight this. I can win. I won't become a killer.*

When he looked up, Greg could see the front lines from his vantage point. Watching the mortars exploding in the distance, he knew Ethan was right. The Alliance needed a slayer. They would choose him.

Ironic. The battle has barely begun and already my soul has been destroyed. The first casualty of war.

As he realized this, a small part of him was excited and looking forward to it.

"Gregory, are you listening to me?" Ethan's voice broke into his thoughts. "I said I want you and Rodrigo to go on a mission to make sure you still have what it takes."

"Where to?" Greg replied. If they wanted a killer, he would show them what he could do.

"Golf Company has been losing a couple marines every night to infiltrators. Stop the raiders. I'll assign a hovercraft to you in a few minutes."

Greg and Rodrigo grabbed their gear and hurried to the hovercraft.

It wasn't long before they were at the company's position. The area had light tree cover, but little elevation. The company was dug in around a small grove of trees.

Greg and Rodrigo did a little questioning as to what exactly had happened, which fighting holes the marines had been killed in, and other details.

When they had finished, the two of them conferred while studying the ground.

"I can't see how they manage to sneak up on them," Rodrigo said. "It's pretty much open ground in front of this grove."

Greg nodded. He looked around. The only place with enough coverage to sneak up on the marines was two kilometers away.

He was about to dismiss that route as a possibility, when it occurred to him that there was no good reason for it *not* to be their route.

"I think the raiders are using that tree line over there." Greg pointed with his finger.

Rodrigo thought about it. "It would make sense. The marines would be looking for them in front of their lines, not behind. Plus, two kilometers is what—twenty minutes, walking? It wouldn't be that far out of their way."

"Let's see if there're any tracks."

They gathered up a squad for security and slowly made their way toward the route they suspected the FDA raiders were using.

When they were a short distance away, Greg ordered the security squad to stop. He and Rodrigo crawled forward to inspect the area.

Moving at a snail's pace, the two snipers were nearly invisible in their Ghillie Suits.

Greg suddenly stopped moving. Rodrigo instantly froze. Greg slowly pointed his finger forward. Following the finger, Rodrigo noticed a faint alien footprint. Rodrigo silently nodded and the two of them started to crawl back.

When they reached the security squad, Greg spoke in a low voice. "We found where the infiltrators are coming from. We're going to move back about five hundred meters. I want you guys behind us so if anyone gets around you can deal with them."

The squad leader gave a thumbs-up to signal his agreement and the small unit went on the move again.

Once Greg and Rodrigo were far enough back, they stopped moving and set up their position. The rest of the squad continued on by, making a defensive position about a hundred meters behind them.

Greg locked his bipod in position, settled in behind the scope, and waited. He and Rodrigo took turns napping until night fell.

As darkness came, Greg decided to turn on his satellite aiming. Each sniper had a panel sown into his Ghillie Suit that reflected a certain frequency of ultraviolet light. An orbiting satellite assigned to a particular sniper would pick up these ultraviolet emissions and lock onto the sniper's coordinates. Since the EMP fields prevented the sniper from sending the satellite any signals, the satellite was programmed to react when the sniper made certain motions.

Grabbing the top of his scope, Greg slid the top half forward. The satellite immediately sent a tight-beamed laser that entered through the opening and filled the scope. When Greg looked through his scope again, he could see a red 3-D image of the area from above, with his aiming post in the middle. Using knobs on the side of the scope, Greg could zoom in and out, and could adjust the image forward or backward, but it would only show the area in his line of sight. To move the image sideways he would have to swing the rifle in the direction he wanted to look at.

Night came, and Greg and Rodrigo kept up their silent vigil. It wasn't until a little past midnight they finally spotted movement.

Greg picked it up first. He zoomed in and discovered it was an FDA soldier.

He notified Rodrigo of the soldier's position and took aim. He moved the inverted post on top of the soldier. The soldier was close, only about four hundred meters away. Greg could now see four more soldiers. They were moving slowly forward, stopping and checking every time they thought they heard something.

Once he was on target, Greg looked above his scope to see if there were any obstacles between him and the target. Seeing none, he lowered his head again and slowly started taking up trigger slack.

A part of Greg was screaming in delight. It couldn't wait to make the kill. *Why not give in? If you're going to lose your soul anyway, why not at least have fun doing it.*

No. I will not surrender. I hate killing. I hate doing this.

There was a sharp crack as Greg's rifle went off, followed a second later by Rodrigo's. Two of the soldiers fell to the ground. The others in the patrol did not hesitate and started running back to where they had come from.

Greg lined up on one of the retreating soldiers and fired again. The soldier stumbled forward a few steps and fell. In his scope Greg saw another of the raiders fall as Rodrigo's bullet found him. Panicked, the last soldier continued running in a straight line. Greg dropped his aimer on the soldier and fired. The round slammed into the soldier like a giant fist, flattening him to the ground.

The two snipers waited several more minutes to see if there were any more soldiers, then ordered the security squad forward to check the area out. The squad confirmed the enemy soldiers were dead, and declared the area secure.

Greg and Rodrigo slowly rose into a low crouch.

Rodrigo turned to Greg. "How do you feel?"

"Like hell," Greg replied.

"Good answer. Come on; let's get back to the HQ."

Chapter 37

Ski Patrol

Carol moved forward swiftly on his cross-country skis across the snow covered ground. Surrounded by mountains, he had no idea where he was other than somewhere in the Alps. Pine trees grew thick in this area, but he had found a game trail that allowed him to traverse the terrain quickly on his skis.

In front of him the point man suddenly stopped. Carol froze and did not start moving again until the point man signaled it was all clear.

Carol was once again on a recon patrol. They were paralleling a road made by the FDA. The lonely road led deep into the heart of the Alps.

Ever since the escalation of the war, the MAA had primarily been raiding enemy supply depots. As a result, the FDA had hidden its supply depots far from prying eyes. The recon teams assigned to each of the Assault Teams were constantly searching for these hidden supplies. Right now, Carol's team was traveling alongside a mountain road in hopes they would find one of these supply depots at the end of it.

To conduct the patrol, Carol had decided they couldn't use any vehicles without compromising their security. He had considered snowshoes, but those were too slow. Instead, Carol chose cross-country skis. Although antiquated, cross-country skis still provided the fastest mode of nonmotorized transportation over snow.

The patrol slowly crested a hill. The point man dropped to the ground and the rest of the team followed him. The point man whispered, "Lead, we have a four-man patrol about three hundred meters out."

Carol crawled to where the point man lay. He scanned the winter landscape before him. Against this white backdrop, the FDA soldiers stood out like a candle in a dark room. The FDA patrol was walking toward them on the game trail Carol was leading his team on.

Speaking very low, the ambush expert said to Carol, "Lead, couldn't we save ourselves a bunch of trouble and capture one of those soldiers? We could interrogate him and find out if there is a supply depot around here. He can also provide us with a more detailed layout of the area than we could ever get from a recon mission."

Thinking about the idea quickly, Carol said, "Okay, let's do this. Ambush, set up the op."

The ambush expert laid out his plan, "We hit them at the bend in the road where the pines are clustered thickest. Lead, Tail, set up on the bend. Point, me, and Weapons will line up on the road in that order. The signal will be when their point man passes the tall dead spruce. Weapons, as soon as they reach the dead spruce you will capture their Tail. Kill the others."

Taking off their skis, the team took a roundabout path that brought them to the bend in the game trail. Moving with extreme care to avoid knocking any snow off the trees, they sneaked underneath the pine trees. The trees had snow-covered branches dropping so low they concealed the recon team from view.

It was not long before they heard the crunch of boots on snow. Marching briskly down the trail came the unsuspecting FDA patrol. Tension mounted as they came closer to the ambush point.

The point man on the FDA patrol crossed the dead spruce, and suddenly the ambush sprung. Carol held down on his trigger, blowing away snow and branches as his bullets raced toward the FDA team.

Greg had been fighting on Earth for almost two weeks. Though he had managed to escape further injury, almost half his squad had not been so lucky. Walters had been hit so badly he had to be evacuated an orbiting battleship. After a few days in modern, and more importantly, electric, facilities, Walters had been able to return to the squad. Fortunately, none of the squad had been hit by small arms fire, so they were all combat ready.

The strain of the constant combat was beginning to tell on Greg. Night had fallen some hours ago and he was only now getting back to base. Flopping down into his fighting hole, he was about to close his eyes when Ramon came over.

"Sergeant Heyligher, we have a mission for you," said Ramon.

"Yes, Staff Sergeant." Greg got up.

Hopping out of his fighting hole, Greg followed Ramon to the command bunker. About halfway over to it, artillery and mortar shells began hitting the base. They crouched down on the ground almost unconsciously. While still terrifying, being shelled had become such a part of daily life it had stopped becoming a noticeable event. A marine scrambling toward a fighting hole was hit, but even that was no longer enough to make them take notice.

Once the shelling had stopped, they got back up and continued on their way to the command bunker and crawled inside. Several field grade officers stood around maps, discussing plans. Overall, the offensive had been going well, but the enemy had so many fortifications it was becoming difficult to maintain the pace. Supplies were also becoming more scarce, but the Second Marines had recently taken a big supply depot, allowing the army to be fully supplied for the next few days.

Ramon walked over to one of the maps on the wall. "A company from First Battalion, Twelfth Marines, has a major sniper problem. In the past two days, five marines, all of them above the rank of sergeant, have been killed by one sniper. From what we can tell, this guy is an expert. He fires twice a day, once in the morning, once in the evening. An exception was made on the second day when a lieutenant exposed himself by standing in plain sight. The company cannot make a sweep of the area, since the sniper would simply disappear, nor can they move to a different position, because they are currently serving as a blocking force to prevent an FDA unit we have encircled from escaping. A hovercraft will take you to the company as soon as you're ready. Any questions?"

"None that can be answered here," said Greg.

Looking around the bunker for a member of his squad, Greg spotted one who had just finished a debriefing. "Hey, Lynch, get over here."

Lance Corporal Lynch dutifully complied. "You wanted me, Sergeant?"

"You're my spotter. We're going after a problem sniper. Got all your stuff together?"

"It's all on me, Sergeant."

"Good. Let's go."

The two of them jogged over to a waiting hovercraft. All hovercrafts were stored in an underground bunker for safety, so they had to make a short dash out of the command bunker, but arrived before the enemy could start shelling them.

Military hovercraft, unlike civilian ones, were fully covered and could reach altitudes of up to two thousand meters, and travel at speeds of nearly Mach 1. They served as the main mode of transportation on the battlefield. The Alliance had several models of hovercraft, including a transport model, a ground-attack model, and a scout model.

In front of the two snipers was a transport model, which was shaped like a flying discus with an elevator to the ground in the middle. Actually, to call it an elevator was to be overly optimistic, since it really wasn't much more than a flat piece of floor that had pistons on each of the corners to raise or lower it.

Stepping onto the elevator, the two of them were lifted into the hovercraft. Greg could tell the pilot was a marine by the camouflage covering on the pilot's helmet, a tribute to past traditions.

As soon as they were on board, the pilot checked to see they were secure in their seats, then took off. It was a short two hour flight.

When they came down to land, Greg looked at the ground below. Though it was dark, he could make out a light forest with knee-high grass and short shrubs covering the landscape. A sniper's playground.

They landed on the backside of a hill. Stepping off the hovercraft, the snipers were greeted by a marine captain.

The captain shouted over the roar of the hovercraft lifting off. "I'm Captain Woodlyn. I take it you're the snipers?"

"That would be us, sir," Greg said.

"Great, now here's the problem. In the past two days, I've lost my XO, my first sergeant, one of my platoon leaders, and a pair of platoon sergeants. We have no idea where the sniper is, but as long as we are on this side of the hill he can't shoot at us. Other than that, we know just about nothing."

"Can I see the bodies, sir?" Greg asked.

"Sure, we have them lined up for graves registration."

Greg and Lynch looked at the entrance holes in the diamond armor, then questioned witnesses as to the exact location and direction the victims were facing when they were killed.

When they finished, the two of them crawled to the edge of the hill. The top of the hill was flat. This was where the marines had set up their base. When the sniper began his reign of terror, the marines had dug in deeper and made a series of trenches and concealed bunkers to allow them to move without sticking their heads above ground.

While the two of them stared down at the forest below them, Greg asked Lynch, "What have you figured out so far?"

"The sniper never occupies the same place twice. He takes the morning shot at first light and waits until daylight is almost gone to make his second shot. It allows him to disappear in the fading light before they can find him. He's out there right now, hiding somewhere."

"Same opinion here. How do we get him?"

"We could wait until he makes another kill tomorrow, get the body, and then figure out were he is for that day. The problem is we want to get him before he makes another kill."

"It's about five hours until daylight. If we move out now, we could get into the forest before he knows we're here."

"If we're going to root this guy out before he makes his shot, we need to get into the woods."

"Then let's go."

———•◦•———

The weapons expert exploded through the low-hanging, snow-covered branches and tackled the tail end man on the enemy patrol. One of the members of the FDA patrol turned to shoot the weapons expert, but before he could get a clear line of fire, Carol cut him down.

Someone fired a rapid series of SMG bursts at Carol's position. Since the shooter could not see Carol, he only succeeded in knocking down snow. The soldier was swiftly silenced by the ambush expert. Combined fire from the tail gunner and the point man dropped the leading soldier.

By now the weapons expert had succeeded in subduing the soldier he had tackled. Other than a few lingering echoes of gunfire, dead silence return to the area.

Carol stood up and walked over to the bodies. While the rest of recon team searched the bodies for anything useful, the weapons expert removed the prisoner's diamond armor and administered a sedative.

Taking a pair of captured rifles, Carol set the repulse-lifters on them to max lift, allowing the rifles to hover at waist level without support. Cutting a cable into three pieces, he used two of them to create a makeshift stretcher. The team placed the captive on the stretcher, and though the rifles dropped low to the ground under the weight, the captive was still above the snow level.

Seeing his idea had worked, Carol took the last length of cable and used it to pull the stretcher.

The recon team reached the hill, where they had taken their skis off. Quickly reattaching their skis, they started back on a different route from the one they had come on.

Skiing fast, they managed to avoid most of the patrols coming to investigate the firing. One patrol, however, spotted them in the distance. The patrol opened up at long range and the recon team returned fire while they skied away. A running gunfight developed, with neither side being able to attain any real degree of accuracy.

Carol tied the rope with which he was dragging the stretcher to his waist. He unslung his rifle from his shoulder and began spraying fire on the advancing patrol. Every time he found a gap in the pine trees, he unleashed a flurry of bullets at the small black dots he could see on the mountain slope.

The small dots were running toward the team, but they were at best making two kilometers per hour, while the recon team was making six kilometers per hour on their skis. Looking at the ground in front of him, Carol saw a long, steep slope ahead. At the end of the slope massive pines grew so thick Carol knew if they could make it to that point, no enemy force would be able to pursue them.

Firing another burst at the approaching FDA forces, Carol skied with a renewed vigor. He did a quick count of the enemy. Only ten black dots—not enough to stop them. They could make it.

The recon team kept up a steady barrage through the trees. Though shots peppered the ground around them, none of the shots landed near enough to cause them concern.

The recon team reached the long slope and their speed kicked up immensely. A few stray shots followed them, but the FDA soon gave up shooting at these extreme ranges. Roaring down the slope, the recon team swooped into the huge pine forest. They had done it. They were safe.

Chapter 38

Duel in Wilderness

Greg and Lynch informed the captain of their plan and climbed down the hill till they got into the middle of the forest before they hid themselves. They knew there was no way they were going to find a good sniper position in the dark, but that was not their goal. Their goal was to get far enough into the forest so they did not have to make a deadly descent under the sniper's watchful eye.

Having found a good hiding spot, they took turns standing guard while the other slept. Between the two of them they managed to get about two hours of sleep. Sleep was as much a weapon as their rifles. Without it they made careless mistakes and couldn't concentrate.

When dawn began to creep over the horizon, they began to move again, searching for a good sniper position. After about thirty minutes, Greg spotted a flock of birds feeding on the carcass of an animal that had been killed. Greg threw a stick into the middle of the birds, spooking them into taking flight. He knew the FDA sniper would spot the birds taking off and realize there was another sniper in the field. A sniper fears nothing more than another sniper, and Greg was counting on the other sniper to try to find and eliminate them.

Although Greg knew exposing his own position was dangerous, the enemy sniper would have to move to get to a place were he could observe the field where the birds were feeding. By then Greg should be in his own position and ready to spot the enemy sniper moving in for the kill.

Looking around, Greg spotted a long ridge that overlooked the site of the carcass. The sniper would naturally head for the high ground. Greg and Lynch slowly crawled to the base of the ridge. It was a light forest, so the trees had a decent spacing between them. This allowed for excellent visibility. Crawling up to a small shrub, Greg and Lynch settled down to wait.

From their position, they could see the entire ridge. Lynch had his spotting scope out and was looking at each blade of grass. His rifle lay where it could be reached by only shifting his hands off the scope a couple of centimeters. A patch of long grass at their backs hid them from anyone who managed to get behind them.

Two hours passed and the only movement they made was with their eyes. They knew by now the enemy sniper had taken up a position on the ridge without their seeing him. Their best chance having passed, the only thing they could do now was to sit tight and look as hard as they could for any movement.

The waiting game had begun. Both sides lay motionless, not daring to make even the slightest bit of movement for fear of detection, memorizing every little detail of the area. If something was out of place, they'd know.

At midday, the sun came out in force and beat down upon the Earth. Sweat began to accumulate on Greg's brow. Unbearable as the heat was, there was nothing that could be done about it. They did their best to endure it.

A gentle breeze blew across the ridge, but the trees at the base prevented it from reaching Greg.

Looking longingly at the wind playing across the grass, Greg spotted something out of place about midway on the ridge. A small bit of grass did not move at all. It had to be the sniper. It was in the middle of a grass field, too far away from any tree to be a stick. The FDA sniper moved sideways a little to compensate for this error, but it was too late. His little movement only confirmed Greg's opinion.

Although the sniper's Ghillie Suit blended in almost perfectly with the long grass, now that Greg knew what to look for the sniper stood out like a sore thumb. It took Greg a few minutes to pick out the sniper's spotter, who was lying less than a meter away from the sniper.

Greg whispered to Lynch the location of the enemy snipers.

After about five minutes, Lynch said quietly, "I got 'em."

"You take the spotter, I got the sniper," Greg whispered back. He knew the instant he fired the spotter would disappear and they would have to start over. If the two of them fired at same time, they could get the sniper team all at once.

While Lynch slowly brought his rifle to bear, Greg dropped his inverted post on the enemy sniper in case the sniper made any sudden moves. Greg gave Lynch a few seconds to get his sight on target.

It was not a long shot, only about fifteen hundred meters. Most sniper duels were fought between one to six kilometers, since any farther out the snipers would not be able to find each other. Greg took a breath, then let half of it out. He slowly took up trigger slack, keeping his post right on the FDA sniper's head. His rifle gave a sharp crack, followed closely by Lynch's.

In their scopes the pair of FDA snipers' arms and legs began to flail and thrash around, letting them know they had both scored head shots.

When the enemy snipers stopped twitching, Greg and Lynch walked over to the bodies. They searched through the pockets of the dead snipers for any intelligence, then ejected their rifle clips and made a short video of the bodies for later identification. The Alliance liked to know which FDA snipers they had to deal with, so they kept a careful record of every enemy sniper killed.

They walked back to the hill after they finished. Captain Woodlyn was waiting for them.

"Did you get him?" he asked.

"We got 'em. There were two, a sniper and a spotter," Greg said.

"How did you do it?" Captain Woodlyn inquired.

"They were in the middle of a ridge, which is why it took us so long to find them. I thought they would be near the top of the ridge where the view was better. Snuck into a field without us seeing them, but the grass moved and they didn't, so we found them in the end."

"I'll call the hovercraft to come pick you guys up. Thanks a bunch."

Greg sat down with his sniper rifle across his knees. Out in the distance the sun was beginning to set, casting its last red rays down on the Earth. Watching the sun slowly fade away, Greg thought, *it was a good day. We took out an expert enemy sniper team, and saved marine lives. That is what it's all about, isn't it; saving marine lives. Whenever I pull that trigger, it has to be to save a marine, not to take a life. Today we got an enemy who was systematically wiping out the leadership of a company. We definitely saved marine lives. It was a good day.*

———

This is highly interesting terrain, Carol thought as he soared through the Alps in a hovercraft. In the middle of the Alps was the FDA supply depot, the location of which they had wrangled out of the prisoner they had taken on the recon patrol.

Since supplies were becoming scarce, they would load up as many supplies as they could carry, then blow up what they could not take. Missions like this had become the primary job of the MAA after the marines had landed. They fought a different war, a war fought behind enemy lines. Attacks had to be made swiftly, and withdrawals even swifter. Hence the reason for the hovercrafts.

The hovercraft was a civilian one that had been left behind when Earth was evacuated. The MAA had modified it into a military weapon. Shaped like a boat with a cabin that jutted out past the aft end, this type of hovercraft served as the pickup truck of the day. To hold cargo, the main body of the hovercraft was scooped out like a truck bed. On a higher level and at the back was the cabin. Underneath the rear half of the cabin the tips of two engines poked forth. From the cabin visibility was good, with a large window in front, a diamond-shaped window on either side, and a sun roof on top.

To make it into a military vehicle, the MAA added four seats to the bed and three machine guns. A machine gun was on the bow and the other two on either side of the bed. The machine gunner had to be standing up to fire, so the gunner's only protection was his rate of fire.

Machine guns fired small twenty-five-round clips strung together on a belt. One clip was inserted in the chamber, emptied almost instantly, and then ejected out the other side as the next clip came into the chamber. Because of the bulk of the system, only vehicles could carry machine guns, and only the MAA regularly used vehicles on the battlefield. This gave them an unexpected edge, the edge Carol was counting on for the mission to succeed.

Zipping along the bottom of a snow-covered valley, they flew so close to the ground they had to dodge large pine trees. It took only three hovercrafts to carry what was left of Assault Team Blue.

Carol was standing against the wall of the hovercraft's bed. Up in the mountain ridges above he thought he spotted a flicker of movement. Suddenly, shots began to ring out from that direction. Several of the bullets pinged off the hovercraft.

"The FDA must have spotted us and sent a force to intercept us," Carol shouted as he dove for one of the machine guns.

Sliding a clip into the chamber, Carol unleashed a thunderous torrent of fire on the enemy, joined by that of other team members. Carol could not actually see the enemy, but he knew they had to be somewhere up on the ridge lines. Sweeping his machine gun back and forth, he had to be hitting something since the enemy's fire was slowing down.

A small black dot appeared on the ridgeline. It was moving, so it had to be an FDA soldier. Swinging his sights over the black dot, Carol held down the trigger until it stopped moving.

The three MAA hovercraft continued speeding along, exchanging fire with an unseen foe. Something was bothering Carol. He couldn't figure out what it was until another bullet pinged off the side of the hovercraft.

That's it. Why aren't they using solid bullets? Every time they hit us they are using ice bullets, which bounce right off. A solid bullet would go straight through the hovercraft. What do they have in store for us?

Looking up ahead, Carol saw a large stone pillar. Suddenly he knew what the enemy's plan was. The instant they passed a highly visible point, such as the stone pillar, they would call in presighted artillery and mortar. In other words, an ambush.

Chapter 39

How John Kept Himself Busy

Standing in an abandoned alley, John waited behind the edge of a building. In five minutes, his target was going to walk from a building at the corner of an L-shaped intersection to a hovercraft. Those few seconds would be the target's weakest moment.

The target was a high-level hustler who had hustled the wrong person. To protect himself from assassins, the target always had fifteen bodyguards around him.

Two of the bodyguards had been police snipers in the past. These two positioned themselves in windows on either side of the L-shaped intersection, allowing them to cover both streets leading to the intersection. John had already located and marked their positions.

Storm clouds gathered over the city. Even without the clouds, the city seemed to have a dark feel to it. John had his two SMGs out, one in each hand. Clutching his SMGs tighter, John tensed himself for the moment when he would spring into action. Twenty seconds to go. Time to get started.

Placing one of his SMGs around the corner, John used his eye-sights to spot one of the snipers. He moved the dot over the sniper's head, then pulled the trigger. The sniper jerked back as the bullet smacked into his head. Leaning out of his window to see what was going on, the second sniper exposed himself to John's fire. John shifted his aim and shot the second sniper, leaving him draped over the window.

Almost immediately after that the target and his escort came out the door. Before they could spot the dead snipers and turn around, John stepped around the corner and brought his second SMG to bear. Firing both SMGs at once, he cut a swath through the middle of the formation. Bodyguards were cut down as they turned to face him.

In the middle of the bodyguards the path of bullets ended. Two shots went flying into the target's chest. Falling over on his back, the target lay dead, as pink, frothy blood poured from the lungs.

Seeing his target fall, John turned around and ran behind the corner. Though most of the bodyguards were still alive, John left the area. His mission wasn't to kill the bodyguards; it was to kill the one they were guarding. Now that he had done that, there was no need to risk death in a firefight.

John found the space pod he had hidden. He made a quick check on the inside and outside to make sure there weren't any tracking devices or dirty bombs. When that was finished, he climbed inside and turned on the autopilot. The pod slowly began to lift off from the planet.

Carol left his machine gun and ran back to the cabin. "Johnston, let me take control."

Johnston climbed out of the cabin and took Carol's place on the machine gun. Dropping into the seat in the cabin, Carol grabbed the controls and pushed the throttle all the way open. As he accelerated past the other hovercraft, he made a fishtail, the signal for "follow me." Somewhat mystified as to his intensions, the other two hovercrafts swung behind Carol. Seeing them form up behind him, Carol turned hard right, pointing straight up a mountain. There was no FDA presence on this mountain and they were able to get over the top before the FDA could readjust to stop them.

Once out of sight of the FDA, Carol led the hovercraft on a circuitous route to the supply depot. His plan seemed to be working. No further encounters were made with the FDA until they reached the mountaintop overlooking the supply depot.

Down below, in a valley surrounded by mountains, was their objective. There was a perimeter fence to keep out raiding parties, but otherwise it was mostly undefended. In clearings between groves of pines lay large piles of supplies. Most of the piles were covered by snow, but a few that had been recently used lay exposed.

The three MAA hovercrafts came roaring down the mountain, guns a-blazing. Smashing through the perimeter fence, they sped through the supply depot, firing as they went. FDA soldiers fired at them from inside the pine groves, but they were able to spot the FDA soldiers' black forms in the woods and sent a torrent of return fire at them.

On each of the hovercrafts, the four team members sitting in the seats now stood. From underneath their seats, they pulled out fearsome new weapons—Magnetically Propelled Grenades. An MPG consisted of a tube with a magnet in the back, and a shaped-charge warhead inserted in the front. When the trigger was pulled, the warhead was magnetically accelerated forward. After the warhead struck an object, it would delay a few seconds to allow for burrowing and then explode.

Firing their MPGs into the supply piles, they were able to destroy them without having to go through the trouble of dismounting and setting the explosives by hand.

MPGs streaked out from the hovercrafts as the machine guns sprayed their deadly loads upon any FDA soldier unlucky enough to get in their way. Constant explosions filled the air as supply piles went up in flames. Nothing escaped their wrath as the hovercrafts swiftly and methodically destroyed the supply depot. When they reached the last supply pile, the hovercrafts stopped and formed a perimeter as some of the team members hopped out and loaded up the supplies.

Knowing he was going to have to wait until the hovercrafts were loaded to take off again, Carol climbed out and helped load. Bullets snapped around him, but he ignored them. Working quickly, they managed to get the vessels loaded within a few minutes.

While the machine guns continued to lay down cover fire, the team members jumped back into the now heavily loaded hovercraft. They could carry about half of the supply pile. Having taken everything they could, they sped away from the supply depot. As they were leaving, one of the team members fired a last MPG into what remained of the supply pile they had raided.

Returning to base by a different route, they avoided any further enemy contact. They did not know it, but they had just completed one of the most successful raids of the war.

Chapter 40

Frontal Assault

"Sergeant Heyligher, I have orders for you, and you're not going to like them," Ramon said.

"How bad could it be?"

"A lot worse than you imagine. Someone up at regiment misunderstood the "scout" part of scout/sniper. The lieutenant tried to explain to him we did our scouting from long ranges, but he wouldn't listen. The regiment is making an advance, and our platoon is walking point."

"Don't they understand we are snipers?" Greg exclaimed. "By sending us on point, that's like ordering our executions. We fight from long ranges; we don't do these sorts of things."

"Lieutenant Derek argued with them, Sergeant. He argued with them all night. In the end, they asked if we had battle rifles. The lieutenant told them we did—then they said there was no good reason why we shouldn't walk point. There was not a thing the lieutenant could do short of refusing a direct order, which is something he took an oath not to do."

After a second of silence, Greg said, "So what's our order of battle?"

"The lieutenant will be in the center with First Squad, I will be with Third Squad on our left flank, and you will lead your squad on our right flank."

The sniper platoon boarded a pair of transport hovercraft and flew to take point for the advance. They landed and began to march forward. For the first two hours they encountered no FDA forces. It was mostly flat terrain, with small depressions and rises breaking up the surface. At ankle high, it wasn't exactly long grass.

When the platoon reached a small canyon with a river at the bottom, instead of trying to find a way around it they went straight down the canyon and up the other side. As they came over the top, there was an odd feeling came over them that something was out of place.

The squads spread out more, but First Squad went too far, leaving Greg's squad unsupported. Greg was about to correct this when Lieutenant Derek, seeing a slight bit of high ground, ordered the platoon to run forward quickly and take it. Something was making Derek feel uneasy and whatever it was, he wanted to deal with it from a good position.

The squads crested the high ground and stopped suddenly. The incline of the other side was so slight it was almost unnoticeable, giving a minimal vantage point.

About fifty meters away the ground was dug up. On top of this dug up ground lay bunkers.

The quiet that had been over the area was shattered by an eruption of gunfire from the bunkers. Greg's fire teams dived for cover in the shallow depressions. Until then the marines had had no idea how flat they could make themselves.

Greg hurled himself into the depression occupied by Rodrigo's fire team. He heard the FDA rifles open up in fully automatic. He started counting, knowing the rifle would run out of ammo in a second and a half. The second and a half passed and the rifle continued firing. Greg got all the way to three seconds before the rifle ran out of ammo.

Taking a quick peek over the edge, Greg saw a line of bunkers stretched out in front of his squad. Each of the bunkers had a rifle attached to it by a swivel mount, and each of the rifles had a monstrously oversized magazine. Greg was quickly driven back to the ground by the supporting infantry in the bunker, who provided cover fire while the automatic-rifleman reloaded.

Ducking back into cover, Greg started to try to get control.

"Schmidt, where are you. Can you maneuver?" he yelled across the battlefield.

Over the sound of the bunkers firing, Schmidt shouted back, "I'm to your right, and Smith's fire team is between you and me. Right now we can't move forward, but if we had to, we could pull back about five meters in relative safety."

"Smith, how's your situation?" Greg said at the top of his lungs.

"We're right between you and Schmidt. They've got us totally pinned down, Sergeant. Can't move forward or backward, can't even get up to return fire."

"I'm with Rodrigo, and we're in the same situation as Smith," said Greg as he began to formulate a plan.

"Smith, can you see Schmidt?" Greg asked.

"I have a clear line of sight with him, Sergeant," Smith yelled.

"Schmidt, I want you to pull back as far as you can. Try to draw the enemy back with you," Greg ordered.

Without another word, Schmidt began to execute Greg's plan. His fire team appeared above the brim of their little piece of coverage and fired a couple of shots at the enemy. They were quickly driven back down behind the brim by a hail of enemy fire. Schmidt did this a couple more times, then began to pull his team back, letting the enemy see little glimpses of them retreating.

Eager to stop the marines from getting away, a squad of six FDA soldiers left the cover of the bunkers to flank the retreating marines. Confident the fire from their bunkers would protect them, they had managed to get directly abreast of Schmidt's old position when Smith's fire team opened fire on them.

Although Smith's fire team could not come out of its position to fire, they could clearly see the small rise Schmidt's fire team had used for coverage. Since the ground was mostly level, they could also see the area beyond Schmidt's old position, and when the FDA squad walked into this area they sprang their ambush.

As soon as the firing started, Schmidt's fire team turned around and added its fire to Smith's, catching the enemy in a neat little crossfire. The FDA squad didn't stand a chance and all six of them were slain before they could mount an effective resistance.

Schmidt's fire team crawled back to its original position. Taking advantage of the loss of the enemy squad in their area, they began to lay down a little bit of cover fire.

Seeing an opportunity, Smith stood up and led his fire team in an assault on the enemy bunkers. They had not gotten more than a few meters when Smith was hit by an enemy automatic-rifle burst and the rest of fire team was sent scrambling back for cover.

Greg saw Smith fall. Looking around for someone to replace Smith, Greg's eyes landed on Lynch.

"Lynch, take command of Smith's fire team," Greg shouted.

"Yes, Sergeant," Lynch answered as he stood up and made a diving roll out of the depression. Sprinting as fast as he could, Lynch tried to dodge the bullets that were snapping at his feet. Leaping the last meter, he landed in a low crouch in the depression Smith's fire team was using for cover.

"What's the situation?" Lynch asked.

"Smith's down, but otherwise we're fine," Sandusky replied.

Lynch took a quick peep over the edge. All his options looked bleak, but as he looked he spotted something that had a chance of succeeding. A small one-man pillbox was covering the blind spot of a bunker. Though they would still have to deal with supporting fire from the bunker on the pillbox's left, the blind spot on the other bunker meant they would be receiving fire from only two enemy positions, as opposed to the three they would have to face anywhere else. Also, the guy in the pillbox would have no one to cover him while he reloaded. Lynch knew he was going to take casualties, but it was their only hope.

Lynch dropped back behind cover. "We're going to attack the small pillbox. Try and keep to the left, and do not stop attacking until we have taken that pillbox. McAlister and I will be running as hard as we can at it, firing as we go. Sandusky and Pierre, the two of you will be going a little slower as you will be doing the fastest leapfrog advance you can do. Everyone got that? Great, let's go."

With that, Lynch started running and firing from the chest, his rifle not quite making it all the way to his shoulder. McAlister, Sandusky, and Pierre came out of the depression behind him.

McAlister pushed himself hard and managed to catch up with Lynch. Though Sandusky and Pierre were doing a leapfrog, their feet never really stopped moving.

The surprise assault combined with the incredible speed of the marines allowed the fire team to make the first fifteen meters without even being fired on. After that, the torrent of fire the marines put out as they were running forced those in the pillbox and bunker to spend a little more time ducking and a little less time firing.

Lynch saw their suicide charge had a chance. As bullets smacked the ground all around him, Lynch did his best to keep his legs pumping and finger pulling. About two-thirds of the way across, a burst of fire caught McAlister in the chest, spinning him around and dropping him to the ground. Ignoring McAlister's death, Lynch kept on running, knowing now was not the time to mourn.

Suddenly the fire from the pillbox stopped as the soldier in the pillbox frantically scrambled to reload his automatic rifle.

Giving all he had to one last push, Lynch reached the pillbox. Sticking his rifle into the firing port, Lynch pulled his trigger until the firing from inside stopped.

Ducking around to the backside of the pillbox, Lynch discovered there was a communications trench system about twenty meters behind the bunkers. All the dirt around the trenches and the bunkers was turned up by the heavy machinery that had been used to make them. It looked like a scene from the trench wars of old.

By then Sandusky and Pierre had joined him. The three marines dropped into a crouch. Lynch took a quick look around. "Okay, we attack the bunkers that are firing at Schmidt's fire team. Let's go."

As they started moving to their right, two FDA soldiers came running out of the back of a bunker.

"Sandusky, get them," Lynch yelled.

Sandusky brought his rifle to bear and fired a few quick shots. The aliens doubled over and fell to the ground. He then chased after Lynch and Pierre.

Meanwhile, Lynch and Pierre had taken up positions behind the bunker that had fired on them during their charge. Lynch turned on his bayonet and slashed the bolt off the door. Pierre kicked the door open and threw a flash-bang into the bunker.

As the flash-bang went off, Sandusky came charging in the door. Three shots were heard and then Sandusky came back out of the door. "It's clear."

They were moving to the next bunker in line when an under-strength squad appeared, coming out of the trenches to reinforce the line.

"Sandusky, Pierre, deal with them. I'll take the bunker," shouted Lynch.

Turning his back on the enemy, Lynch concentrated on the bunker. Cutting the bolt with a quick slash of his bayonet, Lynch kicked the door open and threw in a flash-bang.

He waited for the flash-bang to go off and then burst into the bunker. Inside the bunker he found three soldiers, one of them on his knees and holding his head with his hands, the other two standing somewhat confused. Lynch fired twice into the first, then dropped his aim and killed the kneeling one. The last soldier got off one shot from the hip before Lynch's bullets found him.

Coming back outside, Lynch saw the enemy squad retreating. Sandusky had worked his way around their flank and was pumping out lethal fire on them. Deciding he had taken enough casualties, the FDA squad leader began pulling back.

Lynch opened fire on the retreating soldiers and was able to bring one of them down. Of the FDA squad, only a third made it back alive.

Lynch and his fire team were about to make an assault on a third bunker when Schmidt's fire team arrived.

Schmidt said, "You guys made a hole big enough for us get through, so if you don't mind, we'll finish off the remaining bunkers. Lynch, have your fire team provide security."

While Lynch's fire team watched the trenches, Schmidt's fire team took out the last bunker on the right side. The two fire teams then turned around and began to work on bunkers that had Rodrigo's fire team and Greg pinned down.

They were working on the first one on the left when the FDA soldiers in the second bunker, seeing they were getting methodically destroyed, made a dash for the trenches. Lynch's fire team opened up on them, dropping them like flies.

Hearing the firing, Walters and White came running out of the bunker. Spotting the fleeing enemies, they opened fire, not thinking to get into the prone first. When the marines finished firing, several of the soldiers lay dead on the trail to the trench.

The bunkers having been cleared, Greg and Rodrigo's fire team came running up to join them. When the squad was back together again, Greg asked, "Is that trench occupied?"

"I saw a total of six FDA soldiers make it into the trench, so it has at least a small enemy presence," Lynch said.

"We're going to clear that trench. Sandusky, Walters, you're on point. Move out."

Sandusky and Walters lay down on their backs parallel to the trench and facing opposite directions. Each threw a flash-bang inside the trench. As soon as they heard the explosion, they rolled off the edge and dropped into the trench, landing in a low crouch. The two soldiers facing Sandusky were hurled against the side of the trench by the flurry of bullets he sent into them. Walters made one aimed shot that dropped the Pratin in front of him.

They yelled "Clear," and the rest of the squad leapt into the trench. There was a weak enemy force inside, so clearing it went pretty fast.

Near the end of the trench system, Walters peeked around a corner, then whispered, "Sergeant, we have a mortar battery around the corner. Three soldiers standing guard and a dugout behind them. The guards were whispering about something; I didn't get the full conversation, but they're wondering why they lost contact with their forward observers."

Greg said to Lorenzo, "Do you think you can get the guards without alerting the rest of them?"

"It'll be easy, Sergeant." Lorenzo slowly began creeping forward.

Reaching the corner, Lorenzo paused for a second while he turned on his bayonet, then leapt into action. He sprang for the first FDA soldier, his rifle outstretched.

The bayonet impaled the soldier. Lorenzo used the rifle as a pole vault to get over the soldier's body and landed with a roll. Pulling the rifle out of the dead soldier, Lorenzo made a sweep at the second one.

The soldier grabbed the rifle in midswing and brought his own rifle to bear. Lorenzo dropped his rifle, got a hold on the soldier's forearm and twisted hard, then shoved forward, breaking the soldier's arm. He then fetched him a hard elbow that knocked him to the ground.

In these few seconds the third soldier picked up his weapon and aimed it at Lorenzo. Moving quickly, Lorenzo pushed the weapon aside, but the soldier came up with a hard right knee. Lorenzo spun on one foot to dodge the knee, then carried the spin through and allowed himself to become airborne.

The soldier stopped the first foot that went flying towards him, but Lorenzo used the soldier's grip to support his left foot and keep him airborne as his right foot came around from behind. When the foot connected with the enemy's head, he dropped like a sack of rocks.

The second soldier was getting up, so Lorenzo made a sweeping kick with his leg that knocked his feet from under him. Lorenzo picked up his battle-rifle and ran it through the third soldier before he could reach a weapon. Turning around, Lorenzo stabbed downward to finish off the second, who was lying face down in the dirt.

Lorenzo signaled it was all clear. The squad moved in close to the dugout, shot the hinges off, then threw a flash-bang inside. They went in and killed the rest of the mortar crew.

Greg stepped out of the bunker. "Brauner, destroy the mortars."

Brauner slapped in a clip full of solid shots as the rest of the squad climbed out of the trench. Switching his rifle to fully automatic, Brauner fired a short burst into the base of each of the four mortars. The solid bullets did terrible damage, blasting them in half and utterly destroying the accelerating magnets.

Brauner took a quick look around, and discovered why they had not been fired on by these mortars. The frontline could not be seen from this position, and the mortar men would not be able to fire without an observer.

When he had finished, Brauner climbed out of the trench to rejoin the squad.

Outside the trench, the squad was in the prone, hiding in the grass. They had spotted the rest of the platoon farther on down the trench line. When Brauner rejoined them, the squad slid back into the trench and made a short jog to the platoon.

While the rest of the squad reunited with the other squads to find out who was still alive, Greg spoke to Lieutenant Derek.

"How did you do?" asked Derek.

"We lost two, sir. Smith and McAlister. We did take out a mortar battery."

"You did a lot better than the rest of the platoon. The other squads took a lot more casualties."

"If it wasn't for Lynch and Sandusky, we probably would have had a lot more dead. I want to get those two paired permanently. Lynch has a good tactical mind and Sandusky is something of a superwarrior. The two of them pretty much single-handedly broke through the FDA bunkers and killed most of their soldiers."

"I'll do what I can. In the meantime, have your squad set up a perimeter. I called Battalion and told them we've taken too many casualties to continue. A relief will be here soon."

"Yes sir. By the way sir, where is Staff Sergeant Ramon?"

"He's dead. They got him early in the battle."

"I'm sorry about that, sir." Feelings of pain and hatred began to swell in his chest.

A tear trickled down Lieutenant Derek's face. "You know, I was supposed to be his best man. He and Rosanna had set the wedding date for the day we invaded Earth."

Shaking in silent fury, Greg turned around and ordered his squad to set up defensive positions.

Chapter 41

Surprise

Greg had been at war for at least four weeks now. He was having his first full day of rest at the HQ. Aside from the occasional shelling, everything was relatively peaceful. After having a full night's sleep, Greg was feeling refreshed when he woke in the morning.

That lasted about ten seconds. Suddenly, a heavy bombardment began to fall around the HQ, heavier than anything he had experienced before. A line of shells walked right up to his fighting hole, miraculously missing and continuing to walk into the HQ.

Lance Corporal White—who was sharing the fighting hole with Greg—came awake. "What in the 'verse is that?"

"The biggest shelling I've ever seen in the war."

The mortars and artillery pounded the hill nonstop. Even a couple of battleship shells were fired at them. After a while a messenger came diving into the fighting hole Greg and White were occupying.

The messenger said, "The FDA has just launched a massive offensive. Third Battalion is getting pushed back and the FDA will soon be at the HQ. All snipers need to get in a supporting position and start slowing down the advance."

As soon as he finished speaking, the messenger jumped out of the fighting hole and began running to the next set of snipers, only to be hit by an incoming mortar round.

Greg yelled at the top of his lungs, "Snipers, we have FDA infantry incoming."

He and White then leapt out of their fighting hole and started running away from the front line. They ran until they reached a line of hills behind the HQ, hills that were considerably higher than the HQ hill.

Hiking to near the crest of one of these hills, Greg and White sat down and set up a sniper position. First they opened their rucksacks—which they had had the presence of mind to grab on their way out—and put on their Ghillie

Suits. Next they applied camouflage face paint and assembled their rifles. Once they were finished they laid down in the prone and began to look for the enemy.

The view from the hill was good enough they did not need to use their over-the-horizon satellites. Looking in his scope, Greg could spot soldiers moving in the gaps between the trees in the forest below him. Zooming in a bit more, Greg was able to discern the alien features of the FDA soldiers. Bringing his scope down, Greg spotted the marines of Third Battalion retreating. A little farther back he spotted a defensive line the marines were trying to set up.

Now that he had marked the friendly positions, Greg could fire without fear of hitting a marine. Scanning the forest, Greg picked up a pair of FDA officers consulting a map.

Ever since Ethan's death, Greg had found it harder and harder not give in to anger. He wanted revenge, but knew he could not take it. Greg took several deep breaths to mentally prepare himself for the shot.

Taking careful aim, Greg fired and hit one of the officers in the chest. The second officer instantly hit the deck, which still left him in Greg's sight.

Dropping his inverted post on the officer's head, Greg pulled the trigger and nailed the officer in the back of the head.

White fired, then Greg said, "All right, let's move to a new position."

The two of them grabbed their gear and walked a short distance away until they came upon a small knoll. Climbing to the top of the knoll, the two of them began looking for new targets.

———————

John was sitting behind his desk, viewing information on his new target. Glancing up, he looked through his recently repaired windows at the valley below him. By looking at the sun, he guessed it was about noon. Returning his gaze to the office, he took a quick look at the hologram he had tuned to one of the news channels. He kept a constant eye on the progress of the war, and currently it seemed the Alliance offensive had stalled.

Resuming his work, John stared at the small hologram in front of him. He was using the 'net, and currently he was looking at a site were people posted all sorts of pictures, videos, and personal information about themselves. John had no idea why anyone would give away so much data on themselves. It was as if they were purposely trying to make an assassin's job easier.

Looking at his target's profile, John had been able to figure out this guy was the leader of a large gang. Because of that, it was difficult to find a place were you could hit him alone.

Something caught John's eye. Zooming in, John saw a picture of the target in an apartment with three other aliens, plus a forth in the background. The caption explained he went to his friend's apartment often to relax, and proceeded to name the three aliens in the foreground, plus the one holding the camera. Because the alien in the background was not mentioned, John assumed that was the bodyguard.

This was exactly what John was looking for. Here was a place the gangster often frequented and was lightly guarded.

John quickly looked up the friends and searched until he found a picture of the same apartment, with a caption that said the apartment was where the alien lived. Entering the name of the alien into a universal index, John was able to find the address of the alien's apartment.

Easy kill. Most of the time it takes about a week, but I should be able to get this guy in just a few days.

John gathered his gear and climbed into his space-pod.

Three days later, John was on the top of a building that looked into the apartment's window.

———•———

Greg spotted a patrol of three soldiers moving forward to probe the new marine lines. He notified White of the patrol and the two of them leveled their rifles. Two shots rang out, and two of the patrol collapsed on the ground. The survivor started running back in the direction he had come from. Greg found a clearing along the soldier's path, and waited for the soldier to come. As soon as the soldier entered the clearing, Greg's bullet sent him spinning to the ground.

White found an officer and fired two shots that brought the officer down. They relocated once again, this time setting up in the exposed root system of an oak tree.

Searching the forest for more targets, Greg saw a soldier hold his hand to his head, apparently talking on a speaking rod. Knowing this had to be an officer; Greg placed his inverted post on the officer's chest and waited until the circles his post was making were all inside the officer. He gently pulled the trigger and there was a sharp report from the rifle. Greg's bullet knocked the officer off his feet.

Taking a moment, Greg could hear the other snipers in the platoon opening up on the advancing enemy. Greg switched out his empty clip for a new one while White took his shot. Then the two of them moved to a grove of short trees.

Something in Greg's scope caught his eye. Taking a closer look, he noticed a group of FDA soldiers gathered around one rather fat Waas. Staring at the fat soldier, Greg realized the soldier had two sets of crossed rifles on his collar, the insignia for an infantry major general. Quickly steadying his aim, Greg took a shot that dropped the general to the ground. He moved on to the target nearest the fallen general, a Waas holding the rank of brigadier general. A second shot slew this general alongside the first. A colonel rushed to help the slain generals, and Greg fired again, felling this officer on top of the generals he was attempting to save.

By now the rest of the command staff had disappeared into the woods, but Greg did not mind. To kill two generals on a battlefield was extremely rare, and in one fell swoop Greg had wiped out the leadership of a large FDA unit.

As he scoped out the battlefield, Greg could see targets falling all over the place as the sniper platoon decimated the enemy's leadership. FDA soldiers were milling about, waiting for orders. The Third Battalion finally reorganized and launched a counterattack against the stalled FDA units. Without a cohesive defense, the FDA began to fall back under the marines' assault.

Finally, White made his shot and the two of them changed positions again. Greg moved toward the crest of the hill, making their new position in a patch of shrubs.

Enemies were abundant, but Greg held his fire until he found a worthwhile target. An officer was attempting to rally his troops into a coordinated defense. Greg nailed the officer on his first shot.

Looking at the marine advance, Greg spotted an FDA NCO moving along the faltering FDA lines, encouraging the soldiers to hold fast.

Ethan was probably doing something like that when the FDA got him.

In a burst of anger, Greg snapped a shot off as the NCO was giving encouragement to a pair of soldiers in a fighting hole. The bullets slammed into the NCO's head, causing him to flail wildly as he fell dead on the ground.

White fired twice, getting a hit on both shots. They started to find a new position, but by the time they arrived the FDA had retreated beyond their view, and because of the hill blocking their lane of fire they could not use their satellites.

Greg said to White, "We'll wait for about an hour and then we'll head down to the HQ for a new assignment."

"Yes, Sergeant."

At the end of the hour they returned to the HQ. The shelling had stopped along with the FDA assault, and Greg was able to walk about freely. Lieutenant Derek found Greg and said, "Sergeant Heyligher, I've been looking for you."

"How's it been going, sir."

"Not so well. The FDA has launched a massive offensive across the entire front. We've managed to push them back in most places, but only at great cost. And from what I've heard, they're reorganizing for another attack."

"Well, now that we have forced them to retreat I assume we'll resume the offensive and catch them off guard."

"I doubt it. We're running so low on supplies we've been scraping the bottom of the barrel for some time. Repelling this assault took up what little we had left. The offensive is stalled, at least until we receive reinforcement."

Lieutenant Derek held up his hand for silence, then spoke on his speaking rod for a minute. When he finished, he looked at Greg. "Second Battalion is under attack again, and they're requesting a couple of sniper teams."

"I'll be ready in ten minutes, sir." *By the time this ends, Ethan will probably be avenged many times over.*

Chapter 42

Chilling With an Ice Bullet

After landing on the planet, John set up his position on a building and spent most of three days observing the apartment from there. He decided to use an ice bullet as the method of kill. Ice bullets were utterly untraceable as long as you did not touch them.

Currently, John was carrying his standard load of two SMGs, two pistols, and various grenades and explosives. This community consisted almost entirely of gangsters, so he was taking no chances.

A hovercraft came roaring down the street, bearing the owner of the apartment, John's target, two friends, and one bodyguard.

Showtime, thought John. He waited until they stopped outside apartment before he started to get off the building's roof.

John crawled to the door that opened onto the roof. He had welded this door shut to prevent anyone from accidentally stumbling on him, but it was the work of a moment to remove the welding with acid.

He dashed down the stairs as he knew if he was fast enough he would be in the other apartment before the bodyguard could position himself to watch from the window.

Bursting out of the building, John swiftly crossed the street. Time was of the essence. He drew his pistol and placed the muzzle against were the bolt should be. He fired a few muffled shots, and the door swung open.

No one was in the lobby. Gangsters would not permit someone the opportunity to monitor whether they were present or not.

Marching to the stairwell, John also shot the bolt off this door, then walked slowly and quietly to allow him to get the drop on his target. If he made any noise, the target would immediately attempt to flee through a back door. John had welded this door shut a while ago, but he knew it would not be long until they shot the door to pieces.

John quietly emerged from the stairwell. His target was behind the door in front of him. This was going to an easy kill.

Slapping a breaching charge on the door, he gave the handle a twist and then stepped back. As the timer went down, he drew his SMGs and prepared to make his move.

With a loud BANG, the charge went off, sending a flash-bang into the room. As the flash-bang exploded, John came charging into the dimly lit room.

There were four gangsters in the room other than the target. Bringing his two SMGs to bear, John gunned down two of them before they could recover from the shock of the flash-bang's detonation.

One of the three survivors drew a laser pistol and started firing. John ignored him and concentrated on the target and his bodyguard. Two laser bolts flashed by John's head as he fired a burst into the bodyguard. The bodyguard fell with a spin behind the couch. The target had drawn a pistol and was firing at John as he attempted to leave through the back door.

John aimed his left SMG at the target, and used his eye-sights to aim his right SMG at the laser-wielding thug. He stitched a pattern of ice bullets across his target and sent the laser-armed gangster reeling into the wall with a short burst.

Walking over to the target, John confirmed he was dead. Then he heard the loud wail of a police siren. Someone must have reported the gunfire.

Greg was in the middle of a briefing inside the command bunker. Someone was explaining how the war had gone into stalemate, and how the FDA continued to launch costly assaults in an attempt to break the deadlock.

None of this was new to Greg. He paid no attention. Locked in another of his mental battles, many times now he had killed for revenge. He knew it was wrong, but didn't feel like changing.

Greg suddenly paid attention when the speaker said, "The enemy has found a hole in our defenses and one of their battalions is moving through that gap. They have two companies forward and one in reserve. Sergeant Heyligher, you will take a fire team and halt this advance."

Greg sat up like a thunderbolt. Though this mission was nearly impossible, he said, "Yes sir, I'll get started on it right away." *I wonder how many I'll get this time.*

As Greg began looking for one of his fire teams, Lieutenant Derek intercepted him. "Hey, Sergeant Heyligher, HQ wanted me to give you this."

The device looked like a flare. "What is it sir?"

"It's used for calling in close air support. You attach a speaking wire to it, send it above the EMP field, and it will electronically interpret and broadcast your voice to nearby ground-attack hovercraft. You then direct the hovercraft onto the target and destroy it."

"How does this work better than the fighters?" Greg was referring to the earlier flop in the war when space fighters and bombers had been used for close air support. Since all they used were machine guns, they were next to useless. Shuttles and their missiles were greatly appreciated, but shuttles were too important to expend on close air support.

Lieutenant Derek answered Greg's question, "The ground-attack hovercraft have rockets that are kind of like the MAA's MPGs. The difference is these rockets are coated with ice bullets, like one of the FDA's artillery shells."

Greg handled the device. "How long did it take the Alliance to come up with this?"

"The rocket we made. The close air support radio we found on the bodies of FDA officers. Apparently they use the things for scouting. I probably don't need to say this, but these things are in short supply, so make sure you return it."

As Lieutenant Derek left, Lynch came running up to Greg. "Sergeant, I heard you needed a fire team to stop a battalion. I would like to volunteer my team."

Greg studied Lynch for a second. Ever since the deaths of Smith and McAlister, Lynch, Sandusky, and Pierre had become inseparable. They lived, ate, and fought in their own little circle no one else could penetrate. Even on missions when only a team of two was needed, the three of them always went together. Although this was a little inefficient, the three of them had accomplished things others had considered impossible, and this was exactly the sort of mission that required the impossible.

Greg said at last, "Okay, get your team together, we leave in ten minutes."

"Right away, Sergeant." Lynch hurried away to his team.

⸻◆⸻

John left the room and briskly ran down the stairs to the street. Outside he didn't see any cops. He kept his SMGs drawn because the cops would recognize him anyway.

His space pod was only a block away, but the police would be here in only a few minutes. John continued to walk straight ahead, confident he could handle anything the cops threw at him. His rapidly churning mind quickly worked out a plan as he strode through the street.

Walking for a few more steps, John sprang his plan into action. He knew this section of the city was mostly inhabited by gangsters. Taking aim with his SMGs, John started shooting into the windows of the apartments he passed. Angry gangsters appeared out of the windows, shooting back at John.

Unconcerned, John continued walking down the middle of the street. He stopped shooting altogether once he had enough gangsters firing at him. Listening closely, John heard the police sirens just around the corner. Flipping his SMGs onto full-auto, John sprayed the apartment windows, forcing the gangsters to duck.

Pulling out two explosives, John set the timers to three seconds, then hurled them through windows on opposite sides of the street. As he walked away swiftly, he used the dual-explosions to cover him.

The bombs went off with a huge detonation, sending shards flying at each other. As huge fireballs billowed out of the opposing windows, John strolled nonchalantly around the corner.

When the cops appeared a second later, the gangsters started shooting at the cops. The cops returned fire and a full blown shootout started.

With all confusion behind him, John easily slipped away in his space pod.

Chapter 43

Elephant Valley, Modern Style

Lynch's fire team and Greg were standing a short distance away from the landing zone. In the jungle below them, they could see a trail. The trail split, with one branch leading into a valley with steep, high cliffs. Marching along this trail were the two forward FDA companies, nearly 400 soldiers. This massive column had not yet reached the intersection.

Surveying this, Lynch had a quick conversation with Sandusky and Pierre. "Sergeant, do you mind waiting on the air support for a little bit?"

"What do you have in mind?"

"I won't be able to give you a signal, but I think you'll know when to call in the hovercrafts."

"Alright, go head and do it," Greg trusted that Lynch knew what he was doing.

Without another word, Lynch and his fire team disappeared into the jungle.

Greg moved to a position where he could observe the enemy, then waited. He called in the hovercrafts and had them waiting just out of sight. Looking at the enemy, he saw most of the column had passed the intersection and had decided to continue along in their original direction.

Suddenly, two shots rang out and the leading scouts of the FDA column fell dead. More shots came flying into the column, felling soldiers left and right. The column seemed to hesitate for a few minutes, then decided to avoid these snipers and take the route through the valley. The two snipers continued to hound them on their flanks, herding them like wolves chasing a flock of sheep. Wolves. Predators. Sandusky was a predator. Lynch's plan instantly made sense to Greg.

Once the entire column was inside the valley, Greg's suspicion was proved correct as five shots rang out in four seconds. The first five soldiers in the column were slapped to the ground as the bullets found their mark.

Sandusky's rapid, accurate fire stopped the column in its tracks. Lynch and

Pierre came around and sealed the back of the valley. The two FDA companies were trapped inside the valley while the three of them commenced a dreadful slaughter upon the hapless soldiers. Each of the marine snipers was at least a two kilometers away from the FDA soldiers, so there was no hope of rushing the snipers, nor was there any hope of being able to return fire. Whenever an officer stood to call in fire support, he was instantly picked off. The two companies were going nowhere.

Greg called in the hovercrafts. A flight of four ground-attack hovercrafts came roaring over the jungle. The ground-attack vessels looked exactly like the transport hovercrafts, with the exception of pylons, on which several rocket pods were mounted.

The first hovercraft fired a pair of rockets. Greg followed the luminescent tails given off by the rockets to the ground, then corrected their fire. The next set of rockets landed much closer to the enemy, but still not on target. Greg called in the correction, and this time the rockets landed right on target.

Diving in for the kill, the four hovercrafts unleashed their terrible load on FDA soldiers below. Rockets streaked across the sky, slamming into the FDA positions. Explosion after explosion rocked the ground as the FDA companies were pounded into the dust.

Greg spotted the FDA soldiers quickly scrambling to load their clips of solid shot. They fired in a constant staccato, futilely trying to bring down their attackers. Eventually, one of their bursts connected and a hovercraft shuddered as the rear half of it peeled off. The hovercraft went into a spin and crashed into the jungle floor.

While the other two hovercrafts covered it, the third settled next to the downed hovercraft while one of the crew members pulled out the survivors. Once he was finished, the crew member climbed back aboard his own hovercraft. The heavily loaded vehicle took off, then fired a pair of rockets into the wrecked hovercraft so the enemy would not be able to find anything useful. Turning away, the hovercraft bearing the survivors headed back to base.

The remaining hovercrafts continued to pound the enemy into platoon-sized companies. Watching the slaughter through his scope, Greg saw the FDA soldiers had dropped their weapons and raised their hands.

Greg knew the hovercrafts were going too fast to see the soldiers had surrendered. If he simply kept his mouth shut, he could avenge Ethan, Smith, McAlister, and the entire platoon.

I can't do this. I cannot go down this path.

But you've done it in the past. Why should now be any different?

I was wrong in the past. By saving these soldiers, I can atone for some of what I've done.

How can you take the soldiers prisoner anyway? You don't have enough troops to secure them?

Greg knew the last thought was right. There was no way to secure the prisoners.

Touching his speaking rod, Greg said, "All hovercrafts, cease fire. The enemy has surrendered. I'm going to pop a red smoke. Send a hovercraft to pick me up, over,"

One of the hovercrafts replied, "Sniper, you do understand the smoke will mark your location to FDA artillery and mortars, over?"

"Understood. Popping the smoke now, over." Greg pulled out a red smoke grenade and marked his position. He then pulled down the flarelike radio and secured it to his person.

Within seconds, FDA mortar and artillery rounds began pounding the area around him. Greg weathered the barrage until he spotted the hovercraft coming to pick him up. He stood and made a short dash inside.

As the hovercraft lifted off, Greg told the pilot, "Drop me off by the FDA prisoners. I'm going to walk them back to our lines."

"Are you crazy?" the pilot said. "First off, there're still enough soldiers to overwhelm you. Second, it's a three-day journey back to our lines, and third, there's another company out there, which could overtake and overwhelm you."

"I know."

The hovercraft left Greg in the valley with the FDA soldiers. Armed only with his sniper rifle, Greg walked toward the soldiers. "Who's the officer here?"

A haggard-looking Pratin stepped forward.

"Form these soldiers into a double column. Start marching them down the trail."

Slowly, the soldiers shifted into position and began marching.

———❖———

It was the dark of night, and Carol was once again behind enemy lines with the recon team. He was deployed along with three of the other recon men in an ambush position. The fourth—the weapons expert—was on a hill behind them.

They were overlooking an artillery battery. The war had been in a stalemate for quite some time, and they were told this mission was part of an effort to break the deadlock, but Carol had heard rumors the mission was supporting a retreat from Earth. Either way, didn't matter to him.

The weapons expert fired a MPG into one of the artillery guns. A loud explosion rocked the night as the warhead detonated. Instantly, return fire was sent in the general direction of the weapons expert, but he had relocated. Another MPG flew across the night sky, destroying a second gun. The weapons expert began methodically eliminating the artillery emplacements.

Guarding infantry sent out a patrol to find and eradicate the threat to the guns. Carol heard the patrol advancing toward him. Holding his fire, Carol waited for the signal to initiate the ambush.

One of the FDA soldiers hit a trip-flare. The flare went soaring into the night, then burst into light, illuminating the silhouettes of the FDA patrol. The ambush expert triggered the command detonated mines, then the rest of the recon team opened fire.

Carol let out a long burst that dropped one of the figures in front of him. Another of the soldiers began to run sideways, attempting to get out of the kill zone. Firing at the soldier, Carol saw his bullets impact behind him. Adjusting his aim, Carol fired again and again, increasing his lead each time. Finally, one of the bursts connected and the soldier stumbled forward one more step before falling dead on the ground.

The rest of the enemy patrol had been destroyed by then. The recon team waited a few more minutes for the weapons expert to finish off the artillery battery, then they all disappeared into the woods.

Regrouping at the nearest rally point, Carol checked to make sure the entire team was present, then instructed the point man to lead them out.

Slowly the recon team vanished into the darkness. Traveling through the night, they did not take a break until just before dawn. After a short rest, they began to move again, knowing they could not afford to be caught behind enemy lines in broad daylight.

As the sun was creeping over the horizon, they reached the edge of the clearing. Carol deployed a flare and sent it flying sideways until it was out of sight. Pushing a button, Carol turned the flare on and hoped their extraction crew would spot it.

Nothing happened for a good half hour. Then faintly in the distance came the roar of a military transport hovercraft. There was a light popping as an AA battery fired at the hovercraft, then small explosions as the hovercraft's escorts dealt with the offending AA gun.

Only a few minutes later, Carol heard the roar of the Alliance hovercraft above him. As the elevator lowered, the recon team piled aboard. Carol was the last on in accordance with tradition. The instant his feet hit the elevator, the hovercraft began to lift off.

Leaning back in the relative safety of the hovercraft, Carol was extremely grateful the Alliance was providing support to the MAA.

———•———

Three days later, Greg came marching back into the HQ. Before him were all the prisoners. Not one had escaped or been shot.

As Greg crossed into the perimeter, there was a small committee waiting for him. Lieutenant Derek, Lynch's team, and the hovercraft pilot were in the group.

Derek said, "Heyligher, you're a legend now."

"Thank you, sir."

"I'm not exaggerating. Word got out, and all across the Federation the news played the story of how a single marine sniper was escorting two companies, with a third in close pursuit."

"The third company never got close enough to be much of a threat."

"It was gutsy," the hovercraft pilot said. "That you did it to save aliens makes you a hero."

Greg kept silent. Only Ethan had understood the truth. He was not a hero, he was a murderer. That he saved the soldiers was only an act of penance.

Seeking to change the topic, Greg said, "Lynch, your plan was brilliant. You should have been an officer."

"And miss out on all the action, Sergeant?"

Greg laughed. "By the way, how did you guys get back?"

"A hovercraft extracted us when it was dark, when the FDA couldn't drop mortars on us," Sandusky answered.

"Good thinking."

The four of them headed toward their fighting holes to get some sleep.

Derek pulled Greg aside for a moment. "I'm glad you did that. Ever since the death of Ethan, you seemed like you were close to losing, but now I know you're still you."

"In that valley, I finally realized the truth," Greg replied. "It's not the FDA's fault he died, it's mine. As a matter of fact, the whole war's my fault"

Greg turned away and headed for his fighting hole. Derek briefly considered trying to convince Greg otherwise, but decided against it. Whether or not Greg's opinion was right, it seemed to give him peace, which was all that mattered.

—•—

The hovercraft began to slow down and start descending. Carol looked out the window and noticed they were coming down in an assembly area filled with shuttles being loaded with troops.

"What's going on?" Carol asked the pilot.

"We're evacuating the planet," replied the pilot. "As soon I drop you off I'm going back for another load."

The hovercraft slowed to a stop and descended. Carol and his team exited from the hovercraft, standing slightly uncertain as it lifted off again. After a bit of standing around, Carol joined the growing mass of marines and MAA waiting to board a shuttle to evacuate.

Chapter 44

The Victor's Wreath

General Hadrukc was standing on the bridge of his flagship, staring through the transparent-steel at Earth below. *Down on that planet so many are dying, yet it looks so peaceful from up here. That always has been one of the great paradoxes of land warfare.*

I can't understand why some generals prefer land warfare—you never see your enemy, you only have the reports of others to go on—but then again, I have spent my career as a space officer, so maybe there is something about fighting the enemy on the ground that is fascinating.

How long has the war been going? Let's see, after the first four weeks the Alliance assault stopped because of lack of supplies, and then—against my advice—we launched our own attack. Our attack was stopped by enemy snipers. I wasn't surprised by that, the Alliance has a good sniper program. The attack lasted one week, and both sides have been in a deadlock for—ah, the war has been going on for two months.

An aide interrupted his thoughts, "Sir, we have reports the Alliance is withdrawing. The generals on the planet are requesting permission to pursue the enemy."

"Tell them their permission is denied. The enemy is beginning his retreat and that is something we want him to do."

"Sir, they say the MAA terrorists are leaving in the shuttles with the Alliance."

"They still may not attack, even if that means we have to pass up an opportunity to take the terrorists out."

"I'll inform them immediately, sir."

———◆———

She couldn't believe it. From her vantage point above Earth, the stream of shuttles leaving the planet was clearly visible. Running her eyes over the dashboard, she made a quick check to see if her fighter was still hovering in position. She adjusted a little, using rudders.

In her radar, there were only friendly signatures. All FDA forces were on the other side of the planet.

Slamming her fist on the control panel in disgust, she angrily thought about all the skirmishes the fighters had fought. Although the battleships remained behind Earth, the small spacecraft engaged in constant patrol actions against each other. Thousands of her fellow pilots had died, all for nothing.

A tear began forming in her eye. It wasn't supposed to end this way.

She looked beyond the shuttles. There was no way the FDA would let them go unmolested. To stop them, all available forces were staged for an elaborate ambush. Her flight would be the tip of the spear, the first into battle. That also meant they would have to stay in the fight the longest.

Despite what she'd told her pilots, she didn't expect to survive. Somehow, that comforted her. At least she wouldn't have to live in the shame of defeat.

———•———

Near the end of the day the aide came back and reported the enemy had evacuated Earth.

Here comes the storm, thought Hadrukc.

Ten seconds later the aide returned.

"The Alliance fleet is retreating sir. Generals and ship's captains are all asking permission to pursue the enemy."

"Tell them what I said before, my answer is still no." Hadrukc's weariness with his commanders was almost showing.

Instantly, Hadrukc's personal comm. unit was ringing as every single general called at the same time, each trying to make a personal appeal to Hadrukc.

With a sigh, Hadrukc picked up his comm. unit and set it to universal broadcast. "This is General Hadrukc. If you'll notice, I have the comm. working as a one-way transmitter, so listen to what I have to say before you start speaking. Most of you are asking to pursue the Alliance fleet. My answer is no, and I will tell you why. The enemy was outmaneuvered, plain and simple. They have been forced to retreat without even having the dignity of a glorious battle in which their side was defeated. They lost because we were smarter than they. Their pride is wounded."

He took a breath. "Now, should we attempt to pursue the enemy, this would give him one last chance to avenge his pride. If he succeeded in getting away, he could rightfully say he'd fought a great battle to save himself from the Federation trap. And with this as their motivation, they will cause casualties far out of proportion to their numbers."

Hadrukc continued, "War is not about fighting the enemy at the earliest possible time; it is about fighting the enemy under the most favorable conditions. We know the enemy will strike again at Earth. With this knowledge, we can fortify Earth, prepare elaborate defenses and ambushes, we can do anything we want. Time is on our side, so we lose absolutely nothing by waiting to fight the final battle when the odds are overwhelmingly in our favor. Thank you for listening; I will now hear your complaints."

As he had expected, none of the generals had heard him and had spent the time during his address to formulate their own arguments.

Mentally, he was begging for the Alliance to hurry up and leave so the generals would stop calling. He was forced to endure twenty minutes of agony before the Alliance jumped to midspace and ended the argument.

———

After two months, Greg was finally back in his battleship. Being forced to retreat didn't bother him as much as he thought it would. All of his men, with the exception of Corporal Schmidt, had been wounded, but none had been evacuated. No one could say they had shrunk their duty. They'd done the best they could do, and they knew they would try again. The war was by no means over—only the first battle in the war had finished.

Since the MAA had lost most of its transports, the Alliance had extracted them along side their own forces, and was stuffing them in battleships with the marines until they could reach a space port. Greg had talked Lieutenant Derek into inviting Carol and Assault Team Blue to share their quarters. Only thirteen members of Assault Team Blue were still alive, and combined with the casualties the snipers had taken, things weren't too crowded, but it still was difficult to find a quiet moment.

Slowly reclining into his bunk, Greg tried to close his eyes and get some sleep. The last few weeks had been incredibly hectic. When the enemy made their assault, snipers had been needed all over the front. Usually he did two or three missions a day, spending about twenty hours out in the field. During this time snipers racked up kills in record numbers. In one spectacular sitting Greg had managed to get twenty-eight kills. When the war went into a deadlock, the need for snipers had not diminished as the FDA constantly attacked in attempts to break the deadlock.

Greg was just about to doze off when Lance Corporal White came running in the door. "Congratulations on beating the all-time kill record, Sergeant. We have a party set up for you, and we're all waiting."

Rolling out of the bunk, Greg asked, "When did I beat the kill record?"

"We added up all the kills you made, and discovered you broke the record."

"Is it official?"

"Yeah, it's been official for some time—we just never thought to look at the kill charts the Alliance posted every week. We learned about those charts when we informed Lieutenant Derek of the news, and he told us he had known about it for some time and was wondering why we hadn't had a party yet."

They walked out into the hallway, where not just the squad, but the entire platoon was waiting, along with Carol and Assault Team Blue. Quickly scraped together banners and streamers hung from the wall. Someone started blasting loud music while the platoon did a ridiculous cheer they had made up. Pointless party games started up. In short, it wasn't bad.

Although Greg thought it was tragic they were celebrating his killing beings, he knew the platoon needed the party. All the stress they had built up during the war would be released now.

Carol and Rodrigo accosted him. "Congrats on beating the record," Carol said.

"At the last party, you were telling us you were glad you hadn't beaten the record. What do you think now?" Rodrigo asked.

"I wish I hadn't needed to."

Carol saw a friend from Assault Team Blue and stepped aside to talk with him.

Rodrigo said, "Though you hated it, I think the war was good for you. It allowed you to face your demons, and win."

"Did I?" Greg asked. "Did I win? I broke every rule there is for a sniper. I almost became a maniacal murderer."

"But in the end, you didn't."

Greg was silent for a while. "I suppose that's something."

About midway through the party, Greg received a call. He stepped out for a minute. "This is Sergeant Heyligher."

The voice in the ear receptor said, "Hey, this is John."

A chill came over Greg as John continued, "Congratulations on beating the kill record."

Greg thought for a second John had a tracking device on him or something. "How did you find out? I only learned about it a few minutes ago."

"Oh, you know how the media loves to bash the government. They had a special on how marine snipers were slaughtering FDA troops, how the FDA was helpless against the snipers, and how bad the FDA's own sniper program was. In it they mentioned a Sergeant Heyligher had broken the all time record."

"Interesting. Now I'm notorious. So you just happened to see this media flash a few seconds ago."

"Carol called me earlier and told me about the party. He suggested I give you a call."

"Thanks for doing so."

"Ironic that the two biggest killers of FDA troops are friends. Before I forget, I picked up an interesting tidbit of information. It wasn't the Alliance's fault you guys had to retreat. You were up against a Ribargo, the one that passed the test a while back. I think his name was Hadrukc. Either way, there was nothing you guys could have done against him."

Now this is a valuable bit of information. That the FDA considered us important enough to send a Ribargo says a lot. And John is right, no Ribargo has ever lost, so there was nothing the Alliance could have done to win that battle.

"That'll be useful to know."

"Anytime. Hey, where do you stay when you're on leave? I'll have to drop by and visit sometime."

Greg gave John the location.

"We're responsible for all this, aren't we? Everyone who's dead, it's all because we found Earth," Greg said.

"I told you that'd happen. But that's beside the point. If not us, someone else would've. Those who ordered the mission are most responsible."

"I know. It's still hard to accept."

"You lost someone in your squad, didn't you?"

"Two, actually."

There was a pause.

"Now that you've broken the record, do you understand why I told you not to interfere with the gangsters on Gauss 1?"

Greg swallowed. "To allow yourself to become attached allows you to feel other things, things that will eventually destroy you." He hesitated, then continued, "But stopping the gangsters was still the right thing to do."

"You'll always be an idealist," John said. "I guess it's not too bad to have a few of those around."

The End